THE MAN WHO DEFIED GRAVITY

A Vanessa Mystery

Nov. 2016
To Bryan—
Thank you
for your support.
Madalyn Kinsey

By

Madalyn S. Kinsey

Illustrated by Sharon F. Cazzell

First published by Dog Ear Publishing
4011 Vincennes Rd
Indianapolis, IN 46268
www.dogearpublishing.net

ISBN: 978-1-4575-5024-9

This book is printed on acid-free paper.

Printed in the United States of America

TABLE OF CONTENTS

Special thanks is given to Nils Nordell, Andrew M. Cardimen, Barbara S. Tully, and Kenneth L. Turchi for their editing assistance.

CHAPTER ONE

Rising from the Ashes

It was early on a warm August morning in the summer of 1967. I rolled over and reluctantly opened my eyes. The bright summer sun was already peeking around the edges of the green drapes spanning the high windows in my bedroom. Another day had arrived——another day closer to the end of summer vacation and to the loss of precious freedom. In only a handful of days, I'd be returning to the crowded halls of Eastwood Junior High School and to the drudgery of grades and homework. At least I'd be an eighth grader this year, not an awkward seventh grader struggling to navigate the sprawling school building hoping to find my classroom before the bell rang. Still this had been a very eventful summer, and I didn't want it to end.

I finally got up and stumbled into the bathroom. Yawning, I looked into the large, frameless mirror hanging above the side-by-side sinks on our long pink vanity. I'd just taken a hairbrush out of the drawer to pull through my tousled hair when my mother knocked on the door with an unusual urgency.

"Vanessa! Are you in there?" she shouted. "Hurry up and get dressed. We've got to get out to the farm right away. Something terrible has happened!"

I jerked open the door. "What do you mean terrible? What's wrong? What happened?"

"There was a fire. Only the house was involved, as far as I know. Aunt Louise just called. We need to get out there right away."

I could tell by Mom's voice she was upset.

"A *fire?*" I repeated, swallowing hard. "Did the house burn down? Is everyone okay?"

"Yes, I believe they're all okay. Louise didn't have time to tell me much in all the commotion. Apparently, the cause is somewhat mysterious. We won't know much until we get out there. So hurry. I want to leave in ten minutes!"

She disappeared down the hall. I hurried back into my bedroom and began getting dressed.

I lived in a house my parents built on the north side of Indianapolis, which I shared with my older sister, Karen, who'd be a college sophomore, and two brothers—Brian, who was sixteen, and Bruce, who was seven. Our neighborhood was typically suburban, occupied mostly by families with lots of kids in modest houses on large lots. The neighborhood offered diversions for me, of course, but nothing compared to the fun and adventure I always experienced when I visited my Aunt Louise, Uncle Evert, and my cousins on the farm near Fishers, Indiana.

I first got to know them when I stayed with them for two weeks while my parents were away at the beginning of the summer. They'd recently relocated to Indiana from New Jersey. I became fast friends with my cousin Emma, who was near my age, and my sixteen-year-old cousin Luke and their older siblings, Lars and Margret.

Through them I met a boy named Jim who was sixteen and handsome, kind, and funny. He was good friends with my cousin Luke. I was totally smitten with him. He liked me too, or so he told me on a few occasions. But we hadn't seen each other in several weeks or even spoken on the phone, which was difficult. He'd dated a girl named Monica earlier in the summer, but told me he'd broken up with her for good. I thought that meant he'd be free to date me. Instead, he went on to say he needed to sort things out and wasn't going to date *anyone* for a while, including me. I waited impatiently for a phone call or a letter saying he finally knew what he wanted, and what he wanted was me. But no such letter came, and the phone never rang. I came to understand how life's joy can turn to misery when you're waiting endlessly to hear from someone you long to be with.

I quickly slipped on my new chocolate brown Capri slacks and a yellow-and-brown striped knit top that I had left draped across the rattan chair in my bedroom last night. I ran back into the bathroom and quickly looked in the mirror. I was tall for my age with an extremely fair complexion and long, strawberry-blonde hair that I wore parted down the middle. I wore glasses that my mother promised would be replaced with contact lenses when I turned sixteen. My glasses had amber-colored frames that were reasonably stylish, I guess. My mother didn't allow me to wear much makeup, but she OK'd wearing a little eyeliner and mascara that I carefully put on this morning. I finished with Yardley Slicker pale cotton candy pink lip gloss. I pursed my lips together to blend the gloss, brushed my hair, and was ready to go.

"Should I pack an overnight bag?" I asked Mom as she hurried back and forth from her room to the kitchen in her cotton shirtwaist dress.

"You can throw a pair of pajamas and some underwear in a bag if you want, as long as you do it quickly," she said impatiently. "But I doubt Aunt Louise needs the added stress of another house guest at a time like this. Just be quick about it. We need to leave right away."

It didn't hurt to be prepared. I ran into my room, reached into the closet, and pulled down my brown zippered overnight bag with the orange and yellow flowers on it. I quickly filled it with a few outfits, underwear, my new swimsuit, and assorted odds and ends. I wished I had had more time to think about what to pack, but I heard Mom back the car out of the garage and knew I needed to hurry.

I zipped up the suitcase and carried it into the living room to wait. My younger brother Bruce was watching *Hollywood Squares* on our black-and-white television. Even with the funny wisecracks of comedian Paul Lynde in the center square, my thoughts drifted. I imagined the charred and smoking timbers of the farmhouse. Where would my cousins live now? Would they have to move away? I couldn't bear to think of that happening. This turn of events was a shock, and I felt unsettled and anxious.

Dad was at work, and my sister and older brother were both at their summer jobs. This left only my little brother for my mother to deal with. He said he preferred to go next door to play with his friend Barney rather than come with us. After quickly taking my brother next door, it was finally time for Mom and me to go. I jumped into our beige 1966 Chevrolet, and off we went down our street, across Kessler Boulevard, and then north on Allisonville Road. As we made our way beyond the Indianapolis suburbs, the scenery changed from one-story houses on large, grassy lots like ours, to nothing but fields and wooded ravines as far as the eye could see. A few old farmhouses dotted the landscape. Mom was a good sport and let me listen to the local rock station. I adjusted the dial to WIFE-AM, and "Last Train to Clarksville" by The Monkees, one of my favorite songs, came on. Thinking about the line dance steps I'd learned to it at a slumber party not long ago was a welcome distraction.

We passed fields planted with soybeans and corn, some of which looked almost ready for harvest. Many fields were uncultivated and left to go wild with grass and wildflowers. Mom kept her eyes trained on the road and didn't say much. I was impatient, and it seemed to take longer than usual to get there today.

We finally passed a small private airport called Gatewood Airport and a large farm on the east side of the road near 106th Street. Both belonged to my Uncle Forrest, who lived on the farm with his wife, Aunt Loretta, and my five cousins. They were almost directly across the road from the farm where Uncle Evert lived with Aunt Louise, my mother's older sister. My mother was born and raised here with Aunt Louise, along with three other sisters and their brother, Uncle Forrest. Grandma and Grandpa were no longer living, and now the farm belonged to Aunt Louise and Uncle Evert. Uncle Evert was a water softener contractor and didn't farm the property. He rented some of the fields to other people who cultivated crops on them, but mostly the fields were left to go natural. They weren't currently raising any farm animals either, except for some peacocks who flew into their yard one day and didn't leave.

As Mom turned into the long gravel driveway, I braced myself for what I would see next. I was relieved when I saw the large white barn with the gambrel roof that my grandfather built was untouched; it stood directly in front of us at the end of the lane. A Fishers Fire Department fire engine hummed in front of the one-story farmhouse on the left. The farmhouse was still intact, and I was happy to see its white clapboard walls still standing as we drove up. Then I noticed dark gray smoke ominously billowing from behind the house and out of a hole in the roof over which a fireman stood holding an axe. The separate two-car garage perpendicular to the house didn't appear to be involved in the fire. Nevertheless, someone had pulled the family's red Chevy Bel Air sedan and silver Corvette out and parked them a safe distance away in the grass near the barn. The house and garage were very old and made of wood that would easily burn to the ground if ignited. It appeared the damage wasn't as bad as my imagination had feared.

Mom drove the car up near the barn where it would be out of the way, and turned off the ignition. "We're here," she said, unbuckling her seat belt. "Watch where you step, and stay out of the firemen's way." I got out and stood next to her.

We paused, staring at the chaotic scene and taking it all in. Two firemen came around the corner of the house absorbed in their duties. One held the nozzle of a water hose that snaked across the ground and around the perimeter of the house. Occasional wisps of light gray smoke continued to escape through the hole in the roof and out the windows, all of which were propped open.

Aunt Louise and Uncle Evert were standing in the yard at the back of the house watching the spectacle. Uncle Evert had a full head of silver hair and matching bushy eyebrows that, together with the glasses he wore, gave him the appearance of being older than I suspected he was. When my aunt saw us get out of the car, she crossed the yard, her arms tightly folded in front of her as if to fortify herself. She was tall, like my mother, and had on light tan pants and a dark green man's shirt that was too large for her slim figure. I assumed the shirt belonged to Uncle Evert and she'd grabbed it when the fire started. Her dark blonde hair was cut short in a natural, unfussy style. As she came near I noticed that her usually serene countenance was troubled.

"Sister, thank you for coming," she said, hugging my mother. "For a while there, I thought we were going to lose the house——that we were going to lose everything. We didn't, though. Oh, we lost a few things, of course, but not everything. The volunteer firemen got here pretty quickly and jumped right in. I think they've finally got the fire out. They're working on dousing the last hotspots now." Her voice was soft and sounded weary.

"How much of the house is damaged?" Mom asked, peering at the modest structure with a concerned look.

"We don't know yet," Aunt Louise replied, wiping her brow. "Most of the fire was at the back corner of the house near the boys' bedroom. The fire probably started in the attic on that side of the house. Their room is fairly heavily damaged, and the whole house has smoke damage."

"Are you all okay?" Mom asked, touching Aunt Louise's arm supportively.

"Yes, thank goodness. Everyone got out okay, and that's the important thing. Of course, we were all startled pretty badly when we realized the house was on fire, especially the boys. It happened at about four this morning. The smell of smoke woke us. We knew something was horribly wrong. Luke ran out of the house and could see the flames starting to break through the roof. They still don't know what caused it. There was a small storm last night. Maybe it was lightning. Maybe it was electrical. It's an old house. Who knows?"

Just then, my cousin Emma appeared, racing across the yard toward us. She was twelve, almost thirteen, and slim like her mother, with shoulder-length wavy blonde hair and vivid blue eyes. She had on a blue short-sleeved pajama top, shorts, and thongs.

"Thank God you're here!" she said, running up to me. "Can you believe this? I have no home! I've got nothing to wear but these pajamas I have on."

"Not true, Emma," Aunt Louise said. "The house is still standing. That's a lot better than it might have been. We need to be grateful for that."

"Well, *I'm* not grateful," my cousin Luke complained, walking up behind Emma. He was wearing a faded T-shirt with holes in it and knit pants that I assumed were his pajamas. "My comic book collection was in the closet in my bedroom, and now it's nothing but a big pile of smoky, wet mush. There were some really neat comics in there, too, not to mention my *Thor* collection. This bites!"

Emma's brother Luke had the same wavy white blonde hair she had, only his was always tousled as if it hadn't been combed in weeks, which it probably hadn't. He was about my height and had a muscular and slightly stocky build. He was always in perpetual motion, usually involving his love of the outdoors.

"You mean all of your *Thor* comic books were destroyed?" I joked. "Well, now you'll just have to read *Casper* comics, I guess."

"Oh, real funny, City Slicker," Luke replied, making a face. He had a habit of calling me City Slicker, try as I might to make him stop. "*Casper* is for little kids. That's the sort of thing you'd probably like."

"How much of the house is damaged?" Mom asked, peering at the modest structure.

"Oh, cut that out!" Emma admonished. "Don't start with Vanessa. She just got here, and I, for one, am very glad to see her." She casually slung her arm over my shoulder and glared at him in a show of solidarity.

"Luke, go see if you can help your father," Aunt Louise interrupted. "Make yourself useful." Luke muttered something and then dutifully walked away toward the house.

Just then, I noticed a German shepherd in a fenced area near the barn. I was surprised to see it as I'd never seen it on my prior visits. It was medium-sized with a powerful looking body and tan markings on its face and legs. Dark fur above its eyes made it look as if it was frowning. It paced back and forth inside the enclosure and seemed ready to pounce on anything or anybody who came near.

"Is that your dog?" I asked Emma. "When did you get a dog? What's his name?"

"Oh, that's not *our* dog," Aunt Louise clarified. "He appeared in our yard yesterday afternoon. We figure someone driving by dropped him here to get rid of him. He's mean and ill-tempered. Who'd want a dog like that? Evert asked a couple of neighbors if they recognized him or were missing a dog, but no one seems to know anything about him. We put him in that chicken pen until we can decide what to do with him."

"It looks like he has a collar on," my mother observed. "I can see it from here. Does it have his name on it?"

"No. It's just a black leather collar. There's no name on it or other identification," Aunt Louise replied.

"We call him Dorito, because he loves Doritos," Emma chimed in. "He was kicking up a fuss with us last night when we were trying to get him into that pen. Luke happened to have a small bag of Doritos with him, and the dog snatched it and ate right through the cellophane before he could do anything about it. He loved them!"

"Now, don't go naming that dog and getting attached to it," Aunt Louise cautioned. "We aren't going to keep him. There's something about him that frightens me, and I can't have a dog around that frightens me."

"Oh, Mom," Emma whined. "You can tell he's not a bad dog. He just needs love and understanding."

"You heard what I said," Aunt Louise said firmly. "He's not Dorito or any other name. He's just a dog as far as you're concerned."

A fireman and Uncle Evert came toward us looking as though they had something important on their minds. Aunt Louise excused herself and walked back to meet them. I watched and wondered what was happening.

"Want to see the damage?" Emma asked.

"Is that okay" I asked my mother. I was eager to check out the fire damage close up.

"Sure. Just remember what I told you before, and stay out of the way," Mom said.

I nodded, and then Emma and I walked across the yard to the house. The door at the end of the house where we usually entered through the kitchen stood wide open, and a fireman hurried inside just as we passed. We remained outside and proceeded to the corner of the house where the fire had done the most damage. The exterior white clapboard was scorched with a black residue all the way up to the roofline. The window screens were lying on the ground, no doubt pushed out in haste when the fire started. Curtains, two bedspreads, a rug, assorted stuffed animals, and other odds and ends were strewn all over the grass. Everything was wet and dirty. A fireman was still tromping around on the roof, occasionally whacking away at it with an axe.

"You won't have to move away, will you?" I asked Emma as I studied the scene. "Have your parents said anything about that?"

"What?" she exclaimed, appearing to be taken by surprise. "Why no! No one has said anything like that. Why? Do you think we will? What have you heard? I couldn't bear the idea of leaving here." Her eyes were wide as she pondered the possibility.

"Oh, well, never mind. Forget I brought it up. I'm just talking," I said, doing my best to withdraw the question after witnessing her strong reaction.

"No, I'm not moving. They can move if they want to. But not me!" she said defiantly, still agitated. "I'll sleep outside for the rest of my life if I have to. I'll never move from here. Never!"

"Okay, okay," I said, perplexed about what to say to get her to calm down.

"Are you upsetting my little sister again, City Slicker?" Luke asked as he walked by. His timing couldn't have been worse. "Tsk, tsk. There you go again. Stirring things up, as usual."

"She's not upsetting me!" Emma shouted. "I'm just upset. This fire has upset me. I have a right to be upset, don't I?" Her cheeks were red and she clinched her fists at her sides.

"Fine. Be upset then. But, that won't get you anywhere when it comes to finding out who set this fire," Luke replied matter-of-factly as he studied the scorched side of the house. "Yep. You heard correctly. I said *set*."

"What are you talking about? Someone set the fire?" Emma demanded. "Wasn't it an electrical fire? Or some problem in the attic? Or lightning during the thunderstorm last night? I didn't hear anyone say someone deliberately set the fire. That'd be nuts. We were sleeping in there and could have been killed if we hadn't awakened like we did."

"Nuts you say? Well, explain this to me if you can. I heard someone walking around outside the house just before the fire started. He stepped on a twig or something right under my bedroom window, and it woke me up. That's why I was awake when the fire started and got everyone out of the house so fast. I bet whoever I heard torched the house."

"Oh, now you're just trying to scare us," I said, forcing a small laugh to try to disguise my suspicion that what he was saying might be true. "Why would anyone want to burn down your house? Especially with you guys in it?"

"Hello there, survivors!" someone shouted from out in the yard before Luke could answer. I turned and saw my cousin Daniel approaching us, grinning. He lived across the road with his parents, Uncle Forrest and Aunt Loretta. He was thirteen, slim, and had a full head of brown curly hair and a ready smile. As usual, he was wearing a suede western jacket with fringe, as he almost always did, no matter how hot it was outside. It made me smile to see him wearing it today when it was eighty-some degrees already and getting warmer.

"Hi, Vanessa!" Daniel said as he approached. "Did you come to see what's left of the family homestead?"

"There's lots left," Luke protested. "No one can burn us out of *our* home!"

"Except YOU when you're playing with matches," Daniel joked. He appeared to brace himself for the physical assault Luke frequently inflicted on him, playfully dubbed the "five-minute treatment," but apparently Luke was foregoing the treatment this time.

"Ha, ha. So funny I forgot to laugh," Luke answered flatly, rolling his eyes. "I wouldn't be surprised if what we saw the other night didn't have something to do with this. There's definitely something weird going around here. Maybe someone involved with what we saw didn't want us around to tell anyone, and set the fire to bump us off." His manner was uncharacteristically serious.

"Really? What strange things did you see?" I inquired. "What are you talking about? I'm confused."

He hesitated and looked at me with a strange glint in his eye, almost as though he didn't think he should tell me. "Okay, here goes. Two nights ago Daniel and I were down by the creek until pretty late. I stopped by the barn on the way back to put some stuff away. When I walked out of the barn, I saw some weird lights hovering in the sky way out over the fields." His eyes were big like saucers, and he spoke in hushed tones.

"Weird lights?" Emma asked. "What do you mean? What was weird about them, and why is the first I've heard of this? Are you making this up?" She crossed her arms and gave him a disbelieving look.

"The lights hovered and then zipped straight up and disappeared. No airplane can do that. It was totally silent, too, so it wasn't a plane or a helicopter or anything like that."

Emma appeared skeptical and turned toward Daniel. "Daniel, is this true? I'll believe it if you say you saw this, too."

Daniel shrugged. "I think I'd already gone home. I didn't see it. Sorry."

"Where were these lights hovering?" Emma asked, still unconvinced.

"Over the back field. The one near the old Henderson farm back there," Luke responded, pointing northwest.

"So what do you think it was?" I asked.

"How should I know? It was dark and hard to see, but there was a blue-green glow and it had silver lights. From the way it maneuvered, I think it might have been a UFO," Luke concluded.

"A UFO!" Emma scoffed. "Oh, come on. Now I *really* don't believe anything you're saying."

"Even if you saw some strange lights a couple of days ago, what does that have to do with the fire?" I asked. "I don't see how they're connected."

"I don't know. But, I heard someone——or *something*——last night, and I saw those lights two nights ago. Isn't that all a bit too coincidental?"

"Are you saying——an *alien* from outer space set your house on fire?" I exclaimed. "Oh, come on. You're just having fun with us, aren't you?" I studied Luke's face to confirm my assumption he was playing a prank on Emma and me, but I couldn't tell.

"Why would aliens——if there *are* any in the first place——want to burn down your house?" I continued. "They must have more important inter-stellar things to do, like finding dilithium crystals or warning mankind against our ultimate destruction by the atom bomb. No, if you ask me I think you're just trying to scare us."

"Oh, yeah?" Luke replied. "Well, if you're such a City Slicker know-it-all, like you usually are, let's see if you have the guts to check it out."

"What on earth are you talking about?" I answered. "Check *what* out?"

"The little house is back in that field. I say we all camp out there tonight and see if those lights appear again. We can't sleep in our house the way it is anyway. We can each take turns standing watch," Luke suggested. "And, let me tell you—if I ever see those lights again, I'm going after them. I'll get to the bottom of whatever's going on!"

"What little house?" I asked. This was the first I'd heard of a little house.

"Buzz and Lars just built a playhouse along the dry creek bed in the north field. They got some salvage wood from a neighbor's barn that was torn down," Daniel explained. Buzz was Daniel's older brother, and Lars was Luke and Emma's older brother. They were about nineteen or twenty. "It's got a wood floor and a roof, and a ceiling tall enough to stand in it. It's kinda cool, actually."

"Yeah, Vanessa," Emma chimed in. "It's really cute. I'd love to show it to you. We've talked about sleeping out in it. This would be a perfect night. It'll be fun. What do you say?"

"Is it safe back there? I mean, to sleep back there all by ourselves?" I questioned. "It sounds pretty far from everything. No one could hear us if we had to call for help, could they?"

"Yes, it's safe, City Slicker," Luke said in a mocking tone. "But, if you want to go back to Indianapolis where you'll feel safe with all the street lights and cops patrolling the streets and be bored out of your skull, feel free."

"Stop that. You're so mean," Emma chastised. "Vanessa will stay in the little house with us tonight, won't you, Vanessa?"

I gazed at Emma's expectant face and nodded that I would. I couldn't let her down, but I'd need Mom's permission, of course. It was an intriguing proposition to possibly see a real-life UFO.

"I've got to ask my mother," I said. "She may not go for it."

"Well, okay then. Go ask your mommy," Luke said, smirking.

"Luke!" Emma scolded in a sisterly way. "Give her a break."

Emma looked at me eagerly while I continued thinking. I was hoping to attend the Indiana State Fair with my parents later that week. It ended in only a few more days, and I might miss it if I stayed. And there were things to do before school started on Tuesday.

"I don't know. The more I think about it, maybe I should go home and come back another time to look for those lights. I want to go to the State Fair, and I have other stuff to do," I said.

"Now look, City Slicker. You know we're not going to miss the fair. You can tag along with us. I haven't discussed it with Dad yet, but I know he'll want to go," Luke countered. "So no more excuses. Run along now and ask your mom."

To keep the peace, I went over to my mother, who was standing with Aunt Louise and Uncle Evert near the garage, and asked her about staying. She was against it at first, fearing one more person to account for under these circumstances would burden my aunt and uncle unnecessarily. But Aunt Louise wouldn't hear of it, and insisted I stay. She said she liked having me around, and that I was actually quite helpful. Mom raised a questioning eyebrow when she said I was helpful, but finally and reluctantly said it would be okay, but only for one or two nights. I mentioned Luke's plan for us to sleep in the little house, and all three adults thought that was a great idea. So I was set. I walked back to Luke, Daniel, and Emma to give them the good news, and decided to go with the flow.

"Okay, you guys," I said enthusiastically. "I'm in!"

"Great!" Emma replied.

"All right. Let Project Blue Book commence!" Luke declared. "We'll do our own UFO investigation, right here in Fishers, Indiana."

"What's Project Blue Book?" Emma asked.

"Project Blue Book is run by the U.S. Air Force. It's the official department of the government that investigates UFO sightings to determine if they're real," Daniel explained.

"Oh, yippee," I sighed under my breath.

I hoped all of this UFO talk was a hoax Luke had invented just to scare Emma and me and not the real thing. Even so, I wondered if lights in the sky were all I had to worry about. Maybe there were other things, or people, that could cause problems for four kids sleeping out all alone in a field on a summer evening. It appeared I'd find out.

CHAPTER TWO

The Soggy Aftermath

My mother stayed around for another hour or so talking to my aunt and uncle about the fire. Then she pulled my suitcase out of the back seat, handed it to me, and said good-bye to everyone. Before she left she reminded me to stay out of the way and to not cause my aunt and uncle any additional work. She told me she'd be back to collect me in a couple of days. Usually I'd whine and try to talk her into allowing me to stay longer, but after a night camping in the little house, I might be more than happy to go home to my soft bed.

Not long after Mom left, the firemen rolled up the firehoses and left, rumbling down the driveway in their chrome-trimmed red truck. They said they'd be back tomorrow to check things out and cover the hole in the roof. I guess they wanted to leave it open to allow the last of the smoke to escape and to be certain the fire didn't sneak back and re-ignite itself. Uncle Evert said no one was allowed to sleep in the farmhouse until the firemen came back and declared it was safe.

Two electric pumps were set up in the basement to pump out the water that had collected down there from the fire hoses. The pumped water trickled through hoses pulled through a basement window out to the backyard where it flowed across the grass down to the creek bordering the yard on the south side.

"Can I at least go in there and see if any of my comic books survived?" Luke asked Uncle Evert.

"Yeah, and what about the bathroom?" Emma asked. "Are we allowed to use that? I'm dying. What am I supposed to do? Go in the woods?"

"Okay, okay. I guess there's no reason you can't go into the house and look around and use the bathroom when you need to. Just be careful. There's still a lot of water on the floor throughout the house. Don't hang around in there longer any than you have to, and don't take any showers yet," Uncle Evert instructed.

"Oh, good! Let's go!" Emma exclaimed, practically galloping into the house. "I want to change out of these jammies."

I followed through the side screen door leading to the kitchen. The strong smell of smoke immediately assaulted me, and I clutched my hand up over my nose. The staircase leading down to the cellar was on the right. I could hear the rhythmic hum of the pumps as they did their work in the damp cavern. Straight ahead were two steps leading up to the kitchen and the rest of the house. I went up the steps into the narrow kitchen and surveyed the situation. The gray and white linoleum floor was slick with puddles of water, but nothing else in the room appeared to be burned or to have smoke damage. Two kitchen chairs were shoved aside, probably when the firemen rushed through to get to the fire in the back bedroom. Emma bolted through the kitchen to the bathroom in the hall and slammed the door shut. The bathroom was next to Luke and Lars's bedroom in the back corner of the house. I gazed back toward their bedroom and could see glimpses of the blackened walls, the furniture turned topsy-turvy, and a pile of wet things on the floor.

I proceeded into the dining room. A wide arch separated the dining room from the living room at the front of the house overlooking Allisonville Road. The living room in particular appeared undisturbed, other than the smell of smoke and a general dampness. Emma's bedroom was through an archway off to the right of the living room, separated by old gold brocade curtains that created a makeshift door. I pulled the curtains back and peered in. The sheets on her white canopy bed in the corner were in disarray, giving testament to the haste in which she'd fled, but nothing else appeared out of order.

"Does it look bad in there?" Emma asked, walking up behind me.

She pulled the curtains back, bolted across the room to a small table next to her bed, and picked up a small, leather-bound book lying there.

Unlocking a small brass lock on its side with a little key she took from the drawer, she opened the little tome and carefully examined its gilt-edged pages.

"It's okay. It's okay," she sighed, clasping it to her chest. "I'd absolutely *die* if this had been ruined."

"What is it?" I asked.

"My diary," she explained. "It's very private. All of my secrets are in it. Things I don't want anyone else to read, not even Margret." She locked the diary again and put it back in the drawer along with the little key.

Suddenly, Luke stomped from his room to the middle of the dining room. "Oh, fire gods who plague us. Ye art truly masters of evil!" he bellowed.

"What on earth is wrong with you?" Emma shouted. She and I ran between the curtains to the living room to find Luke holding a soggy stack of comic books.

"Look at these comic books! Did the firemen have to dump all of the White River on us just to put out one measly little fire? This bites so bad! So much for years of collecting." He dropped the dripping mess into a pile on the floor and sorrowfully gazed down on it as if bidding farewell to the favorite family pet.

Emma looked at me and shrugged. "It doesn't seem too bad to me. Who cares about a bunch of silly old comic books? I was scared the whole house was going to burn down."

"I'll bet it was really scary," I sympathized as we walked back into her bedroom, leaving Luke to deal with his loss. "I can't imagine waking up with my house on fire. I used to worry about that happening all the time when I was a kid. I'd wake up in the middle of the night and be afraid to fall back asleep for fear the house would catch fire while I slept. My mother had to reassure me all the time that it wouldn't."

"Well, it happened to *me*," Emma said, making a face. She walked to the dresser and pulled out a pair of red shorts and a striped T shirt and quickly changed into them.

Suddenly, there was a terrible commotion outside. It sounded as though Uncle Evert was arguing with someone. Emma and I darted through the gold curtains to the dining room window to see what was going on. Uncle Evert was standing in the driveway talking to an old man dressed in rumpled clothes. The elderly gentleman had Dorito, the German shepherd, on a leash.

"You must get control over your *Kinder*——I mean children——*Herr* Larsson," the old man said in a heavy German accent, pointing at Uncle Evert in a threatening way. "I've been all over Hamilton County searching for Fritz. I have better things to do than waste my time rounding up *mein Hund*."

"Your dog must have jumped the fence or found some other way to get out on its own. You have no reason to conclude that any of my kids let him out. I doubt they've ever even seen your dog before," Uncle Evert replied calmly.

Suddenly, the dog lunged toward Uncle Evert and strained against his leash, barking and then letting out a low growl. It was as though he were reflecting the angry attitude of his master. Uncle Evert flinched and took two steps backward.

"Down Fritz! *Platz*! *Sitz*!" the old man commanded. He gave the leash a hard jerk, and the dog whimpered and sat quietly, as instructed.

"*Das ist absurd!* Fritz is too wise to jump the fence," the old man continued angrily. "I have seen your kids back in the fields near my property doing God knows what. They are nothing but undisciplined, teenaged troublemakers. I know the truth is that they let him out. There is no other way it could have happened. Now you tell those *Kinder* to stay off my property and away from my farm, or there will be trouble. I guarantee it, *Herr* Larsson. *Ich warne Sie*!"

The old man didn't give Uncle Evert a chance to rebut, and turned abruptly and walked to his old Ford pickup truck parked half-way down the driveway, taking Dorito——or Fritz——with him. He started the truck and made a sharp U-turn, his tires kicking gravel into the grass, and sped away.

Emma and I ran out of the house and rushed over to Uncle Evert. Aunt Louise and Luke did the same.

"Who was *that*?" Aunt Louise asked, watching the old Ford pickup race away.

"Yeah, who's the crazy Nazi?" Luke inquired. "What's his problem? Is he mad we won World War II or something?"

"He said his name is Kleinschmidt, and that he bought the Henderson farm just north of here a little more than a year ago," Uncle Evert replied.

"The Henderson farm?" Aunt Louise repeated. "I've wondered who moved in there. I've never seen Mr. Kleinschmidt before. He must keep to himself."

"Except for today," Luke quipped.

"He claims you let his dog out, Luke. Did you?" Uncle Evert asked pointedly.

"Heck no, Dad," Luke answered. "Why would I do that? That's not the kind of dog I'd want around here. Too mean. Why's that old geezer picking on *me*?"

"That's what I told him—that you didn't let it out," Uncle Evert said, peering at Luke as though he could tell just by looking at him whether he was lying. "You kids don't hang around near his property, do you?"

"Not really. But the little house Buzz and Lars just built isn't too far from where he lives. We've been hanging around there a little lately, sure. I can't help it if Colonel Klink lives nearby."

"Well, stay as far away from him and his farm as you can. I don't care much for Mr. Kleinschmidt and don't want to tangle with him again if I can help it. Don't give him any reason to come back here," Uncle Evert directed.

"You got it, Dad," Luke replied. "You and I see eye-to-eye on that."

Emma and I went back into the house to continue looking around, while Aunt Louise checked the closets and the kitchen cupboards for what she could salvage. She exclaimed "Oh, my!" every now and then. Almost all of the food in the kitchen was ruined, except for a few cans of Campbell's soup and four or five cans of Stokely-Van Camp lima beans and creamed corn, all of which Aunt Louise stacked on the small kitchen table. The electricity had been off for several hours, so just about everything in the old refrigerator was spoiled. Emma discovered a half-eaten bag of Chips Ahoy! chocolate chip cookies left sitting on the green couch in the living room before the fire. The bag had miraculously escaped getting wet or smashed in the chaos.

"Mmm! Want one?" she asked, munching on a cookie. I dug my hand into the bag and pulled out two. They weren't terribly fresh and had a slightly smoky flavor, but were edible and I was hungry.

I walked back to Luke's room to get a better look and peeked in. The walls were totally blackened by the flames and covered with soot. Wet, dirty clothes, sheets, shoes, and books lay in a heap in the middle of the room. Large areas of the ceiling were missing, leaving gaps that extended through the attic to the roof, and there were openings where the firemen had cut holes in the roof that allowed the sky to peek through. Scorched shirts, pants, and jackets still hung on their wire hangers in the doorless closet. The bunk bed mattresses, blackened with soot, were thrown topsy-turvy into the corner of the room. The room was a wreck. A lot of repairs would definitely be needed.

Luke and Uncle Evert busied themselves carrying the formal dining room table and chairs and some other smaller pieces of furniture out to the yard. The pungent smoke lingering in the house began to make my eyes water, and I went outside and sat down on one of the dining chairs placed on the uneven ground. Soon, Emma's older sister and brother, Margret and Lars, arrived in a red Ford Falcon station wagon they borrowed from Uncle Forrest. Uncle Evert had sent them off to Kenley's Super Market in Noblesville to purchase supplies. They dropped the four or five brown paper bags full of food on the dining table.

"This certainly is a unique predicament," Lars said, gazing at the house. He was about twenty, tall and slim, with straight dark hair parted on the side. "Has anyone figured out where we're going to stay until the house is habitable again? Are we going to a hotel?"

"Wendy says I can stay with her for as long as I want," Margret replied.

Margret was nineteen, with straight dark blonde hair that fell to her waist. Her bangs were cut long and the crown of her hair was teased in the Mod style of the trendsetters on Carnaby Street in London. She was surprisingly well dressed for someone who'd just escaped a fire in the middle of the night, wearing a cream-and-red striped knit shirt under a navy A-line jumper with white knee socks and flats. She told me later she borrowed the clothes from our cousin Wendy who lived across the road with her brother Daniel and the rest of their family.

"We're not going anywhere. We're going to stay right here!" Uncle Evert declared with his usual determination. He was holding two long wooden poles he'd gotten from the barn. "Help me set these up."

"What're those for? Those aren't tent poles, are they? You can't mean we're going to live in tents! That's not civilized," Lars complained.

"Oh, come on. It'll be just like Boy Scout camp," Luke fired up. "Sounds like fun to me!"

"Your grandparents slept outside all summer many years ago while they rebuilt after the top floor of this house burned. If they could do it, so can you," Uncle Evert said. "Now help me get these tent poles in the ground."

While Lars, Luke, and Uncle Evert dealt with setting up the tent in just the right spot, Emma and I helped Aunt Louise unpack the groceries and make honey loaf lunch meat sandwiches on slices of white Wonder Bread smothered with French's mustard with a slice of American cheese. Everyone gobbled them down without complaint, and then helped devour a big bag of Mikesell's potato chips.

The day passed quickly as I helped my aunt and uncle clean up the yard and sort through what could be salvaged. Before long it was early evening. There was no trace of any rain or unfavorable weather, and the temperature was warm—-perfect for sleeping outside. I hadn't seen the little house yet, and was curious what I was in for tonight as far as sleeping arrangements went. Daniel reappeared just before sundown. Not long after that Luke, Daniel, Emma, and I left for the little house, each armed with a clean sheet or old quilt Aunt Louise managed to find in the back of the closet in Emma's room. Aunt Louise also found an unopened bag of marshmallows in the kitchen and gave it to us to take, together with several bottles of Coca-Cola.

We crossed the yard, passed the barn, and crossed two grassy fields until we finally came to an area where the ground sloped gently downhill to a dry creek bed and then rose to a small ridge of land on the opposite side. There, at last, along the dry creek bed, was the little house. The structure was much larger than a typical playhouse, and was the size of a small house that real people might live in. It was built with unpainted weathered wood, with a peaked roof and a wooden floor. Large windows were cut out on either side of the door opening, and there were small windows on its two side walls, although there was no glass in any of them and no actual door. An old elm tree arched over the house completing its picturesque setting.

"There's the castle where you'll be sleeping tonight," Luke said, nodding toward the small structure. "What'd ya think?"

"Hmmm. Looks very nice," I said diplomatically. I wasn't ready to commit whole-heartedly until I'd had a chance to thoroughly check it out.

I was relieved when I saw the large white barn with the gambrel roof that my grandfather built was untouched.

We walked down to the little cottage and I looked inside. The wooden floor was built about ten inches off the ground. Luke and Daniel stepped up first and went inside, and Emma and I followed. The house had only one room that was surprisingly roomy and pleasant, with a ceiling high enough to comfortably accommodate a tall adult. A doorway in the back corner led to an adjoining smaller room that had four walls, but no roof or floor.

"Buzz hasn't gotten around to finishing that room yet," Daniel explained. "He says it's going to be the bedroom."

I took in the views from the windows and could see plenty of fields with tall grasses and some trees, as well as the back of the barn far in the distance, but no other house, barn, or structure. It felt so secluded that I could almost imagine being a pioneer on the prairie as I surveyed the scene.

"Why did Buzz build this? I don't think you said," I asked.

"You know Buzz," Daniel explained. "My brother's got to be doing something all the time or he goes nuts."

"Don't forget that Lars helped him build this," Emma added.

"Hey. You want to see Old Man Kleinschmidt's place?" Luke asked. "You can see it from the top of the ridge outside. Come on, I'll show you."

"You'd better remember what Dad said," Emma said. "He said to stay away from Mr. Kleinschmidt."

"Aw, we aren't going to bother the old man. We're just going to look," Luke said, with a devilish glint in his eyes.

"Who's Mr. Kleinschmidt?" Daniel asked.

"He's the old dude who bought the Henderson farm. He paid us a visit earlier today. Quite a charming man, I must say," Luke replied sarcastically.

"Charming? What do you mean?" Daniel asked, looking confused.

"Oh, just ignore him," Emma replied. "He's kidding, as usual."

Luke darted out the door and was taking long strides up the ridge before we could say another word. We followed, and before long we were standing on the crest of the ridge next to him.

"Look. Down there," he said, pointing north.

In the distance was a small, two-story farmhouse with white paint and black shutters. Several farm buildings stood near the house, and high chain-link fences surrounded the house and the buildings in a complicated design that appeared to be designed to prevent anyone from entering.

"What's with all those crazy fences?" Daniel pondered. "Almost looks like a military installation or something. What's in there that's so important?"

"It's just an old guy," Luke answered dismissively. "He's got nothing important, I'm sure, except his false teeth and walker!" He let out a burst of laughter, and then continued. "He's just paranoid like old people sometimes are."

"Look! There's the German shepherd," I said. "Fritz. See him?" In a separate fenced area, Fritz milled around the way dogs do.

"Yep, there's the devil dog," Luke answered. "I see him."

As we watched, Mr. Kleinschmidt walked out of the house carrying a bucket and walked over to Fritz's pen and entered. He put the bucket down, and Fritz began to wolf down its contents. But as if he had radar, the dog suddenly stopped eating, looked in our direction, and began barking. Mr. Kleinschmidt quickly took note of Fritz's warning and peered intently in our direction, trying his best to see what—or who—the dog was alerting him to.

"Whoops! We're busted!" Luke said, falling to his stomach. "Quick, you guys! Get down!" He gestured for us to get down.

"Why? What have *we* done?" Daniel asked while slowly getting to his knees and then onto his stomach. "What's going on?"

"I'm not going to get down there and get the one clean shirt I have all dirty," Emma protested. "I'm going back to the little house. You can stay up here if you want. He's just a crazy old man and there's nothing to see. Come on, Vanessa. Let's go."

"Spoil sports!" Luke jeered as we walked away.

Emma and I made our way back down the ridge to the little house and sat together in the doorway.

"So, what's the deal with that old guy?" Daniel asked as he and Luke arrived back at the little house moments later. "Why are you afraid of him? Why'd we have to drop to the ground like that?"

"Who, me? I'm not afraid of that old Nazi," Luke replied, puffing out his chest slightly as he spoke. "It's just that he's a little off his rocker and has it in for me for some crazy reason. On top of that, he's got a mean dog. That's all. I didn't want him to see me and get more crazy ideas again about accusing me of things I didn't do."

Daniel looked at him as though he didn't believe him and shrugged.

"What's with the shrug? Do I have to give you the five-minute treatment, or something?" Luke taunted, looking sternly at Daniel. "Don't make me do that to you, son. Don't make me."

"Okay, okay. Have it your way, I believe you. You're not afraid of the old guy," Daniel replied, leaning away from Luke. "Chill out, dude, will ya?"

Luke seemed satisfied with Daniel's response for the time being and relaxed. We decided to make a campfire, so we fanned out and collected twigs and small limbs. The boys built a small fire near the little house door and we sat around it as the evening darkness crept in. We roasted marshmallows on long twigs that Luke sharpened to a point with his Swiss army knife, and passed around the Coke bottles. We laughed, told stories, and discussed the house fire and how scary it had been.

"What if you hadn't wakened us? We might have all died in the fire," Emma said, staring into the fire. "I don't think I'll ever be able to get a good night's sleep in that house now. I'll be too worried about another fire starting." She seemed tearful and fiddled with a long piece of grass. "When I saw Dad running back inside into the smoke to save Karma, I thought I might never see him or the cat again, and I couldn't take it," she continued.

"Oh, now, Sis," Luke replied. "That fire was a fluke. We'll figure out what started it, and fix the problem. It'll be okay."

Luke was being uncharacteristically consoling. I looked across the campfire and smiled at him.

"That reminds me—who's going to take the first watch for those colored lights?" Luke asked. "That's the reason we're out here, isn't it?"

"Not me," Emma replied, yawning. "I'm too tired tonight to stay up looking for some goofy lights you say you've seen that I don't believe you ever saw."

"Well, you'll miss seeing them, but you're dismissed because you almost got toasted in a fire this morning. Vanessa, Daniel, and I will just have to share the burden, won't we guys?"

"Well, I don't think...I mean...couldn't you guys handle it without me?" I pleaded, trying my best to look sympathetic.

"Oh, you're hopeless, City Slicker," Luke answered. "Just forget it. Daniel and I will handle this all by ourselves, as usual."

"Good. Have fun. Try not to get beamed up into a flying saucer," I replied. "I understand they like to perform experiments on Earthling boys. If you're not back here by morning, I'll know what happened."

"Ha, ha," Luke replied flatly.

Not long after, Emma went inside the little house and rolled up in her sheet on the floor. I followed shortly, while the boys remained outside poking at the fire with their sticks. Emma fell asleep right away, judging from her regular, deep breathing.

As I lay on the floor, I wondered if there really were colored lights, and if there were, would they come back tonight. We were far back in the fields where no one would be able to hear us call for help if we needed it. It was pitch dark outside except for the solitary light of our campfire. Anyone, or *anything*, could be out there. As my mind raced with these thoughts, the floor underneath me grew more and more hard and uncomfortable. I lay on my back, and then on my side, and then on my back again, but no position was comfortable. How would I be able to endure the night? I could see that sleeping in the little house wasn't such a great idea. Why did I agree to it? As I watched the shadows of the camp fire reflect off the back wall, I somehow, mercifully, fell asleep, and slept surprisingly well, until...

CHAPTER THREE

Blue-Green Lights in the Sky

Luke was screaming his head off as he practically flew down the side of the ridge to the door of the little house and fell inside. It was the middle of the night, and the campfire had burned down to nothing but a few smoldering embers.

"Hurry! Get up! Hurry! You've got to see this. You won't believe it! Come on. Get up!" he shouted, breathing heavily.

My eyes snapped open at the sound of his booming voice, and I sat up with a start. My sheet had become wrapped around my ankles during the night, explaining why my shoulders were cold, and I worked to untangle myself. Daniel had been asleep on the other side of the room, and he quickly scrambled to his feet.

"Oh, go away!" Emma mumbled. She rolled over and squinted at us, then tugged her sheet up around her ears, turned on her side, and fell back asleep.

"Forget her. Come on, City Slicker. You like to solve puzzles, don't you? You've got to see this!" Luke urged. "Vanessa! Let's go! Come *on*!"

I stood up, yawning and a bit dazed. My shoulder was stiff from sleeping on my side and I was still half asleep. While I was still collecting myself, Luke darted out the door with Daniel close behind. I stumbled out and followed them as they clambered up the ridge. Luke stopped at the crest, crouched down, and pointed into the sky.

"There! What'd I tell you? What do you say about that?" he asked. He was almost breathless with excitement.

I looked up and was amazed by what I saw. There, in the distant sky, was something large silently hovering about as high as a low-flying plane. It had bluish-green lights and barely moved, as though suspended by an unseen cord. It was difficult to see clearly in the dark, but I could make out the silhouette of a round craft about the size of large truck. It had no wings or propellers and didn't look like anything I'd ever seen.

"Wha....what on earth is *that*?" I blurted as I crouched low to avoid being seen by anyone who might be inside the hovering object. I gulped, remembering the scene from the movie *The Day the Earth Stood Still* when an alien named Klaatu came to earth and landed his flying saucer on the mall in Washington, D.C. Everyone in the movie went nuts with fear and ran in all directions like ants. But that was only a movie, and everyone knows aliens don't *really* come to earth. Or, do they? What was I seeing here and now? A UFO? Was Klaatu coming to earth for real this time? That couldn't be, but it clearly wasn't a plane or a helicopter. What else could it be? A ripple of sheer panic ran through me, and I felt slightly light-headed.

"That's the same thing I saw the other night," Luke whispered. "Notice how silent it is? That's no airplane, I guarantee it."

"Then what is it?" I gasped as I watched the blue-green lights pulse slightly, then become a silver glow. "Maybe we should get out of here."

"Is it my imagination, or does it seem like it's hovering over Kleinschmidt's farm? It's hard to tell for sure at this distance, but it sure seems like it might be," Luke observed, ignoring my suggestion to flee.

"Yeah, I think you're right," Daniel agreed.

"Should we warn Mr. Kleinschmidt—you know—let him know it's there right over his farm?" I asked.

"You know, now that I think about it, maybe Kleinschmidt's an alien, and they've come to take him back to their planet," Daniel suggested.

"If only that were true. They'd be doing all of us a big favor!" Luke joked.

"How do you know it's not true?" Daniel replied. The two boys chuckled together.

"You guys!" I whispered loudly. "Stop joking around. This is serious."

"Calm down, City Slicker. Kleinschmidt probably already knows it's there. I mean, it's kinda hard to miss," Luke pointed out.

We continued kneeling for several minutes with our eyes riveted on the spectacle hovering in the sky. Would it land? Would green men emerge with laser guns and start zapping every living thing they encountered?

I didn't know what we should do, but it seemed as though we should do something to warn the world that this thing—whatever it was—was there. Was anyone else in Hamilton County seeing it? Surely someone would call the proper authorities to report it. Then again, it was the middle of the night. Maybe no one else was awake to see it. That meant it was up to us to take proper action to save the Earth. Who would believe us when we told them? A photo would be persuasive, but we didn't have a camera, and even if we did, the chances of getting a good photograph at this distance at night weren't good. How would we be able to convince anyone of what we were seeing? It was too incredible for *me* to believe, and I was looking right at it!

I couldn't take my eyes off of whatever it was. I expected to see it swoop like a flash into the sky at any moment and disappear into a mere pinpoint of light, but it didn't. Would it land and spill open with dozens of large-headed green men looking to colonize the Earth? It didn't do that either. My feeling of panic began to overtake me, and just when I contemplated dashing off to the farmhouse to alert Uncle Evert and Aunt Louise, the blue-green lights began to fade. Then, abruptly and suddenly, everything went totally dark. The craft—or whatever we were looking at—disappeared before our very eyes. None of us spoke, waiting for what would happen next, but the night was silent, except for the crickets, and the sky empty. Several minutes passed, and the lights didn't reappear. The show was apparently over—for now.

"Where'd it go?" I asked quietly. "Is it gone?"

"I think so," Luke answered. "Just like last time, it doesn't stay around very long."

We waited on the crest of the ridge in the tall grass for another half hour or so to see if it would reappear. My gaze was locked onto the area where the lights had been. But I saw and heard nothing more. We finally gave up and ambled back down the ridge to the little house.

"There must be a logical explanation for what we just saw," Luke said as we walked along. "After all, we're not crazy hippies having a drug-induced hallucination, you know."

"I wish!" Daniel joked, making a peace sign with two fingers.

"Right. As if, Mr. Squeaky-Clean," Luke chortled.

"What if this is the end of the world, like in the movie *Invaders from Mars*? Those lights could have been a Martian ship dropping off green people with giant heads who want to take over our planet," I cautioned. "Maybe they beamed down a landing party, and we didn't see them do it. They could be out in the fields watching us right now!" I checked over my shoulder for any movement or other indication of someone following us.

"Oh, calm down, City Slicker, will ya?" Luke replied. "If they were going to do anything, they'd have done it by now, don't you think? After all, I saw those same lights two nights ago. Let's just go back to the little house and get some sleep for now and deal with it tomorrow. Okay?"

Let's just get some sleep? Was Luke serious? I didn't want to go back to the little house. It was much too close to where we'd seen the UFO. But what else could I do? I could either make my way back to the farmhouse where everyone would be asleep and wake them up and tell them a crazy story about lights in the sky, or I could try to sleep in the little house and wait until morning. On top of that, if I stayed, maybe Luke wouldn't call me by that dreaded *City Slicker* name anymore. So I decided to stay.

Back at the little house, Emma was still sound asleep. She'd never believe what we had just seen when I told her tomorrow. Too bad she slept through it all and missed witnessing the phenomenon. I smoothed out my sheet on the floor and did my best to wrap myself snugly in it. Being nestled in something, even something as flimsy as a sheet, was strangely comforting. Instead of situating themselves for sleep, Luke sat on the floor leaning against one of the side walls and fiddled with his pocket knife. Daniel sat leaning against the adjacent wall.

"Go ahead and sleep and I'll keep an eye on things," Luke instructed Daniel.

"That's all right. I don't feel like sleeping," Daniel replied.

I didn't feel like sleeping either. Try as I did, I was too worked up to relax and nod off. I attempted to force myself to listen to the rhythmic songs of the crickets in the trees as a distraction, but I couldn't crowd out thoughts about that "thing" in the sky. Would it return as we slept? What would we do if it did? Would the aliens find us here in the little house? Were they walking around outside this very minute? We'd be sitting ducks if they came for us. I stayed on alert listening for the crunching sounds of approaching footsteps that I assumed were inevitable. But then I had a thought: What if aliens float a few inches off the ground and don't make walking sounds? We'd never hear them sneak up on us!

Thoughts about running back to the farmhouse ran through my mind again, but I didn't act on them. All I had to do was cope until morning, which couldn't come fast enough. What time was it? It was too dark to be able to read my watch. It had to be almost daybreak. Surely the sun would peek through the darkness any minute, and this uncomfortable night would finally end. Please!

CHAPTER FOUR

Shed Those Dowdy Feathers and Fly

I fell into a troubled sleep sometime during the night. In the morning, the rhythmic sounds of Luke digging around in the campfire embers awakened me. The bright sun was up and the world looked normal again. It hadn't come to an end during the night after all! I sighed with relief and grabbed my eye glasses lying on the floor next to me and slid them on. Emma was still blissfully asleep wrapped in her pink sheet. Daniel lay on the opposite side of the room using his wadded up fringed frontier coat as a pillow.

"Hey, you sleepyheads in there!" Luke shouted. "Get up. We have things to do today! We can't dawdle here all day."

I stumbled to my feet and stretched. I was hungry, and felt rumpled, tired, and dirty, as if I'd been on a hike all night.

"What time is it?" Emma asked, rolling over. "I slept like a log!" She smiled and stretched contentedly.

"Yes, you sure did," Luke replied, leaning through the door. "Too bad you missed the UFO."

"What? A UFO? No way," she scoffed. Then, looking at me, she asked, "Was there *really* a UFO?"

I nodded. "Yep. There was. For real."

A look of surprise crossed her face. She paused and studied each of our faces, then jumped up and clumsily folded her sheet. "Oh, you guys. Very funny. Ha, ha. Nice try."

"But—-we *did* see something," Luke insisted. "Up in the sky."

"Oh sure you did," she replied. "Cut it out."

"Have it your way," Luke replied. He resumed poking at the dead embers.

We collected our trash and bedding, and then made our way across the fields to the farmhouse.

"Okay, come on, tell me for real. Did you see the colored lights again last night? Did you?" Emma asked as we walked along.

"I already told you we did," Luke answered impatiently. "Are you hard of hearing or something?"

"Then why didn't you wake me up?" she complained. "I wanted to see it, too, you know."

"We tried, but you were in your zombie mode and insisted we let you sleep. You know what they say—you snooze, you lose. You snore, you don't score. Catch some zzzs, wake up with fleas," Luke taunted.

"All right, already!" Emma shouted, glaring at him. "Stop it with the stupid rhymes. I get it."

"Wait! I have one more. You snore, you bore — *me*!" Luke continued, laughing. Emma punched him in the arm, and he playfully pretended it hurt.

I studied the blue sky and wondered if whatever I'd seen was up there waiting to swoop down and perform experiments on us. Or maybe it was hiding behind the clouds, observing us and waiting for just the right moment to descend. Perhaps it had zipped away faster than the speed of light to explore another universe and was gone forever. I was uncomfortable not knowing what to expect next.

As we approached the large green tent set up in the farmhouse side yard, Lars was busy cooking breakfast on a Coleman camp stove sitting on a small table in front of the tent. I could smell the delicious aroma of bacon almost as soon as I turned the corner of the barn. Like thirsty cattle stampeding to a stream, we practically knocked each other over running to the dining room table to eat.

"Mmm...bacon!" Luke said, plucking a crisp slice from a paper plate and popping it into his mouth.

"Hey, cut that out! That's *my* breakfast. You can make your own when I'm done," Lars protested, threatening to smack Luke's hand with the spatula.

The family radio was sitting on the dining room table, and I smiled at how appropriate it was when "I Can't Get No Satisfaction" by the Rolling Stones came on.

Aunt Louise was in the tent straightening things up. When she heard us, she lifted the tent flap and walked out. "Good morning, everyone. How'd you sleep? I think it'll take my back some time to adjust to that hard cot. I don't know how young men in the army manage to get any sleep on them."

"Well, I didn't sleep too well, either, and it wasn't because of a hard cot," Luke offered. "Did any of you see something unusual in the sky late last night?"

Uncle Evert appeared from the garage carrying a large water jug just in time to hear the question. "I heard one or two planes going over to Gatewood Airport, but that's about it. You know how they come and go at all hours." He placed the jug on the table.

"No, not a plane. Something *else*," Luke hinted in an ominous voice.

"What do you mean? What else could there be in the sky?" Uncle Evert asked.

"Come on, Dad. You're not thinking hard enough," Luke coaxed.

"Oh, for crying out loud," Lars exclaimed as he stirred scrambled eggs on the stove. "Are you hinting that you saw a UFO or something ridiculous like that last night?"

"Well, yes, as a matter of fact that's exactly what I'm saying. It was hovering over Kleinschmidt's farm," Luke answered with an air of indignation. "Come on, guys. Isn't that right? Back me up here." He gestured at Daniel and me, and we nodded in agreement on cue.

"With blue-green lights," I added, thinking an additional detail might add credibility.

"Probably just swamp gas or a weather balloon," Lars replied dryly as he dished the eggs onto a plate. "People see strange lights in the sky all the time, and there's always a logical explanation. Those people think they've seen a UFO, too, but it never is."

"There's no swamp back there. How do you come up with swamp gas as an explanation?" Luke shot back. "And, who would launch a weather balloon around here? Those are stupid ideas and don't explain it."

"You're free to believe you saw whatever you think you saw. Just don't expect everyone to agree with you," Uncle Evert cautioned.

"I know, Dad, but I know what I saw," Luke protested. "It was really something to see, too. It had lights, and it hovered and then suddenly disappeared. Maybe we should call the sheriff or something and report it."

"Call the sheriff? He'd be furious we wasted his time," Uncle Evert replied.

"Hey— the Beatles' manager, Brian Epstein, just died," Lars interrupted, his eyes fixed on the pages of the newspaper he was reading while he ate. "Says here they found him dead in his bedroom. They think it was a sleeping pill overdose. He was only thirty-two. Wow."

"Margret and Wendy will be upset," Daniel observed. "They're crazy for the Beatles. They're always saying the Fab Four are outta sight."

"Does that mean the Beatles will break up?" Emma asked.

"No. They'll find another manager and keep going. It'd be my guess the Beatles have another three or four years before they fade into oblivion," Uncle Evert opined.

"They'll disappear from the music scene soon, no doubt about it, with or without Brian Epstein," Lars said, still reading.

Luke shook his head with exasperation. "Is that all you guys have to say about what we saw last night? Seriously? Well, so be it." He gazed mournfully at the smoke-stained walls of the house, and then plopped down in a dining chair. "I'd go to my room, if I had one," he said wistfully. "A prophet is without honor in his own country."

"Are you quoting the Bible?" Daniel smirked. "Never thought I'd ever witness that from a heathen like you!"

"Luke, make yourself some breakfast. A person always sees things more clearly when he's got a full stomach," Aunt Louise suggested, patting his shoulder as she walked by.

Daniel left to go home, while Luke did as Aunt Louise suggested, and went over to the Coleman stove to cook eggs and bacon. It quickly became apparent he was a novice at cooking. Emma and I agreed to be his assistant chefs on the condition he share the food with us. When we finally sat down to eat, I was glad for hot food again.

After I ate, I took my little suitcase into the bathroom, splashed some water on my face, and changed into my new brown cotton slacks and yellow knit top. I pulled my hair back into a thick pony tail, and carefully put on my eyeliner. I didn't know what today would bring, and I wanted to be ready.

"Hey, City Slicker," Luke said when I emerged from the house. "I was just on the phone with Jim, and he said to say hi."

I was delighted and stunned to hear Jim's name spoken, and that he was sending me a greeting. I gulped and did my best to appear cool and collected. No need to reveal to the others that the mere mention of Jim's name made my stomach turn inside out. Emma knew how I felt, of course. She shot me a knowing look and smiled.

"You...you were on the phone with Jim?" I replied. "You mean....the phone's working?" I wasn't really interested whether the phone was working or not, but thought it would throw everyone off if I talked about that. I could sneak in a question about Jim later.

"Well, yeah," Luke said. "I picked up the receiver and heard a dial tone, so I dialed his number to see if it worked, and he answered. So, I guess that means it's working again. The phone lines must be separate from the electrical lines."

"Well, that's good. By the way, how is Jim?" I asked as casually as I could. Now I was really getting down to what I cared about.

"He's the same," Luke said with annoying brevity. Then he added, "His shoulder's still sore from that crash a few weeks ago. He thinks it might mean he can't play ball when school starts again. At least not as pitcher."

"Bummer," I murmured.

I'd heard about the crash from Emma. A few weeks ago Jim lost control of his bike while going down the hill on Eller Road to 116th Street. He flew over the handle bars, landed on his shoulder, and seriously damaged his rotator cuff. I worried about how he was doing, but stopped myself from asking more questions. I could have asked if he was on his way over, or if he asked about me and how I was doing, or if he asked how long I'd be visiting. I could have asked if he'd gone back to seeing his old girlfriend Monica. But I didn't. I had to admit my self-control was improving when it came to *talking* about him, even if I wasn't making much progress when it came to thinking about him, which I did all the time. I sat down at the table and focused on the red-and-white checked vinyl tablecloth so no one could read the thoughts I was certain were written all over my face. Luke didn't offer any more information about Jim. I wished he had.

As the day progressed, I did my best to help Aunt Louise and Uncle Evert organize their lives around their new living arrangements. Emma and I helped Aunt Louise sort through stacks of clothes to decide which were too damaged by smoke and soot to be kept, and which could be salvaged with a good washing. Aunt Louise carried large loads of clothes out of the house and dumped them on the dining room table. We picked up each piece, studied it, and gave it a good sniff. I'm not sure how helpful Emma and I were; Aunt Louise seemed to have her own opinion about each piece. Nonetheless, we were at least able to help her fold the clothes she wanted to save and place them into plastic laundry baskets and paper bags to take to the coin-operated laundry in Noblesville.

Just when we were almost done sorting, Margret arrived from being over at Wendy's for the night, and said she wanted to sort through her own clothes, which we hadn't touched yet. She went inside and returned with a large bundle of clothes and starting sorting. She stopped for a moment and fiddled with the radio. When the DJ announced the WIBC call letters, she appeared satisfied and resumed sorting, with a little dancing thrown in to the strains of "Georgy Girl" by the Seekers.

"Hey, Vanessa. Do you want this?" Margret asked, holding up a navy crocheted vest. "You can have it if you want. I've got another one that's almost identical that I like a little better for me."

"Really? Well sure!" I said, eagerly taking it. It was the kind of stylish vest shown in *Glamour* or *Mademoiselle* that was long and looked great with short skirts or bell bottoms, and I was delighted to get it. "Groovy!" I said, putting it on.

I ran over to the garage windows to see my reflection. I could see enough to know it looked great, even over my yellow top, and I spun around happily. Margret laughed and clapped her hands together.

"I love it!" I declared, almost caressing it. "Thanks!" I felt older in it, and that was a good feeling.

Meanwhile, Uncle Evert, Lars, and Luke worked on placing plywood boards over the windows that were broken out in the fire. Uncle Evert stood on a tall ladder with a hammer and nails, while the two boys held the heavy boards in place below. One by one, the windows in the boys' room and in the middle bedroom were boarded up.

After a few hours, an insurance agent arrived and walked around and through the house, checking out the damage and taking photographs. Just as he left, a man in an old pickup truck with *Anderson Construction* painted on the door arrived and talked with Uncle Evert about making repairs to the house. It was a busy day at the Larsson house.

After the Anderson Construction man left, Uncle Evert strolled out of the house and called out, "Who's in favor of going for a bite of lunch?"

"Where're you thinking of going?" Luke asked.

"Does it really matter?" Uncle Evert answered. "Since when do you care what you eat as long as there's plenty of it?" Luke just smiled and shrugged. "I think it'd do us all some good to take a break and get away from here for a couple of hours," my uncle added.

"I could use a change of scenery, but count me out," Lars said. "I'm waiting for a phone call from Wilking Music to find out about restoring the piano."

"Sorry, but count me out, too, Dad," Margret chimed in. "I'm going back over to Wendy's to hand-launder a few of my things. She said I could use her laundry and she'd help me with some of this."

"I'll go Dad," Emma shouted. "I'm starving." I was, too, and nodded that I'd go.

"Okay. Who else?" Uncle Evert asked, rubbing his hands together.

"I'm going to take these clothes up to the laundry in Noblesville and get the smoke and soot out as soon as possible, so I'll see you later," Aunt Louise said.

"Well, okay then. Luke and girls, into the van!" Uncle Evert commanded.

Emma and I took our positions in the back seat of Uncle Evert's Econoline van. He used it in his business and it was big, blue, and boxy, with a large area in the back accessed by double doors. Luke and Uncle Evert jumped into the front seats and we were ready to go.

The van rolled along the gravel driveway, around the turnaround, and down to Allisonville Road. We turned left and proceeded north. It was nice to get away from the farm and the fire and the UFO for a little while. I wondered where we were going, but it didn't matter. Anywhere with hot food would be good, as far as I was concerned. As I rode along, thoughts of Jim collided with thoughts of the UFO. I wondered if I'd ever see either of them again and was both anxious and excited that I might.

CHAPTER FIVE

May Loved Jim Dandy

Allisonville Road became 10th Street as we approached the heart of Noblesville, Indiana. We proceeded past Walnut, Vine, Mulberry, Cherry, and Maple Streets, and finally came to Conner Street where Uncle Evert turned east. We drove a short distance and finally came to Jim Dandy Drive-In and Coffee Shop. The restaurant's tall neon sign with the distinctive large red "V" was topped by a rotating white box bearing the image of a blond boy in blue overalls. The building had large windows in the front and an unusual white zig-zag roofline. Uncle Evert turned into the parking lot in front and parked.

Without further prompting, Emma, Luke, and I jumped out of the van and entered the restaurant through its main door on the side which was ornamented by tall glass panels. The room was filled with booths at the front buzzing with diners, with a long counter for individual diners at the back. Numerous barrel-shaped light pendants hung from the ceiling, and tall windows extended up to the vaulted ceiling at the front. The inviting aromas of coffee, hamburgers, and french fries were punctuated by the dusky odor of cigarette smoke that hung visibly in the air.

"Have a seat anywhere you can find one, honey," a waitress greeted us as she sped by holding a platter of food in each hand. "There's an empty booth over by the windows. I'll be with you in a jiffy." She nodded toward a booth near the front windows, so we made our way to it and sat down. The table still held several dishes, crumpled paper napkins, and half-empty soda glasses.

"Let me get rid of these for you," the waitress said, re-appearing suddenly. She stacked the dishes and took them away, then returned, wiped down the table, and passed around large paper menus. "What would you like to drink?" she asked, holding an order pad and pen at the ready.

"I'll have a chocolate malt," Luke said, his eyes shining.

"I'll have a Coke," Emma chimed in.

"Me, too," I said next.

"Just a cup of coffee for me—black," Uncle Evert said.

"Okay. Got it," the waitress said, hurrying away.

I opened my menu and studied it. A giant photograph of the Jim Dandy—a double decker hamburger piled high with all the trimmings—dominated one of the pages. It featured two hamburger patties with American cheese on a double-decker bun with lettuce, pickles, and the restaurant's special sauce.

"I'm starving. I'm going to have that huge Jim Dandy burger," Luke announced, his eyes fixed on the photo of the sandwich. "I can't wait to get my mouth around that! No, wait. Maybe I'll have the Jimbo instead. That looks pretty mammoth, also."

The Jimbo was pictured on the page opposite the Jim Dandy. It was a large submarine sandwich on an oblong bun, generously filled with large amounts of salami, ham, bacon, cheese, lettuce, and pickles.

"Why don't you get both?" Emma asked sarcastically. "Then you won't have to decide."

"Great idea!" Luke answered. "I'll have both, with a large french fry."

"I have a quiz show question for you," Uncle Evert asked, changing the subject while we waited for the waitress to return. "I bet you don't know how this place got its name, do you?"

"No. Can't say that I do," Luke answered. "And I can't say that I care," he added, still staring at the menu.

"Luke!" Emma blurted. "Don't speak to Dad that way."

"Okay, okay. Hmm. Jim Dandy. Sounds familiar, but why?" Luke said, drumming his fingers on the table. "Let me think."

"Jim Dandy. Isn't that a saying?" Emma offered. "Like when a person says 'I feel Jim Dandy today.'"

"Yes, that's close, but not quite the correct answer. How about you, Vanessa? Do you want to take a stab at it?" Uncle Evert asked, shifting his gaze to me. Luke hummed the background music used during the Final Jeopardy question in the TV game show, *Jeopardy!*

I searched my mind. "Um, well," I said, stalling. "Well, isn't there ...isn't there a song called 'Jim Dandy'?"

"Correct!" Uncle Evert exclaimed. "Vanessa got the answer! The owners named this place after the song 'Jim Dandy,' which was a very popular pop song when they opened in the late '50s," Uncle Evert explained. "Vanessa wins a piece of pie."

"Okay, genius. Just be prepared to share it with me," Luke warned, casting his eyes back down on the open menu. A large photo of strawberry pie also appeared in the menu. From the looks of its generous size, there would be more than enough of it to share.

"I'm going to go to the phone to make a call about an afternoon delivery I have to make today," Uncle Evert said. "You kids go ahead and order when the waitress comes back. Don't wait for me."

He got up and walked to a pay phone hanging on the wall near the entrance. After thumbing through a phone book lying on a shelf under the phone, he picked up the receiver and dialed. While he was gone, the waitress returned with our drinks and took our orders.

I looked around and noticed that a large number of teenagers were there. One girl in particular sitting in a booth on the other side of the restaurant caught my eye because she kept staring at us. She was about sixteen and sitting with two girls about the same age. She'd talk to them, then look over at us, then resume talking to her friends again. This went on for so long that I wondered what was going on. She was average in height and slightly plump, wore glasses, and had brown hair that flipped up at the shoulder. She wasn't a great beauty, but was pleasant looking and had a friendly air about her.

"Why is that girl over there looking at us?" I asked. "Do you know her?"

"Who?" Luke asked, turning around to see who I meant. He quickly turned back and put his hand up against the side of his face to try to hide himself.

"Oh, that's Bunny Bibble," Emma explained. "She's in Luke's class. Her real name is Bernadette. People used to call her Bernie and she hated it. She said it sounded like a boy's name. So, she started calling herself Bunny and it caught on. I think it's a cute name. Was she really looking over here?"

"She sure was. I think she was looking at Luke," I theorized.

"Hogwash!" Luke exclaimed. "Why would Bernie-the-Bruiser be looking at *me?*"

"I don't know, but here she comes," I said. Bunny was standing and moving in our direction.

"Don't you dare call her that mean name to her face," Emma warned. "That's a terrible name to call someone."

"She's taking her chances if she dares to come over here," Luke said. "I can't be held responsible for what I say if she does." He scrunched down in his seat and stared at the table, as if trying to will himself to disappear.

"Hi, Emma. Hi, Luke," Bunny said as she bravely strolled up to our table. She gave Luke a big smile.

"Hi, Bunny," Emma replied. "This is our cousin, Vanessa. What's new?"

She smiled and nodded hello to me. Then she turned toward Luke, who was still looking down at the table. "Not much. Say, Luke. Are you going to take second-year algebra with Mrs. Swanson this year? I hope so. Maybe we can study together sometime," she said. "I'm just terrible at math, and you were pretty good in first-year algebra last year, as I recall. I'd really appreciate your help if you can spare some time. Well, see you around." She went on to the ladies' room in the back of the restaurant.

Luke's face was bright red. It made me laugh to think Bunny had a crush on *him,* of all people.

"Ha! You have a *girlfriend,*" Emma taunted. "She must be really desperate!" Emma let out a large and sustained howl of laugher.

"You were pretty good in first year algebra?" I repeated in a mocking tone. "She can't be serious."

"Cut it out, you guys," Luke demanded angrily. "Bernie's *not* my girlfriend. No way. Don't you ever say she is, either, if you know what's good for you."

"I think thou dost protest too much," I said, laughing. "Bunny Larsson. It has a nice ring to it, doesn't it, Emma?"

"I mean it, you guys," Luke growled. "She's not my speed. No way. She's scary. I'd only choose her to be on my wrestling team if I needed another bad ass. Not to date like a real girl."

"You're so mean," Emma said, frowning. "She's a nice girl. Stop saying those mean things about her."

Luke was usually so fearless and brash. I'd never seen him put off by anyone before, but then again, I'd never known anyone to be romantically interested in him before. It was amusing to watch him sweat at the idea of being the object of affection. Bunny was a brave girl to go after him, and I had to admire her courage. Maybe that was the only kind of girl who could domesticate him. Moments later she walked out of the ladies' room and gazed back at him on her way to rejoin her friends.

Not long after, Jim walked through the restaurant's front door with two boys. They sat down at a booth on the other side of the room. Jim was facing me, but he was too absorbed talking to his friends to notice us. He looked good, as usual. His dark curly hair fell across the forehead of his handsome face, and he was dressed in a dark T-shirt and jeans that looked good on his tall, athletic build.

"There's Jim over there," Emma said softly to me. "Did you see him?"

"Where?" Luke asked loudly. He turned and looked over his shoulder. "Oh, yeah. He's with Ryker and Wade. They're all on the varsity baseball team at school. He must not have seen me over here."

"Why doesn't he come over?" I pondered out loud. "You guys aren't on the outs again, are you, Luke?"

"Of course not. We're solid," he answered. "Why're you so hot to have him come over here? Don't tell me you still have a thing for him. You don't, do you? Haven't you learned your lesson, City Slicker?" He shook his head with exasperation.

"Oh, leave her alone, stump head," Emma defended. "You know she's over him. Take a chill pill."

"Sis, you'd better quit calling me stump head, or I'll...," Luke chided.

"Then stop acting like one," she replied with a smirk.

"No, I don't still have a thing for him, if you must know," I interrupted. "I was just wondering why he didn't come over to say hi, that's all." I did my best to sound breezy and easy.

"Yeah, so relax Max. Or, should I say relax, stump head? That doesn't rhyme though," Emma said, tossing her hair defiantly.

Luke looked as though he would explode and was about to reply when Jim approached our table.

"Well, hello everyone!" Jim said, standing in the aisle. "May I sit down?"

"Sure," Luke said, scooting over to make room. "I could use the help. What's up?"

Jim slid down next to Luke and looked across the table at me and smiled. His eyes twinkled and his smile was warm and sincere. "First things first," Jim said. "How are you, Vanessa? Good to see you." He reached across the table and stopped just short of touching my hand, then drew back. "Good to see you, too, Emma. Why are you two ladies hanging out with this crazy Swede here?"

"We came with my dad. He's on the phone over there," Emma said, pointing toward her father who was still on the phone. "We had a fire at our house and have to eat out until they fix it and we can use the kitchen again."

Jim looked surprised. "That's right! I heard there was a fire at your house. Why did you want to burn your house down?" Jim ribbed, turning to Luke. "They send little boys to the juvenile center in Indianapolis for that, you know."

"Ha! Very funny," Luke said. Then, becoming solemn, he continued, "But, seriously, man, I think someone *did* set that fire on purpose. It's kinda freaking me out, frankly."

"What are you talking about?" Jim asked. "Is this a gag? I heard they think it was caused by lightning or faulty wiring or something. No one said anything about *arson*."

"I'm deadly serious. Something's going on at our farm, and whatever it is, it isn't good," Luke continued with a straight face. "I could use your help."

"What's going on at your farm? You should have told me before. Of course I'll help you," Jim said, looking sincerely concerned.

"I've seen something really weird in the sky twice that I know isn't a plane or a helicopter," Luke continued. "Nessie saw it, too. Didn't you, Ness? Tell him."

I should explain that "Nessie" and "Nessie Monster" were nicknames Luke called me from time to time in addition to City Slicker. They were derived from the name Vanessa, of course, but also served to slyly conjure up images of the mythical Loch Ness Monster rumored to be lurking in Scotland's Loch Ness. I didn't mind being called Nessie or even Nessie Monster, but detested being called City Slicker.

I nodded. "It hovered and had blue-green and silver lights," I replied.

"There's got to be a rational explanation. I know you have a vivid imagination, but that'd be crazy. You aren't suggesting you saw a UFO, are you?" Jim asked.

Luke paused. "I don't know what I saw. Whatever it was, Nessie and Daniel saw it, too. If you come by late tonight, you can probably see it, too. I've seen it twice." Luke was met with disbelieving silence, and then continued, "Dude, I'm serious about this, and it's got me going mental."

Just then, one of Jim's friends walked up to our table.

"Sorry to interrupt Jim-bo," the boy said. "But Wade and I are going to split soon. He told his mother he'd be home with the car by three."

"Okay, I'll be right there," Jim said. "Oh, by the way everyone, this is Ryker. Ryker, I believe you know Luke from school. This is his sister Emma and his cousin, Vanessa."

Ryker was medium height and build, with short wiry brown hair and piercing blue eyes.

"Sure. Hi," Ryker said to all of us, a little shyly. Then, looking at me, he added, "You've got a lot of hair. A *lot*. You know?"

I laughed, feeling slightly self-conscious. It was true my pony tail was thick, although I had very little do with that. It was just the luck of genetics. "Yeah, I guess I do," I replied, laughing nervously.

"You could be a superhero with all that thick red hair. You know, like Batgirl, or Poison Ivy. They're both from the Batman series," Ryker observed, looking quite pleased with himself.

"Or Jean Grey from X-Men," Jim added. "Or Pepper Pots."

"Don't forget about Medusa," Ryker continued. "Or the Black Widow."

"Dudes, are you smoking something? Red hair or not, Nessie could never be a superhero," Luke scoffed. "So cut it out. You're making me sick with all this talk."

"I don't know," Jim pondered, looking me over in a way that made me self-conscious. "I think Vanessa would make a very fine superhero."

"Yeah. Rad Red. That's what I'll call her. Rad Red!" Ryker exclaimed, appearing quite pleased with himself.

Suddenly, everyone was looking at me. I felt my face getting as red as my hair. "Come on you guys," I coaxed. "I'm no superhero. Let's talk about something else. Okay?"

"Ha! At last you and I see eye-to-eye on something, Nessie Monster," Luke agreed.

"Well, I disagree, Miss Rad Red. I think you're definitely superhero material, but I've got to take off now, so we'll have to leave it at that for now," Jim said, getting up to leave. "It was good seeing you, Vanessa. Are you going to be around for a few days?"

"Who cares about Vanessa? Aren't you coming over tonight?" Luke interrupted. "You know—to continue that *othe*r thing we were just talking about? Come any time right after dark. We can build a big bonfire back in the field like we've done before."

"Okay. I guess so. I'll call you if I can't make it. Sounds as though I'll be seeing you tonight, Rad Red. Bye, Emma."

He looked at me and smiled as he walked away. It made me feel good to think maybe he still had a connection to me. I watched him return with Ryker to their booth and sit down.

"Ha. Did you hear that?" Luke teased. "You? A superhero? What a crock. That Ryker is one weird dude. I don't know him that well. He hangs out with Jim mostly."

"Don't you know about the superpowers Rad Red's ponytail has?" I said as I pulled my ponytail over my shoulder and menacingly stroked it like a cat. "Don't underestimate the power of Rad Red's pony tail."

"*That's* your superpower? Your *hair*?" Luke mocked. "Good grief! Lame, as usual."

"Ha! I'd give anything to see you give Luke a good whopping with that!" Emma said, laughing. "Go ahead and try it out right here, why don't you? Do it!"

"Cut it out," Luke said, rolling his eyes.

Just then, Uncle Evert came back to the booth and sat down. "Mrs. Duffy is a very talkative lady. I thought she'd never let me off the phone," he said. He took a sip from his coffee mug. "Goodness! This coffee's cold now," he exclaimed.

The waitress was right behind him with our food. She placed the dishes around the table and replaced Uncle Evert's coffee. At the end of the meal, Uncle Evert felt charitable and ordered us each a piece of strawberry pie so we didn't have to share. It wasn't necessary, though. I didn't eat too much of mine, or many of the fries, even though I wanted to. I had to think of my figure if Jim was going to come over tonight.

CHAPTER SIX

The Bird's the Word

After we left Jim Dandy's, Uncle Evert took us straight back to the farm. Lars was sitting at the dining table in the yard reading a book when we arrived and didn't look up. He appeared to be oblivious that we'd pulled up.

"What're you reading that's got you so mesmerized?" Uncle Evert asked as he got out of the van and strolled up the walk.

"It's that new thriller, *Rosemary's Baby*. About a young couple in New York City who move into an apartment building filled with creepy old people who belong to an evil cult," Lars explained. He turned the book around and gazed at the eerie image of a Victorian building on the cover. "I can see why it's a best seller. Very suspenseful."

"That's all well and good, but I wanted you to start cleaning debris out of the house while we were away," Uncle Evert said. "Don't you remember that little conversation we had?"

"I would have, but we had visitors," Lars said, standing and stretching. "The fire marshal just left and said the house is safe now if we want to move back into that wretched place. A utility man also came and turned the electricity back on."

"Thank goodness!" Emma exclaimed. "We're back to normal. At last!"

"Well, not quite, Princess. I still want everyone to stay out of the house for a few more days, except for using the bathroom as necessary," Uncle Evert said. "It never hurts to be extra careful. It's still too damp and smoky in there to be healthy, in my opinion."

"Can we at least take showers now?" Emma asked.

"Yes, you can do that, as long as you keep them short," Uncle Evert cautioned.

"But Dad. The final episode of *The Fugitive* is on tonight," Luke protested. "Don't you want to find out if Dr. Kimble finally catches the one-armed man who killed his wife? I've got to see it. I've got to know!

"Let's see if the TV works first and then I'll consider it," Uncle Evert said. "It may have been damaged in the fire and not work."

"I'm going to check it out right now. I bet we can get it working again if we need to. Come on, Dad," Luke urged, charging into the house. Uncle Evert followed him inside.

"Want to walk down to the creek and hang out for a while?" Emma asked. "I'd like to get away from everyone for a while."

That sounded fine to me. We walked toward the barn, passed through the gate, and crossed a field of ankle-high weeds that crunched under foot as we walked along. It wasn't too long before we approached the old cemetery that was practically located smack dab in the middle of the farm along the creek. You had to pass it to go just about anywhere on the property. It was small and encircled by an old, wrought-iron fence with a gate that hung by a single rusty hinge. No one had been buried there for almost seventy years, and no one ever visited anyone buried there. There was a melancholy, abandoned feeling to it. Perhaps being surrounded by woods and a creek contributed to the eerie atmosphere that hung over it. I'd checked it out already on previous visits, but I never got totally at ease with it. Every time I passed by, I had to remind myself not to let it frighten me.

"Shall we go in?" Emma asked, gesturing toward the cemetery gate. "You can give your respects to Private Parker."

Private James Parker was a Civil War soldier buried in the cemetery. He was the only person buried there with the surname of Parker and the only Civil War soldier. His grave was alone in a corner under a half-dead tree on a rocky hillside. It always struck me as sad that he was placed in such a craggy, forlorn area. It almost appeared that he was located as far from the others as possible. Until just a few months ago, Emma believed that the ghost of Private Parker haunted the area. Perhaps it still did.

"Okay, if you want to," I replied, even though I thought we were going to the creek, not to the cemetery. "It's too early in the day for ghosts to be roaming around, so we should be all right."

Until just a few months ago, Emma believed that the ghost of Private Parker haunted the area. Perhaps it still did.

"If you say so," she replied, making a spooky face and then laughing in a weird way that took me a little aback.

We squeezed through the gate that was stuck open in the mud just far enough to allow a person through if you held your breath. There were several small, light-gray headstones lined up in two or three rows. Most were fairly slim slabs that stood only ten or eleven inches above the ground. A few were taller and were made out of granite with elaborate carved details. Those must have belonged to the wealthy people, I figured. The cemetery also had the distinction of being the location of the grave of Leonard Eller, who settled the area in 1823.

"Here's poor Private James Parker, the Civil War deserter," Emma lamented, walking over to a small white headstone marked "Jas. Parker, died 1865, 39 Indiana Infantry, Company E."

"Yes, poor James Parker," I echoed. "Do you feel he's still haunting you, or has he finally gone far, far away to ghost heaven?"

"I don't know," Emma said, thinking as she peered pensively down at his grave. "I guess I'd have to say he's still hanging around, even with all you and I did to try to put him at rest by proving he wasn't a deserter the way people thought he was."

"Hanging around? Does that mean you've seen him recently?" I asked. The hair on back my neck stood on end, and I looked around anxiously for a glimpse of a ghostly white vapor.

"No, nothing like that. It's just a feeling I get every now and then that makes me think he's nearby," she explained. "But it doesn't bother me. Not like it used to, anyway." She had a faraway look as she spoke.

"Why doesn't it bother you?" I asked.

"Because he's not as angry as he used to be. He seems more peaceful. Can't you feel it?" She gave me a look as though there were no way I wasn't experiencing the same sensations she was.

"Um. I'd have to think about that," I said. The truth was, I didn't feel anything, except a desire to get the heck out of there.

"Oh, Nessie," Emma giggled. "I forgot how you are. You don't like ghosts so much."

"I like them as much as the next person," I defended. "It's just that...."

Emma shook her head. "That's okay. You don't have to live with him like I do. I'm okay now with having him around. Really I am."

She smiled and gazed up into the trees at the edge of the cemetery as though listening to a secret melody only she could hear.

"You're the one who should be the superhero, not me," I suggested. "If my house were as close to a cemetery as yours, I don't know if I'd be as brave."

"Okay, if you say so. What superpowers shall I have?" Emma asked playfully.

"Hmm. Let me see. How about paranormal superpowers? You know, the ability to see dead people on the other side. What do you think?"

"I like it!" she said. "Now all we have to do is come up with my superhero's name."

"How about Ethereal Emma?" I suggested.

"That's okay, but it doesn't sound fierce enough. How about ...Mystic Millicent?" she replied.

"I like it!" I said. "We can work up a back story for you, Mystic Millicent. You know, explaining what happened to give you your superpowers the way comic books always do."

"Okay Rad Red. Let's go down to the creek and talk about it," she said, laughing.

We exited the cemetery and continued walking down the hill a short distance to the small creek that snaked through the farm. It was about thirty to forty feet wide at its widest point, and about eight to ten feet deep, depending where along its curving channel you measured. The fast flood waters of countless spring storms had carved out deep juts along its banks, some of which stood three to four feet above the water's surface. The water was murky, and I'd never known anyone to swim in it. But it was definitely a popular spot for fishing, even though the fish were tiny and not the kind anyone would eat.

"It's very pretty here," I said, taking a deep breath and gazing down the course of the creek. "Especially on a sunny day like today. The way the light hits the water makes the surface look like shimmering jewels."

"Let's sit down here," Emma suggested, plopping down on a grassy spot along the bank. "We should have brought fishing poles. Too bad we didn't."

"I don't mind just sitting here like this," I said. "It's nice just to look at nature."

The tall grass smelled fresh and felt comfortable beneath me. Small purple and white wild asters dotted the deep green of the grass, and I plucked one and rolled the stem between my fingers. I gazed upstream at the old sycamore tree leaning over the water at such an extreme angle that I marveled it didn't crash into the water. It was hollow in part, and you could crawl inside to a giant hole over the water.

"I'm not as zonked from being up most of the night as I thought I'd be," I said, staring up at the puffy clouds.

"Oh, you mean you didn't sleep because of the UFO. *That* again," she replied dryly. Then, turning to me, she asked in a serious tone, "Come on, you can tell me the truth. You didn't see anything, did you? I promise not to rat you out to my crazy brother. Pinky swear. Tell me the truth."

"I *am* telling you the truth, Emma. I saw the lights hovering in the sky for a few minutes, and then I saw them suddenly disappear. It scared me to death. I'm totally freaked out just remembering it."

She stared down at the water and tossed a small pebble in. I watched the ripples flow outward and crash into the creek bank.

"I'm still worried the UFO will come back tonight, or even this afternoon while we're sitting here. How do we know they won't kidnap us, or take over our government, or take over the whole darn planet while they're at it?" I said as I gazed nervously at the billowing white clouds floating overhead. It was making me crazy not knowing what I'd seen, but I knew whatever I saw was still up there somewhere and could reappear in a heartbeat.

"Well, if it turns out there really was a UFO, I want them to make me their alien queen, not someone they do experiments on. If they make me their queen, it's okay with me if they beam me up," Emma proclaimed.

"Okay. That sounds reasonable," I scoffed. "Be sure to tell them you're royalty when you meet them, and not lab bait. I'm sure they'll do exactly as you say."

"Darn right they will!" she declared. "Or, I'm not going away with them. Plain and simple."

"Feisty Earth girl!" I added. "Mystic Millicent's not taking guff from no stinkin' aliens." I made a fist, and she fell backward on the grass laughing.

"Stop it, stop it!" she said, holding her middle as she continued laughing. "You're making my stomach hurt!"

The water was murky, and I'd never known anyone to swim in it.

After about another hour of staring at the water and exchanging mindless chitchat, we decided to go back to the farmhouse by way of the little house. I wanted to see it again in the middle of the day when there was no threat of an alien lurking around. We walked back past the cemetery and then cut a hard left to cross the field to the hollow where the little house was nestled. As the compact structure came into view, I was struck by how charming and peaceful it was—so different from last night when it had only been a place of isolation and danger. We walked down the hill to the front of it.

"We ought to have a picnic back here sometime while you're visiting," Emma suggested as she looked inside through the front door. "We could even do it today if you want to. You know, bring dinner back here to eat. It'd be fun. Maybe Luke and Daniel could join us."

"Yeah, that sounds great. There's a nice feeling here. Kind of homey," I observed. "It's like a clubhouse where you can hang out."

"I hope Buzz and Lars finish the bedroom soon," she said, walking around to the bedroom area. "When they're finished Mom says we can bring some old furniture back here and really make it our own little hangout."

We circled around the little house, and then I climbed the small ridge where Luke, Daniel, and I had stood to observe the UFO. I wanted to see what the view looked like during the day, to try to judge where the UFO had been hovering. But just as I got to the top of the hill, I was greeted by a hideous scene.

"Oh, my god!" I screamed. "What is *this*?"

On the ground, to my horror, were more than thirty dead birds scattered all over. There were birds of all kinds—starlings, sparrows, wrens, and robins, all fully intact, as though something had mysteriously killed them in mid-flight. What could have caused this? I stopped dead in my tracks, not wanting to inadvertently step on any.

"What is what?" Emma shouted from behind. She scurried up the knoll and scanned the area. "Something really strange has happened here. Let's get out of here." Her eyes were big and she seemed upset.

"There aren't any electrical lines around here to electrocute them. Could they have been poisoned? How? Why?"

"I don't know. Let's just get out of here," she said, pivoting to go back down the hill.

We took off in a slow jog across the field toward the farmhouse. By the time we were almost behind the barn, it finally felt far enough away from that hideous scene to slow down. Someone or *something* had caused those birds to die since this morning, and all I knew was that I was going to stay far, far away from the little house from here on out.

CHAPTER SEVEN

Little Children Laugh at Him behind His Back

When Emma and I finally arrived at the makeshift camp in the farmhouse yard, Aunt Louise was busy washing dishes in a large rubber tub set up in the yard. After each dish was thoroughly washed in the soapy water, she'd rinse it with the garden hose and stack it in a wire rack on a workbench borrowed from the garage. Luke was sitting at the dining room table fiddling with an assortment of comic books spread out all around him. No one else but Aunt Louise and Luke appeared to be around. The radio was now plugged into an incredibly long extension cord leading into the house and played "Penny Lane" by the Beatles.

"What's got you guys so worked up?" Luke asked, not looking up at us as he smoothed the cover of a damp *Thor* comic book.

"There are a bunch of dead birds back by the little house lying all over the ground," Emma reported breathlessly. "You didn't have anything to do with that, did you? You didn't shoot them with your BB gun or do something else to kill them, did you? It was horrible to see those poor little things dead all over the ground."

"Hey, take a chill pill, will ya? I've been here ever since we got back from Jim Dandy's, isn't that true, Mom?" Luke replied as he continued tinkering with the comic books. "Besides, I have more important things to do than to kill a bunch of birds."

"Well, how did it happen, then?" Emma demanded.

"How should I know?" Luke replied, peering closely at another comic book on the table. "Do I look like a psychic or something?"

"Could it have been caused by something connected to the UFO we saw last night?" I suggested.

"Hmm. Could be. We don't know what we saw, so it's hard to say. But then again, sometimes flocks of birds mysteriously just up and die. The lead bird loses its radar and flies them into walls and glass windows. That happens mostly in the city, though. Not in the country," Luke conjectured.

"I agree that it sounds strange," Aunt Louise said, turning from the wash basin. "Let's ask your father to go back there in a little while and see what he thinks caused it. I really don't think there's anything to worry about, though. There must be a reasonable explanation for it."

"You didn't see a green man while you were back there, did you?" Luke teased. "With a gigantic forehead and big bug eyes? Maybe he killed those birds using laser beams from his eyes!"

"Stop horsing around. This is serious," Emma demanded. "All those poor birds. It was gruesome."

"You're an *edgy little* Emma today, aren't you?" Luke continued teasing.

Emma glared at him. "Edgy? You'd better stop calling me things like that or you'll be a *lifeless little* Luke," she returned.

"Great news everybody. The TV's working again!" Uncle Evert announced, bursting through the screen door with an air of victory. "I don't know what I did exactly, but it worked. That's one less repair we'll have to pay for."

"Way to go, Dad," Luke said, holding up his hand to do a high five. "I knew you could do it. Now we can watch *The Fugitive* tonight and find out if Lieutenant Gerard finally catches Dr. Kimble."

"I'll be really disappointed if they don't find the one-armed man so Dr. Kimble can be free to live his life again," Aunt Louise said as she resumed washing dishes. "You can tell by the character he's demonstrated time and time again that he isn't capable of killing anyone, much less his own wife."

"You're such a bleeding heart, Louise," Uncle Evert teased, walking to the table and sitting. "I read an interview with David Janssen in this week's *TV Guide*, and he pretty much hinted that Dr. Kimble did it."

"I don't believe it!" Aunt Louise protested. "I'm an excellent judge of character, and that's just not possible."

"Well, your wires may be crossed on this one," Uncle Evert said, taking a sip from an RC Cola bottle sitting on the table. "Those Hollywood writers have their own ideas about things."

"Hi, everyone," Daniel said, emerging from around the corner of the house holding a large model airplane and carrying a tool case about the size of a lunchbox. I was surprised to see he was wearing a blue Civil War shirt with yellow chevrons on the sleeves instead of his usual fringed suede jacket.

"What do you have there?" Luke asked.

"This is a radio controlled plane I built with Buzz. I just finished it," he explained. "The paint's barely dry."

He carefully set the plane down on the dining room table and then stepped away and gave it an admiring gaze. It had a wing span of about thirty inches and was painted red with a mustard yellow stripe down the side. It was an impressive accomplishment in my book.

"I thought I'd bring it over here to try it out in the flying circle. It's never been in the air before. Want to fly it with me?" he asked Luke.

"Sure. I have to let these comic books air out, so I might as well. Nobody touch these comic books while I'm away, okay?" Luke said, rising from his seat and leaving the comic books laid out in rows on the table. "You girls can come, too, if you don't get in the way," he added, to my surprise.

"Not interested. We have better things to do," Emma said, sitting down at the table. "Don't we, Vanessa?"

"Oh, come with us," Daniel urged. "I could use some help getting this thing in the air. These kinds of planes have a habit of running off course, and I'll need people around to catch it if it goes haywire." He smiled so sweetly the way only he could, that I hoped Emma would change her mind. I wouldn't feel right about going if she didn't go, too.

"Well, okay. I guess so, but only for a little while," she said after a long pause. "I need to tell Dad about the dead birds I saw today."

"You go ahead, I'll fill your father in on the details about the birds," Aunt Louise urged. "You children need to enjoy the day, so scoot and enjoy yourselves." She gestured with her hands for us to go.

The four of us crossed the yard, passed the barn, and then traversed the field on the other side of the barn until we came to an area where the grass and weeds had been cut short in a giant circle almost as wide as our backyard at home. Daniel knelt, carefully set his plane on the ground at the edge of the circle, and opened the tool chest. As he set about filling the small motor with gas from a tiny rubber bulb, Luke stood over him observing every careful detail of the pre-flight preparation.

Not too far off was the little house, the hill where I'd discovered the dead birds, and beyond that the cluttered and fenced barn yard of Mr. Kleinschmidt's farm. I could see the numerous fences and weathered structures on the German's property, and caught a glimpse of his dog running back and forth in its fenced pen. Even on a sunny afternoon like today, the dark and decrepit buildings had a decidedly foreboding appearance.

"That's the Kleinschmidt farm over there in the distance, isn't it?" I remarked, pointing. "I think I can see Fritz running around over there."

Luke stood and looked. "Yep. That's the old Nazi's place." Turning squarely in the direction of the farm, he made a gesture that involved flicking his four fingers together under his chin. "There. Take that, old geezer."

"What was that about?" I asked, dumbfounded by his actions.

"I was telling him to flake off," Luke replied.

"You're wasting your time," Daniel observed. "He can't see you from way over there."

"You think not? I wonder. I'll bet he's watching every little move we make with those beady old Nazi eyes of his this very minute," Luke replied.

"What makes you say that? Do you see him?" Emma asked. She stood up straight and peered at the farm as if she expected to see the old man standing at the edge of the yard looking right back at us.

"Some things you just know," Luke replied, returning his full attention to the plane.

"Are we here to talk about that old sourpuss, or are we here to fly this plane?" Daniel asked. He stood up and gently turned the propeller blade with his index finger. "I'm ready! Are you all ready to witness my marvelous flying machine?" He had a big smile and his eyes twinkled with expectation.

"Okay, Wilbur Wright. Let 'er rip!" Luke coaxed.

We all stood behind Daniel as he wound the propeller several times and then knelt down and let the plane go. Like a shot it rolled several yards in an arc off to the right and then nosed into the ground where it ended its journey.

"That was a dud," Daniel said, running to retrieve the plane. He picked it up and examined it, and then nodded to us. "It's okay," he declared happily.

He walked back to where we stood, wound the propeller several times again, and then knelt down and let it go. Once again, it rolled forward several yards, nosed down into the grass, and stopped.

"Maybe you should try throwing it into the air," Luke suggested after several more failed attempts. "I don't see how you're going to get it airborne from down on the ground."

"But if I throw it up, it might crash and really get damaged if the motor doesn't take hold," Daniel said, mulling over the idea.

"It might, but nothing else seems to be working," Luke observed. "Want me to do it for you?"

"No, no. I'll do it," Daniel said. "You can hold the radio controls, though. Until I get it going, that is, and then you have to give them back to me. Here."

He handed Luke a little black box with a lever, then stood gazing down at the plane in his hands as though he were taking one last look at it before it might be damaged and never look the same again. Then, without saying a word, he wound the propeller several times, ran forward, and threw the plane up into the sky as hard as he could, like an athlete throwing a javelin.

The little engine began to buzz as it took hold and carried the plane upward. Daniel jumped with glee at finally achieving success. He rushed over to Luke, who was busy manipulating the lever on the little black box and thoroughly enjoying himself. The plane went higher and higher and then faithfully to the right and to the left as Luke manipulated the lever.

"Okay. Give it to me!" Daniel demanded impatiently, reaching for the box. "Hurry!"

"I've got this!" Luke said, his face reflecting the rapture of a kid with a new toy. "Give me a second."

Daniel frowned, sensing Luke's determination to retain the controls. "Come on! Give it back. What a double-cross."

"You can fly it the next time, and I'll do the throwing," Luke said, his eyes glued on the plane as he moved the lever this way and that.

Daniel had no choice but to let Luke have his way. The plane made large loops and flew without faltering. It flew down to the edge of the field, and then soared back over our heads and came back around. Time and time again the buzzing plane completed its circular journey. With each pass, Luke became more emboldened and sent the plane farther down the field before directing it back over our heads, and then over toward the barn and back again to complete another loop. He eventually flew it so far that it approached the edge of Kleinschmidt's farm. The little motor kept up its steady hum, and the plane flew without faltering.

"This is fun!" Luke shouted. "I could do this all day."

"Just pay attention and don't crack up," Daniel warned, watching every move Luke made.

As his confidence grew, so did Luke's recklessness, and on one pass as a joke he flew the plane so low it almost touched the top of Daniel's head. Luke laughed uproariously when Daniel suddenly ducked to the ground and grabbed the top of his head.

"Hey! Cut that out. That's dangerous!" Daniel chastised, stroking the top of his head to confirm it was okay. "Don't fool around like that. You could hurt someone—or my plane!"

"Okay, okay. How long will this thing fly?" Luke asked as he moved the lever to make the plane climb.

Daniel was about to answer when the plane's little engine suddenly sputtered. The plane was just approaching the edge of the field not far from Kleinschmidt's farm. I was relieved when the buzzing of the engine resumed again and the plane regained altitude. But it wasn't long before it faltered again as the gas finally ran out, and the fragile plane began to descend to the ground.

"Quick! Run down there and catch it!" Luke shouted, frantically moving the lever to try to keep the plane airborne. "I think it's going to crash!"

In a split second, Daniel, Emma, and I ran down the long field, watching for the plane over our heads as it continued to descend. When I was finally almost at the fence dividing the two farms, I looked up and saw the plane falling straight down like a rock directly over me.

"Catch it, Nessie! Catch it!" Luke exhorted. "Don't let it hit the ground."

I closed my eyes and reached up to grab it like a football player completing a pass. I almost had it within my grasp and was pleased I was going to be able to save the day, when it deflected off the tips of my fingers and got away. It floated over the fence and fell to the ground on other side, nose first. I ran up to the fence and peered over just as Daniel and Emma came up behind me. There it was, nose down in the mud on the forbidden property of Old Man Kleinschmidt, with a broken wing.

"Crap," Luke lamented as he rushed up and looked through the fence. "Way to go, City Slicker."

"Leave Vanessa alone," Emma countered. "You were the one who flew the plane all the way down here like a drunken air traffic controller. You flew it too close to Kleinschmidt's property."

"My plane! Look what happened to *my plane*!" Daniel moaned as he stared at it through the fence. "What do I do now? This was the first time I ever flew it—or should I say, that *anyone* ever flew it."

"Go over and get it. What're you waiting for?" Luke said, stepping forward to climb the fence. The fence was very tall and had barbed wire wound around the top like a prison compound. "Come on. Let's do this before the crazy German comes out to see why his dog's barking." Fritz had witnessed the crash and was barking up a storm in his pen up near the house.

"Okay. But I don't have a good feeling about this," Daniel hesitated. "On top of everything else, I don't like the looks of that stuff wound around the top up there. Is that barbed wire?"

"I agree. I don't think you should go over there," I warned. "I mean ...didn't Uncle Evert say not to bother Mr. Kleinschmidt? That must include staying off his property."

"Seriously, City Slicker? You're the reason we're in this situation. If you didn't catch like a girl, we wouldn't be here!" Luke mocked.

"Aw, leave Nessie alone, Luke. She did the best she could. Let's just get this over with," Daniel urged as he stepped toward the fence to climb it.

The two boys climbed the fence as Emma and I stood in a worried state below. They carefully made their way up, and then slowly and painstakingly maneuvered around the rings of barbed wire at the top. Finally, they were clear and jumped down on the other side and stood by the fence as they assessed the situation. I anxiously scanned the area up by the house and was relieved not to see any sign of Mr. Kleinschmidt. Still I knew he had to be around and could appear at any moment. Meanwhile, Fritz was going crazy over the intrusion. His barking became more intense, and he continually jumped up and down along the edge of his enclosure as if determined to find a way to get to us. He looked ferocious and ready to kill.

"Shh, puppy!" Luke whispered loudly, putting his finger up to his lips. "Hush!"

Suddenly, a voice with a thick German accent rang out. "*Ruhig, Fritz! Sitz!*" Fritz immediately became quiet and sat, but still glowered at us as though he wanted to eat us for lunch.

"What are you boys doing in my yard?" Mr. Kleinschmidt demanded, walking sternly toward Luke and Daniel through the numerous fences between the house and the outer fence where the boys entered. "You're trespassing and I have every right to turn you over to the authorities. Explain yourselves! Speak. *Schnell!*"

Luke and Daniel stood frozen. Daniel's jaw dropped and his eyes got big.

"I ...I came to get my plane. It's over there, see?" Daniel said finally. He pointed toward the plane as it lay crashed on its nose. "It flew into your yard by accident. I'm really sorry."

"I see," Mr. Kleinschmidt said, walking up to us. Then, turning toward Luke, he asked, "You're Luke Larsson, aren't you?"

"*Ja* . . . I mean, yes" Luke answered. He nervously put his hands into his pockets and looked down.

"I warned your father yesterday about you. I told him you were a juvenile delinquent," Mr. Kleinschmidt scolded. "Now get back over that fence and stay there. I don't want to see either of you on my property ever again!" He came toward the boys with such a fierce attitude that they practically ran to get back to the fence.

"Can. ...can I have my plane back, please?" Daniel asked sheepishly as he pointed at it again. "I made it. It ...it's mine. I didn't mean for it to come into your yard."

"*Nein!* It's in my yard, so it's mine now," Mr. Kleinschmidt said, waving his hand dismissively. "You boys need to be taught a lesson. Now away with you! *Schnell!*"

The boys climbed back over the fence as Mr. Kleinschmidt stood watching with his hands on his hips. It was difficult to see much from where I stood, but I could see his face was old and craggy, with heavy eye brows that arched upward giving him an almost sinister appearance. His wispy gray hair fell just below a well-worn brown fedora, and his dark work pants were faded and had a patch sewn over one of the knees. His dark shirt was similarly well-worn and faded, with an emblem stitched over the pocket I couldn't see well enough to read.

The boys complied with his instructions and slowly made their way up the fence. They carefully and slowly maneuvered around the barbed wire at the top again, but this time Daniel cut his hand as he was making the transition over to the other side. He recoiled momentarily from the sting, but continued on.

"Let's go," Luke said in an exasperated tone after he and Daniel were back on the ground again on our side. "Let's get out of here."

The old German stood watching as we walked away. It appeared he wouldn't move until we were totally out of his sight, just in case we sneaked back, I suppose. I peeked over my shoulder when we'd taken a few steps to see if he was still there, and he was. It was unnerving to be watched so intensely. Daniel stopped to pick up his tool chest and to collect the rest of his things when we got back to the flying circle, and then we continued on to the farmhouse.

"That's *my* plane. It's no fair for that old goofball to keep it. He has no right to do that," Daniel protested as we walked along. "Just because it flew into his yard? That's totally bogus."

"I'm sorry I didn't catch it," I said, walking up next to him. "I tried. I really did."

"That terrible catch of yours reminded me of Fred Merkle pulling the Merkle Boner that cost the New York Giants the 1908 National League pennant," Luke chastised.

I had no idea what the Merkle Boner was, but I knew it couldn't be good.

"Don't pick on Vanessa," Daniel said. "I'll talk to my dad. He'll know what to do. He'll get it back for me."

"Hold up there, Dude. If you tell your dad what happened, he might tell *my* dad," Luke reasoned. "I'll get in a heck of a lot of trouble if my dad finds out I was on Kleinschmidt's property, no matter what the reason."

"What else can I do to get it back?" Daniel asked. "I can't leave my plane with that crazy old fossil."

"Let me come up with a plan first, before you say anything to anyone," Luke coaxed. "I'll give it some thought. You know me. I always come up with *something*."

"Oh, brother," Daniel said, rolling his eyes. "Okay, I'll wait, but don't take too long to come up with something. Kleinschmidt might throw away what's left of the plane if I don't get it back soon. It could be in his garbage can right now for all I know."

"Good. Thanks for being a champ!" Luke replied, giving Daniel a hearty slap on the back. Then, turning toward Emma and me, he added, "You girls are under strict orders to keep our little visit today quiet, too. Got that?"

"Maybe," Emma replied flatly.

"Say what?!" Luke grunted.

"I won't make a peep today, but I can't guarantee what I might do tomorrow," Emma said with a mischievous smile. Luke gave her a long stare, but continued walking.

"How's the cut on your hand. Is it bad?" I asked Daniel, looking down to see if he was bleeding.

"Nah, it's a tiny cut. That stuff was sharp, but I'll be fine," Daniel said, holding out his hand to show me. "As long as I get my plane back, that is."

As we turned the corner to pass the barn, I looked back one last time. The Kleinschmidt farm was too far away to see if Mr. Kleinschmidt was still standing at the fence watching us, but I figured he probably was. Just like Luke, I could sense the old man scrutinizing our every move, and it gave me the willies.

CHAPTER EIGHT

Light My Fire

August days are wonderful because they seem to go on forever, especially when you're a teenager. Today was one of those days. Even though the sun had changed positions as early evening approached, there was still plenty of daylight left, and I was glad of that. I didn't want night to come too quickly. Darkness meant the UFO might reappear, and I hoped I'd never, *ever*, see that again. Another reason was that school would resume the day after Labor Day, which was less than one week away, so every minute of every remaining day of vacation had to be enjoyed and savored to the fullest.

When Luke, Daniel, Emma, and I got back to the house, the Anderson Construction truck was parked in the driveway, and two men were covering the big gash in the roof with plywood. A dumpster had been delivered and was parked on a grassy space on the other side of the driveway. Uncle Evert and a man with a dark tan I'd never seen before were busy dumping buckets of debris and ruined things into it. It didn't seem as though we'd been gone very long, and yet a lot had occurred in our absence. The radio was still on and tuned to a rock station playing "Light My Fire" by the Doors. I wondered if the DJ was psychic.

"Lars! Get out here and lend a hand, will you?" Uncle Evert yelled over his shoulder as he exited through the screen door holding two buckets full of debris "You've fussed with that piano long enough!"

"I'll be out in just a minute. I'm setting up the fan on the piano keys to help dry them out," Lars yelled back from inside the house. "It's what the Wilking Music people said to do."

"That darned piano!" Uncle Evert groused under his breath as he lugged two heavy buckets across the driveway to the dumpster. "Luke, grab a bucket," he ordered as Luke checked on his comic books lying on the table.

"I've got to get home," Daniel said, barely pausing to say good-bye. "I'll see you later."

"See you, Dude. Remember what we discussed," Luke called after him. "No spilling the beans."

Daniel made his way to the path in the back yard leading down to Allisonville Road and disappeared into the green underbrush.

"What beans?" Uncle Evert asked, pausing at the door before going back into the house. "What are you two up to?"

"Nothing, Dad," Luke said, laughing nervously. "Just comic book trading stuff."

Uncle Evert made a stern face as if to warn Luke he'd better be telling the truth, but I suspected he knew Luke was fibbing.

The rest of the afternoon, Uncle Evert, Luke, Lars, and the workmen labored on the house, while Emma and I helped sort through more soiled clothes with Aunt Louise, or helped her fold those recently laundered. After we were done with that, Emma and I sat at the dining table and listened to the radio while we observed the men continue to carry loads to the dumpster. The AM station we were listening to was WIFE-AM. Not long after we began listening, the DJ announced that the station was conducting a special promotion. He said their DJs were driving around to public swimming pools handing out transistor radios. The only catch was that the radios could only receive WIFE's frequency. When I heard this I just had to have one! The DJ further said they were on their way to the swimming pool at Forest Park in Noblesville. Forest Park wasn't too far from the farm. If we could get there, maybe I could get one of those coveted little radios. I didn't own a radio, and would be very proud to show off my treasure to the other kids when school started.

"If your dad took us to Forest Park, I might be able to get one of those radios," I remarked to Emma. "Do you think he would if you asked?"

She watched her father dump another load into the dumpster and then return to the house to start the cycle over again. "I don't know. He seems pretty busy," she observed. "It's getting kinda late, too. Even if we got Dad to take us, how do we know the DJ will still be up there? How many radios are they giving away? They might run out before we get there."

"You're probably right, but I'd sure like to give it a try," I said. "Think of it. A *real* transistor radio! For *free*! Don't you want one as much as I do?"

She looked at me and shrugged. "I don't know," she said. "I can listen to the radio we have out here on the table just fine."

I decided to ignore her lukewarm attitude, and press on. "Come on, Emmie. Go ask your dad, will you? He'll do anything for you, if you ask. I've seen you in action, and you're good at getting your way."

She smiled slyly. "Oh, okay," she said. "But don't blame me when he says no."

She walked over to Uncle Evert as he approached the door, spoke with him briefly, and then returned to the table and sat down.

"Well? What'd he say?" I asked impatiently. "Did you get it squared away for us? Are we going?"

"He said he'll take us to the swimming pool up there tomorrow if we still want to go," she said, avoiding eye contact. She knew I was disappointed.

"Tomorrow?" I brooded. "That'll be too late."

"What's the matter, Nessie?" Luke asked, passing by the table with a load of debris. "I've noticed you're often in a distressed state of being. What is it about you that causes you and those around you so much suffering?"

I knew he was enjoying taunting me, and ignored it. "Radio station WIFE-AM is at the pool at Forest Park handing out free transistor radios *right now*!" I said, hoping he'd be equally obsessed with getting one and help me. "I thought it'd be kinda neat to go up there and get one, but we don't have a way to get there."

"Wow. That's kinda cool," Luke agreed. "But, I don't think you can talk Dad into anything right now except clearing debris out of the house. He's on the war path to get the job done while he's got the Anderson Construction guys here and there's any daylight left. Those guys aren't cheap."

"I suppose you're right," I said, finally accepting the folly of my scheme. I knew down deep that more pressing issues confronted Uncle

Evert than helping me score a giveaway radio. "It'd be so cool to have my very own transistor radio. I guess I'll just have to keep wishing for one."

"Yeah. Having something cool like that just isn't your speed, City Slicker. Might as well accept the fact it's not in the cards for you," Luke joked. The phone rang and he went inside to answer it.

"Sorry, Vanessa," Emma said, looking apologetic. "Couldn't you baby sit and save up enough money to buy one?"

"I suppose. Don't worry about it. I'll get over it," I said. Getting a *free* radio handed to you for just showing up at a swimming pool had an appeal that saving up to buy one didn't.

Just then Luke flew out the screen door. "Jim just confirmed he's coming for the bonfire. He's got a special errand to run first, and then he'll be here," he announced. This was great news.

The afternoon passed, and eventually the workmen departed. Emma, Luke, and I gathered around the dining room table. The table, almost laughably out of place sitting in the yard, had become the unofficial lounging spot. As dusk arrived, Aunt Louise lit several candles and placed them on the table. The tents had been taken down and put away, and all of the furniture brought outside had been returned to where it belonged inside, except for the dining room table and chairs. It didn't appear that Uncle Evert and Aunt Louise were in any rush to take the table inside. It hardly ever rained this time of year, and the days and evenings were warm and pleasant. I could imagine they might choose to eat outside for a few more days, or even weeks, until the fall rains came.

"I wonder what's holding Jim up," Luke pondered when it became dark. "He's late."

Emma, Luke, and I played a TV theme song trivia game we made up while we waited for Jim. Luke said he didn't want to start the bonfire without him. Finally, I heard the crunch of wheels rolling up the driveway, and the familiar screech of bicycle brakes, and then saw Jim in the dim light propping his bicycle against the garage wall. He was here at last! I took a deep breath, smoothed back my hair, and straightened my ponytail.

"Hi everyone!" he said, walking into the yard. "Mind if I join you?"

"What took you so long?" Luke asked bluntly. "We've been waiting eons for you."

"Sorry. It's my parents. They're arguing again. My mom wouldn't let me leave until I did some stuff around the house for her. I think it was just an excuse to keep me there so she doesn't have to be alone with Dad," Jim said, taking a seat at the table.

"Gee, Dude, that's rough. Well, let's head out. Help me get the gear from the tool room," Luke said. "You, too, Daniel."

Luke, Jim, and Daniel went into the garage and rummaged around, emerging with tarps, two canvas folding chairs, an axe, and several newspapers, which I assumed were going to be used to help start the fire. Emma ran into the house and emerged with a paper grocery bag filled with bottles of RC Cola, a half-eaten bag of Oreo cookies, and a bottle opener.

Jim smiled at me, and I felt my cheeks grow warm. He seemed somehow different on this visit—friendly, but distant, the way he'd be if we were meeting for the very first time. We'd lost the casual ease of two people who'd once meant something special to each other. I suppose that was to be expected. Even though we'd expressed so many affectionate thoughts to each other in the past, those days were gone; I could tell. I returned the smile and did my best to hide my disappointment that the special magic we'd once shared had evaporated.

"Let's go," Luke charged, pointing toward the barn. "Operation Night Vision, here we come!"

We crossed the yard, passed by the barn, and went through the gate to a field behind the barn.

"Tell me again what our mission is tonight?" Jim asked as we walked along.

"I want you to see those lights in the sky I've seen, and help me figure out what they are," Luke explained.

"I see," Jim said, holding back a chuckle. "What are we supposed to do if we see them? We can't exactly chase whatever it is if it's in the sky, you know. We're just puny Earthbound humans."

"I know," Luke replied, sounding unsure. "Frankly, I haven't thought it through that far. Mostly, I guess, I want you to witness what I saw. I need someone to verify I'm not seeing things. Nessie saw it too, but no one will believe her. You know how she is."

"I beg your pardon!" I complained. "What do you mean by that?"

"See what I mean?" Luke remarked to Jim. "Clueless."

"Luke, you're incorrigible!" Jim answered, laughing. "He's just kidding," he said to me.

Luke led us to a spot where there were a few pieces of charred wood and stones from past camp fires, and a two large logs arranged for seating. The cemetery lay only a few hundred yards farther to the left of us, and the creek just beyond that. The little house and the flying circle where we'd flown Daniel's model plane were located far off to the right in an adjoining field, with the Kleinschmidt farm just beyond that.

"Okay, Merriweather Lewis, famous frontier guide. I guess you're telling us this is the spot," Jim said, laying the folding chairs on the ground.

"Did Luke tell you about all the dead birds we saw today near the little house?" Emma asked Jim, not wasting a moment to inform him.

"No, he didn't," Jim answered. "I thought you were only being visited by aliens. Now there's a mysterious bird kill going on, too? Maybe the aliens from the UFO killed them."

"You know what I think? I think Kleinschmidt probably killed them," Luke said as he laid a folded tarp on the ground. "He's mean enough to kill innocent little birds."

"Who's Kleinschmidt?" Jim asked. "Someone from school?"

"No, he's the old geezer who bought the Henderson farm just north of here," Luke explained. "He came to our house yesterday and accused me of letting his killer dog out of his yard. Why did he blame me? What'd I ever do to him?"

"He said Luke was a juvenile delinquent," Emma added, smiling. "Can you believe that?"

"Sounds like an insightful person," Jim said, nodding. "He seems to have sized you up pretty accurately."

"Ha. Ha," Luke responded. "You're so funny, Jim-bo." Luke made a gesture I didn't see that made Jim chortle.

"And, he won't give Daniel his model plane back even though it flew into his yard by accident," Emma said.

"Really? What a grouch. What's the deal with him?" Jim asked.

"He has a real heavy German accent," Emma continued. "He sounds a little like Colonel Klink on *Hogan's Heroes*."

"Yeah. I bet he's an escaped Nazi running from Nazi hunters," Luke ventured. "Living right here in Indiana under our noses. I'm not just saying that, either. No one seems to know anything about him. My parents don't, anyway. He's got his farm set up like a prison camp with lots of fences and barbed wire. Something's definitely strange with him."

"If he's running from Nazi hunters, he wouldn't come over and pick a fight with your family, would he?" Jim observed.

"He's crazy—who knows what he'd do? Well, okay, back to work everyone. Fan out and collect firewood before it gets too dark to see in front of your noses. Pick up only the old, dry stuff," Luke instructed us.

There was just enough light from the bright moon to make out what was near us if we looked closely. We walked across the field toward the woods near the cemetery where Luke quickly spotted a log about five feet long. He and Jim carried it back to the campsite where Luke chopped it up with the axe, while Jim turned his attention to the newspaper and twigs to start the fire. Before long, a nice little blaze began to take shape. I took a seat on one of the big logs and watched the warm glow of the fire grow as the boys fed it. The wood snapped and belched embers into the night sky as it began to burn.

"There you go!" Luke exclaimed victoriously as he stood back and observed the flames grow higher. "Come on baby! Light my fire!"

"Ah, Jim Morrison and the Doors," Jim sighed. "What a band! I dig that song."

Jim pulled out a folding chair next to me and sat down. He reached into his back pocket, pulled something out, and leaned toward me holding it out. "By the way, Vanessa. Is this yours?" he asked. I looked down and was speechless when I saw a silver GE 10 Transistor radio lying in his palm. "Well, aren't you going take it? I believe it's yours," he said with a big grin.

"What? Are you giving it to *me*?" I asked, looking up at him.

"Sure. Don't you want it?" he asked. He looked quite pleased with himself.

"Of course I do!" I said. I gently took it from his warm hand and rolled the round tuning disc on the side. Static noise immediately poured out of the small speaker. "Where did you get this? I don't understand."

"A little birdie told me you were all done in over not being able to get up to Forest Park today to get one, so I went up there and got one for you on my way over. That's why I was a little late."

"I...I can't believe it!" I gushed. I continued playing with the tuning disc until I was finally able to tune in radio station WIFE. It was playing "Downtown" by Petula Clark. The signal was surprisingly strong for this time of night, and it came in loud and clear. "But why?" I asked. "You went up there just to get this for *me*?"

I couldn't believe my good fortune. I studied every square inch of it, using the light of the fire to check out its shiny silver mesh grill and the over-sized "10" and General Electric logo molded into its plastic casing. But why did Jim go out of his way to be so kind to me? Did this mean he still had feelings for me?

"Are you serious?" Luke blurted, looking across the fire at the radio. "Is this the *special* errand you said you had to do?"

"I was up that direction anyway, so why not get one and make Vanessa happy? I should tell you it only picks up WIFE's signal," Jim warned me. "I don't know how they managed to make it do that, but they did. Some people complained about that, but mostly people appeared happy just to get one."

"Oh, I don't care about that," I giggled happily. "I don't know what to say. Thank you so much! I don't know why you went to the trouble just for me, but I'm so grateful you did."

I wanted to kiss him on the cheek, but resisted the impulse, thinking it might be too bold the way things were between us. I smiled and grinned at him gratefully, instead. I was delighted with my gift.

"Yeah, I don't know why you went to the trouble, either," Luke chimed in. "What a sap!" Then, he added, "Did you get one for me?"

"Sorry, old buddy. It was one per customer only. They were almost out of them as it was."

I looked into the fire and felt happy. The strains of "All You Need is Love" by the Beatles flowed out of the little radio and echoed through the night.

Suddenly, I heard the distinctive sounds of someone walking toward us. I couldn't see who it was, but the person was definitely advancing quickly, and coming from the direction of the woods.

"Did you hear that?" Luke exclaimed, jumping to his feet. The rest of us instinctively did the same thing. It was too dark to see anything.

"Who is it? Who's there? Identify yourself!" Luke demanded in a deep voice he made as gruff as possible. No answer came and the sounds intensified. "Speak up! Who's there?"

Two or three seconds that seemed like minutes passed without a reply.

"Whoever you are, you'd better speak up, or you'll regret it!" Luke shouted, his voice slightly wavering.

"Yeah? Exactly *how* will I regret it?" Daniel quipped, stepping into the light. He was wearing his signature fringed suede jacket and carrying a cloth bag that had a slight bulge in it. "My, aren't you jumpy? You act like you're Jim Bowie defending the Alamo."

"You blockhead!" Luke chastised. "Don't sneak up on us like that. I have a lot on my mind right now, and I'm sure you scared the crap out of Nessie and Emma. I ought to give you the five-minute treatment just for good measure."

"How else am I supposed to bring this homemade rhubarb pie to you?" Daniel bantered playfully as he held up the cloth bag. "My Mom just baked it. Aunt Louise said I should bring it to out to you guys back here. Don't you want it?"

"I, for one, sure do," Jim said, retaking his seat in the folding chair. "Thanks for bringing it to us. But you did give us all a start there, my friend. Maybe until we figure out what's going on around here you should shout out that you're coming to let the others know it's just you, and not someone on a different team."

"And, by 'team,' just so you know, he means that you're from planet Earth, and not from planet Doofus," Luke said, retaking his seat. "Although, in your case, it's a toss-up."

"Knock it off, Luke. Let's have some pie," Emma said, her eyes riveted on the cloth bag resting on the ground.

Daniel reached into the bag and pulled out paper plates, plastic forks, and the coveted pie wrapped in several sheets of aluminum foil. Steadying the pie on one of the logs, Daniel carefully peeled off the foil and sliced into the golden crust, allowing the deep maroon filling of baked rhubarb to spill out. He clumsily moved each slice onto a plate and passed them around.

"Be sure to thank your mom," Jim said, taking a bite from the pie on his plate.

"I sure will," Daniel replied, putting a forkful into his mouth.

"I could use a napkin," I said. "Did you bring any, Daniel?"

"Just use your shirt like this, City Slicker," Luke suggested, demonstrating by pulling his shirt tail up and wiping his mouth with it.

"You're uncouth!" Emma declared flatly. "No class at all."

"Uncouth? Not at all. I'm just resourceful," Luke countered. A trickle of rhubarb juice ran from the corner of his mouth, and he wiped it on his sleeve. "Voilà!" he said with a smile of self-satisfaction.

"I don't see how Bunny Bibble could have a crush on you. She's obviously never seen you out like this," Emma jeered. "Or when you're eating."

"What's this?" Jim asked, looking up. "Bunny Bibble has a crush on Luke?" He burst out laughing, and tossed his head back gleefully. "That's too funny. Is the feeling mutual? I think you'd make a very nice couple. Don't you agree, ladies?"

"I told you not to mention her name—-*ever*!" Luke scolded Emma. "You've violated my trust. From now on you're banished from my inner sanctum."

"Fine with me!" Emma exclaimed. "I don't want anything to do with your inner sanctum, whatever *that* is, or your inner ...anything else!"

Jim, Emma, and I looked at each other and laughed, as Luke frowned disapprovingly. The more Luke scowled and objected to our delight, the more we died laughing. It felt wonderful sitting so near to Jim as we chatted and joked. It was just like old times.

"I'm having a really good time tonight," Jim said, looking at me with those handsome, expressive eyes of his, made even more inviting by the way the firelight reflected in them.

"Me, too," I said, gazing back at him.

I had carefully propped my new radio against the back side of the log we were sitting on so it was safely away from the heat of the fire. At that moment, the station played "You Keep Me Hangin' On" by The Supremes. The lyrics about being hopelessly stuck in a relationship seemed strangely appropriate.

"Look at those stars way up there, a million light years away," Daniel observed. His head was craned back looking skyward. The sky was beautiful and clear. The stars sparkled like a million sequins sewn on a dark velvet gown. "Some of those twinkling lights are stars or planets, but I bet some of 'em are spacecraft bolting through the galaxy on their way here this very minute," he continued. "It could happen, you know. A real flying saucer crashed on a ranch in New Mexico a few years ago. It did! I read about it in an old *Popular Mechanics* magazine today."

"I read about that somewhere, too. It was on a ranch in Roswell, New Mexico, wasn't it? A few years after World War II," Luke continued. "They found alien bodies and all kinds of stuff. It was in all of the newspapers."

"Eeew! Alien bodies? Really?" Emma asked. "That's gross. What happen to them?"

"Some people believe they're on ice in the sub-basement of Wright Patterson Air Force Base in Dayton," Daniel replied.

"Cool! Can we go there and see them sometime?" I asked.

"Nope. The government says they don't exist, so there's nothing to see. They've denied the crash ever happened," Luke explained. "Just like there was no second gunman on the grassy knoll in Dallas when President Kennedy was shot. Right." Luke made an "okay" gesture with his fingers and winked.

"The government says it was a weather balloon that crashed in Roswell and not a UFO," Daniel said. "But if it was just a weather balloon, then why did men in black come to the rancher's house where the crash occurred and threaten him to keep quiet about what he'd seen?"

I looked up at the stars and watched for one of them to move and plunge downward to our little corner of Indiana, but none did. Not right then, anyway. I knew it was probably only a matter of time until the UFO I saw last night reappeared, because Luke had seen it twice already. I grew increasingly edgy as the night wore on knowing that the later it got, the more likely the UFO would appear.

Eventually, the fire began to die down as all of the wood we'd gathered was burned.

"Shall we gather more firewood and build this thing up again?" Luke asked, standing and stretching. "Or call it quits? What do you think?"

"Didn't you build this bonfire so we could hang out here until the UFO returns no matter how late it gets" Jim asked. "I say we gather more firewood and stay put to see this thing through."

"Yeah. I agree. You girls can go back to the house if you want. We'll hang here for a while," Luke suggested. "Heck, we may sit out here all night waiting for the UFO to come back."

"I'm psyched to chase it if it reappears, so I'll stay," Daniel said.

Emma reluctantly agreed to stay a bit longer, too, which pleased me. I was enjoying being with everyone around the fire. So the three boys strolled through the dark toward the woods to collect more kindling and logs. Suddenly, they stopped abruptly as if confronted by someone in the trees that I couldn't see. Luke's voice boomed out, "Who's there? Who are you?" They stood fixed in their tracks and peered intently into the woods.

"What are you doing here? Who are you?" Luke demanded again. Then, just as suddenly as they had stopped, they all ran into the woods as though chasing something or someone, and disappeared.

"What is it? What's wrong?" I shouted to them, standing and straining to see.

Emma was on her feet, also. "I think they saw something in the woods," she whispered.

"They definitely saw something. Should we run back to the house and get help?" I asked.

"No, let's wait a minute and see if they come back," Emma proposed. "Luke could be playing games with us and only pretending to be chasing someone. He's like that, you know."

I did what she suggested and stayed firmly planted by the fire, even though it didn't seem as though Luke was playing a practical joke. A few minutes later I heard a voice cry out. It sounded like someone in trouble, and it sounded like Jim. I was shaken. What was going on? Should I go after them to help, or make a run for the house? I didn't know which to do. I trained my eyes on the spot where the boys disappeared into the woods, hoping they'd run back out laughing and saying it was all one hilarious prank. But the seconds ticked away, and there was no sight or further sound from any of them.

CHAPTER NINE

'Cause You're Playing with Fire

Time slowed to an excruciating pace while Emma and I anxiously stood by the edge of the bonfire's waning embers waiting for the boys to re-emerge from the woods. Everything was silent, except for the tinny sound of rock songs coming from my new radio.

"Okay, this is officially getting strange," Emma whispered. "Maybe we should go back to the house now." She quickly gathered the empty RC Cola bottles and other debris and stuffed everything into the brown paper bag.

"Do you think we should go after them? Maybe they need help," I suggested before I'd thoroughly considered what I was suggesting. The last thing I wanted to do was go charging off into that dark woods right now. I turned off the radio and slipped it into my back pocket to be ready just in case.

"You can if you want to, but I'm not going into those woods this late," she answered. That settled that. There was no way I was going into the woods without her. "If you're coming, let's go. We don't need to do anything with the fire. It'll burn itself out," she said anxiously.

We turned and started across the field toward the house. I felt uncomfortable leaving the boys behind, but I wanted to get out of there. We were approaching the gate next to the barn when I heard Luke's voice from behind us.

"Hey! Where're you going?" he shouted. "Hold up there."

Emma and I turned and saw Luke, Daniel, and Jim running toward us. I was never so happy to see their eager faces. They looked okay, but Jim had mud caked all over the bottom of his jeans and was cradling his right arm.

"Why did you guys run into the woods? What happened?" I asked. "We were worried. Are you okay?"

"Jungle Jim there slipped along the side of the creek and fell in," Luke replied. "Some frontier man he'd make!"

"I'm not sure 'slipped' is exactly the word I'd use to describe what happened. I'd say 'pushed' is more accurate," Jim said, shooting Luke a dirty look.

"Hey, you slowed down without signaling. I can't help it if I crashed into you," Luke shrugged. "Didn't they teach you in driver's ed to signal before jamming on the brakes like that?"

"Are you hurt?" I asked. Jim moved his arm slightly and a look of pain flashed across his face.

"My shoulder's still sore from the bike crash, and being pushed into the creek by a certain person didn't help it any. I should be fine, though. I'm pretty tough," Jim said reassuringly. He continued making small circular movements to check his condition.

"What were you guys chasing in the woods, anyway?" Emma asked.

"I saw a strange-looking man just as we walked up to the edge of the woods," Daniel said. "I think he may have been spying on us."

"Was it a kid like us, or a man?" I asked just to be sure.

"It was a man all right. Judging by what I could see in the dark, he had a big build," Luke replied.

"Maybe we should get back to the house and talk there," I suggested. I didn't want to stand around if a strange man was lurking nearby.

"Oh, you can relax, City Slicker. We chased him off. He's long gone," Luke said assuredly.

"He ran across the creek and sprinted through the woods on the other side before we could catch up to him. He probably had his car stashed somewhere along 106th Street and made a fast get away," Daniel continued. "It was strange, though, how he knew the woods so well. He knew the best route through the underbrush to 106th Street, that's for sure. He got through there awfully fast."

"Yeah, we stopped to fish Jim out of the creek or we might have caught that sucker," Luke complained. "It's really too bad we didn't catch him, you know? I was up for letting him know we don't like trespassers."

"Did you recognize him?" I asked. "Maybe he lives around here, especially since he knew the way through the woods so well."

"No, I didn't recognize him. Did either of you guys?" Luke answered, looking at Daniel and Jim, both of whom shook their heads.

"What'd he look like?" I asked. "It wasn't Old Man Kleinschmidt, was it?"

"No, it was definitely *not* the old man. He was much younger and totally bald with a skull tattoo on the side of his head," Daniel said without hesitating. Luke looked at him with surprise. "Why are you looking at me like that? I'm not making this up. He had a big ol' tattoo right on the side of his head. I swear! It was huge and its mouth was wide open ready to bite. Real creepy. You couldn't miss it," Daniel insisted. He demonstrated where the tattoo was by gesturing to his own head.

"How on earth could you see all of that in the dark?" Luke challenged.

"I almost caught up with him while you were pulling Jim out of the creek," Daniel explained. "I have the vision of an Indian scout, you know. I can see things in the dark most people can't."

A man with a skull tattoo? This didn't sound good. There was no way a man like that was just strolling around in the woods tonight without a reason. He had to be up to something sinister. I felt a chill run through me, and wanted to get to the house even more quickly.

"Oh, well. Let's go to the house and look after Jim's shoulder," I suggested.

"I appreciate your concern, Vanessa, but we had a plan to wait for the UFO tonight and I plan on seeing it through, if you guys still want to. Don't let my shoulder derail us. I can deal with it. Really. I'm good to go," Jim insisted, but wincing a little.

Luke shook his head. "Nah. We're done for tonight, I'm afraid. There's a chance that guy might still be out there and could make trouble for us. Besides, Nessie's right for once. Your shoulder needs attention. I'm afraid we have no choice but to call it off for tonight."

Jim reluctantly nodded in agreement, and we all made our way back to the house. We told Uncle Evert about the strange man in the woods right away. Uncle Evert said he'd report him to the sheriff first thing in the morning, and tell him about the dead birds, too. He didn't seem too concerned about the skull tattoo guy, but I figured that was only his outward appearance. He probably didn't want to worry us, especially because everyone was practically living outside while the house was being repaired.

Meanwhile, Uncle Evert fashioned an arm sling out of an old burlap bag he found in the workshop, and slipped it over Jim's shoulder. He insisted on driving Jim home, saying he shouldn't be on his bike with a bad shoulder, especially in the dark. Jim could pick up his bike tomorrow. Jim resisted at first, but wisely gave in and accepted the offer.

"I had a really good time tonight," Jim said to me just before getting into Uncle Evert's van.

"I'm glad," I said. "Thanks again for the neat radio. I hope your shoulder's okay."

"It'll be okay. I'll get even with Luke for pushing me into the creek, never fear," he replied, winking and giving my hand a quick squeeze.

Aunt Louise said Emma and I could sleep in Emma's room if we wanted to, as long as we kept the windows open and the floor fan running to air out any lingering smoke fumes. The curtains had been taken down to be laundered, and the rug thrown out after Aunt Louise determined it had absorbed too much of the smell of smoke to be salvageable. Emma and I put the freshly laundered bed linens on the bed, and then went back outside and joined Aunt Louise, Luke, and Lars sitting around the dining room table. I gazed in the direction of the field where we'd been, and wondered if that man was still out there watching us.

"Well, Dr. Kimble finally caught the one-armed man who killed his wife," Aunt Louise informed us. "On *The Fugitive* tonight." She leaned down and stroked the back of a black cat who preened and curled around her leg.

"So, you were right about Dr. Kimble, weren't you, Mom?" Lars replied. "You must be happy about that."

"I have a talent for understanding people and animals. Take little Karma here. We get along pretty well. She and I knew each other in a past life, so that's probably why," Aunt Louise said, picking up the purring cat and placing it on her lap.

I'd never heard anyone speak of having a past life before, much less knowing a cat in it. I studied Aunt Louise and concluded she was being serious. My cousins accepted her statement without comment, so she must have mentioned the concept to them before.

"How do you know you knew each other in a past life?" I asked. I was curious to learn how.

"Oh, you just know. Something inside tells you," she said, stroking the cat's whiskers. "Don't you agree, Karma?" She smiled and looked down at the cat who looked up at her adoringly.

"Did you know any of us in a past life?" I inquired.

She looked around the table and pondered the question carefully. "No. This is my first time with all of you, I'm pretty sure," she concluded, speaking slowly and solemnly.

"Can you tell me if I'm going to spend any more lives with you, Mom? I'm just asking so I can be prepared," Luke quipped. He laughed and looked around the table to see if we were as amused by his comment as he was.

"If I have anything to say about it, this will be the one and only time," Aunt Louise returned. She delivered the statement in a very matter-of-fact tone.

Luke puckered his mouth and looked stunned. "Gee, thanks, Mom," he replied sheepishly.

Lars let out a hearty laugh and slapped the table. "Ha! Touché, dear Mother," he congratulated her. "It's a joy to witness you eviscerate your offspring so handily."

Luke glowered at him and crossed his arms defiantly. "What the heck does eviscerate mean? Why can't you speak English like the rest of us?" Luke muttered.

"I'm not trying to be hurtful, Son. I'm just telling it like it is. I see no reason that the spiritual growth of either of us would be enhanced by being reincarnated together again," Aunt Louise explained as she continued petting the cat. "That's all."

"So you're telling me you were spiritually benefited from being reincarnated from a past life with Karma—a *cat*? And, yet you wouldn't be benefitted from being reincarnated again with me—your own *son*? Your own flesh and blood?" Luke challenged. He appeared to be taking his mother's remarks very personally.

"Let it go, Brother. You're not going to win," Lars laughed.

"What can I say?" Aunt Louise replied as she continued scratching Karma's whiskers. "I'm just telling it the way it is."

It wasn't much longer until I heard Uncle Evert's van roll up the driveway. I felt safer knowing he was home. Luke gave up quizzing his mother about their next lives, and everyone said goodnight and found a place to sleep for the night. Margret was staying with Wendy across the street again. Aunt Louise and Uncle Evert moved back into their middle bedroom, while Luke and Lars drew straws to determine which of them got to sleep on the green couch or on the floor in the living room. I was glad to be in a real bed again in Emma's room, but I had a restless night thinking about who might be outside our open windows. Only window screens separated us from anyone who might want to climb in, and that did little to quiet my concerns.

I was glad when morning came and I opened my eyes to see the bright light of a new day. Uncle Evert was on the phone at the desk on the other side of the gold curtains. He was talking with the sheriff about the man in the woods. The sheriff would surely come out, find that guy if he was still around, and drag him away. That would be such a relief! Then, I'd only have to worry about the colored lights hovering in the sky.

Yawning, I stretched and walked into the living room in my pink pajamas. Lars was sitting on the green couch reading *Time* magazine which had drawings of the recent Twelfth Street race riots in Detroit on the cover.

"Hi, Vanessa," he said, not looking up from the magazine. "Sleep okay?"

"Yes, I guess. Okay, not really," I replied, taking a seat in the dragon chair. It was a mahogany chair made in China carved to look like serpents with mother-of-pearl eyes were snaking around the arms. "Is the sheriff on his way over? I thought I heard Uncle Evert on the phone talking to him."

"I don't think so," Lars replied, turning a page of the magazine. "You'll have to ask my father to be certain, of course, but I gather it's the sheriff's opinion that man you encountered last night was probably just a teenager pulling a prank. Not worth his time to come out to investigate."

"What?" I said, shaking my head in disbelief.

"The sheriff probably thinks you guys are a bunch of teenagers overreacting to another kid trying to eavesdrop on you," Lars explained. "But don't worry too much about that man. After Luke and the others chased him, he probably got the message to clear out."

I was stunned and disappointed. I sat silently and thought about it. Maybe it was just a kid watching or sneaking up on us as part of a prank, and nothing more sinister than that. Daniel could have been seeing things when he thought he saw the skull tattoo on the man. After all, it was dark and difficult to see your own hand, much less something like a tattoo on a person running from you. Still I didn't totally buy into the sheriff's explanation. They saw a man, not a boy, so the teenager-prank theory didn't hold water. But I was just a visitor here. There was nothing I could do. I got up and walked through the kitchen, down the steps, and outside. Aunt Louise was seated alone at the dining room table reading a book with the drawing of a large peach on it entitled *James and the Giant Peach*.

"Good morning," she greeted me heartily. "We have some Quisp cereal today if you'd like some." She lifted a blue box adorned with the image of a cross-eyed cartoon character depicting an alien with a small propeller on his head. "Each piece of the cereal is supposed to resemble a flying saucer. Want to give it a try?" I took note of the irony.

I had just poured the little golden disks into my bowl when I heard Luke shouting in the distance. He was running fast toward us from the field behind the barn.

"Someone trashed the little house during the night," he yelled when he was near, breathing hard. "They took a crowbar to one of the walls and pulled it down. The roof's caved in, too. There's something sticky all over the floor and stuff painted on the walls. It's a mess!"

"But why?" I asked, jumping up from my seat. "Who do you think did it?"

"You can't be serious!" Lars bellowed, bursting out of the house having overheard Luke's report. "Buzz and I just finished building that only a few days ago. Why would someone do this?" He darted across the yard toward the field, each purposeful step conveying his apprehension about what he would find.

I ran back inside the farmhouse, grabbed some clothes from my suitcase, and locked myself in the bathroom to change. When I emerged seconds later, Emma was standing by the door, dressed and ready to go.

We ran past the barn and crossed the two fields until we reached the little house, or what was left of it. Someone had viciously inflicted as much damage as possible. Half of the roof was caved in and an entire wall had been pulled down. There was a dead possum inside; the stench was oppressive and hung in the air. Amazingly, the floor was still intact, although covered with grease and oil. Uncle Evert arrived moments later.

"Someone really wanted to spoil our fun out here, that's all I can say," Luke lamented as he walked around the sad remains of the playhouse.

"We can clean it up," Lars declared, studying the damage. "We're not licked. Not by a long shot. Not rebuilding would be giving in to the vile hoodlum who did this, and I won't do that." His words were slow and deliberate, and tinged with anger.

I was intrigued by the paint designs on the walls, which appeared random, except in one place where something was crudely written in a foreign language that looked vaguely like Russian, although I didn't really know what Russian looked like.

Luke peered in the direction of Mr. Kleinschmidt's farm. "The old Nazi did this; you can bet on it. That kraut probably didn't like our bonfire last night and all the noise we made, so he got even and did this."

"Mr. Kleinschmidt, you mean?" Emma asked.

"Of course that's who I mean!" Luke answered sharply.

"Do you have any proof he did it?" Lars challenged. "Maybe some kids did it, or that man you saw running around in the woods. You can't just assume someone did something based on preconceived notions about them."

"Oh, yes I can!" Luke insisted.

"Why?" Emma asked.

"'Cause I know he did it!" Luke exclaimed impatiently.

"Surely even a mean old geezer like Kleinschmidt wouldn't do something as low as this," Uncle Evert said, looking toward the Kleinschmidt farm and thinking. "Maybe I'll have the sheriff come out and look around after all. This constitutes property damage, and that's a whole different animal from merely seeing a stranger walking in the woods."

Suddenly, another section of the roof fell in with an unexpected "kaboom!" It startled me and I jumped. It seemed to be the last straw for Luke.

"This is war!" Luke blurted. He turned and bolted back toward the farmhouse.

"What's he going to do?" I asked.

"Who can say?" Lars replied, watching Luke disappear across the field. "But whatever it is, it won't be good. I guarantee it."

CHAPTER TEN

A House is Not a Home

Daniel met us near the barn as Uncle Evert, Lars, Emma, and I were returning to the farmhouse. He looked shocked when we told him the little house had been vandalized and virtually destroyed.

"Luke's mad as a hornet! Says he's going after the dirtbag who did it," Emma reported. "I haven't seen him *this* crazy in a long time."

"He'll blow off steam and calm down after a bit," Uncle Evert said. "That kid has strong feelings about certain things, sometimes too strong."

"I don't see what his beef is about. I'm the one who spent weeks of my life out there building that house with Buzz," Lars said. "You don't see me bouncing off the roof over it."

"You might say it's a question of temperament and maturity," Uncle Evert explained. "He's got too much of one and not enough of the other."

We were all nodding in agreement when Luke came walking toward us carrying a rifle. His stride was quick and he had a determined expression on his face. It startled me to see him with a rifle, and I wondered what he was going to do with it.

"Now, Luke. Where are you going and just what do you intend to do with that?" Uncle Evert asked sternly. Uncle Evert stepped sideways and blocked Luke from passing.

"Calm down, Dad. This is just a BB gun. I'm headed down to the creek to shoot at these plastic soldiers," Luke explained. He held up his other hand which was holding a small brown paper bag that I presumed was filled with the toy soldiers. "Thought it'd make me feel better to shoot at something."

"Oh. Well, then go ahead. Get it out of your system," Uncle Evert said, stepping aside.

"I'll go with you," Daniel volunteered.

"Yeah. Come along Daniel Boone. You can wade into the creek to fish these guys out after I pop them in," Luke said as he resumed his rapid strides. Daniel made a face, but walked on alongside him anyway.

"He could hurt someone with that gun, Dad, even though it's just a BB gun," Lars warned. "Should he be allowed to be unsupervised with it, in light of what happened today and how he reacted? He might go gunning for Mr. Kleinschmidt."

Uncle Evert watched Luke and Daniel as they walked away. "He's got Daniel with him, and if I know Daniel, he won't allow anything to go too far off the rails without coming to tell me. I trust Luke. He'll behave," Uncle Evert assured us.

"I hope you're right," Lars said. "I'd hate for Luke to be guilty of murder. It's so unseemly to have a relative in prison."

When we got to the house, Margret was in the bedroom she shared with Emma looking through the dresser. She had on a black and white one-piece swimsuit with a short white terrycloth robe over it and blue rubber thongs. Emma and I heard her when we entered the house, and went to the bedroom to see what she was doing. With her active social life, I never seemed to see enough of my older cousin for my taste.

"Hi, you guys. Want to go swimming? I'm meeting Wendy at Northern Beach today if you want to come along," Margret said. She opened and closed a drawer. "Have you seen the Coppertone? I can't seem to find it."

"I'd love to go!" Emma exclaimed. "That's what Vanessa and I planned to do today. We were thinking of going to the pool at Forest Park, but Northern Beach is just as good. We'll get into our suits and be ready to go in nothing flat."

I was happy my mother hadn't made the dreaded phone call informing me she was on her way to collect me home. Until then, as far as I was concerned, I could go to the pool or do whatever with my cousins. I reached into my suitcase and took out my new turquoise polka dot swimsuit my mother had purchased at L.S. Ayres at Glendale Shopping Center for me earlier in the summer. It had several rows of small ruffles in contrasting fabric around the hips, which I hoped gave my slim figure a hint of curves. Emma emerged from the bathroom wearing a cute emerald-green two-piece suit with white trim.

"Look at you two stylish ladies! We could do a *Seventeen* magazine swimsuit photo spread right here, you both look so good," Margret said as she walked up with a straw beach tote and sunglasses perched on her head. She handed each of us a colorful beach towel.

"Oh, I don't think so," I said, giggling self-consciously. "Me? Model in a *swimsuit*? That'd never happen in a million years!"

"Oh, Vanessa! You're just too hard on yourself," Margret laughed.

We walked out to the red Chevy Bel Air and got in. Margret drove us up Allisonville Road and across 116th Street until we crossed White River. Not long after that she turned into Northern Beach. The park bordered White River and had lots of grassy areas and large shady hickory, elm, and maple trees. Built in the 1920s, it had several picnic shelters and other buildings that had the look of that era, one of which was the poolhouse. She pulled up to the front and we made our way in.

The slap of our thongs against our feet sounded like little motorboats as we walked up to the teenaged boy sitting at the window just inside the door where you paid the entry fee. He had sandy-colored hair and a bad case of acne, and grinned at me non-stop as we approached, making me very uncomfortable.

"Well hello there, pretty lady. You new around here?" he asked. He was chewing gum and boldly looked me up and down in a way some might consider rude.

"No...I'm with my cousins...they live here...," I stuttered self-consciously, not knowing what to say.

Margret paid the entry fee of twenty cents per person for all of us. His strange eyes were fixed on me, and I was relieved when we walked through the turnstile and went on our way. After we walked through the locker room and the showers, we stepped outside to the pool area.

The pool was shaped like a giant kidney bean and was made out of rough brown concrete full of lots of little pebbles, giving it a rough texture. It had three or four six-foot water sprinklers made from ordinary pipe out of which water continuously rained on swimmers. Its best feature were the two water slides standing in the middle, each curling twice before depositing swimmers into the water. Kids were constantly scurrying up the ladders to the tops of the slides, and then flying out below with gleeful yells and a loud splash.

I looked across the pool and there he was—talking to Monica!

It was crowded today, with a lot of people making good use of what remained of the summer. We finally found three unoccupied pool chairs under the leafy limbs of a large maple tree reaching over from the other side of the fence encircling the pool area. We placed our towels on the chairs and sat down. Margret began pulling things out of her beach tote, including the copper-colored plastic Coppertone bottle.

"You guys go ahead. I'm going to get some sun," she said. She began spreading the lotion on her legs and arms with long strokes.

Emma stood up and jumped in, and I quickly followed. The water was warm and inviting. I stood up in the chest-high water and looked around at the people milling along the side. Jim's summer job was in maintenance at that pool. It'd sure be a nice bonus to run into him today, especially after the pleasant evening we shared last night before the chase after the man in the woods. Unfortunately, there was no sign of him. Perhaps his injured shoulder had kept him home.

"Want to go down the slide?" Emma asked, bobbing over to me.

"Sure. Let's go," I said. I had just started to swim toward the slide, when Emma grabbed my arm.

"Wait a minute," she said with a strange look on her face.

"What's wrong?" I asked. "Are you all right?"

"Look. There's *Monica*," she said, pointing with her hand low in the water.

Sure enough, Jim's old girlfriend, Monica, was walking along the side of the pool with two girlfriends. They must have just arrived. I watched them strut their stuff as they slowly made their way around the perimeter of the pool looking for just the right place to sit. They finally settled on three unoccupied chairs on the opposite side of the pool from where we were sitting.

Monica was petite and very curvy, with long, glossy, dark brown hair. She had on high heeled sandals and a bright red two-piece swimsuit that matched her long manicured nails. I noticed she was wearing the gold chain with the gold heart Jim had given her earlier this summer when they were dating. If they'd truly broken up, why was she still wearing it? Had they reconciled? Well, if they had, it was none of my business. I had no claim on him. Oh, sure, he'd been friendly enough last night and gave me the radio, but there'd been no kiss good night or even a hug. Maybe that was why. It was just my tough luck that she came to the pool today. Seeing her made me feel hopelessly inadequate.

"Don't let her bother you," Emma urged. "You're much prettier than she is."

I let out a burst of laughter. I knew that wasn't true, but Emma was so dear and loyal to say it. "You're goofy. *She's* magazine material. I'm not," I replied. Emma started to refute what I said, but I wouldn't let her. "And that's okay. I have *personality*, and that's worth much, much more than sexy good looks. Right?"

I thought if I said it out loud, my psyche would hear it and believe it. But saying it wasn't working, and I'd have to repeat it a million more times before my inner self would believe it.

"Right on, Cuz!" Emma said, playfully smacking the water. "Girl power!"

"Right. Girl Power! Go, Mystic Millicent!" I said, slapping the water.

"Go, Rad Red!" Emma returned in kind.

We splashed around in the water a few more times to demonstrate our fierceness, and giggled with self-satisfaction. Another hour went by as we continued playing in the water. I practiced diving off the side of the pool and holding my breath underwater for as long as I could. I did my best to forget Monica was there, and focused on having a good time.

When we got back to our chairs, Wendy had arrived and was sitting next to Margret. They glistened from having rubbed suntan lotion and baby oil all over their bodies. Their heads were laid back against their chairs, and their eyes were closed as they let the sun do its work.

"Hi, kids!" Wendy said cheerfully when we walked up and sat down. She sat up and gave us both a big smile. "This is one of the last days you'll have to work on your tans. After the pool closes next week, it'll be back to being pale and washed out again until next year."

Wendy was a little shorter than Margret and about the same age. Her dark blonde hair was straight and long, and she wore it parted down the middle with long bangs in the same style. She had athletic legs, and they were very tan, just like the rest of her.

"I don't really tan," I confessed. "I burn and then I turn this ashen color again."

Wendy peeked at me with one eye, looked me up and down, and chuckled. "You really *are* a ghostly pale redhead, aren't you? Oh well, don't worry about it. Tans are highly overrated and make you old and wrinkly before your time."

Just then, Ryker, Jim's friend, and another boy walked by. Ryker was wearing bright red, white, and blue swim trunks that had a built-in white belt and came almost to his knees. They were decidedly longer than the shorter, spandex-style swim trunks worn by most of the other boys. Even so, he didn't appear at all self-conscious in them. You had to give him credit for that.

"Hey, Rad Red, how you doin'?" he asked me cheerfully. Then, he turned toward Emma. "Hey, Emma. Looking good."

I was uncharacteristically tongue-tied. "Hi," I mumbled. Emma looked up and silently scowled at him.

"Catching some rays here at the pool today, eh, ladies?" he continued. "Groovy. I dig those rays, too."

He nodded nervously and smiled non-stop, but didn't seem too concerned that neither Emma nor I was very talkative. He seemed determined to ignore our signals, and stayed planted in front of us. "Well, see you around," he said after a few more awkward moments struggling for something to say. Waving, he finally walked on with his friend.

"Who was *that*?" Wendy asked, smiling slyly. "And, why did he call you Rad Red, Vanessa? Is he your new boyfriend? He's kind of cute— in an offbeat kind-of-way. Personally, I go for that Bohemian type."

"That was no one," I replied. "He's one of Jim Sparks's friends. That's all."

"He's goofy and annoying," Emma chimed in. "I can't believe someone as nice as Jim hangs out with a total weirdo like him."

"I see. Speaking of Jim Sparks, isn't that him over there?" Wendy asked, gesturing across the pool.

I looked across the pool and there he was—talking to Monica! He was wearing a work shirt and khaki slacks. My heart jumped into my throat and I suddenly felt faint. I was jealous beyond description. How could he be over there talking to *her*? Monica was on her feet standing next to him, touching his arm every so often and laughing and smiling in an overly-animated fashion. He appeared to be enjoying every minute of it.

"Uh, oh," Emma uttered under her breath.

"Oh, yeah. That's Jim all right," I managed to squeak out.

Wendy and Margret were aware of my crush on Jim from earlier this summer.

"She's a real piece of work, isn't she?" Wendy said as she observed them. "A real man trap. What a flirt!"

Margret opened her eyes and gazed across the pool. "I've seen her all over town riding around with Vinny Shoals on the back of his motorcycle."

I couldn't take my eyes off of them. They must be back together, and that was why she was wearing his heart necklace. If that was the case, why did he lead me on last night by giving me the radio? I suddenly felt sick to my stomach.

"Speaking of tans, I think I'm getting too much sun now," Margret complained, sitting up straight in her chair. "Why didn't I bring my big floppy hat? My face is going to be burned to a crisp unless I get out of the sun."

"Well, where's your hat? If it's in the car I'll get it for you," Wendy offered. "I don't mind stretching my legs a bit."

"Thanks, I can get it. But I might as well leave if I have to go out to the parking lot to get the hat. What do you think? Are you guys ready to leave?" she asked Emma and me. I was surprised she suggested leaving so early, and wondered if it was because of me.

"Sure," Emma replied. I nodded in agreement

We packed up our things, said good-bye to Wendy, and made our way through the poolhouse and out to the car. I was grateful Margret had suggested leaving. I didn't know if she wanted to leave because she was genuinely ready to go, or because she wanted to spare me further exposure to the Jim and Monica Show. It was like her to be thoughtful like that. Whatever the reason, the important thing was that I was getting away from there, and that now I could breathe again.

CHAPTER ELEVEN

Look At That Caveman Go!

When we arrived back at the farm, Mr. Kleinschmidt was standing in front with Uncle Evert. His old Ford pickup truck was parked in the turnaround with Fritz sitting patiently in the passenger seat. Luke stood near them looking guilty. You didn't have to be a psychic to see something was very wrong. Margret cautiously guided the car to the driveway leading to the barn and parked. Even from there you could hear the heated conversation between the two men.

"I promise I'll take care of this, Kleinschmidt. Luke'll learn a lesson he'll never forget, I assure you. There's no need to get the authorities involved, and I'd ask you as a personal favor not to," Uncle Evert pleaded.

"That's what you told me before, Larsson. If you ask me, I don't think you can handle that boy," Mr. Kleinschmidt argued. "Shooting at my dog and property with a BB gun? That conduct is simply unacceptable."

"Yes, you're absolutely correct," Uncle Evert replied. "Unacceptable is the correct word for it. I'll make certain nothing like this ever happens again. Please, allow me to handle this in my own way. He'll be punished severely, I promise."

Mr. Kleinschmidt scowled at Luke. "Okay. I'll give you one more chance, *Herr* Larsson, but if he steps out of line again, I'm taking the matter straight to the authorities. I have spoken my piece and I mean what I say. *Ich warne Sie*!"

"Yes, yes," Uncle Evert replied. "Thank you, Mr. Kleinschmidt. I appreciate your understanding." He reached out to shake Mr.

Kleinschmidt's hand, but the old man ignored the gesture, leaving Uncle Evert standing there awkwardly.

"Understanding? Ha! You people in this country are soft and don't know how to instill discipline in your children. They are growing up to be thugs and criminals, just like your boy there."

"Now, Mr. Kleinschmidt, I'd ask you to watch your words. That's my son you're talking about," Uncle Evert said, starting to get angry. "We've had our conversation, and I'll do as I said I would. You should probably leave now."

"Oh, I'm leaving all right. You just be sure to do as you promised, *Herr* Larsson," Mr. Kleinschmidt growled. "You get that boy under control...or else!"

He walked to his truck and got in, slamming the creaky door. It looked as though Uncle Evert was going to say something more, but before he could, Kleinschmidt fired up the noisy old truck and it began to move. I could have sworn Fritz gave me a dirty look as they drove by me as I stood watching by the corner of the garage.

"Into the house, Mister. We need to talk. *Now*!" Uncle Evert brusquely commanded after Kleinschmidt was gone. Luke sheepishly walked into the house, and Uncle Evert followed close behind.

"Uh, oh. Luke's done something again," Emma said softly. "I'd hate to be him right now."

"You oaf! Why would you go over there when I specifically told you not to?" I heard Uncle Evert chastising Luke through the open windows. "It's not like you to disobey me like that. I'm deeply disappointed in you."

Emma and I sat at the table outside. I was anxious to get out of my wet bathing suit, but didn't want to go inside until Uncle Evert was done with Luke. "Luke's taking a real tongue lashing in there," Emma observed. "Dad's *really* mad."

"I know. I can hear," I said. "Wonder what he did?"

"I think I heard Dad say he went over to the fence along the old German's property and shot BBs at Kleinschmidt's barns and at Fritz," she reported.

"At the *dog*? That doesn't sound like something Luke would do. The rest sounds possible, but not that. He loves animals too much," I replied. "Doesn't he?"

"Maybe, but he's off his rocker when it comes to that old geezer," Emma said. "I believe he'd do just about anything where that old guy is concerned. It's like he's in a private war with him."

"The old man doesn't like him much, either," I observed. "I think they both hate each other."

Uncle Evert continued lecturing Luke for several more minutes. Finally, Uncle Evert emerged from the house with an "everyone out of my way" look on his face, and walked directly into the workroom in the garage and moved things around noisily. A couple of minutes later, Luke came out looking defeated and walked over to us.

"What happened?" Emma asked him. "What did Dad say?"

"It's totally unfair. I didn't do what that old Nazi said I did, but Dad won't believe me," Luke complained. "I'm a martyr. A victim of an adult conspiracy against me."

"Luke! Get to the barn. *Now*!" Uncle Evert bellowed from inside the workroom.

"Why do you have to go to the barn?" Emma whispered.

"Dad says I have to move all of the bales of hay from the south side of the hayloft to the north side so he can replace some rotted floor boards on the south side. He says the work will reform me and make me a better person," Luke said softly so as not to be heard. "This bites. I was supposed to join up with Jim and some guys later on. I'll be lucky to be done moving the bales by dark."

"I know. You'd better get busy. You'll have to move a whole lot of bales before you're a better person, that's for sure," Emma teased.

"Too funny, Sis," Luke said flatly. "Hey, look what Daniel and I found down by the creek today. You don't deserve to see it, but I'll let you cause that's the kind of nice guy I am."

He pulled a silver coin out of his pocket and handed it to Emma. I leaned over and studied it. It had the letters "CCCP," a small star, and the image of a man with a raised arm on the front. There was also odd writing on the back in a language I didn't recognize. I thought that it might be Russian.

"What do you make of that?" he asked. He seemed very excited about the discovery.

"What is it?" I asked. "Is that Russian writing on it?"

"Yeah, I think so. Weird, huh?" he said.

"What would a coin from the Soviet Union be doing down by our creek?" Emma asked.

"*Exactly*," Luke replied, drawing the word out for emphasis. "I think this means there are a bunch of Commies running around in our woods!"

"Or coin collectors! They can be very troublesome," I taunted playfully.

"Laugh all you want. Russkies could be down by *our* creek plotting a Communist takeover of Fishers. Go ahead and make jokes. You'll see." He took the coin back from Emma and put it in his pocket. "Well, might as well get started. Those bales aren't going to move themselves."

"Hey. One question. Did you really shoot at the dog?" I asked. "That's pretty despicable if you did."

"Heck, no. I'd never do something inhumane like that," Luke insisted. "I don't love that German hound, but I wouldn't shoot at him."

"What were you doing over at Kleinschmidt's property, then? I thought you said you were going down to the creek to shoot plastic soldiers," I asked.

"I did! We took turns shooting at them near the hollow sycamore tree until we lost them all in the creek. I tried to get Daniel to go under and fish them out, but he wouldn't, the sissy! Complained he would get too wet. So we went over to the little house. He wanted to see what the damage looked like."

"Okay. But you still haven't explained how you ended up at Kleinschmidt's. You *were* at Kleinschmidt's, weren't you?" Emma asked.

"We messed around at the little house for a while, and then I thought I saw something going on over at the old Nazi's place, so we went over to the fence to check it out. But I never shot at Fritz or at anything else on his property, I swear."

"What do you mean you saw something going on? What'd you see?" Emma questioned.

"That's just it. I couldn't see much. He's got a real operation going on over there, but I can't tell what it's for. Lots of buildings and screened areas. He's got things over there I've never noticed before that just don't add up," he said. "I think that's why he keeps making up these wild stories that I'm shooting at his dog. Maybe he wants to keep me away. I don't know."

"What could he be hiding?" I asked. "He's a hateful, old man, for sure, but he seems harmless enough. You're not still blaming him for the damage to the little house, are you?"

"I can't put my finger on what it is he's doing yet, but I will," Luke said, gazing into the distance. "I'll need more intel."

"You better not nose around there anymore, Luke. Dad's fed up with all of this, I can tell. I haven't seen him this angry in a long time. I don't usually care if you get in trouble, but all of this fuss you're causing is stressing me out," Emma complained.

"Well, boo hoo, sissy pants!" Luke said, smiling. "Heaven forbid I should do anything to stress you out. Even if it helps defend me from unfair attacks by old Germans!"

Just then Uncle Evert walked out of the workroom and stood at the edge of the walkway with his hands on his hips. "Luke, do you remember what we talked about? I want those bales moved by sundown. If you know what's good for you, you'll get moving right now. Don't test me."

"Okay, okay. I'm going," Luke grumbled. He sauntered across the yard toward the barn, mumbling under his breath the whole way.

A few minutes later, Lars drove up in Uncle Evert's van. He had on blue overalls that he wore whenever he worked on jobs or made deliveries for Uncle Evert's water softening business.

"What're you girls up to sitting out here?" Lars asked, walking over to us. "Have you seen Dad? I need to tell him when I made the delivery today to Mrs. Haygood, she said she has a job for him."

"I think he's in the workroom in the garage," Emma replied. "Or at least he was a few minutes ago. Be careful, though. He's really mad. Luke goofed up with the BB gun and got in big trouble."

"Oh, no. What now? Did he go after Mr. Kleinschmidt? He did, didn't he? I knew he would. I told Dad not to let him have that gun," Lars said. "Did the sheriff have to come out?"

"No, nothing that serious. He didn't hurt Kleinschmidt, but the old man was just here claiming he took shots at his dog with the BB gun. It was really horrible," Emma said.

"Well, at least the old guy's still alive," Lars said. "I'm not a fan of the gentleman, but I don't want Luke to go to jail for knocking him off."

"What are we going to do with Luke?" Emma continued. "I heard him say some mean things to Jim and some other boys last week about a boy in their class named Todd Yamaguchi just because the boy's parents are Japanese. He's got a grudge against anyone with Japanese blood because of what they did during World War II. And against Germans, like Kleinschmidt, for kind of the same reason."

"Yes, well, our brother isn't very enlightened when it comes to accepting people from other walks of life. Maybe he'll mature and get half a brain one of these days. Until then, we'll just have to try to steer him straight when we can," Lars said. "Well, I've got to find Dad. See you girls later."

I looked down at my watch and saw that it was almost 3:30. I knew that meant the popular daytime TV show *Dark Shadows* would just be starting. I had a crush on one of the principal characters, Barnabas Collins, a vampire in the fictional setting of Collinsport, Maine. Not only was he dark and brooding with the classic set of fangs and sweeping black cape, he also had unrequited romantic longings and heroic impulses that made him irresistible.

"Do you want to watch *Dark Shadows*? It's about time for it to be on," I suggested. "I'd like to see if Dr. Hoffman is able to cure Barnabas from being a vampire. The last time I tuned in, the treatments the doctor was giving him weren't working, and were making him prematurely age. He could die from old age and be off the show! I'd die if they killed him off."

"Sure," Emma said. "They wouldn't really kill Barnabas, would they? He's much too popular."

"You're probably right, but you never know with daytime TV," I said. "I don't want to miss it if it happens."

I went inside to Emma's bedroom and changed into my brown slacks and a blue button down shirt. Emma went to the kitchen to make a grape drink for us using Fizzies pellets she dropped into glasses of water. We grabbed a box of Bugles snack chips and went to the couch, turned the TV to Channel 13, and sat down. The dark images of Collinwood Mansion appeared on the screen, and I settled back. At the conclusion of the show, Barnabas lived on, although in a vampire-kind-of-way. *The Dating Game* came on after that, and we amused ourselves guessing which bachelor each contestant would choose. I never chose the same boy the girl contestant did—not ever, strangely.

As early evening approached, Aunt Louise cooked a skillet of sloppy joe meat on the stove. An open bag of Chesty brand potato chips was sitting on the dining room table outside, and Emma and I helped ourselves to some.

Suddenly, I heard a bicycle come up the gravel driveway, and then the loud squeak of a bicycle hand brake. Could it be Jim coming to visit Luke? I turned expectantly to see him. But it was Ryker, not Jim. He had a worried look on his face as he walked toward Uncle Evert working in the driveway.

"Hello, Mr. Larsson," Ryker said. "Is Luke around?" He gazed around the yard.

"No, he's doing some chores out in the barn. I'll be sure to tell him you dropped by when he's done with them," Uncle Evert said.

"Do...do you think it'd be okay if I went out to talk to him?' Ryker asked.

I expected Uncle Evert to tell Ryker he'd have to see Luke another time. But Aunt Louise came to the door and spoke to Ryker before Uncle Evert could answer.

"Sure. Go right ahead, young man. Luke needs to come in for dinner right away. Would you please tell him that when you speak to him?" she said.

"Oh, Louise. Please!" Uncle Evert thundered. "Must you interfere?"

"The boy needs to eat, Evert," Aunt Louise replied in a matter-of-fact way. "Emma, you and Vanessa accompany Ryker out to the barn to get Luke, please. Make sure he comes in for dinner, won't you?"

I didn't fully comprehend why Emma and I needed to get involved in the drama, but we dutifully stood to do as we were told. I sensed my aunt and uncle were going to have a discussion after we left. Emma remained silent as we walked to the barn, refusing to acknowledge Ryker.

"Your hair's not in a ponytail," Ryker observed as we walked along. He was right. I'd let my hair down after we got back from the pool to let it dry, and it fell loose almost to my waist. "I've never seen you without your ponytail. Rad Red always has a ponytail."

"Well, the Invisible Woman doesn't," Emma chirped up. "She has short blonde hair like mine." She shook her curly blonde hair and gave him a sly look.

A look of surprise washed over Ryker's face, and he smiled. "Okay. Now that you mention it, I guess you could be Sue Storm, the Invisible Woman. You're certainly athletic enough, and okay looking, I guess,"

Ryker replied. He gave Emma a sidelong glance as if it was the first time he'd really looked at her.

"Whatever," Emma replied as we came to the barn. "I don't want to play your silly game. I was just saying I could be a superhero if I wanted to be. But I'm me, and that's who I want to be. Not Sue Storm or anyone else."

She tossed the words out so breezily it seemed as though she didn't care how Ryker reacted to them. Instead of being offended, he seemed more intrigued by her.

The air in the barn was woodsy, with the smells of damp earth, hay, and animals, even though, as far as I knew, the barn hadn't housed any animals, other than an occasional horse, since my grandfather retired from farming several years ago. It had no electric lights and was dim inside. I had to pay close attention not to trip over the lawn mower, a farm wagon, and a rusty piece of farm equipment as we made our way to the back near the two empty stalls where the ladder to the hayloft was located. The ladder consisted of flat wooden slats nailed into the wall that extended up to a square opening cut in the hayloft floor.

Emma looked up at the hayloft opening. "Hey, Luke! Are you up there?" she shouted. "Hey, Luke! You have a visitor!"

After a few moments, Luke's head appeared in the opening looking down at us. "Hey, hi, Ryker. What's up? Does Dad know you guys are out here?"

"Yeah, Mom said we should come out here and tell you to come to the house for dinner," Emma replied.

"Well, come on up first. I want to show you something," he beckoned.

One by one we climbed the ladder and popped through the opening and stood up on the hayloft floor.

"Well, what is it? Dinner's ready and I'm hungry," Emma complained impatiently.

"Look at that!" Luke said, holding his hand out proudly toward a tall pile of hay bales on one side of the hayloft floor. "Isn't it genius?"

"What?" Ryker replied. "We've all seen hay stacked in a barn before."

"Oh, no. Don't you see it? I made a maze out of the bales. See? You go through it on your knees. Start over there where the floor height changes." He pointed to an opening in the honey-colored wall of bales. "I'd love to have someone try it out."

"Oh, I get it. A tunnel made out of hay bales. Very nice. I'll test it out for you," Ryker said enthusiastically. In an instant, he'd fallen to his knees and disappeared into the dusty organic structure.

"You guys want to give it a try, too?" Luke inquired with a big smile. "I dare you to get all the way through without getting stuck."

Emma stood with her arms crossed. "So, this is what you've been doing out here all this time? Dad's really going to bite your head off when he sees this."

"Why should he care how I stacked the bales? He told me to clear the floor on the other side, and I did." He pointed to a large section of the floor that was completely empty.

Luke seemed delighted to track Ryker's progress through the maze. You could tell where he was by the thumping sounds his legs and feet made against the wooden floor as he crawled through. At a certain paint, Luke whispered "Watch this!" to Emma and me, and then he kicked a heavy bale in the back of the structure into position.

"Hey. I can't see. I'm trapped in a dead end. Hey, Luke! What do I do now?" Ryker immediately yelled from deep inside the structure. "Hey, Luke! Give me a hand, will you?"

"Ha! He's in what I like to refer to as Dead Man's Dead End!" Luke declared gleefully. "Let's see how long it takes him to work his way of that. I bet he can't!" Luke gazed down at his masterpiece with delight, and plopped himself down on a bale.

"Hey! Luke! Let me out!" Ryker called again. "It's dark in here, dude."

I could sense Emma was losing patience with her brother. "Come on, Luke. Dinner's ready. You better hurry. Mom stuck her neck out so you can eat with us," Emma warned.

"Okay, okay. But I can't leave Ryker in there, can I? Wait just a second, will you? You'll get wrinkles if you keep frowning like that, Sis." He went back to the bale he'd just positioned to trap Ryker, and pulled it away.

"Ack! You're a caveman and you'll always be a caveman," Emma retorted. "You can just stay in your cave made of hay for all I care." She walked to the ladder to leave.

Before Luke could respond, Ryker appeared through an opening on an upper area of the structure and crawled along a shelf made of bales. "Dude! This is epic! There's a ramp in there that takes you up to a second level," he reported. His face was animated with excitement. He continued crawling along the open area and disappeared back into the maze. I was impressed Luke was capable of designing and constructing such a complicated structure all by himself in a single afternoon.

"A ramp?" Emma asked, raising an eyebrow as she stood at the top of the ladder before descending.

"Yeah. I borrowed it from the peacock cage," he replied. "He should be coming out at the end any second. Are you sure you ladies don't want to give the maze a whirl?"

"Not now. We've got to get going," Emma pressed.

Emma began climbing down the ladder just as Ryker crawled out of an opening on the other side of the maze and jumped to his feet. I paused at the top of the ladder to hear what he had to say.

"That totally blew the doors off! Way to go, dude!" he exclaimed, walking over to Luke. "Gimme some skin, Son!" He and Luke did a low hand sliding gesture I'd never seen, but one that they'd obviously executed before. "That dead end had me racked up, but I got out of it somehow. A totally rad experience, dude!"

"Pretty neat dead end, isn't it? There's a trick to it, but I can't tell you what it is," Luke boasted.

"Can we go now, puleese?" Emma coaxed from below.

"Okay, okay. I'm coming, Princess," Luke reassured as he turned to walk to the ladder.

"The Invisible Woman over there is cute, but bossy, isn't she?" Ryker commented as he walked with Luke to the ladder.

"You don't know the half of it!" Luke replied with a sigh. "Wait. Did you call her *cute*?"

Ryker smiled and nodded.

"I really wish I could make myself disappear right now," Emma commented to me with a dour look as we waited below.

Ryker ignored Emma's lack of interest in him and walked cheerfully with Luke, Emma, and me through the grass to the farmhouse just as the sun was starting to set. The warm glow of lights in the house fell on the ground outside, and three large candles clustered in the middle of the table were lighted.

"Say, Ryker. You didn't say what brought you over here tonight. I thought we were going to meet up at Jim's house later. What's up?" Luke asked as we approached the back wall of the garage.

"Jim said you've seen some strange lights in the sky recently. Is that true?" Ryker started.

"Yeah, I've seen them a couple of times. Why?" Luke answered. He looked confused by Ryker's question and a bit cautious about the reason for the line of questioning.

"I've seen them, too, but I haven't mentioned them to anyone before, because I didn't want people to think I'm a candidate for the funny farm," Ryker confessed. "But when Jim couldn't meet for ball practice this morning because of his bum shoulder, he told me in confidence that he was with you last night waiting to see those hovering lights."

Luke stopped in his tracks. "What? You've seen them, too?" he exclaimed. "I've been wondering if anyone else around here has seen them. You can't miss them. Wow. This is cool."

"Yep. I sure have. My family doesn't live that far from here, you know. Just north along Eller Road," Ryker said, pointing. "I was sleeping in our yard in my new pup tent a couple of nights ago, breaking it in, you know, and I saw the lights. I hiked across the fields to see what they were, and I think I know."

"You do? Well? Don't keep me waiting, son. What are they?" Luke asked, so impatient he practically grabbed Ryker by the collar. "Those lights have been driving me crazy."

CHAPTER TWELVE

You Can't Hurry Love

Just as Emma, Luke, Ryker, and I approached the encampment in the yard, Lars left the dining table to go inside holding a folded copy of the *Indianapolis Star* newspaper. "It's about time you guys showed up. Mom's been waiting for you," he groused as the screen door slammed behind him.

Hearing us, Aunt Louise came out of the house and greeted us. "There you are. Sit down and I'll get your dinner," she said. "Ryker, have you had dinner yet? Even if you have, why don't you stay and eat something? Young people like you need to eat. Sit down all of you."

The boys sat down at the dining room table while Aunt Louise assembled sloppy joe sandwiches with potato salad in the kitchen. Emma and I carried out the plates and a green bottle of Mountain Dew for each of the four of us. "Help yourselves to the potato chips," Aunt Louise shouted through the screen door, referring to what was left of the bag of Chesty brand potato chips sitting in the middle of the table.

"Let's go over this again," Luke said, talking to Ryker with his mouth full. "You walked across the field and managed to get pretty close to whatever it was hovering in the sky? Is that correct?"

"Yeah. That's right. I got close enough so that it was almost directly over my head. I could see the blue-green lights turn silver and then back to blue-green again and see the outline of a circular craft. It was freaky, I'm telling you. I thought I was in a science fiction movie," Ryker said.

"You said you figured out what it is. Tell me. What is it?" Luke asked, leaning forward eagerly as he waited for the answer.

"I think it's....it's something coming from Kleinschmidt's farm," he replied. "Yeah. That's what I think."

"I wondered the same thing, but how? He's an old man. How could he have something to do with a UFO?" Luke pondered, looking away and shaking his head. "Do you think he might be an alien? Maybe those alien guys are meeting with him every night? He doesn't look like an alien. He's got to have something to do with that UFO, but how?"

"It doesn't make sense, but think about it. It always seems to be hovering over Kleinschmidt's farm or pretty close to it, doesn't it?" Ryker said, looking at Luke intently. "He only moved here recently, right? No one knows anything about him—-where he's from and why he came here. Does he have any family? Maybe the aliens dropped him here and gave him the appearance of an old German man as a disguise."

"Well, they sure goofed if they thought he'd blend in and be inconspicuous, that's for sure," Luke replied, laughing. "But he's definitely got something going on at his farm that he doesn't want anyone to know about. I could tell that this afternoon when I snooped around near there. I didn't even put one foot on his property, and he got all bent out of shape and ran over here and ratted me out to my dad. And he made up this nonsense that I was shooting BBs at his dog. I sure wish I could go over there and really get a good look around."

"Dad would have your head on a stick for sure if you did that," Emma reminded him. "You should leave the UFO and Mr. Kleinschmidt for someone else to worry about."

"You know, Sis, I'd leave him alone if he hadn't declared war on me. He made it personal, so I'm going to see this thing through," Luke stated. Then he added, "No matter what the consequences."

"If you ever want to go over there, let me know. I don't mind getting in trouble with my dad. He always says I'm a member of the depraved hippie generation, anyway, so it doesn't really matter what I do," Ryker said. "Well, I've got to go. Thanks for the good eats. My mom said to be home by sundown for dinner, and it's almost dark, so I'd better go. See you guys later."

He walked to the garage and mounted his bike, which was propped against the wall. "'Bye, Sue Storm!" he shouted as he started to pedal away. "It's been great eating dinner with a superhero like you!" he added.

"I am *not* Sue Storm. I'm Emma!" Emma shouted back.

"Ha! Sassy! I dig that in a chick!" Ryker grinned and blew Emma a kiss, and then rode on down the driveway. "Peace, baby!" he shouted before turning onto Allisonville Road.

"That guy is *so* annoying! I don't see how you can be friends with him!" Emma complained. "You really should pick better friends."

"What did someone tell me recently? Oh, yeah—I think, 'Thou dost protest too much'?" Luke said, his face beaming with the joy of teasing his younger sister. "Now that the shoe's on the other foot, how does it feel?"

"Oh shut up!" Emma replied, tossing her head.

"He thinks you're cute. Who knows why—-maybe he needs glasses—but I wouldn't scoff at that. With your scary looks, you may not get a better offer," Luke continued.

"If you don't shut up right now, I'll tell Dad about how you wasted all afternoon building your ridiculous hay fort," Emma returned, pursing her lips together.

"It's not a fort, moron. It's a *maze*," Luke responded with dead seriousness. "There's a lot more engineering with a maze than there is with a fort."

"Luke, did you finish the job in the barn?" Uncle Evert asked, walking out of the workroom. "I hope for your sake you weren't fooling around out there."

Emma's eyes opened wide, and she shot Luke a sly smile. "Yes, Dad. I finished the job. The floor on the south side is totally clear and ready for you to work on," he replied politely.

Uncle Evert nodded. "Good, good. You'll help me replace those bad boards tomorrow, then." He turned and walked back into the workroom.

"Wait 'til Dad sees your fort out there," Emma whispered behind Luke. "You're a dead man walking."

"Why should he mind?" Luke said, turning around.

Suddenly, Uncle Evert reappeared. "It's been an unsettling few days around here, hasn't it? I think you kids deserve a distraction. The ABC Drive-In is showing *The Dirty Dozen* tonight. It's almost dark, but I'll bet we can still find a spot to park if we hustle. Anyone interested?"

"A World War II movie with Lee Marvin, Telly Savalas, and Charles Bronson? With all those bad asses in it, you can definitely count me in," Luke replied with a pumped fist.

I wasn't as sure. I loved to go to the movies, but a *war* movie? I looked at Emma to gauge her reaction and was surprised to see her look interested. "That sounds great!" she chimed in.

"Okay, then. You've got exactly three minutes to get yourselves ready and in the van. We're not waiting for any stragglers," Uncle Evert said with a wink.

I ran inside and grabbed my zippered coin purse and ran back outside. Luke was already sitting in the front passenger seat with the door open, impatiently waiting for the rest of us. Emma and I took our customary positions in the back seat. A few seconds later, Uncle Evert stepped up into the van and turned on the engine. He proceeded around the circle and down the driveway.

"Isn't Lars coming with us?" Emma asked. "He'll be sorry to miss the movie."

"No. He's going to a chamber music concert tonight at the Second Presbyterian Church in Indianapolis. It's just us four chickens tonight, I'm afraid," Uncle Evert explained.

"Good. I like to stretch out," Luke said.

Uncle Evert turned left and proceeded north on Allisonville to the east side of Noblesville. There, between Indiana 37 and Cumberland Road was the drive-in. You couldn't miss the large neon A, B, and C block letters that were stacked vertically on a pole near the street. We turned onto the gravel driveway and pulled up to a small brick building where Uncle Evert paid our admission to get in. It was a one-price-per-vehicle night. We proceeded along the driveway to the area where rows of cars were parked facing the huge white movie screen. We were arriving late, and almost all of the spots to park were filled. Uncle Evert drove down one row and then up another until he finally found a spot and parked. After he turned off the engine, he took the speaker off a metal pole, hooked it onto his partially open window, and turned the small knob to adjust the volume. Wile E. Coyote was about to be clobbered by the ubiquitous anvil in a Road Runner cartoon already in progress on the screen.

After two more Bugs Bunny cartoons and a feature involving an animated box of popcorn and a cup of cola singing together, Luke stated he was hungry. Uncle Evert responded by digging deep into his pockets and producing a handful of change. He handed it to Luke and instructed him to use it to purchase refreshments for all of us. Together we made our way back toward the snack bar. It was in a concrete block building with a flat roof situated in the middle of the field of parked cars. The projection room was on one side, and the snack bar and restrooms on the other.

"Hurry, Luke!" Emma urged as we moved in and out of the parked cars. "I don't want to miss the beginning of the movie."

"They'll run movie previews for at least ten more minutes. We've got plenty of time," Luke reassured her.

I looked back at the screen and caught the trailer for *Wait Until Dark* staring Audrey Hepburn and Alan Arkin. "*The blinds moving up and down...the squeaking shoes...and then the knife whistling past her ear!*" the announcer said in a deep, chilling voice.

"Oh, my goodness!" Emma exclaimed. "Audrey plays a blind woman trapped alone with the bad guy in her apartment. I've got to see that when it comes out!"

Next up was the movie trailer for *Bonnie and Clyde* starring Faye Dunaway and Warren Beatty. "*They're Young. They're in Love. And they kill people*," the announcer said ominously.

"That one looks pretty violent, but I like the flapper clothes Faye Dunaway wears in it, so I might see it," I said.

"Come on you guys. Try to focus," Luke said as we walked up to the snack bar window. "How about popcorn and a Coke for everyone?" he suggested.

"And a box of Good & Plenty for me," Emma added. "I like licorice. How about you, Vanessa? Do you want some Good & Plenty, too?" She was so content I could swear she was humming under her breath.

I shook my head. Luke rolled his eyes and gave our order to the girl in a white polo shirt and khaki shorts standing in the window, who dutifully turned and quickly set about filling it. Moments later he handed Emma and me our Cokes and bags of popcorn. He'd also purchased a hot dog for himself and a purple box of Good & Plenty for Emma.

We were organizing ourselves to return to the van when three boys in T-shirts and jeans walked up behind us. They were about Luke's age and were very loud and fidgety. One of them had a bad case of acne, and another held a lighted cigarette between two fingers with dirty nails.

"Well, look who it is everyone. It's Larsson. This must be one big loser of a movie if Loser Larsson is here to see it," one of the boys taunted. The other two boys, who were chatting together and not paying particular attention, suddenly became silent and stared coldly at Luke. Luke started to walk away when the boy who spoke blocked him. "Where're you going, Larsson?" he demanded. "Running away?"

The boys seemed serious in their hostile attitude. I was taken off guard by the sudden confrontation. It had been a beautiful evening so far. What was happening?

"Knock it off, Hawes," Luke demanded sternly. "You're a douche. You know what you can do to yourself, so why don't you go do it, and leave me alone?"

The other two boys walked up and the three of them made a tight semi-circle around Luke. I was stunned by this unexpected encounter and didn't know what to do. Emma and I stood there frozen, a large cup of Coke and a bag of popcorn in each hand, helpless to stop the harassment.

"Oh, tough guy, huh?" Hawes said as he bumped Luke's arm, causing some of his Coke to spill. "What's the matter, Larsson? Can't hold your cup? Look at that everyone! Loser Larsson's too scared to hold his cup steady."

Another boy forcefully plunged his hand into Luke's bag of popcorn, spilling kernels on the ground. With a slow flourish, he pulled out several kernels and stuck them into his own mouth. "Mind if I help myself to some popcorn, Larsson?" he said with a mocking sneer.

"Cut it out!" Emma suddenly exclaimed. "Leave my brother alone!"

The boys turned and stared blankly at Emma. They seemed to have been oblivious to her presence until that very moment. "Look at that, will you? Your little sister told us to leave you alone. Isn't that sweet? Is she your bodyguard, Larsson?" Hawes jeered. The boys made a forced and hollow laugh. "How pathetic!" Hawes continued.

"Listen, you morons. I've had it with you. Step aside and leave us alone," Luke said in a low voice. "You're nothing but low-life scum."

Suddenly, Luke fell to the ground, his Coke and popcorn spilling everywhere and his hot dog flying out of his hand. He grabbed his midsection in pain.

"Oops. I guess I slipped," one of the boys said, smiling a sick smile and his hand in a fist.

"Come on, Larsson. Get up and let's see what you're made of," Hawes challenged. "What are you doing crawling around in the dirt like that?"

We proceeded along the driveway to the area where rows of cars were parked facing the huge white movie screen.

Suddenly, Hawes, too, fell to the ground. He looked startled. A split second later, a shower of Coke drenched the head as well as the face of one of the other boys. The third boy stood motionless watching as his friends were assaulted.

"Cut it out, Hawes," Bunny Bibble scolded, stepping forward holding an empty Coke cup. I realized she'd been standing behind Hawes and must have used the old knee trick like the one my brother once taught me to cause him to fall. "You, too, Clyde and Roscoe. You guys are mean bullies. Knock it off!"

"You frump! Mind your own business!" Hawes said, starting to get up. But before he could, Bunny stepped on his fingers. He cried out and fell back to the ground. "There's a name for what you are!" he said, looking up at Bunny with a ferocious glare.

"You're fine down there for now, Hawes," she directed. "Just stay there in the dirt. It's where you belong."

"I ought to teach you a lesson, you fat shrew!" the boy with Coke dripping from his face threatened. He took his sleeve and wiped his face, and then took a step toward her as though he were going to punch her. In a flash, she took his hand, twisted it around and pressed his middle finger down in a skillfully executed self-defense move. He was as incapacitated as if he'd been hit over the head with a brick, only she'd accomplished the task with much less force. "Ouch, ouch!" he cried as she continued twisting his middle finger further. "Cut it out, Bibble. You're too rough!"

"Oh, yeah? I thought you liked it rough, Roscoe," she taunted. "That's what the girls all say, anyway."

"What's going on here?" Jim asked, suddenly appearing with Ryker and another boy. He gazed around at Luke and Hawes on the ground, Roscoe whimpering in pain as Bunny twisted his hand, and Emma, Clyde, and me standing in awe watching Bunny subdue the boys.

"The guys and I were just goofing around. Bunny misunderstood and butted in," Luke said, scrambling to his feet. "You know how women are. They always overreact. I had everything under control until she came along. I don't know why she thought she had to meddle in things that are none of her business." He dusted himself off and avoided looking in Bunny's direction.

Bunny dropped Roscoe's hand like a spent match and made a strange face as though trying to process what Luke had just said.

"Meddle? Did you say *meddle*?" she repeated angrily. She looked at Luke with such hurt in her eyes that I felt terrible for her. She turned abruptly and walked away without saying another word.

"Luke! Why'd you say that? Bunny did you...a favor...," Emma started, her voice trailing off. She stopped speaking when Luke threw her a stern look indicating she should shut up.

Seeing they were outnumbered, Hawes, Clyde, and Roscoe gave up, but before they did, Hawes took a parting shot. "We're not finished with you yet, Larsson," he said with a sneer. "We'll see you later." They glared at us as they slowly walked away, using as much swagger as they could muster.

"Get lost!" Luke shouted after them. He took a deep breath, and then turned to Jim and the other guys.

"Are you okay?" Jim asked. He looked down at all the food spilled on the ground. "Did they do that?"

"I'm fine as fine can be," Luke said, tossing his head back and forcing a smile. "Nothing to worry about. So, what are you guys doing tonight?" he asked. I could tell he was doing his best to appear cool, collected, and in charge.

"We thought we'd take in this movie since it's so cheap tonight with the one-price-per-car thing. Want to come sit with us in my dad's truck, Luke?" Jim asked. "You girls are welcome to join us, too. There's room for everyone—if Luke's willing to sit on the hood!"

"You girls ought to come," Ryker coaxed. "Why don't you?" He shot Emma a goofy smile, which she returned with a frown.

How wonderful it would be to snuggle up next to Jim in the cramped seat of his truck. It seemed like a heavenly way to spend an evening. But before I could accept his offer, Emma spoke, bursting my bubble of romantic bliss.

"No, we've got to go back to our van and keep my dad company," Emma explained. "He's waiting for us over there." She gestured with her cup in the direction of the van. "He'd be lonely if we didn't watch the movie with him."

"Sure. I understand. Well, maybe another time then," Jim said. He trained his gaze on me for a long, drawn-out moment, which just about killed me. I wanted to sit with him. But I had to be mindful that Emma was my friend and host, and I couldn't abandon her.

"If you change your mind, we're in a green Chevrolet pickup truck in the second row near the aisle," Jim said. "It has a red ball stuck on the radio antenna. You can't miss it."

I promised we'd find their truck if we changed our minds. Emma and I walked back through the rows of cars to her dad's van. The movie was well underway by now. Major Reisman was in the midst of training the twelve convicts freed from prison to assist him accomplish a suicide mission to blow up a chateau where several Nazi officers were scheduled to meet.

"Those boys back there sure were mean. I think they're in Luke's class at school. They seemed to have some grudge against him. Good thing Bunny helped out," Emma said as we watched the movie.

"Poor Bunny. I don't think Luke will ever have anything to do with her now," I said.

"Why not?" she asked. "She was terrific!"

"It bothered him too much that she got the upper hand with those bullies," I explained. "That's why he was so mean to her."

"I'd think he'd be glad she helped him," Emma continued.

"That's just the way boys are," I sighed. "That's just the way they are."

"Are you ladies going to talk through the whole movie?" Uncle Evert asked. He squeezed Emma's shoulder good-naturedly.

Several minutes later the convicts blew up the chateau with the Nazis in the wine cellar. As the movie progressed to its conclusion, the Dirty Dozen were killed one-by-one serving in the line of duty. Only one, portrayed by actor Charles Bronson, survived and returned to freedom in London.

The theater turned on bright lights on tall poles positioned around the parking area as the credits rolled. Emma stretched and sighed. "I loved that movie, didn't you?" she asked, looking at me enthusiastically with her bright blue eyes.

The movie had been a little violent for my taste, and I was surprised by her positive reaction to it. "Sure," I replied.

"Yeah," she sighed again. "It was really good."

I didn't know what to say, so I just nodded.

CHAPTER THIRTEEN

Another Sleepy, Dusty, Distressing Day

Luke ran up alongside the van just as Uncle Evert was about to merge into the bumper-to-bumper traffic snaking through the parking lot to exit the theater. He jumped into the front seat and slammed the door. He didn't say much, which was okay. It was late and none of us was particularly chatty. The scene I'd witnessed with Luke being bullied played over and over in my mind. Who would have thought someone as bold and aggressive as Luke could be the target of harassment? I wondered if Jim and the guys had ribbed him about Bunny as they sat in their truck. I hoped not. He'd been through enough tonight.

Besides, she'd been fearless, and I admired her for that. The more I thought about it, the more I was convinced Bunny would make an excellent girlfriend for Luke. It took an independent, confident person like her to push against Luke's crazy energy. It was a match made in heaven. As I gazed out the window at the lights of Noblesville going by, I made up my mind that if there were ever anything I could do to help bring them together, I'd do it, even though I knew the odds of that happening were slim.

It got darker and more deserted the farther from the theater we proceeded. It was very late, and we passed few cars after we left the Noblesville area. As we approached the farm, I wondered if I'd be able to see the UFO. I studied the sky to the northwest and focused on every light

I saw, but didn't see anything suspicious—only house lights and an occasional truck or car proceeding along a road in the distance.

"Are you going back to the field tonight to look for the UFO?" I asked Luke when we were getting out of the van back at the farm.

"I might. Why do you ask?" he replied.

"I don't know. I was just wondering," I said. "I'd kinda like to see it again, but I don't want to spend the whole night sitting in a field waiting for it."

"Well, I'm going to bed," Emma said, looking sleepy as she walked by us. "I don't believe there really is a UFO anyway." She went on into the house.

"You should go to bed, too," Luke said. "I'm going back there with a blanket for the night and see how it goes. I want to test Ryker's theory. It's hard to believe whatever we saw was something Kleinschmidt invented. How does a burned-out old Hun like him have the science to do that? No, I've got to get to the bottom of this."

"Okay, but come to the house and wake me if it returns," I asked. "I'll come out to see it if you do."

"Right," he replied sarcastically. "Big talk for a City Slicker." He turned and walked toward the barn.

Emma and I changed into our pajamas and climbed into the white canopy bed. Margret wasn't around, so I assumed she was staying at Wendy's again. The house had a quiet feel as everyone settled in for the night. I could hear Uncle Evert's deep baritone voice speaking quietly to Aunt Louise in the next bedroom. Lars was reclining on the green couch eating popcorn and watching *The Tonight Show Starring Johnny Carson* with the sound turned low. I could make out comedian Don Rickles calling someone a "hockey puck" followed by the roar of the audience as they laughed. I wasn't a big fan of Don Rickles, especially after what happened tonight to Luke. The comedian got laughs by ridiculing people and calling them derogatory names, which wasn't much different from what any run-of-the-mill bully did. Except, when Don Rickles did it, people were in stiches with laughter and handed him big checks.

Emma reached over to the small table next to her bed and picked up her dark blue leather-bound diary and unlocked the small brass lock with the little key she kept in the drawer. Using the light of the small lamp next to the bed, she opened the book with its gold-rimmed pages and began scribbling on a blank page.

"What're you writing?" I asked after watching her for several minutes. "Are you telling your diary how much you liked *The Dirty Dozen*?" I smiled teasingly, but I wasn't sure if she saw me.

"Yes, I liked it, but I know you didn't like it as much as I did," she said without taking her eyes off the page as she continued writing. "If you must know, I'm not writing too much about the movie. Mostly, I'm writing about those boys who made trouble for us."

"Oh, yes. Those mean boys. They scared me," I said. "You were fearless, though. What got into you? You really blasted them to leave Luke alone. You didn't seem intimidated by them at all."

She stopped writing and looked at me. "I don't know. Something inside me just snapped, I guess. There's a girl in my choir at school who calls me names and tries to make trouble for me at almost every rehearsal. It really starts to get to me as much as I try not to let it, you know? She almost makes me dread going back to school—and I like school, and I really love being in choir! When those boys started bullying Luke, it really hit a nerve. I hate bullies, and wanted them to stop."

"What's the name of that girl at school?" I asked. This was the first I'd heard of her.

"It doesn't matter what her name is, because I've decided I'm not going to let her bully me anymore. She can try all she wants, but it won't work."

"Good for you!" I cheered. "Half the battle is how you react to her stuff. You can always tell her you're the Invisible Woman and will punch out her lights if she doesn't watch it."

"Oh, you and Ryker! Very funny," she said, rolling her eyes. "I auditioned for choir at school a couple of weeks ago, and hopefully she and I won't be in the same choir this year, so that should help some. I'm supposed to call the school tomorrow to find out which choir I'm assigned to. I've got my fingers crossed that I'll get into the swing choir."

She continued writing for several more minutes, and then locked the small diary and turned off the light. I turned on my side and fell asleep.

The next thing I knew, it was morning. Emma was already out of bed, so I got up and walked through the house in my pink pajamas and found her outside. She was sitting at the dining room table with Lars and Luke eating cereal. Lars was reading the newspaper and Luke a comic book. The radio was on and the popular new song "Ode to Billie Joe" was playing.

"Here she is! Princess Sleepyhead," Luke said, looking up as I approached.

"You didn't come get me last night," I said. "You promised you would."

"No reason to," he replied. "No one came to the party, if you catch my drift. The sky was empty." Then he added, "And for the record, I didn't promise anything."

Stretching, I looked over and was surprised to see the sheriff's car sitting in the driveway. I sat down and took the box of Apple Jacks sitting on the table and poured the orange Os into an empty bowl, which I assumed was intended for me.

"Why is the sheriff here? Is someone in trouble?" I asked. I quickly scanned the yard and area near the barn and didn't see the sheriff or anyone else, including Uncle Evert or Aunt Louise.

"Yes, one would naturally assume, given the history of those residing in this house, that the sheriff had come to arrest one of our happy clan, but fortunately, that's not the case today," Lars replied.

"I— didn't mean it—that way," I stammered.

"No, this time the good constable's here to search the creek area for the man Luke saw a couple nights ago," Lars continued. "I think Dad's going to show him the damage to the little house, too."

"You mean they're looking for the guy with the skull tattoo on the side of his head?" Emma asked. "Ooh! It gives me shiver to even think of him. I sure hope he's not around here anymore."

"Can you believe it? Dad told me I had to stay here while he shows the sheriff around," Luke complained, brusquely turning a comic book page and then another. "I'm not a kid. I should be allowed to go with them. *I'm* the one who chased the guy, for the record."

"Well, if you ask me, the sheriff took too long to come out. There's very little chance anything is left back there to find," Lars opined.

"At least it hasn't rained to wash away any footprints and other evidence like that," Luke observed. "I sure hope they find some answers. That guy was menacing and lurking way too close to our house."

"I overheard the sheriff say he received a complaint from a lady living along Eller Road about someone trying to break in her back door," Lars continued. "I think that convinced the sheriff someone might be hanging around this area who shouldn't be, so he finally came out to look around."

"I'm glad the sheriff came to look around," I said. "Maybe the man with the skull tattoo had something to do with your house fire. Have you ever thought of that? Maybe he set it."

"Sure, City Slicker. And he could be a psycho-pyro who was irresistibly drawn to our bonfire, too," Luke joked.

I frowned and took a bite of my Apple Jacks. "Well, it's a lot more likely the skull tattoo guy set the fire than that an *alien* did," I grumbled.

I was glad the sheriff had finally come to look for that strange man. I was also preoccupied with other concerns as well, such as what had happened last night at the drive-in between Luke and those mean boys. I decided to just jump into it with him.

"So what was last night about?" I asked quietly. "Who were those boys picking on you?"

Luke sat silently looking down at his comic book, pretending not to hear me. Lars raised his eyebrow and looked up from his newspaper.

"Hey, Luke. I asked you a question. Aren't you going to answer me?" I persisted.

"No. I'm not," Luke replied, still looking down at his comic book. "None of your business, Nessie Monster. Stay out of it."

"Well, I think it is *my* business," Emma joined in. "I was scared. I thought they were really going to hurt you. If Bunny hadn't come along..."

"Shut up already about Bunny, will you? Geez!" Luke exploded. He ran his hands nervously through his tousled hair. "Look. I've got it under control. Really, you guys, I don't need your help or Bunny's help or anyone else's help. Just leave me alone, will you?"

"What's going on, Luke? Should you talk to Dad about this?" Lars asked. "Are you being bullied by someone?"

"No. Heck no. Bullied. Me? Are you forgetting what a bad ass I am?" Luke answered, a bit unconvincingly. "There's no way anyone can bully me, and I pity any dumb ass who tries."

"Who were those boys?" Emma asked. "You seemed to know them."

"Yeah, I know them. They're in my class at school, and they like to pick on people, especially guys like me who aren't particularly big. They think they can push people around, but I can handle them just fine. There's no way they're going to bully me," Luke declared with such determination I almost believed him. But I was there last night and saw that it wasn't as easy as Luke wanted us, or himself, to believe.

"Okay. But if it gets worse, or you can't handle them alone, you've got to go to Dad, okay? I want you to promise me you will," Lars said. He gave Luke a prolonged and concerned stare.

"All right. I promise. Now can we drop it?" Luke demanded impatiently.

"I think I'll take a karate class so I can whup people just like Bunny did," Emma said, slicing the air with a pretend karate chop. "She was amazing." Her eyes lit up as she continued doing karate chops.

"Yes, she sure was. She was fierce!" I agreed enthusiastically.

"Who's this Bunny person you're talking about?" Lars inquired.

"Okay, okay. Bernie the Bruiser—Bunny—whatever her name is—was really something. I agree. Now can we shut up about her? Okay?" Luke said, looking tortured.

"She really cares for you, you know," I said softly, leaning over to Luke.

That was apparently the last straw for him, and he got up, grabbed his comic book, and marched into the house, slamming the screen door behind him.

Moments later Daniel walked across the yard. He was wearing his Civil War shirt again, but had added a red bandanna around his neck. "Hi everyone. Is Luke home?" he asked.

"Yes, he's inside, but you'd better watch what you say to him. He's a bit ill-tempered this morning," Lars cautioned.

"Yeah. Whatever you do, don't use the word *bunny* around him," I added. Emma giggled.

Confused, Daniel shrugged and went inside. About that time, Uncle Evert and the sheriff came walking in from the fields and paused near the corner of the garage. "Sorry we didn't find more, Mr. Larsson," the sheriff said. "I think we gave the area a pretty thorough going-over, if I do say so. I'll keep my file open for a few more days in case anything new pops up. Just give me a call if it does."

"Thanks for coming out, Sam," Uncle Evert said, shaking the sheriff's hand. "I just wished we could have found something that would help us identify who that man was. There's no way to know if that bootprint we found along the creek belongs to him or not. It certainly left unusual tread marks."

"I'd put it out of my mind if I were you, Mr. Larsson. Whoever he was, he's probably moved on by now. We have situations like this come up with some regularity, being out here in the country. People without homes—-we used to call them hoboes—-come through looking to steal a chicken or something easy to pawn. They keep moving and go on to the next town after a day or so. I took down the dimensions of the boot print and a description of the unusual tread in it. I'll put that, together with a description of the strange markings on the playhouse wall, in your file. But I'm fairly certain we won't need it."

The two men walked to the sheriff's vehicle. "I hope you're right, Sam. I've got my family's safety to think about."

"Like I said, give me a call if you have any additional concerns. If you're worried, until we're absolutely certain this person had moved on, keep the family close by the house and be sure to lock up at night," the sheriff said, getting into his car. He turned on the engine, continued around the circle, and left.

Uncle Evert stood rubbing his chin slowly as if contemplating the situation. I wondered if Luke had mentioned to him that he found a Soviet coin along the creek yesterday. I didn't know if that would be helpful information or not, but it seemed like an unusual thing to find and something Uncle Evert should know about. He walked on toward the barn, and I made a mental note to ask Luke about it when I saw him next.

"There's a coupon for the State Fair in the *Star* today," Lars said out of the blue. "Says it's good to get in free of charge on Saturday." He ripped the coupon out of the newspaper and handed it to Emma. "Why don't you get Dad to take you and Vanessa? I'm going down with Buzz and some guys to the Herman Hermits and The Who concert tomorrow. Maybe Luke and Daniel would want to go with you. It's going to close after this weekend, so Saturday would be a good day to go."

The mention of the Indiana State Fair brought an eager smile to my face. I especially enjoyed the Midway with the bumper cars, the Spider, and the Ferris Wheel, among other rides. And the food! The cotton candy, corn dogs, and lemon shake-ups were among several tasty treats I enjoyed that were available only once a year when I went to the fair.

"Well, I'd better get going," Lars said. "Got to deliver a water softener to a contractor in Tipton for Dad today. Have a good day, ladies." He got up and walked out to the barn.

Daniel and Luke came out of the house making a minor commotion. "I've waited long enough," Daniel said with an irritated tone that was unusual for him. "I want my plane back. Kleinschmidt has no right to keep it. My friend Joey says if something that belongs to you flies into your neighbor's yard accidentally—like a baseball or a model plane—it still belongs to you, and you can go onto your neighbor's property to get it back. That's the law, he says. So I'm going to go over there and get my plane back right now."

"So you're taking legal advice now from *Joey*, of all people? The mental midget? Where'd he pick up that little legal tidbit, from *Perry Mason*?" Luke scoffed. "I don't care what the law is. I've told you a million times, my dad will kill me if I get near Kleinschmidt's property ever again. You can go ahead—but I'm not going. Aren't you afraid you'll get in trouble with your own father?"

"My dad can't stand the old guy after Kleinschmidt came over and complained there were planes from Gatewood Airport flying too low over his farm. He and Dad really got into it," Daniel said. "He thinks people are watching him from the air or something."

"I see. Air reconnaissance and delusions people are snooping on him. Paranoid old sucker, isn't he?" Luke said, shaking his head. "Must be an old person's thing to think everyone wants to know your business. I tell you what. I'll walk back there with you just to keep you company, but you're on your own once we get there. Capeesh?"

"Okay. Let's go then," Daniel said, starting to walk with purpose in the direction of the fields.

"Wait a minute. You might need a distraction for Fritz. I'll go get some Doritos," Luke said. He bounded back into the house to retrieve the snack chips.

"We'll come with you," Emma volunteered out of the blue. "It'll take us just a minute to get dressed. Stay right here and don't go anywhere until we get back." She gave me a knowing look as she popped out of her seat and stepped toward the door. I wondered what she was up to.

"That's all right. You guys finish breakfast. We'll see you later, alligator," Luke shouted breezily from the kitchen.

"Hurry, Vanessa! Pull on some clothes and be quick about it. I have a feeling they'll get in trouble if we don't go with them," Emma whispered to me as she ran to the bathroom with her clothes and slammed the door.

I wasn't certain what compelled Emma to want to be her brother's keeper today, but I complied and ran to her bedroom and quickly slipped into my jeans, a striped T-shirt, and my white sneakers. Then I brushed my hair up into a high ponytail. Moments later, we burst out the screen door, breathless and fully clothed for the day, only to find that the boys had left without us.

"Gosh darn it! Where'd they go?" she said, looking around. "Come on. We know they went back to Kleinschmidt's farm. Let's just hope we can catch up with them before they do something stupid." She started off at a quick pace, almost a slow jog, toward the fields.

"You think they'll do something stupid?" I asked, running up beside her.

"Is the sky blue?" she replied. Her eyes had a worried look in them.

CHAPTER FOURTEEN

Up on the Roof

Emma and I were walking so fast we practically flew past the barn and across the field where we'd had the bonfire two nights before. In the distance I could see Daniel's red bandanna bobbing along as he and Luke made their way back to the fence along Kleinschmidt's property line. It was reassuring to know they hadn't had time to reach their destination yet. Still, I was filled with feelings of foreboding as Emma and I approached the old man's property. If it were up to me, I'd never go near the old man and his property.

"Luke! Wait up!" Emma shouted. The boys turned and looked back at us. Emma broke into a fast jog and I followed suit.

"Shh! Keep it down, will you? Do you want the old Nazi to know we're out here?" Luke chastised as we ran up, breathing hard.

"And you don't think the old Nazi can't see that bandanna?" Emma pointed out, gesturing to the scarf around Daniel's neck.

Luke turned and looked at the bandanna, and made a face. "Oh, for Pete's sake, take that silly thing off, will ya?" he said, apparently noticing it for the first time. "Do you want to be like the British at the Battle of New Orleans? They made very nice targets in their red coats and were massacred, remember?"

"I love that song, 'The Battle of New Orleans,'" I commented enthusiastically. "*We fired our guns and the British kept a-comin,*'" I sang softly.

"Hey, City Slicker. Snap out of it. We came here to do a job, not to sing silly songs," Luke scolded. I immediately became silent and mouthed the word *sorry*.

"Okay, Colonel Jackson. What's the game plan?" Daniel asked, starting to hum the same song under his breath.

"Are you all talk, or are you going over the fence like you said you were going to and demand your plane back from the old Nazi?" Luke asked. "That's the *law*, isn't it?"

"Well, maybe I'll just climb over and see if I can find it on my own without bothering the old gentleman," Daniel suggested. "He's kinda cantankerous and might not like visitors."

"Yeah. And he won't like trespassers, either," I added.

Daniel looked off toward the complex system of fences and dark outbuildings on Mr. Kleinschmidt's property and seemed to have second thoughts. I had a difficult time believing he was really going to do as Luke had said, and I hoped he'd reconsider. Even if he got over the fence without Mr. Kleinschmidt's knowing, how would he know where to look for the plane? Maybe the old guy had thrown it in the trash already. Even though Daniel had made it and taken time and trouble to do so, it was just a model plane, after all, and could be replaced. I wasn't sure the risk and trouble were worth it.

"Okay. I'm ready," Daniel said finally, with the resolve of an Olympic diver about to plunge off the high board. "I'm going to climb over and look around. If I don't find it pretty fast, I'll give up and climb back and be done with it."

He took a step toward the fence, placed his foot in an opening in the mesh of the chain-link fencing, and started to climb. I was about to say something to stop him, but Luke spoke first.

"Wait a minute!" Luke said. "I've got a better idea. How about if you break in there by climbing that tree down there instead? You know—climb the tree and then shimmy down onto the roof of that outbuilding?"

He pointed to a towering white oak tree standing about fifty yards farther down along the fence. Even though its massive trunk was on our side of the fence, its large limbs spread high above the fence and over to Kleinschmidt's property about as far as a particularly strange-looking outbuilding whose windows were painted black to prevent people from seeing in.

"What? That's too complicated. I'll just climb the fence," Daniel insisted. "I climbed this thing the other day and I can do it again." He started toward the fence again.

"Wait. Come back. Think again. You may have climbed the fence the other day, but the old guy caught you, didn't he? That big barn over there blocks that tree from view from Kleinschmidt's house and he won't see you in it, I bet. And, see how that one limb is almost directly over that strange-looking outbuilding? You could climb down out of the tree onto the roof of it and get in that way. You could bypass a lot of those nasty fences and the barbed wire at the top of this one if you do that," Luke explained.

Luke made a valid point about the fences. Mr. Kleinschmidt had constructed his chain-link enclosures and barricades in a dizzying pattern. Daniel obviously didn't possess the keys to the numerous gates, and would have to climb more fences than just the tall outer one to get to any of the buildings that might contain his plane.

"How do you think I could get up into that monster tree? That first branch is super high up. I'd need a rope, and I didn't bring one."

"There's a rope in our barn. I'll get it for you. Wait just a second, and I'll be back," Luke said, running back toward the barn before Daniel could object.

Daniel looked taken aback by Luke's insistence that he climb the tree. While we waited for Luke to return, Daniel, Emma, and I walked down to the white oak tree in question and made ourselves comfortable sitting in the tall grass under its massive branches. I pulled my new transistor radio out of my pocket and turned it on. "Up on the Roof" performed by the Drifters came on. I kept the volume low so Mr. Kleinschmidt wouldn't hear it.

"Daniel, this is crazy. Let's go to Forest Park and forget about stealing your plane back. We could hike and do all kinds of fun stuff," Emma said, taking advantage of the lull in the action to try to talk some sense into him. "You'll build a bigger and better plane, and you'll forget all about this one. It isn't worth getting hurt or in trouble, is it?"

"I know. But it's the principle of the thing. He took something that belongs to me, and I can't let it go," Daniel confided. "If he hadn't been so mean about it, maybe I wouldn't care so much. But I do."

"I know. Kleinschmidt's a bully, and believe me, I hate bullies. But don't give him another opportunity to bully you," Emma urged.

Daniel was about to reply when Luke walked up with a thick coil of rope hanging over his shoulder. He dropped the rope to the ground and started unwinding it.

"Okay, let's get this show on the road," Luke said. He looked up at the tree and studied it. The lowest limb was at least twelve to fifteen feet overhead.

Suddenly, Emma remembered something. "What time does it say on your watch, Vanessa? Is it eleven yet?" she asked.

"It's five minutes 'til," I said.

"Oh, gosh darn it, I have to go. I'm supposed to call Mrs. Mason at eleven to find out which choir I'll be in next year. I'm late. I'll come back right after the phone call," she said. She took off running across the field.

"Good riddance. Now where were we?" Luke teased, taking the rope and winding it in a circular fashion like a cowboy's lasso. "Do me a favor, will ya, Nessie Monster? Turn that darned radio off, will you? You might as well shout to the old man with a bull horn that we're out here." I dutifully turned off the radio and popped it into my back pocket.

Luke threw the rope high into the tree, and it fell back to the earth without going over the limb as he'd planned. He threw the rope again and then again, and each time it fell back without hitting its mark. I began to hope he'd never be able to throw it high enough and would give up. Unfortunately, on the fifth attempt, it hit its target and went over. He pulled down taut on the rope to fix it securely.

"Okay, Daniel Boone. Up you go," Luke ordered, steadying the rope. "Use this one when you get to the other side to climb down on the roof of that outbuilding over there." He wrapped a second rope around Daniel's waist and secured it tightly so it wouldn't slip.

"Aye, aye Cap'n," Daniel said with a small salute. "Here goes nothing. I sure hope you're right about this being the best way in."

Daniel began climbing the rope while Luke held the bottom so it wouldn't dance all over and make climbing more difficult. Up, up Daniel ascended until he reached the top, where he pulled himself up onto the long, straight limb and stood up. After he'd steadied himself, he jumped up and down playfully and looked down at us grinning.

"You ought to see the view from up here. It's great!" he said triumphantly. "I can almost see the hangars at Gatewood Airport from here." A few leaves, dislodged by the shaking, fell gently to the ground.

"Cut it out!" Luke admonished in a loud whisper. "Be quiet and don't call attention to yourself, Doofus McGee! Get to work."

Daniel stopped fooling around and began to move carefully across the limb like a tightrope performer. He held onto the trunk and then to some smaller limbs as he slowly and skillfully inched his way along, eventually crossing high above the fence, and then transferred onto another branch that swayed high over Kleinschmidt's property. Soon he was directly over the targeted outbuilding. He unfastened the rope Luke had wrapped around his waist and carefully knelt down and began tying it to the limb. Meanwhile, to my surprise, Luke began shimmying up the rope on our side of the fence.

"Luke! What're you doing?" I shouted, forgetting that I might be heard by the Nazi. "I thought only Daniel was going over. Your dad will *kill* you! Get down!"

"I can't allow the boy to have all of the fun, can I?" he replied as he continued climbing. He had a twinkle of adventure in his eyes as he rhythmically pulled himself up the rope.

When Luke finally got to the top, he pulled himself up and stood on the limb, just as Daniel had done. Once he'd gotten his feet steady underneath him, he began inching toward the spot where Daniel was still working to attach the second rope. Finally, the two boys were standing together high over Kleinschmidt's outbuilding. They reminded me of trapeze performers sharing a platform high over the big top. I gazed nervously at the house to see if Mr. Kleinschmidt had noticed them. Happily, the house and farm yard were quiet, and there was no sign of the old man or even of Fritz.

Daniel continued tying off the second rope as Luke stood over him watching. Jerking it a few times until apparently satisfied it was fastened securely, Daniel began to slowly slide down, with Luke close behind. I held my breath. They were descending into hostile Kleinschmidt territory. How this would play out concerned me, for whatever grievances Mr. Kleinschmidt might have had against Luke in the past would be compounded triple-fold should he discover Luke had brazenly trespassed onto his property like this.

Suddenly, the rope snapped, releasing Luke and Daniel into the air. With arms and legs flailing, they fell at least eight or ten feet onto the roof of the outbuilding. They crashed through an opening in the weathered roof and plummeted inside. The sounds of clanging metal, shattering glass, and splintering wood spilled out.

"Oh, my God!" I screamed. "Help! Help!" I shouted, even though there was no one around to hear. Where was Mr. Kleinschmidt? I called his name, but he didn't emerge despite my yelling. I pressed against the chain-link fence and struggled to see. "Luke! Daniel!" I shouted again. Were they hurt? Why didn't they answer me? "Luke! Daniel! Are you all right?" I shouted again. Suddenly, the door to the house opened, and Mr. Kleinschmidt's dark form appeared.

"Help, Mr. Kleinschmidt! Luke and Daniel fell through the roof!" I shouted, pointing to the outbuilding. "Please help them!" I pleaded.

Mr. Kleinschmidt stood silently in the shadow of his doorway and looked toward the weathered frame structure trying to assess the situation. Fritz pushed past him and ran across the yard to the outbuilding where he barked and scratched against the door obsessively trying to get in. After assessing the situation, the old man hurried in his shuffling, awkward way to the outbuilding and unlocked the door and went inside, with Fritz on his heels.

I waited apprehensively for what would happen next. There was yelling and Fritz's incessant, wild barking, together with more clanging, banging, and crashing sounds of metal and glass objects falling, breaking, and being moved around. This was followed by the sound of a scuffle. After a prolonged and heated exchange of voices, the barking and shouting ceased and everything became strangely silent. As the moments ticked by, I just knew something terrible had happened to my cousins.

I continued pressing against the fence and craned my head to see, but the outbuilding was set too far back to see much, and the open door blocked my view of what was going on inside. Finally Luke and Daniel, with his hand up to his bloody nose, stumbled out of the building, with Mr. Kleinschmidt and Fritz bringing up the rear. The boys appeared dazed and subdued. Kleinschmidt gestured that they should go up to his house, and they dutifully turned toward the somber two-story structure and began to walk. I continued standing by the fence, uncertain I should speak up. Eventually, I couldn't restrain myself.

"Luke! Daniel! Are you okay?" I shouted through the fence.

The two boys and Mr. Kleinschmidt turned and looked at me. Mr. Kleinschmidt shook his head as if he'd just remembered an unpleasant obligation he had to attend to. He began walking toward me through the complicated course of the various fences that crossed his yard, using the keys on a large key ring attached to his belt by a chain to unlock the gate in each span of fencing as he went. Maybe I should have run back to the farmhouse instead of waiting for him to reach me, which would take a few seconds. I didn't know what to do, and I froze.

"Well, *Fräulein*, why don't you come in and join your young friends," Kleinschmidt said in a low voice when he finally reached me. "*Kommen sie hier, bitte.*" He stepped to a gate in the outer fence I'd never focused on before that moment, selected a key on the large key ring attached to his belt, and unlocked it. "Enter, *bitte*," he said in a stern voice, pushing it open. He didn't smile and seemed impatient for me to hurry through.

I looked up at his weathered face and his deep set eyes staring at me coldly from their recessed sockets, and pondered what to do. I definitely didn't want to cross that threshold. Why was he making me? What would he do to me? Did we—the undisciplined neighborhood kids, in his words—bother him once too often, so that now he'd teach us a lesson we'd never forget, just as he told Uncle Evert he'd do? All I had to do was turn and run. Turn and run. There was no way he had the ability to give me any serious chase. That was all. "Do it!" an inner voice urged. "Turn and run! Do it *now*!"

I almost did, until I looked over and saw Luke and Daniel watching me. They were probably wondering what I was going to do next, just as I was. Perhaps they wondered why I hadn't already high-tailed it out of there. I knew they'd never leave me if the tables were turned. Emma knew where we were and would bring help if we didn't return to the farmhouse soon. The last thing I wanted was my cousins to see me be a coward. Even though I knew I'd never be a fearless daredevil like they were, I'd worked too hard to try to overcome my city slicker image.

So, I looked the old man straight in the eye and walked through the gate. He slammed it behind and me and locked it. "Come with me, *Fräulein*," he growled.

CHAPTER FIFTEEN

Let Me Play among the Stars

"*Kommen sie hier, Fräulein,*" Kleinschmidt said, guiding me back through the maze of fences as the boys watched and waited. "You shall all come to the house, yes?" he said in a booming voice when we finally reached the boys. It was clear it more than a request. He led us up a stone path to a white two-story frame house with black shutters. There were no bushes, shrubs, or flowers in the yard, but the grass and trees were neat and trimmed. There was definitely nothing decorative or colorful when it came to Mr. Kleinschmidt's yard or the outside of his house.

He walked up to the screen door, and he held it open for us. "Enter," he said simply. We dutifully walked inside and stood in the dimly lit entryway to await further instructions. Daniel still held his nose as it continued bleeding. The old man closed the heavy outer door behind us and turned the lock with a loud "clunk." It was dark and gloomy in the house and smelled of cooked cabbage. "Come," he said, ushering us down a short hallway into a small living room at the front. "Sit," he said. He took a seat in a large brown leather chair with well-worn arms and back indicating it was his favorite, while Fritz assumed his place at his feet. The old man reached into his back pocket and took out a handkerchief and handed to Daniel. "For your nose," he said. "You're bleeding on my carpet."

I took a seat on a small red velvet chair with slender wooden legs situated closest to the door. Luke and Daniel sat on a brown sofa near Mr. Kleinschmidt's chair. The room had a large multi-paned window that looked out on a gravel driveway and sprawling green yard at the front of the house, but the heavy brocade curtains framing it severely limited the amount of light allowed in. The massive fieldstone fireplace had black iron andirons shaped like dragons. A large, ornate wooden clock with carved acorns, leaves, and a stag's head hung on the wall behind us, ticking loudly. A table near the window was covered with stacks of books, a few framed photographs, and other odds and ends. A large red-and-blue Oriental rug covered most of the wooden floor, with smaller rugs placed over the larger rug in certain places, perhaps to hide worn areas. Several small etchings and mountain scenes, which I assumed depicted places in Germany, hung on the walls. In the middle of the wall was a photograph in an ornate oval frame of a middle-aged woman wearing a dress with a large, white lace collar.

"You are wondering why I brought you here, yes?" Mr. Kleinschmidt asked in his heavy German accent. "I am wondering something also. I am wondering why you came onto my property and destroyed the roof of my building. Perhaps one of you can explain this to me?"

"Are you holding us prisoner?" Luke blurted boldly. "'Cause you can't do that. This is the United States and that's kidnapping. I demand that you let us go— *right now*!"

"Yes, you're always the one, the troublemaker, aren't you?" Kleinschmidt replied. He gazed coldly at Luke. "Let me remind you. It was you who came onto my property, not the other way around. You must be taught to respect your elders and their property."

"Oh, I respect my elders, all right, just some more than others," Luke replied with a scornful attitude I'd never witnessed in him before. "Especially those who fought for our country, not against it."

Mr. Kleinschmidt looked stunned by the comment, and then smiled a hollow smile. "I see. So that's how it is, is it?" He laced his fingers together in a commanding manner.

"I don't know what you mean by that. You're the one who declared war on me, not the other way around, if you want to get personal about it. Now, just let us go, and we'll call it even," Luke said. I was worried his blunt talk would make the old man even angrier than he already was.

"I'm afraid I can't do that," Kleinschmidt replied with an icy directness. "Not yet."

Daniel's nose stopped bleeding, and he reached out to Mr. Kleinschmidt with the soiled handkerchief to return it. "Thank you for the kerchief. I'm okay now," Daniel said politely. Kleinschmidt took it and immediately dropped the soiled cloth on the table. "May I say something?" Daniel continued. "It was my idea, not Luke's, to come here today. I came to get my model airplane—-the one you kept after it flew into your yard the other day. I'm sorry it flew into your yard, but I really need to get it back. So, may I have it—please?"

Kleinschmidt said nothing, but snapped to his feet, causing me to gasp quietly. What was he going to do? He was difficult to gauge because his stern face always seemed to exude anger and displeasure. He took a step forward, and I instinctively leaned back in my chair, not certain what his next actions might be. He walked past me out of the room without saying a word and disappeared down the dark hallway.

"Don't antagonize him!" I whispered to Luke, taking the opportunity for a quick conversation while we were alone.

"Why didn't you run back to the house when you had the chance?" Luke whispered back. "What a dunderhead. You could have brought us help."

"I thought I'd stay and help you," I replied emphatically, though quietly. "I thought that's what you wanted me to do."

Luke rolled his eyes. "Yeah, as if *you* could help us!"

"Shh! He's coming back," Daniel warned. "Stop talking."

Mr. Kleinschmidt's heavy footsteps came near and he entered the room. I looked up and was stunned by what I saw. The old man stood in the doorway holding Daniel's plane! The wing that had been broken in the crash was repaired and the paint retouched, and it looked as good as new. "Here," he said, handing it to Daniel. "You should be careful who you let fly this in the future. Some people are very reckless, and they'll destroy your things if you let them."

Daniel stood and accepted the plane from Mr. Kleinschmidt, looking dumbfounded. "Thank you," Daniel stammered. "Thank you for repairing it." He studied the repaired wing very carefully, then sat down and gently rested the plane on his lap. "Why did you do this?" he asked. "I...I don't understand."

"I enjoy the model building, just like you," Kleinschmidt replied. "And, well, you remind me of someone I used to know." He gazed toward the framed photographs sitting on the table.

"Who?" Daniel asked. "Someone in one of those photographs over there?"

"Yes. My son Wilhelm," Kleinschmidt replied. He walked over to the table and picked up one of the framed photographs and lovingly looked down at it. "He had curly brown hair like you, and the same big smile and carefree spirit. He liked to make model airplanes, too."

"What happened to him?" Daniel asked. "If you don't mind my asking, that is."

"He died during the war. He was only thirteen," the old man said, still gazing fondly at the photograph. "He was our only child—my only son."

"I'm sorry," Daniel replied. The old man looked so sad that I felt a twinge of sympathy for him.

"There was so little one could do then, medically speaking, in our little town, with the war on and limited medicine available to us. He was gone in a whisper." He paused and continued looking at the photo, and then abruptly placed it back on the table and turned back to us. "But let us not dwell on the past. We're here to discuss the three of you and what you're going to do to correct the wrong you've committed."

He suddenly began coughing to the point of almost gagging. He reached into his pocket, took out a fresh handkerchief, and held it up to his mouth. "Excuse me," he said in a hoarse voice. "I've not been well."

"Did your son's illness occur while you were off fighting for Germany in the war?" Luke asked.

Kleinschmidt dabbed his mouth and gave Luke a knowing look. "You're trying to find out what I did during the war, aren't you? You want to know if I was a Nazi soldier who fought against your countrymen, don't you?"

"Well, yeah, sort of. I assume you served in the German army," Luke replied. "And, now you're living next door to us here in Indiana, and I was just wondering why."

"My past is none of your business, and I have no obligation to tell you. But I have nothing to hide. Yes, I was a member of the German military. But I was a scientist—a physicist to be precise—and served as such, not as a soldier. All that mattered to me was that I was able to pursue my research, and that's what I did for the Third Reich in the way my superiors asked me to. When the war was over, I was required to work for your government. Then I came here to Indiana. That is the answer you've been seeking. Now I must insist we discuss the three of you and what you will do to fix the damage to my building."

Now that I was sitting across from Kleinschmidt, I could see that he looked sickly, with puffy eyes and a painfully thin and wizened body. He was sallow, and his left hand shook slightly.

"Are you saying the Third Reich used your brain—your intellect—to invent stuff for them?" Luke asked.

"Yes, you could say that. At your age, you think strength and personal physical power rule, like in the day of the caveman. It is different in the modern world, where scientists are a very valuable commodity. It is the intellect that ultimately gives men the power to rule, not their brawn," Kleinschmidt stated.

"Ha! I think he called you a caveman," I said, giggling nervously. I tended to make jokes at inappropriate moments when I was nervous. Kleinschmidt ignored me, but Luke shot me a disapproving frown.

"I would have given your plane to you when it crashed in my yard if it weren't for the way your wayward friend here behaved," Kleinschmidt said to Daniel. He gestured toward Luke when he said "your wayward friend."

"May I ask one more question? Do you live alone?" I asked. Looking around, it was difficult to tell if a woman lived there. The way Luke and Daniel looked at me, I could tell they thought it was a stupid question.

"Ah, it is always the females who think of such questions. Yes, *Fräulein,* I live alone. I had a wife of many years, Hilde, but she died shortly after we moved here," Kleinschmidt said. "Now that is enough of the questions. It is time for you to hear what you will do for me."

The three of us exchanged worried looks. The old man had another bad coughing spell, and then he spoke.

"You will come tomorrow and work on the roof of the building you damaged until it is completely repaired and do other chores for me until I feel you've fully repaid your debt to me. I will meet you at the gate along the back fence where the *Fräulein* entered today at precisely nine o'clock tomorrow morning, and you will stay until the work is completed to my satisfaction. If you do not do this, I will report you to the local sheriff for trespass and vandalism and insist on prosecution. Do you understand? Is this agreed?"

Well, so much for making friends with the old guy. We nodded yes, although I didn't understand why I should be required to participate. I hadn't trespassed or climbed the tree or fallen through the roof.

"Do I have to come back?" I asked timidly. "I mean—-I didn't do anything. You didn't mean to include me, did you?"

"Yes, *Fräulein*, you must return, too. You must learn that you will suffer the consequences of the actions of those with whom you associate. Thus you will choose your friends more wisely in the future."

I didn't like his answer, but I doubted he'd really go to the sheriff if I didn't show up. Although he'd done a nice thing to fix Daniel's plane, he still intimidated me, and I found him unpleasant. On top of that, everything on his property had an eerie, depressing feeling that gave me the creeps. I didn't want to come back.

"Is that machine we saw in the building we crashed into part of your research?" Luke asked as we were about to leave. "It sure looks like nothing I've ever seen."

Kleinschmidt was very displeased with Luke's question. "That machine and anything else you may have seen here is none of your business. You must not mention what you saw today or anything else you may see here to anyone. Not to *anyon*e, is that clear? Not to your father, mother, brother, sister, or friends. Your safety and theirs depends on it. You must promise this to me. Do you promise? Do you?"

Kleinschmidt demanded our oath with such intensity that he was practically shouting at us. We all mumbled in the affirmative and then stood up to leave. At that point I just wanted to get out of there and would have agreed to just about anything. I suspect Luke and Daniel felt the same way.

CHAPTER SIXTEEN

Wise Men Say

Mr. Kleinschmidt led us through the complex course of fences to the outer fence, unlocked the outer gate, and pushed it open. "I'll see you here tomorrow at nine. Not a minute after or I go to the authorities. *Auf wiedersehen.*" We eagerly walked through, and then he locked it and methodically made his way back to his house.

"Well, that certainly was interesting," Luke remarked after Kleinschmidt disappeared into his house. "What do you make of *that*?"

Daniel and I shrugged. "I feel sorry for the old guy," Daniel said unexpectedly. "I mean, he's sick, he's old, and living alone. No wonder he's so mean sometimes."

Luke shook his head. "I don't feel sorry for him in the slightest. He's still as mean as ever. Didn't you hear the scolding he so very kindly threw our way as we were leaving? Nope. You just like him because he likes *you*. From now own I'm going to call you Wilhelm Junior, the Nazi lover. Nessie, what's the word for *junior* in German? You seem to always know these things."

"I believe it's *junior*," I replied flatly.

"Really? Huh. Go figure," Luke replied.

Daniel looked at his cousin and sighed. "Luke, you can't hate him just because he was a Nazi. Lots of people were Nazis. The war ended more than twenty years ago. A lot of time has passed since then. He wasn't even a gun-shooting kind of Nazi."

"I don't care. He should have stayed in Germany where he belongs, instead of coming here to Indiana and building a compound that looks like a concentration camp practically in our backyard," Luke ranted. "Why did he come here in the first place?"

"Who knows? He said he did research for the Nazis. I wonder if he worked on what they called *Die Glocke*, or the bell. I read in *Popular Mechanics* that the Nazis were designing a super weapon using anti-gravity technology called *Die Glocke* around the time the war was ending. Didn't he say he was a physicist? Those were the type of scientists who worked on that project. That'd be so cool if he was one of them," Daniel said.

"What's anti-gravity?" I asked.

"It's the concept of zero gravity. In elementary terms, it means that objects move from simply being free from the pull of gravity, rather than from the propulsion of an engine powered by fuel," Daniel explained.

"Why is that such a big deal?" I asked.

"Because with zero-gravity you don't need fuel to power engines, so anything is possible. Even time travel can be possible, they say," Daniel continued, his eyes getting big as he thought about it. "He would have been a big deal in his day if he worked on that. Those German physicists and rocket scientists came up with lots of neat stuff that we think of as science fiction, but it's real. Luke, you can't hate him just for being German. That's not right."

"I don't hate him for being German. I hate him for being a Nazi," Luke replied coldly. "Now let's go back to the house. I'm hungry."

Daniel shook his head and laughed. "That's what I like about you, Cousin. You take a position and stick to it. Right or wrong."

Luke made a face, but seemed willing to discontinue the debate for now. We began walking back to the farmhouse, but then Luke stopped abruptly. He appeared to have something else to discuss.

"Listen you guys," he said. "Dad must never know what just happened or that we're going back to Kleinschmidt's in the morning. I need your blood oath you won't tell or let it slip out."

"Sure," Daniel and I said in unison, nodding.

"Really, you guys. You can't let me down about this. Dad has just about run out of things to give me as punishment. One more dust-up with him, and he'll have me paint the entire house or sit out the wrestling season. I mean it!"

"Can I tell Emma?" I asked. "After all, she was with us until she had to make that call."

Luke rolled his eyes. "If you must. I know you girls have to discuss *everything*. But make sure she knows to keep her yap shut about it."

I agreed and we continued on. As we approached the farmhouse, I perked up when I saw Jim sitting with Emma at the table. They were eating strawberries topped off with Reddi-Wip topping from an aerosol can sitting on the table. I was surprised to see Emma enjoying her treat so calmly instead of rushing back to Kleinschmidt's farm to check on us, as I had expected her to do. No one else was around, and the radio was on, as usual. Daniel gently placed the plane on the table and sat down.

"Hey, you guys! Good to see you. Where've you been?" Jim asked.

Luke gazed around the yard to make certain there was no one else around. "Uh, we were held prisoner by the old Nazi in his house. We could have been killed or tortured," he said. He walked next to his sister and looked down at her as she continued eating, ignoring him. "We were hoping *someone* would come looking for us, but I guess that was a silly notion."

"Are you possibly referring to *me*?" Emma said, taking another bite of strawberries.

"Yes, you. Who knows what the crazy old guy might have done to us? Why didn't you come back to the fence like you said you would?" Luke demanded.

"Mom sliced up these strawberries while I was on the phone and said I should eat them while they're fresh. I figured it's not my job to bail you out of the crazy stuff you do. I knew Vanessa would come back to the house for help if anything went wrong, and she didn't, so everything must have been okay."

I shook my head. "I got stuck in the house, too, and couldn't go for help. The old man came to the fence and made me go inside," I said. Emma looked surprised. "It's a long story," I added.

"I had no idea you guys were in trouble like that, or I would have come back there to help you myself," Jim piped up. "I was told you'd be back shortly, and decided to wait for you here so I wouldn't miss you."

"And so you could eat strawberries," Luke added flatly.

"Sorry, dude," Jim said, smiling apologetically and holding up his spoon. "They're really good. You ought to have some before I eat them all."

"What happened back there?' Emma asked. "Did the old man catch you trying to steal your plane back? I see you got it." She gazed at the plane and looked confused. "Wait! The wing isn't broken. Wasn't one wing broken? How'd you get it repaired so fast?"

"Well, it's an interesting story..." Daniel started to explain.

"*I'll* tell the story," Luke interrupted. "Okay, here's what happened...," he began.

While Luke summarized the details of our encounter, I sat down next to Jim and helped myself to a bowlful of strawberries. It was a hot afternoon, but a soft breeze blew through the yard, making the leaves move gracefully in the trees overhead. "California Dreamin'" by the Mamas & the Papas came on the radio, and the lyric, "*All the leaves are brown and the sky is gray,*" reminded me that summer would eventually come to an end, like it or not. I didn't want to be reminded of that, though. So, I put another generous squirt of Reddi-Wip topping on my strawberries to drown out all thoughts of fall. Jim observed what I had done and chuckled good-naturedly at my excess.

"Okay, well, I'll see you guys later. I'm going to take my plane home now," Daniel announced after Luke finally finished telling his enhanced version of the story. He picked up the model and carefully walked with it resting in both hands.

"Bye, Wilhelm Junior!" Luke yelled. "You know what they call people like you—*collaborator*. You're a turncoat collaborator! That's what you are."

Daniel let out a howl as he walked across the yard to the trail leading down to the road. "Whatever!" he yelled back.

"What was that strange machine you said you saw in that outbuilding? What did it look like?" Jim asked. "You said the old man went ape when you asked about it, didn't you?"

"It was covered by a big tarp, so I couldn't see it very well. But it was about nine feet high and twelve feet across and had a roundish shape," Luke explained. "There were lots of metal canisters stored in the building and electrical control panels. It kinda looked like Dr. No's control room in the James Bond movie. Really! I've never seen anything like that whole set up before."

"What do you suppose he uses that machine for?" Jim asked.

"I guess he must conduct his experiments in there. I wasn't in the building very long and was trying to keep that crazy dog off of me, so I didn't have much time to look around. Fritz had me pinned into a corner and would have chewed my arm off if I hadn't brought those Doritos with me. On top of that, Daniel had fallen on something and bashed his nose, and I was concerned about him, too," Luke explained. "The building had a glass ceiling that was probably retractable. That's what we fell through."

"The old man said we shouldn't talk about what you saw in there to anyone," I reminded him. "Didn't he say our safety depended on staying quiet about it? Maybe we should do as he said and stop talking about it."

"That's peculiar," Jim observed. "He actually said your *safety* depends on it? That sounds like a line out of *Dr. No* for sure. It could just be eccentric inventor talk."

"That's what I thought," Luke agreed. "He's a bit extreme in just about everything he says and does. Maybe he's delusional and thinks he's living in a thriller movie. He didn't appear at all well. Maybe his mind is slightly off-kilter."

"Do you think he has anything to do with that UFO you guys have seen? He said he was a physicist, didn't he?" Jim asked. "Could he have any possible connection to what you saw? What about that glass ceiling? Could he possibly fly the machine you saw out through that?"

"I don't see how what I saw in the sky was man-made, and it certainly wasn't built by an old geezer living by himself on a farm in Fishers, Indiana," Luke scoffed. "If he could make that metal machine of his fly like the one I saw, he wouldn't be hanging out around here. He'd be working for the government in a secret lab in a mountain somewhere, driving slick custom cars and surrounded by lots of sexy chicks."

"That only happens in the movies, doofus. You're going back there tomorrow to fix the roof, right? You can look around then," Jim strategized. "It's a perfect opportunity."

"Yeah and don't think I won't," Luke said, nodding emphatically. "I'm going to look into every nook and cranny. I'm certain that stuff he said about our safety was just mumbo-jumbo to keep us from snooping around."

Just then Uncle Evert drove up after doing a job in Noblesville. Emma asked him if he'd take us to Forest Park for the afternoon. I was pleased when Jim said he'd come along with us. I felt our bond returning.

The four of us piled into the van, with Luke in the front passenger seat and Emma, Jim, and me in the back. We went north on Allisonville Road and turned on Conner Street and drove past the stately Noblesville courthouse with its striking Second Empire architecture, mansard roof, and three-story bell tower. After we crossed White River, Uncle Evert turned north on Cicero Road until we came to the two fieldstone gates that marked the park's entrance. We proceeded up the gently sloping road lined with old-style light posts to the picnic area where the burnished metal curly slide stood among the tables. Uncle Evert parked the van under a tree and we all piled out.

"Okay, kids. We're here. Go have fun, but be back here at the van by five," Uncle Evert said, reaching for a copy of the *Indianapolis Star* and unfolding it.

"I don't feel like swimming today," Luke said, squinting at the pool in the distance. "Why don't we just hike? Whaddaya say Jim-bo?"

"Sure. That sounds good. How about you, Vanessa?" Jim asked. "Do you want to hike with us? And Emma, how about you?"

"Sounds good," I replied enthusiastically. "I love hiking."

"You do?" Emma asked, surprised. "Well, okay. Count me in, too, then."

I could tell Luke wasn't happy that Emma and I were going to hang out with him. He took off striding across the picnic area at such a high speed it was almost as though he was in a race, or perhaps trying to shake us off. He made his way to the interurban train tracks that ran along the western edge of the park that were no longer used and looked down the deserted corridor.

"Come on, Luke," Emma complained. "Let's do something. These train tracks are *bor-ing*."

"You can do whatever you want, but I'm going to follow these tracks down to the river. I'm in the mood to hike and may follow the river all the way to Potter's Bridge," Luke said. "Right, Jim-bo? So you girls should find something else to do unless you think you want to hike that far. Knowing City Slicker, I seriously doubt that you do."

I peered at the side of Jim's handsome face as he watched Luke throw a rock down the tracks, and reached over and gently touched his hand to hold it. To my surprise, he pulled away. It was subtle, but there was no mistaking that he purposely avoided holding hands with me. I was stunned and embarrassed. I moved away from him and felt my cheeks grow warm. He looked at me and seemed to understand my reaction. I could tell he felt bad about it.

"Want to go get a Sno-Cone at the refreshment stand?" he blurted. "My treat?"

"Sure," I answered meekly, confused about what was going on.

"Luke! Vanessa and I are going to go get a Sno-Cone. We'll catch up with you and Emma at Potter's Bridge later," he shouted.

"Good idea. I'll come with you," Luke suggested. "I like Sno-Cones, too."

"No, go ahead and hike on down to the bridge and we'll be there in a little bit. I lost a bet to Vanessa and I have to make good on my wager," Jim insisted, waving him on.

Emma looked at me with her hands on her hips and her lips pursed as though she considered herself dealt a particularly bad hand. I could read her mind and knew she didn't want to spend the afternoon alone with her brother hiking along White River all the way to Potter's Bridge. But I wanted her to take the hint and leave me alone with Jim, just this once. She seemed to get it, and turned and began walking away along the tracks with Luke.

"Sheesh! You think you're going to spend the afternoon with one of your best buddies, and then he ditches you for the Nessie Monster, of all people," I overheard Luke complaining as he walked away with Emma.

"Oh, be quiet. How do you think I feel about it?" she replied.

Luke punched her playfully in the arm, and she responded by swinging at him. She almost smacked him in the side of the face, but he jumped out of the way just in time. They continued on, arguing and swatting playfully at each other.

Jim and I walked back to the small concession stand located under a large oak tree near the playground. It felt awkward to be with him now. I thought about making small talk, but didn't feel like it. We got our Sno-Cones with the bright blue syrup and then walked to a nearby bench.

"Want to sit?" he asked, plucking an empty paper cup off the seat and dropping it into the nearby waste bin.

The curly slide was only a few yards away, and it provided a welcome distraction as we sat on the bench and picked at our snow cones.

"I used to slide down that thing for hours when I was a kid," Jim reminisced. "To think I could be so completely and utterly happy doing something so simple. It sure was great to be a kid."

I nodded. I couldn't shake the terrible feeling he was going to tell me something I didn't want to know.

"Sorry about that back there," he said finally after an awkward period of silence. "I didn't mean to be rude."

"Oh—it's all right. Don't mention it," I said. The truth was that I really didn't want him to mention it. I was embarrassed enough already.

He turned and looked at me with those striking hazel eyes of his. "It's not that I didn't want to hold your hand. You know I did. It's just that it wouldn't be fair to you if I did," he explained.

Here it came. I knew what he was going to tell me—that he was back with Monica—that she'd won the Jim lottery. Okay, so be it. I knew it was a long shot for me, but it was a difficult blow to take just the same. I wanted to curl up and die.

"I see. You've decided to date Monica again?" I asked, almost choking on the words I didn't ever want to say. "I understand."

"Oh, no. That's not why. And by the way, I'm not dating *her*," he said, almost scoffing at the idea. "In fact, I believe she's with Vinny Shoals now." I felt my spirits rising. This might mean there was a chance for me after all. "Monica's not the reason. It's my dad." He paused to collect himself.

"Your dad? Is he okay?" I asked, feeling foolish I'd been so selfish when his father could be ill or dying.

"Oh, yes. Dad's perfectly fine. What I'm trying to say is that he lost his job at Delco in Kokomo. He says he quit, but I don't think he's telling Mom and me the whole story."

"Oh, sorry," I said, confused about how his father's employment status could prevent us from dating.

"So, we're going to be moving soon. I didn't want to get something started with you and then blindside you and move away."

Moving away? That didn't sound like an insurmountable hurdle. We were already living in different cities and going to different high schools. We could surely work this out.

"Dad says he's always wanted to move to a place with warmer weather, like Arizona. So that's what we're going to do. We're moving to Arizona—Phoenix to be exact."

Phoenix? Did I hear that correctly? That was a zillion miles away. This couldn't be happening. I felt light-headed and my heart was racing.

"Maybe your dad could get his job back? Maybe he'll reconsider and you'll stay?" I suggested, employing my best denial-coping skills.

"I've asked my father that same question more than once, and I always get the same answer—we're moving no matter what. My sister's been crying all over the place about leaving her friends, and my mom and dad have been arguing night and day. Believe me, it's no fun to live at my house right now."

I couldn't believe my ears. Surely something would happen to change this, but what? I couldn't lose him. I felt like weeping, but held it in.

"When will you be moving?" I asked. I wasn't certain I wanted to hear the answer, but I had to know.

"At first, my parents said we wouldn't move until our house sold, but now the plan is for my dad and me to go out to Arizona next week so that I can start the new school year out there. My sister will stay behind with my mom until the house is sold, and then they'll join us. Dad and I are going to stay with my uncle outside of Phoenix until Dad finds a job and a house for us."

Jim looked as though his eyes were tearing up, but I couldn't be certain. I slipped my hand through his arm, and he put his hand on mine. It hurt to see him so sad and forlorn. I'd never seen him that way before, and it broke my heart.

"I was going to be the captain of the varsity baseball team this year, and had lots of other things to look forward to. It'll be rough," Jim lamented, gazing off into the distance.

"Does Luke know?" I asked.

"No, not really. He knows Dad lost his job, and knows my dad's wanted to move to Arizona for a long time. But he doesn't know it's a done deal. No one does, except you, and I'd really appreciate it if you wouldn't tell anyone. People will know soon enough. I wanted to tell you today because, well, because I didn't want you to be hurt. It's been driving me crazy to be around you and not able to touch you and be close the way I want to. I feel better now that I've told you the whole story. But you know Luke. He'll go bonkers like he usually does. I'd rather break it to him in my own way. Okay?"

"Sure, sure," I said, nodding. "I won't say a word."

This meant I wouldn't be able to confide in Emma, which would be rough, because I needed someone to help me talk this through. He was asking a lot of me to keep quiet, which wasn't my strong suit, but I'd just have to do it. We sat silently for several minutes, enjoying being together. Then, out of the blue, he leaned over and gave me a quick kiss on the lips. It was a sweet kiss and seemed heartfelt. Then he laughed.

"Uh, oh. Whadya know? Mrs. Henderson from chemistry class is sitting on a bench near the carousel over there," he said, pointing to an older woman sitting on the other side of the playground. "That kiss probably gave her fits!" He laughed again and squeezed my hand.

"We can write letters to each other, can't we?" I suggested. "I really love receiving letters, and I have pretty scented onion skin stationery you'll just love. Wait until you see it."

"Oh, sure. But I'm not really very good at writing letters. It's not that I don't want to write, it's just that it's hard to actually sit down and do it," he said. "You know it doesn't mean I don't care about you, right?" He looked at me apologetically.

"I know. But maybe you could write a short one every now and then?" I gazed at him and could tell by the look on his face that it was a futile wish. "Oh, never mind. It was just a suggestion," I relented.

"We can talk on the phone every now and then, although my dad goes bonkers over long distance charges, so we'll have to keep our conversations short," he said.

We relaxed and sat close as we enjoyed what was left of the afternoon. It was pleasant enough watching the kids on the playground and the birds walking in circles searching for bits of discarded food, but I couldn't stop thinking. What would I do without him in my life? Phoenix was so far away that we'd inevitably grow apart no matter how hard we tried not to. Letters and an occasional phone call wouldn't be enough. This was a curve ball I hadn't ever imagined, and it would take some time to absorb. The end of summer was coming far too quickly, and with it a farewell to more than just endless carefree summer days.

CHAPTER SEVENTEEN

Don't Leave Me, Baby

Emma and Luke returned to the playground sooner than I expected, putting an end to my time alone with Jim. They brought along Ryker, Luke's friend, who they'd encountered while Luke was trying to goad Emma out into White River to help snag an old Coleman cooler he spotted bobbing down the middle of the waterway. Ryker appeared just in time to go out on the slippery stones along the river to grab it while Luke waited downstream to get a second shot at it if Ryker failed.

"You're a brute!" Emma complained to her brother as they walked up. "Why did you want that old smelly thing anyway? I might have fallen in and drowned for all you care. And, for what?"

Luke stood holding the blue-and-white metal cooler with a big grin. The cooler wasn't huge, but it could hold something about the size of a Thanksgiving turkey. It was rusted and had two big dents on one side that looked as though someone had tried to kick it in. "Free stuff is always the best!" he boasted.

"No, dude. You should get rid of that nasty thing. Someone fishing along the river had some really smelly bait in there and probably threw it into the river to get rid of it," Ryker urged.

Luke lifted the lid slightly and a horrible odor escaped that was so powerful I could smell it from several feet away. A look of disgust came over Luke's formerly happy face. "Ooh! That *is* bad!" he said. I was certain he was going to put in the trash, but he didn't. "But with a little airing out, it'll be good as new," he concluded, grinning proudly again.

Emma, Jim, Ryker, and I shook our heads in disbelief. Luke was going to keep his dubious trophy, and that was all there was to it. The downside was that he had to lug the thing with him wherever he went, which put a damper on any further hiking or exploring in the park.

"Just put it under this bench, and you can come back for it before you leave. It'll be safe there," Jim suggested. "After all, who'd have the bad judgment to take it?"

"Oh, real funny," Luke replied. "No, I'm going to keep it with me. Someone will steal it for sure if I leave it anywhere."

"How about taking it to the van?" I proposed. "Uncle Evert will keep an eye on it for you."

Luke pondered my suggestion. "Nah, I'm not sure I want to spring it on Dad just yet. I'm happy keeping it with me," he replied.

After a brief discussion, everyone agreed there wasn't much reason to stay at the park under these terms, so we agreed to go back to the van ahead of schedule and go home.

"Sue Storm, may I say you're looking very super today," Ryker said as we walked along, shooting Emma a big smile.

Emma rolled her eyes and scowled. "Are you seriously going to start that again?" she groaned. "Will you *puleese* cut it out? I'm Emma, not Sue Storm, or the Invisible Woman, or anyone else."

"Okay, okay," Ryker said, seemingly unfazed by her rejection. "Have it your way. I could call you Elusive Emma, but I think I'll call you Enchanted Emma instead. Yeah, that's it. Enchanted Emma. It suits you. Is it okay with you if I do that?"

She turned and looked at him quizzically, and then smiled. "Well, if you have to, I guess that'd be all right," she answered. "At least my real name is part of it. I'd rather be plain old Emma, though."

"I can't call you plain old Emma, because you're much too pretty to be called plain," Ryker replied. Emma giggled.

Jim and I exchanged a look of surprise. Perhaps Ryker was beginning to reach the impenetrable heart of Miss Emma Larsson, as unlikely as that was.

"Let's see," Ryker continued, encouraged by his unexpected success. "What shall we make your superpower? Oh! I've got it! Your superpower will be lightning bolts that strike men blind with love. That's why you're Enchanted Emma. Men fall helplessly in love with you when you toss your lightning bolts. They're rendered helpless to resist your commands." He made the sound of lightning bolts crashing around him and pretended to be hit by lightning in his heart.

"Oh, gag! Dude, you're making me nauseated. What's come over you lately? Cut it out!" Luke scolded.

"Ha! Don't forget I fished that filthy cooler out of the drink for you," Ryker protested. "You owe me."

"I do not!" Luke retorted. "I would have caught it farther downstream if you hadn't nabbed it."

"Yeah, so you say. Well, I've got to go back and get my bike where I locked it, so I'll see you all later," Ryker replied. "Especially you, Enchanted Emma. Be careful with those lightning bolts of yours. They're very powerful!" He grabbed his heart playfully and made more exploding sounds as he walked away. "Enchanted Emma strikes again with her lightning bolts and blue eyes!"

"What is wrong with that boy?" Luke remarked after Ryker had gone. "I used to think he was a regular guy. Now I'm not so sure."

"I think it's pretty obvious," Jim replied, smiling. "He's been struck by lightning, like he said. He's one smitten guy."

Emma appeared to be distracted and not listening. "I guess he's not so bad when you get to know him," she remarked quietly.

"What? Egad! Am I the only normal person around here?" Luke exclaimed, shaking his head.

Jim and I burst out laughing, while Emma smiled sheepishly. "I think he's kind of funny," she said. "Well, isn't he?"

Luke was speechless, which was unusual for him. When we got to the van, Uncle Evert was sitting inside with the door open reading the paper and drinking a bottle of Coke. When he saw Luke approaching with the cooler, he immediately and firmly declared he wouldn't allow Luke to stink up his van by taking it home with him.

"But Dad," Luke pleaded. "I went to a lot of trouble to fish this out of the river. I know I can get it back in good shape with just a little work."

"Next time you'll have the good sense to leave it in the river," Uncle Evert said. "Now get rid of it and let's go."

"Why discard a perfectly good item like this? It has value, Dad. Really it does," Luke persisted.

After a few minutes of further conversation with his father, Luke realized Uncle Evert was even more stubborn then he was, and that further arguing would be futile. Reluctantly, he placed the rusty chest on the edge of the curb with exaggerated care, then walked solemnly back to the van and got in. As we drove away, he kept his eyes trained on the abandoned cooler, even turning to catch once last glimpse of it as we drove down the drive to Cicero Road.

"Someone's going to get one swell cooler," Luke protested as we drove through downtown Noblesville on our way back to the farm. My uncle ignored the comment, while the three of us in the back seat did our best to stifle our laughter.

Uncle Evert stopped to let Jim out at the corner of Allisonville Road and 126th Street as we passed by so he could walk home, which Jim insisted he preferred instead of being driven there. I'd never seen where Jim lived, and was disappointed not to have the opportunity to see it today, but Jim was determined not to have us drive him home. I wondered if it had something to do with how his parents were getting along. He'd told me at the park that they were arguing a lot lately and he probably didn't want us to see how it was for him at home. You never know what kind of situation a person is coping with at home.

After we dropped him off and were underway again, I wanted to say something to Luke and Emma about Jim moving away, which dominated my thoughts, but I managed to stop myself. Even when Emma asked me later what Jim and I had discussed for so long on the bench, whether we were back together, or if he was seeing Monica again, I managed not to reveal anything. It just about killed me. It would have been comforting to talk with someone about it. I could tell Emma was hurt I wouldn't tell her more.

"And I thought you and I were close friends who can share things," she groused when I told her I had nothing to tell. It made me sad she was so upset, but she'd understand later when I was free to explain.

The rest of the day passed quickly. Margret returned home around five o'clock from working for Mrs. Patterson, the elderly woman for whom she did errands and household chores twice a week, and volunteered to make dinner for everyone. She made Campbell's chicken noodle soup and grilled American cheese sandwiches on Wonder bread. Lars arrived, and we all took our places around the dining room table in the yard to eat. All of the Larssons were in attendance, which was unusual and very nice. It was a warm evening, and the late afternoon light was golden, the way it often is this time of the year. "The Beat Goes On" sung by Sonny and Cher played on the radio as we dug into our meal. The song has only recently been released, and I tapped my toes to the distinctive bass line as I ate.

Suddenly, the distinctive sounds of gunshots rang out in the distance. First one, then another and then a third. It was jarring and startled me. Everyone stopped eating and peered toward the barn and the fields to try to see what was going on.

"What was that?" Luke shouted, standing.

"Sounds as though someone's hunting back in the woods," Lars suggested as he continued calmly eating.

"I didn't give anyone permission to hunt on our property," Uncle Evert said, scowling angrily. "Whoever it is, they're trespassing, and they're going to hear from me about this."

Another shot rang out. Who was shooting? What was happening? I was starting to feel something wasn't quite right.

"Those don't sound like shots from a rifle," Lars said. "More like from a handgun."

"Who'd hunt with a handgun?" Luke pondered. "Maybe it's not a hunter who's doing the shooting."

"Who else would be shooting, then?" Emma asked.

"I don't know. There's been plenty of weird stuff going on around here lately. Maybe it's the skull tattoo guy shooting at ghosts in the cemetery," Luke suggested flippantly.

"Do you think so? Really?" Emma asked. "I thought the sheriff said the tattooed guy probably moved on and isn't around anymore." A look of consternation came over her.

"What does the sheriff know? He probably just said that to make us feel better, and had no idea whether it was true or not," Luke conjectured.

"What?" Emma blurted. "Really? Would he do that? I hadn't thought of that."

Aunt Louise interrupted the conversion. "Luke, eat your dinner and stop scaring your sister. It's got to be hunters. Don't you agree, Evert?"

"I can't say for sure. Maybe we should play it safe and all go inside to have our dessert. I wouldn't want anyone to get accidentally hit by a stray bullet," Uncle Evert urged, suddenly sounding serious. He stood and started toward the door. Aunt Louise picked up her plate and instructed us to follow her lead and take our plates and glasses into the house. Just as the screen door closed behind the last of us, another shot rang out.

"Wow! Did you hear that? Someone's really letting loose back there with those bullets," Luke said. "I feel sorry for the bird or rabbit the hunter's gunning for."

"I'm going to call the sheriff right now and have him come out and look around before whoever it is back there gets away," Uncle Evert said, walking to the desk. He put his plate down and starting dialing the phone. "This has got to stop."

Luke followed his father to the phone. "I'll bet you anything it's that skull tattoo guy doing the shooting," Luke said. "I never thought he'd left. I don't know what he's shooting at, but he looked crazy enough to shoot at just about anything."

The sheriff arrived within minutes. Uncle Evert met him the driveway and then they walked together back toward the barn and disappeared behind it. By then, the sounds of shooting had stopped. This time, the sheriff had an air of urgency and concern.

"Is it safe for Dad to go back in the fields with the sheriff like that?" Emma asked as she stood at the window looking out. "He could get hurt, couldn't he? Isn't it the sheriff's job to go back to the woods and look around? Why does Dad have to go with him?"

"Your father knows what he's doing. Come away from the window and help clean up the kitchen," Aunt Louise directed.

Emma reluctantly left her post at the window and walked into the kitchen. As she and I washed the dishes and put them away, I, too, wondered how safe it was for my uncle to be walking in the fields when a crazy shooter was back there. I was glad the sheriff was with him, but that didn't necessarily guarantee Uncle Evert's safety. Surely together they would find the shooter and either contain him or shoo him out of the area. It occurred to me that the farmhouse was isolated, and anyone, including deranged criminals, could come onto the farm from just about any direction. Fortunately, that'd never happened before to my knowledge, if you didn't count the skull tattoo guy, but there was always a first time.

It had been quiet outside for some time now, so Emma, Luke, and I went outside after we'd put the last clean dish away. We sat down at the table. Believing there was nothing too serious to worry about, Lars left in the Corvette to see the new movie *Casino Royale*, a spy spoof about an aging Sir James Bond, with friends at the Carmel Theater, and Margret departed to meet Wendy at a club in Broad Ripple.

Eventually the sheriff and Uncle Evert walked back through the field behind the barn and stood in the driveway talking. The sun was setting, and I was relieved to see my uncle had returned safely. Moments later the sheriff left, and Uncle Evert walked back to the side yard where we were sitting. He was quite relaxed and at ease—not at all the way I'd expect him to be if he'd just chased a trespasser off the farm.

"Well?" Luke asked impatiently. "Did you find that guy with the skull tattoo? Did the sheriff tell him to leave?"

"No. We didn't find a soul back there. We walked all over the property and down along the creek. No one was there. It was the darnedest thing."

"Did you happen to check with Mr. Kleinschmidt to see if he heard the shooting?" Luke asked. "He must have heard it. Those shots sounded as though they could have been fired from pretty close to his farm."

"Yes, as a matter of fact. The sheriff knocked on his front door—God knows you can't get through all those fences in the back of his property—but he didn't answer. He must have been out," Uncle Evert said. "You kids stay close to the house for the rest of the night, okay? No bonfires or ghost hunts or midnight hikes for now."

"Dad, I'm frightened," Emma stammered. "You mean someone could still be out there? Do you think the skull tattoo guy is still hanging around?"

"No, Princess. I highly doubt that. The sheriff and I walked over the entire property and didn't see a trace of anyone. I just want you to stay close by tonight, that's all. Well, I've got an errand to run and I'll be back later. Remember what I said," he added. He walked out to the van and left. It made me a little uncomfortable to see him leave us alone.

There wasn't much the rest of us could do for now, so Luke, Emma, and I went inside the house and turned on the TV. The last summer re-run of *Star Trek* before the new season began aired tonight. Emma turned the dial to Channel 6. The episode was called "The City on the Edge of Forever" and featured Captain Kirk and Mr. Spock time traveling back to 1930s New York to find Dr. McCoy, who accidentally time traveled there through a portal called the Guardian. Kirk fell in love with a woman running a mission for the poor, played by the glamorous Joan Collins. He had to allow her to be run down and killed by a truck because it would have altered the course of history if he'd saved her. According to the show, if she'd lived, she would have organized an anti-war movement causing the United States to enter World War II too late, allowing the Nazis to discover the atom bomb and win World War II.

The show really made an impression on me. I'd never thought about time travel and how if you went back in time and changed the course of anything, no matter how seemingly insignificant, the course of history would change from that moment on. For example, if Jim's father hadn't lost his job at Delco, Jim wouldn't be moving away, and we'd be together. My dream to be with him was shattered from that one event. I was just like Captain Kirk—deprived of my heart's desire by a cruel twist of destiny.

"Those darned Nazis! They're always the bad guys. Thank goodness we won the war. Now if only we didn't have to live next door to one of them!" Luke complained as the credits for the show ran across the screen.

"There you go again. You need to take a lesson from Martin Luther King and become more tolerant," I suggested.

"What do you mean? I'm just like Martin Luther King. I have a dream—a dream that one day I won't have to be put up with people who annoy me," Luke returned.

"Is that all you can say? I don't know why we bother," Emma lamented.

Uncle Evert returned just as the show was ending. I soon realized that the errand he was on was destined to delight Luke. Luke let out a piercing howl of glee when he walked outside. It startled me, especially given what had happened earlier in the evening. Emma and I rushed to the screen door to see what had happened.

"Dad! You did it! My cooler! What happened to change your mind?" Luke shouted when he saw the battered Coleman sitting on the sidewalk near the garage.

"Well, I was near the park this evening, and it was still there sitting on the curb where you left it, so I took that as I sign you should have it. But you must never, absolutely *never*, bring it into the house," Uncle Evert said. "I mean n-e-v-e-r, young man."

Luke eagerly opened the chest, and then made a face and slammed it shut.

"It was still there because no one else would be stupid enough to take it," I said through the screen door where Emma and I stood watching them.

"I agree. You're a big freakin' weirdo," Emma remarked "That thing is disgusting. You've got Dad wrapped around your finger."

Luke didn't seem to care what anyone said. He was happy.

That night I slept fitfully. There was a lot on my mind. I couldn't adjust to the idea of Jim's moving away. On top of that, I was worried about our safety. The doors to the house were left unlocked as usual, and this weighed heavily on me. Emma didn't seem too concerned and slept like a rock. As I tossed and turned and gazed sleeplessly around her room, I did my best not to look in the direction of the closet. I thought about the black, cavernous space inside. The first time I visited her, Emma told me Margret had seen glowing red eyes in there. She swore it was true. To this day I'd never seen them, but there was always a first time for everything. I looked away and tightly squeezed my eyes closed. On top of everything else, I didn't want tonight to be the night I saw those incandescent scarlet orbs staring at me through the darkness.

CHAPTER EIGHTEEN

Secret Agent Man

Bright and early the next morning, Luke, Daniel, and I walked through the fields to the gate at Kleinschmidt's farm, dutifully keeping our appointment with the old man, as instructed. To make sure my aunt and uncle didn't know where we were going, Luke told his mother that he and Daniel were showing me an old Indian campsite they'd uncovered down by the creek. Emma wasn't coming, too, because she'd already seen it and wasn't interested. Aunt Louise didn't question this, and simply noted it was good we were getting fresh air. Uncle Evert would have been more difficult to convince, so it was our good fortune he'd left for an appointment earlier this morning.

I wasn't exactly certain why I had to go to the gate with the boys. The old man said I should be more careful who my friends are, but I couldn't exactly choose my cousins, could I? Still I guess I didn't mind too much. This would give me an opportunity to explore Kleinschmidt's compound, which intrigued me. In particular, I was curious to see the contraption in the building we were going to repair.

Luke complained the whole way there, of course. He said this was going to cause him to miss a fishing trip to Griffy Lake with his friend Joey, whom I'd never met. As we approached the gate, it seemed odd that Mr. Kleinschmidt wasn't standing there waiting for us, as I'd expected. There was no sign of him at all.

"What time is it now?" Luke asked impatiently after we'd stood by the fence for a few minutes.

"Ten after nine," I replied. I pulled my transistor radio out of my pocket and turned it on, and Johnny Rivers was singing "Secret Agent Man."

"So, the old guy warns us not to be late, but he can be as late as he wants? Is that the way he's going to play it?" Luke complained.

"Maybe he forgot we were coming?" I suggested.

"Fat chance of that," Luke replied.

"Does the 10-minute rule apply like in school? You know—if the teacher doesn't show, after ten minutes you're dismissed?" Daniel asked, drumming his fingers against the gate. He continued peering in through the links of the fence.

"I don't think so. We should probably wait just a little while longer," I suggested, swaying to the music with the radio in my hand.

"Cut out that dancing, will ya, City Slicker? You look like an injured goose jerking around like that," Luke chided. "You'd think a city slicker would know how to dance, what with all of the nightlife down there in the big city of Indianapolis. Guess not."

I stopped moving and stared at him, then resumed dancing, purposely exaggerating my moves just to aggravate him. He rolled his eyes. "Be sure to dance like that on your next date and watch the poor sucker run for the door, why don't you?" he wisecracked.

"Very funny. Hey, that gate wouldn't be unlocked, would it?" I asked. "Did someone try it?" I wanted to get on with things. "Maybe he left it unlocked for us and wants us to go on in."

"There's no way the old Nazi is going to leave this fortress unlocked," Luke scoffed.

"Let's see," Daniel said. He reached down and turned the lever on the gate, and to my amazement, it creaked open.

"Well, saints preserve us, would you look at that? Shall we go in?" Luke suggested.

"Do you think we should?" Daniel asked. "Maybe he doesn't know it's unlocked? I can't believe he left it unlocked on our account. He told us to meet him here at the gate—not inside."

"You guys can do whatever you want, but I'm going in," Luke replied, boldly walking through the gate. Daniel and I exchanged perplexed glances, then followed him in.

"Okay. Now what?" Daniel asked once we were all inside. "I sure hope the old guy's okay. He didn't look so good yesterday."

"I don't know. Serves him right if he's sick. He said to repair that roof, didn't he? So let's go over there and get on it," Luke said. "I have plans for this afternoon."

"What are we going to repair it with?" Daniel asked as we made our way through the system of fences toward the damaged outbuilding. Curiously, the gate in each fence was also unlocked.

"I don't know anything about repairing the kind of roofs that open and close," Daniel continued.

A stack of plywood sheets, some boards, a bundle of asphalt shingles, and other roofing supplies were stacked by the door of the outbuilding.

"See? He was expecting us. I told you so," Luke said. "There's even a ladder over there," he said, pointing to a wooden ladder lying on the ground nearby. "I guess he expects us to just do it on our own. Let's get started and do the best we can. If we hurry, maybe I can still make it to Griffy Lake this afternoon."

Luke walked back to get the ladder, while Daniel leaned down to take stock of what we had in the way of building materials. I turned and studied Mr. Kleinschmidt's house. It was eerily quiet up there, with the drapes and the heavy outer door closed. And yet it was a very warm morning when most people had all of their doors and windows open. I spotted Fritz tied up next to the front door, staring quietly at the door instead of barking at us as he normally would. Why wasn't he barking at us? Several minutes passed while we moved around working and talking, and still Mr. Kleinschmidt didn't appear. Surely he knew we were there. That just didn't seem like him, and I couldn't dismiss my concern that something was wrong.

"Hey, you guys. Fritz is tied up over by the door. I almost didn't notice him. Doesn't it seem strange he's not barking his head off at us?" I observed.

"Nah. Maybe he was out all night at the bars and is too tired to bark," Luke quipped as he carried some boards up the ladder. "The nightlife in Indianapolis can do that to you."

"That does seem strange," Daniel agreed, looking over at Fritz by the door.

"I'm going to knock on his door and see if Mr. Kleinschmidt answers. I want to make sure he's okay," I said.

"Oh, there you go messing things up for us, Nessie Monster. Don't call that old guy out here. He'll criticize us and make our day even worse than it is already," Luke scolded from up on the roof.

"I'm at least going to see if I can see him through one of the windows. It isn't like him not to be out here making sure everything is the way he likes it," I insisted.

"I'll come with you," Daniel volunteered.

As Daniel and I walked up the steps to the house, I was anxious Fritz would bark and snap at us, but instead he whimpered strangely and allowed us to get to the door easily. The dog was on a leash and sat facing the door as though preoccupied with something behind it. Daniel pulled a Dorito chip out of his pocket and offered it to the dog. Fritz was barely interested and allowed Daniel to pet him on the head.

"Good boy," Daniel said as he examined the leash. "Why did your master put you on this thing? Why aren't you inside or in your pen? What's going on, fella?"

I knocked on the door and waited, but there was no answer and no sound of anyone stirring inside. I knocked again and again, and still there was no answer.

"I'll look through the small window in the door," Daniel suggested. "Maybe I'll be able to see something." He jumped up several times, catching a glimpse inside each time.

"Well, do you see anything?" I asked impatiently.

"Oh, my god!" Daniel blurted. "The skull tattoo guy is in there, and he's holding a gun to Kleinschmidt's head. Quick, get away from the door before he sees us!"

I turned, but before I could take a single step, the door flew open, and the most hideous face I'd ever seen peered down at me. A skull tattoo covered nearly the entire side of his bald head. The man had an icy, ruthless look in his eyes that made me shiver, a few missing teeth, and a scar and other marks on his face that indicated he had seen much violence. He was tall and quite muscular, and wore a dirty shirt unbuttoned almost to the waist, revealing an even filthier undershirt beneath.

"Come in curious children," he said in a heavy Russian accent. He held a pistol aimed directly at me and smiled sarcastically. "Join us, won't you?"

In a flash Daniel leaned down and released Fritz from his leash. The dog instantly sprang into action and locked his powerful jaws around the man's wrist. The man winced in pain, dropped the gun, and fell backward to the floor. Fritz pushed forward and jumped on the man as he writhed on the floor, growling angrily and biting him with the intense fury of a dog defending his home and master.

"Pull him off! Pull him off!" the man pleaded. "Help! Help me!"

I stood motionless, stunned and unsure what to do. Daniel tried to pull the dog off, but he was determined to destroy the man who'd threatened his master, and wouldn't budge. Fritz and the man were a blur of motion as they wrestled on the floor and rolled from side to side. Time and time again the man pleaded for help. Daniel continued pulling on the dog's collar without results. Even Luke, who heard the commotion and ran to the house, couldn't pull him off.

"Fritz! *Aus*! Get off! *Halten*! *Setzen*!" Kleinschmidt firmly commanded as he hobbled toward the tangle of dog and man. It was then that I noticed his left ankle was wrapped with strips of cloth, and he appeared to be in great pain with each step. He reached down and grabbed Fritz's collar and successfully pulled the loyal dog off the man.

"*Braver Hund*! Good dog," Kleinschmidt praised the canine. The dog immediately retreated to his master's side and sat obediently, his chest heaving from exertion and his frothy tongue hanging out. Kleinschmidt took the leash from the door, clipped it to the dog's collar, and held it tightly in his hand.

Daniel quickly picked up the pistol and aimed it at the man. The man slowly got to his feet and grimaced in pain, holding his left arm. I was finally face-to-face with skull tattoo guy, and even though he was injured and Daniel had a gun, I was intimidated by him and wondered what he'd do next.

"Stay where you are," Daniel warned. "I know how to use this."

"How amusing. Listen to the little boy. He thinks he can tell me what to do. Ha!" the man jeered. He started to move toward us.

"I mean it. Stay where you are," Daniel demanded as he held the gun aimed at the man's midsection. "Who are you? What do you want?"

"Wouldn't you like to know, curious child," the man replied with a snort of derision. He looked at each us, laughed, and then, after a brief pause, suddenly sprinted out through the yard toward the outer gate.

"Don't let him get away!" Kleinschmidt yelled. "Shoot him! Shoot him!"

Daniel turned and was frozen, the gun useless in his hand. The man made his way through the system of fences and finally reached the outer gate as we watched, helpless to stop him.

"Shoot! What's wrong with you? Can't you see he's getting away?" Kleinschmidt admonished again. "You must stop him!"

The old man grabbed the gun out of Daniel's hand and turned to shoot. By then, though, it was too late. The skull tattoo guy had run out of the outer gate and was proceeding across the field toward the creek.

"I'm sorry. I...I couldn't shoot. I can't kill a human being," Daniel stammered.

Fritz seemed to know he had to take matters into his own hands. He jerked his leash out of Kleinschmidt's hand with a single, forceful tug, and took off running through the fences toward the outer gate in hot pursuit, his leash trailing behind him.

"Fritz! Come back! *Komm*! *Hier*!" Kleinschmidt shouted, to no avail. The dog continued out the outer gate and disappeared running across field. "This is no good. Fritz could get hurt."

"We've got to follow them," Luke said, running down the steps. "This is our chance to capture skull tattoo guy and be done with him once and for all. Come on you guys!"

I didn't want any part of following the man, but Luke and Daniel took off running after him, so I felt compelled to follow. I left Kleinschmidt on his stoop and ran. When I was finally out in the field, I could see Fritz quickly closing in on the man, with the boys not too far behind. The man seemed to know he couldn't outrun the dog and changed course. Instead of running toward the creek, which would take him to 106th Street where I presume he had a vehicle parked but require going through the thick undergrowth, he ran toward our barn, which wasn't too far away, and fled inside. By the time I got there, Fritz was panting heavily and barking at the base of the ladder leading to the hayloft.

"What are we going to do now?" I asked as we stood looking up at the opening in the floor. "Did that man with the tattoo run up there?"

"Yeah. I think so," Luke whispered. "Did you bring the gun?"

"No. Was I supposed to?" I asked. I made an apologetic face, and Luke looked away in disappointment. "Kleinschmidt has it, I think," I added.

"Great. Okay, run to the house and get my dad and tell him to come out here right away. Tell him to bring his rifle. Do you think you can do that? I'll try to get the guy to go into the maze and then I'll trap him in the secret dead end and keep him there until you get back. Now go! Be quick about it!" Luke urged. "Daniel, you stay down here and guard the ladder with Fritz in case my plan doesn't work. Do whatever you have to do so the guy doesn't get away."

I ran to the house, frantic that it was up to me to save my family. No one was sitting at the table in the yard, so I ran inside, clambered up the stairs, and found Lars sitting alone on the couch reading *Rosemary's Baby.*

"Hurry, hurry!" I entreated, barely able to catch my breath. "There's a Soviet spy hiding in the barn! Get the rifle and come with me. Hurry!" I turned to go, expecting Lars to immediately jump up and follow, but to my surprise he didn't move.

"Of course there is. And why, may I ask, is there a Soviet spy hiding in our barn?" Lars asked, calmly looking at me over the top of his book.

"We chased him up in the hayloft, and Luke is setting a trap for him to keep him there until I bring help back. Come on! Hurry before he gets away!" I implored, gesturing for him to put a move on it.

"And, which Soviet spy is it? Is it Illya Kuryakin from *The Man From U.N.C.L.E.*? I know you and Emma think he's cute. Are you girls playing some sort of international spy game?"

"No! I'm not playing a game. It's a real Soviet spy, I swear! You know—the guy with the skull tattoo that Daniel saw down by the creek? Please come! We don't have much time," I pleaded. I couldn't believe how difficult it was to convince him that this was real and not a game. "Is Uncle Evert around?" I asked, gazing quickly around the house hoping to see him. Maybe *he'd* believe me. "Luke asked me to get him."

"No. Just me, I'm afraid. He went with Mom and Emma to the grocery. They should be back soon," Lars said, resuming reading.

"Okay, will you please come with me?" I begged. "I swear I'm telling the truth. Luke's up there alone with the Russian and could get hurt."

Lars made a face, and then got up and slipped on his loafers. "Okay, I'll take the bait and come. But this better not be a prank," he warned.

"Great! You'll need the rifle," I reminded him. He gave me a strange look.

"Am I supposed to capture this guy with Dad's hunting rifle? That old thing might blow up in my face. This seems dangerous and a bit too much like *Secret Agent* for my taste," Lars complained. "Tell me again why you guys chased this guy into our barn, assuming there really *is* a man out there?"

"It's a long story. Just come, and bring the rife. Maybe you can fake him out with it," I suggested. The tattoo guy frightened me, and I hoped my cousins, working together, could subdue and take him prisoner, but they'd definitely need firepower to accomplish that.

We went outside and Lars stopped in the workroom in the garage as we passed by. He emerged with a rifle with a very long barrel that looked old, even to someone like me who didn't know much about firearms. He checked to see if it was loaded, and seemed satisfied that it was. We proceeded on toward the barn, walking quickly. I took note of every small noise and movement in case the skull tattoo guy was on the loose and hiding in the bushes to ambush us.

"I think he's up in the hayloft," I whispered as we approached the main door of the barn.

Lars cautiously entered with me following on his heels. Our steps were slow, quiet, and deliberate as we made our way back to the hayloft ladder. I surveyed the ceiling as I made my way around the tractor and the lawn mower, hoping to catch a glimpse of the situation overhead through small gaps in the hayloft floor. But I couldn't see or hear anything up there. I worried about Luke. We found Daniel standing faithfully at his post at the bottom of the ladder, with Fritz next to him at full attention on all fours staring intently at the hole in the hayloft floor. You could tell the dog hadn't lost his resolve to devour the Soviet if he got the opportunity. It was deadly silent overhead, which was unsettling.

"What's the situation?" Lars whispered to Daniel. Daniel shrugged.

"It's been pretty quiet," Daniel answered softly so as not to be overheard. "I heard Luke goad the guy to chase him through the hay maze, and it sounded like the guy might have done it. There was a crashing noise and someone yelled. I haven't heard or seen anything since."

Lars looked up at the hole in the floor and seemed to anxiously ponder what he should do. If I were he, I wouldn't dare ascend those steps. Not in a million years! Even having that old rifle wouldn't make a difference to me. But his little brother was up there and something had to be done. So with the rifle in one hand he began climbing the steps. When he got high enough to see into the loft, he stopped and gazed around the area. Then he continued on until he was standing on the hayloft floor. He took his time before he walked further. I braced myself, wondering if I'd hear the sudden crack of the rifle discharging. But there was only silence, which was unnerving.

"Luke! Luke! Are you up here?" Lars shouted.

"Over here!" Luke answered back. "By the entrance to the maze. I've got the Soviet dude trapped in the Dead Man's Dead End, and I have to stay here sitting on this hay bale to hold it in place so he can't get out. Hurry!"

I heard Lars walk across the wooden floor. Finally, Lars made his move, and he cocked the rifle.

"Okay, Russian. Crawl out slowly. I've got a rifle, so don't try anything," Lars commanded as authoritatively as he could muster.

There was a prolonged silence, and nothing happened. I wanted to go part of the way up the ladder to get a peek, but thought better of it.

"I mean it, Soviet! Do you understand me? Come on out now. Slowly," Lars commanded again.

Again, there was silence, with no rustling or thumping sounds of a man crawling out of the maze, as I'd expected. Why didn't the Soviet come out? What was he planning to do?

"Why don't you come out, Russkie? Are you too frightened? We made you guys back off during the Cuban Missile Crisis, and we can do it again right here in Indiana. Come on out and show us what you've got, you coward," Luke chimed in mockingly.

Daniel chortled with his hand over his mouth. "Oh, burn!" he said softly. "The skull tattoo guy won't like that."

"Well, Igor, are you coming out, or are we going to have to come in and get you?" Luke demanded impatiently after the skull tattoo guy still didn't emerge.

A few more seconds elapsed, and still nothing happened. "Okay, keep the rifle aimed at the maze, Lars. I'll get him to come out. There's more than one way to crack an egg in this kitchen," Luke said.

"Luke, be careful. That guy has age and probably some weight on his side, and might overpower you. Don't do anything foolish," Lars cautioned.

"Oh, I won't. I'm a varsity wrestler, don't forget," Luke boasted. I rolled my eyes.

One-by-one, I heard the bales fall on the opposite side of the hayloft floor as Luke disassembled his masterpiece one bale at a time in order to expose the Russian hiding in the trap he'd set.

"Well….where is he, anyway? What the heck?" Luke exclaimed after he'd tossed several bales to the other side of the floor, virtually taking the maze apart entirely. "Where the heck did he go? Igor, are you in here?"

Upon hearing that, it seemed safe to go up, and Daniel and I hurried up the ladder. I was surprised to see the maze reduced to a heap of hay bales thrown in all directions. Lars looked perplexed, still holding the rifle ready to fire while Luke continued to sort through the bales.

"He *has* to be in here somewhere! He just has to be. I heard him crawl in behind me!" Luke cried as he moved one bale and then another. "I dared him to catch me, and I'm pretty sure he crawled in right behind me. I went out my secret exit and then moved those bales in place in the dead end. This just doesn't add up. How'd he get out, and where'd he go?"

"He obviously got away. He probably got out of your foolproof dead end and jumped out a window onto the top of the peacock cage and got away while you were fooling around with that dead-end stuff. What made you think a thug like him could be imprisoned by mere bales of hay?" Lars asked in an exasperated tone, finally lowering the rifle barrel. "Assuming there really was a man in the first place."

"Oh, there was a man all right. And he was up here. Maybe we should make sure he isn't hiding somewhere else up here," Luke urged.

The boys fanned out and looked around, but the skull tattoo guy simply wasn't there. You could easily see all around the hayloft and up into the ceiling rafters. There was no place to hide. However he did it, the skull tattoo guy managed to get out of the maze and make a clean exit without being detected.

"I don't get it. Why didn't Fritz chase him?" Luke asked, totally bewildered. "Didn't he see him? I thought dogs had super eyesight and super noses. Couldn't he smell the Russkie getting away?"

"The dog probably couldn't see him from where he was inside by the ladder, and was too far away to smell him," Daniel explained.

"*Now* what're we doing to do?" Luke asked, looking exhausted. "That Igor is a menace and he's on the loose!"

"Why do you call him Igor?" I asked. "How do you know what his name is?"

"I don't, but it's a lot better than calling him 'Russkie scumbag,' isn't it?" he replied.

"Well, I'm going back to the house," Lars said, going to the ladder and taking a step down. "This has been very invigorating, to say the least."

"Watch out when you get back to the house. He might be hiding in there waiting to ambush you," Luke warned.

"I doubt it," Lars said from the bottom of the ladder. "Surely he's not that dumb."

"How'd he do it?" Luke pondered, sitting on a bale. "I thought I had a trap set for sure. There must have been a design flaw in there someplace."

"Dude, you got to figure a big man like that Soviet can kick out a few crummy bales of hay to free himself," Daniel conjectured. "He probably managed to get out while you were still inside the maze and didn't see him. You should just be glad he didn't rough you up. He must have been more interested in getting away than taking the time to bump you off."

"I suppose so," Luke said, looking dejected. "But the Dead Man's Dead End trapped Ryker cold. It did, I swear! I had to let him out or he'd still be there today."

"Yeah, but that's Ryker. He could get tangled up putting on his own pants in the morning," Daniel laughed.

Just then Fritz barked from down below as if to remind us he was there.

"I think we should find Uncle Evert and have him take Fritz back to Mr. Kleinschmidt right away," I suggested. "Igor might have run back to Mr. Kleinschmidt's house for all we know, and the old guy could be in trouble."

"Okay, you guys stay with Fritz, and I'll run back to the house and see if Dad's home," Luke said.

We all went down the ladder. Fritz seemed glad to see us, but wouldn't stop looking up at the hole in the floor. He probably wondered what had happened to the man he'd chased up there. Daniel took hold of his leash as Luke sprinted across the yard to the farmhouse. When Luke returned a few minutes later, he had Jim with him.

"Hi, you guys," Jim said. He looked at me and smiled. "I dropped by to see if you were done with the roofing project. Luke told me a few of the details about the chase with the skull tattoo guy. Man! That sounds like something right out of *The Man From U.N.C.L.E.*"

"Okay, now listen up. We've got to act quickly. Dad's not home yet, so I say we go on ahead to Kleinschmidt's on our own. I told Lars where we were going, and he said he'd send Dad to Kleinschmidt's just as soon as he gets home," Luke proposed. "Jim, you can come along with us. You've got to see Kleinschmidt's farm and the layout up close. It's unreal."

"Maybe we should wait?" I suggested. I didn't want another encounter with the Soviet without some help from an able-bodied adult. As a matter of fact, I still felt a bit jangled from the one we'd just had.

"Oh, City Slicker. You're such a scaredy cat! We'll be fine. The Soviet dude is probably long gone by now," Luke scoffed. "Let's go."

He started out across the field with Jim by his side and Daniel following with Fritz. "Coming or staying, Nessie Monster?" Luke asked over his shoulder when he'd noticed I'd remained planted were I was by the barn.

I took a deep breath. "Oh, coming…I guess," I stammered reluctantly. I took a step to follow them.

"Attagirl," Luke replied with a smile.

CHAPTER NINETEEN

Operation Paper Clip

As Jim, Luke, Daniel and I approached Kleinschmidt's outer gate, I wondered if it would still be unlocked. Surely Kleinschmidt wouldn't have left it that way, especially with the Soviet on the loose. On the other hand, he had a very swollen left ankle and might have found it too difficult to walk all the way to the back of his property to lock it.

"Darn, it's locked," Luke said as he tried to turn the lever on the gate. "Hey! Old man! Open up! We're returning your dog!" he shouted, jiggling the gate's lever repeatedly.

Suddenly, the door to the house opened, and Kleinschmidt's dark form appeared. He looked even more gaunt and weak than he did this morning, if that were possible. A pistol was conspicuously tucked into the waist band of his faded dark work pants. He paused in the doorway as if to brace himself, and then slowly limped to the gate using an elaborately carved wooden cane to steady himself. Fritz burst out barking the instant he saw him, and jumped up against the gate as if beckoning his master to hurry.

"*Ja, ja, Fritz, mein Hund*. I'm coming," the old man reassured the dog. He carefully unlocked the gate and let us in, then shut it again and turned the lock. Fritz almost knocked Mr. Kleinschmidt down when he rushed up to greet him, wagging his tail and thrusting his face into the old man's palm. Daniel handed the leash to him. "Well? And what happened with the chasing of the Soviet gentleman?" the old man asked immediately. "Did you catch him? Where is he?"

"He...he got away," Luke confessed sheepishly. "We did the best we could, or should I say the best *I* could. But somehow he got away and disappeared. I'm really sorry." I was shocked. I never thought I'd hear Luke apologize to the old German.

"*Ja, ja.* I am not surprised," he replied, nodding. "You are still children and he is an evil grown man. This is the way things go." His hollow eyes looked disappointed, and he gazed back over the gate as if checking to see if the skull tattoo guy might still be lurking in the bushes.

"We're not going to stop looking for him though," Luke reassured him. "When my dad gets home I'll see what he thinks we should do and we'll do it. We won't give up."

"Who is this young man?" Kleinschmidt asked, looking at Jim.

"My name is Jim," Jim said. "I'm a friend."

"I see. Well, you should all go home now and stay far away from here. The Soviet man might return to get what he came for, and you won't be safe if you are here. I give you my thanks for bringing Fritz home, but now you must go. Good day." He turned to limp back to the gate to let us out.

"But what about the roof? Don't you want us to repair it?" Daniel asked.

"No. Not today. Circumstances have changed, and that can wait," the old man replied.

He started to unlock the gate to let us out, but was interrupted by a coughing spell that seemed to go on for some time. It was a deep, dry, rattling cough—not the kind a person gets with the flu. He took out his handkerchief and wiped his mouth. I thought I saw a trace of blood on it. After the cough passed, he took another step toward the gate, but suddenly faltered and almost fell. Daniel caught his arm and helped him stay upright.

"*Danke*, Daniel," he said. "I've not been feeling so well lately. And now with this ankle...."

"What happened to you?" Daniel asked, still holding on to the old man. "Do you want to sit down?"

"*Ja*. Help me back to the house, *bitte*," he requested.

Daniel and Kleinschmidt slowly walked through the fences back to the house, while Luke, Jim, and I followed. It occurred to me that the old man was correct, that it wasn't safe for us to be there. The skull tattoo guy obviously wanted something badly from Mr. Kleinschmidt, and he might return to get it. We interrupted him the last time he came to get whatever it was he came for, and he might not treat us so well if we were in his way a second time. So I didn't want to hang around too long.

We all made our way into the house, through the dimly lit entryway, down the short hallway, and into the small living room. Daniel gently lowered the old man into his large, brown leather chair, as Fritz took his positon at his master's feet. I sat in the small red velvet chair, while Luke, Daniel, and Jim sat together on the brown sofa. Kleinschmidt reached into his back pocket and took out his handkerchief again and coughed briefly into it, then returned it to his pants. He leaned back in the chair and closed his eyes. We remained silent as we waited for Kleinschmidt to speak. The only sound came from the large, ornate wooden clock with the stag's head on the wall as it ticked away and then sounded the hour with a deep bass chime.

"What happened to your ankle?" Daniel asked finally, breaking the silence.

Kleinschmidt opened his eyes and gazed out the large window overlooking his front yard. "The Soviet man and I exchanged gun fire, and I was hit in the ankle," he replied without the slightest trace of emotion.

"So, those gun shots we heard last night—that was you and the Soviet dude shooting it out?" Luke asked. He seemed excited to finally learn the source of those disturbing shooting noises.

"*Ja*," the old man said, nodding. "I found him trying to break into my laboratory. When he would not leave, I had to make him leave."

"My father and the sheriff came to your house to check on you, but you didn't answer the front door. They thought you weren't home," Luke said. "Why didn't you answer the door? They could have helped you."

"This is not a matter for the sheriff or your father. I must handle this on my own," the old man said wearily.

"What does the Soviet guy want from you?" Daniel asked. I was glad he posed the question.

Kleinschmidt paused, and then answered. "He wants the secrets of my research."

We looked at each other, and I knew we all had the same thought. *What are the secrets of your research?* But none of us dared ask.

"Now, you must go. Thank you for bringing my dog home."

He tried to get up, but struggled and fell back into his chair. "I must ask you to let yourselves out please. You must go now and not mention me to anyone—not to the sheriff or to your father—not to anyone. This is extremely important, for your safety as well as theirs. Do you promise to do as I ask?"

Yet another coughing spell came over him. It made me sad to see the old man in such obvious poor health, struggling to stop the coughing and to breathe. It didn't feel right to leave him there, all alone and helpless. He'd be a sitting duck if the skull tattoo guy returned, which he probably would. My conscience wouldn't allow me to do what he asked.

"No. I, for one, won't promise that. Not until your tell me what the Soviet dude is after and what's going on," Luke replied defiantly. I was secretly glad he was so outspoken. Like it or not, we'd all been drawn into Mr. Kleinschmidt's world, and I couldn't leave without knowing why the skull tattoo guy was menacing him.

"Ah, yes. The brash one. You remind me of many men I knew once in my country. The men who rushed forward when others drew back. The ones who took too many risks. There's a place for men like you as leaders in the world, but you must learn to temper your impulses first," the old man counseled.

"Well, thanks for that, I guess," Luke muttered.

"Mr. Kleinschmidt, we want to help you," I started. "The Soviet man knows where we live and who we are. We're already in danger, even if we were to leave right now and say nothing to my uncle or the sheriff," I argued. "You must help us defend ourselves by telling us more about yourself and what's going on."

A look of concern came over Kleinschmidt's face as he pondered my statement. "Yes, *Fräulein*, you are correct. I have placed you all in danger, and for this I apologize."

"Can you please tell us your story, then?" Daniel asked.

Kleinschmidt gazed fondly at Daniel, and then closed his eyes and said nothing for what seemed like a long time. I began to wonder if he had passed out and almost got up to check on him. But he finally opened his eyes and spoke.

"I'm too sick and old to do what I had planned, so I am going to tell you about myself as you request. But after I am done, you must leave and never come back to this house or to this farm. This must be understood, *ja*?" he warned. "What is done is done, and while you may be in danger at this moment, I believe I can cause the Soviet man and his colleagues to stay away from you." He stopped to gather his strength.

"Okay. Please continue," Daniel urged, leaning forward in his seat.

After a few moments, the old man continued. "Do you remember that I told you I am a physicist? After the war, your government brought me and my family here to the United States to conduct research for your government in a program I believe they called Operation Paper Clip. It was a form of peacetime imprisonment, in a sense. Your government made many German scientists do this."

"You say you worked for *our* government?" Luke asked. "How is that possible? Where?"

Another coughing spell came on. After it subsided, the old man continued.

"I worked on zero-gravity propulsion research for the U.S. Air Force for four years, and then for Modern Propulsion Laboratories in Maryland for many more years after that. The U.S. government initially moved me and my family to the United States from a village in Austria where we were hiding in 1945 when the Soviets were advancing. The Soviets were known for their cruelty and might have killed all of us to prevent us from using our knowledge of zero-gravity theories."

"Sorry to interrupt, but may I ask a question? Is zero-gravity the same thing as anti-gravity?" Daniel asked. "I think I read something about anti-gravity research in *Popular Mechanics* magazine. Weren't the Nazi's working on developing anti-gravity weapons around the time the war ended?"

"Yes. Some people use the terms interchangeably, although I don't," Kleinschmidt answered. "Some people describe it as a change in the space-time continuum in such a way that it defies gravity."

"I saw a re-run of *Man in Space* not long ago on *Walt Disney,* and anti-gravity was mentioned. Is that the kind of stuff *you* worked on?" Luke asked, his eyes widening as if seeing the old man in a different light for the first time.

"I wasn't a rocket scientist like Wernher von Braun, who is in charge of America's Saturn V program and who, I understand, was shown on that show," answered Kleinschmidt. "But he and I are similar in that he was also brought to the United States to continue his research as part of Operation Paper Clip. My own work has other applications that are closely related, though. But we're getting off track. Perhaps I should end my story here."

"No, no. If you don't mind, sir, please continue. *Please*," Daniel urged. "How did you happen to come to Indiana and to this farm?"

The old man coughed a bit, and then took a sip of something clear that was in a short glass on the table next to him. He cleared his throat and continued.

"My time left on this Earth is short, and for some reason I feel you might as well know the whole story. My real name is Karl Weidmann, not Klaus Kleinschmidt. My research at Modern Propulsion Laboratories was on the verge of proving the existence of zero-gravity five years ago, when the company suddenly discontinued the program and disavowed ever having worked on a zero-gravity project. They even made me sign an oath not to ever discuss what I did there. I was stopped from continuing my research just at the moment of a major breakthrough.

"So I changed my name and came here. I needed a place where I could blend in and continue my research and experiments without being noticed. I needed to disappear from both the Soviets and from your government. I knew about Indiana from a great-uncle who moved here many years ago and ran a meat market in Noblesville. In a vast agricultural area like this in the middle of the U.S., for the most part a person can go about their business without being observed. Unfortunately, the Soviets found me last week and have been getting bold. They want the results of my research and will go to any lengths to get it. And then you children started watching me and playing nearby. Suddenly, it got very uncomfortable for me. I've done my best to drive you away, but that hasn't worked, and here we find ourselves today."

"So, the UFOs I've seen silently hovering in the sky for several nights—are you responsible for those?" Luke asked excitedly. "Is the contraption in the building we fell into a UFO?"

Kleinschmidt smiled with great pride and nodded. "Your term 'UFO' isn't what I call it, but as I understand your question—*ja*, that is my craft that works by zero-gravity technology. I finally made a breakthrough three weeks ago and got the technology to work. I was testing it in the middle of the night to avoid being seen, to the extent I could."

"Wow! Now things are starting to make sense," Luke replied, nodding.

"I saw scores of dead birds on my family's property near here. What happened to them? Do you know about them?" I asked.

"*Ja*, unfortunately the effects of zero-gravity experiments can be deadly to birds and small animals," he replied. "It can also affect the health of humans, as it did my wife and now me."

"What about the vandalism at our playhouse. Did you do that, too?" Luke asked.

"*Nein*, I would never do such a thing to the property of another person. It would be my guess that the Soviet agent did that. Your playhouse is very close to my farm. Just as much as I didn't want you to see too much, the Soviet didn't either. In my case, I didn't want you children to get caught in the middle."

"Well, what do you know? All this time, and I thought you did it," Luke admitted. "I'm sorry. I guess you never know about people." This was the second time he apologized to the old German.

"If you wanted us to stay away so much, why did you make us come back here this morning to fix the roof and do chores for you?" Daniel inquired. "Of course, we didn't mind, but...."

"That was my mistake. I wanted you to learn a lesson about responsibility, but I was also weak. Daniel, you may recall that I told you that you remind me of my son Wilhelm. He meant so much to me, and I wasn't thinking straight. I see I was wrong to require that you return, but I have a plan that will make it right and get you out of harm's way, I promise."

He pulled out his handkerchief and dabbed his eyes and mouth. He appeared to be physically uncomfortable and in pain, and was perspiring profusely.

"Did the Soviet set the fire at my parents' house, too?" Luke asked.

"Hard to say. What would he gain by doing that?" the old man observed. "I suppose he might have been trying to scare you and your family in order to drive you away. The same reason he tried to destroy your little house."

"Maybe it was a lightning strike after all," I suggested. "That's what the firemen thought, didn't they?"

"Yeah, but I know I heard someone walking around outside my window, and a supposed lightning strike a few minutes later seems like too much of a coincidence," Luke replied.

"Do you mind if I ask—-what kind of illness do you have, other than your ankle?" Daniel asked, leaning toward the old man.

"I'm afraid I'm suffering from complications caused by exposure to thorium, beryllium, and mercury used in my research. I don't have long to live," he said a bit sadly. "It has been my heartfelt hope to return to my hometown in Germany—to Augsburg—before I die. But first I must get the results of my research into the hands of the right people, and time is running out for me more quickly than I had thought. I must leave soon if I am to make it back to the old country."

He leaned back and took a deep breath. I could see that all this talking was sapping him of what little strength and energy he had left.

"When you say into the hands of the right people, do you mean the United States government?" I asked.

"No, *Fräulein*, no. Into the hands of a fellow physicist named Otto Richter, a man I worked with at Modern Propulsion. He will know what to do with it. What I have discovered is too powerful and dangerous. I trust no one else to use the technology for peaceful purposes. If I can't get it to *Herr* Richter for any reason, then I'll have to destroy it to prevent the Soviets or any other people, including your own government, from using it for destructive purposes."

"How are you going to get the data to him? Are you going to mail it to him, or travel to see him in person?" Daniel asked.

"Otto and I are to meet in person at the Indiana State Fair tomorrow. It's far too important to be sent through the mail, and I'm much too old and sick to make the journey to carry it to him in Maryland. If I'm able to travel at all, it must be to use what little strength I have left to go back to the old country. With my declining health, it may be too late to even do that."

"Why at the State Fair?" Luke asked. "Is there an anti-gravity show there this year?"

Daniel scowled and mouthed the words "*be serious.*" Luke looked perplexed and mouthed the word "*okay*" back. Kleinschmidt didn't appear to notice their exchange.

"No, he will be there to introduce a new, highly efficient and powerful engine developed by Modern Propulsion Laboratories for agricultural equipment. We are to meet at one o'clock by the Reynolds Farm Equipment display to make the hand-off. The crowds there will help shield us from being seen. After that, my work here is done, and I hope to return to my beloved country to live out the rest of what remains of my life."

"Why not just have Mr. Richter come here?" I asked. "Wouldn't that be easier?" I didn't see how Mr. Kleinschmidt, in his fragile condition and with an injured ankle, would be able to walk through the fairgrounds to make that rendezvous.

"With the Soviet watching me, he can't risk coming here. The Soviet government might keep me alive to interpret and explain my research to them, but they wouldn't hesitate to harm my dear friend Otto, especially if they suspected he was in possession of my research data. That is why the gentleman with the tattoo didn't kill me this morning. They need me—at least for now."

"But how will you get to the State Fair the way you are? There are long distances to walk, and long lines of people. You'll never be able to do it," I said. I didn't want to be a downer, but there were obvious realities to consider.

"Yes. I'm afraid you are correct, *Fräulein*. I appear to have no choice but to destroy my laboratory, all of my research data, and the craft that I built. That's all that's left to do, because I am unable, with my declining health, to get to *Herr* Richter tomorrow. Once the Soviets realize my research results are destroyed, they'll return to Moscow and have no reason to bother all of you further. Then, I can return to my beloved Augsburg, and you can return to your happy and safe country life. That is how I plan to make things right for you."

He sighed heavily and stared blankly out the window. To think that his life's work—the years of dedicated research— would be destroyed just when everything was coming together to harness zero-gravity technology must have been devastating for him. On top of that, sacrificing his life and his wife's life— cut short from the effects of prolonged exposure to toxic metals and substances—for nothing must have been a bitter pill. It didn't seem right that he should die like this, and that his research should be lost forever. Mankind for decades has sought to harness zero-gravity, and Mr. Kleinschmidt had succeeded! His breakthrough had to be preserved. But how?

Luke looked as though he were about to burst forth with an idea. He stared down at the floor, deep in thought, tapping his foot nervously.

"I'll take the data to Mr. Richter for you tomorrow," Luke blurted. "You can trust me to do it, I swear."

"Luke, don't be stupid. This isn't kid stuff we're talking about," Jim cautioned.

"I know this is serious stuff. I can get the job done," Luke said. "Please give me a shot at it, sir."

Mr. Kleinschmidt looked stunned and studied Luke carefully. "You are indeed the brash one," the old man said, shaking his head. "As I said before, you take risks before you understand the consequences. No, it is not possible for you to take my research data to *Herr* Richter tomorrow. You could be captured or harmed by the Soviet agent. I can't be a part of putting you in that kind of danger. *Nein*. That is totally out of the question."

"What other option do you have?" Luke argued. "Do really want to destroy all of your life's research when I can deliver it into trusted hands for you? I've seen for myself what you've invented, and it's too fantastic to destroy. You say I'm brash. Well, okay, I'm brash. But that's a good trait to have for a job like this, isn't it? I have the determination and the courage to get the job done for you. Please let me try. I'm not afraid."

Mr. Kleinschmidt took a labored breath and closed his eyes.

"If you don't give it to me, the skull tattoo guy will come back again and take it from you, won't he?" Luke added. "You know he will. Do you want the Soviets to get it? At least this way, there's a chance that Mr. Richter will get it."

The old man opened his eyes and peered intently at Luke. "It would need to be stored in a safe place overnight. Where in your parents' farmhouse could you possibly keep it safe should the Soviet man come tonight to take it from you?" the old man asked.

"I have the perfect place," Luke answered, sitting forward eagerly upon sensing Mr. Kleinschmidt was coming around.

"Where?" Kleinschmidt asked flatly. He coughed and took another sip from his glass.

"There's this really great cooler I found down by the river...," he began. The rest of us moaned spontaneously. "Okay, to tell you the truth, it's really disgusting and smells putrid. But that's the point. No one would ever think anything important was in it. Especially if I stack some bait and other smelly stuff on top."

"A cooler? I see. A youthful approach, to say the least. I am distressed that you and your family are already in danger and will be even more so if I let you take the data out of this house. But I am ill and have no choice but to agree to allow you to take it to *Herr* Richter tomorrow. So, I'll agree on one condition with which you must pledge to comply," Mr. Kleinschmidt said slowly and carefully. Luke leaned forward and hung on the old man's every word.

"You must take every precaution not to let anyone outside of those in this room know you have the data. This is the only way to keep yourself and your family safe. Do you agree to this, brash one?" Mr. Kleinschmidt asked, his eyes locked on Luke.

I was surprised Kleinschmidt agreed. This meant Luke would have custody of very important documents for almost one whole day, and then would have to get them to the rendezvous spot by one o'clock tomorrow. Luke was taking on a big responsibility, not to mention a dangerous one.

"Yes, yes I will!" Luke swore enthusiastically. "You can count on me, *Herr* Kleinschmidt! I'll get the job done for you."

"*Ja*, just remember what I said about considering your actions before you take them," Kleinschmidt advised. "You are still young, and I wish for you to live to be an old man. Remember, the future of the world now rests on your shoulders. If this information falls into the wrong hands, mankind may be enslaved by evil forever, or even extinguished."

Having finished his cautionary remarks, Mr. Kleinschmidt struggled to his feet. Steadying himself with his cane, he walked slowly to an ornately framed oil painting of a mountain meadow scene. He pulled the frame forward revealing a wall safe behind it, spun the dial, and tugged open the safe's door. I was fascinated to see what anti-gravity data looked like, and observed him closely. He took out a thick bundle wrapped in a beige leather folder bound by leather straps, then lumbered back and feebly lowered himself into his chair.

"Here are the schematics and the results of my research. This is the only copy that exists. I am entrusting you with the one and only copy," he underscored, handing the precious package of documents to Luke. After he caught his breath, he continued. "You must never open this or look at the data inside. Never. No matter how curious to see it you may be. The less you know about what's in this package, the safer you'll be. Do you understand? Never break the seal on the outside of this folder. Never. Your life, and the lives of those around you, depends on it."

"Yes," Luke replied solemnly.

There the old man was again, reminding us that our lives depended on this or that. Now that I knew what was going on, perhaps he was more right about that than I'd given him credit for.

"*Herr* Richter will be at the Reynolds Farm Equipment display at precisely one o'clock tomorrow. You'll be able to identify him by his bushy moustache and a loden-green hat with a short feather on the side. He never fails to wear his hat. He'll be expecting me, not you, so you'll have to explain to him who you are and why I couldn't come," the old man instructed. "If you need to, use the German word '*Frieden*' as a password, and he'll know that I sent you."

"What does that word—*Frieden*—mean?" Luke asked. "Am I pronouncing it correctly? Free-din."

"*Ja*, you are pronouncing it fine. It means peace," Kleinschmidt explained.

Another coughing spell suddenly came over the old man, and he took out his handkerchief and coughed into it repeatedly. He was barely able to choke out the words, "God be with you," before he collapsed. His eyes rolled back in their sockets, he dropped the handkerchief, and passed out.

Luke, Jim, and Daniel jumped up and checked his wrists and neck for a pulse.

"Is...is he dead?" I asked, shaken.

"Thank God, he's still alive," Luke reported finally, his fingers still resting on the old man's neck. "It's faint, but he's got a pulse."

"I don't care what he said about not wanting doctors, I think we ought to get him to the hospital right away," Jim insisted. "Besides, if we leave him here, he'll be a sitting duck for the skull tattoo guy, and who knows what he might do to him this time."

"I agree. We can't leave him alone here like this," Daniel said. "I'll call Riverview Hospital and see if they can send an ambulance right away."

"We'll take Fritz back to our house while the poor guy's in the hospital," Luke offered.

The dog, sensing something was seriously wrong with his master, sat with his nose resting on the old man's thigh, gazing up at him with sad brown eyes.

Daniel walked down the hall and disappeared into another room, and then returned with a perplexed look on his face. "Does anyone see a phone around here?" he asked. "I can't find one."

"Is that a phone over there?" I asked, pointing to a small table by the large living room window.

Daniel walked over and found the phone, and then looked below the table and produced a phone book containing telephone numbers for Fishers and Noblesville. He quickly paged through the book and then picked up the receiver and carefully entered the number on the rotary dial.

"I hope you know what you're doing," Jim said to Luke, who was examining the outside of the leather bundle with fascination. "You're playing with fire, you know."

"Yep. This should be fun," Luke replied, laughing a slightly forced laugh. "Just up my alley, you know, since I'm the brash one, according to Mr. Kleinschmidt. I feel as though I'm in an episode of *Secret Agent* or *The Man From U.N.C.L.E.*"

"Right," Jim said, unconvinced. "Except in your case, you're Luke Oh-No instead of Napoleon Solo."

"Ha, ha. Funny, funny," Luke smirked, taking the leather folder back from Jim.

"The ambulance is on its way," Daniel confirmed, placing the receiver back in its cradle. "They said they'd be just fifteen minutes."

Suddenly, there was a loud knock on the front door. We immediately stopped talking and froze.

CHAPTER TWENTY

Gotta Get Away

After a slight pause, there was another loud and forceful knock at Mr. Kleinschmidt's front door.

"Do you think it's the Soviet?" Daniel whispered with an alarmed look on his face.

"Nah. Igor's not polite enough to knock," Luke replied softly.

"What should we do?" I whispered. "I don't think we should open it, do you?"

"Maybe whoever it is will go away if we're quiet and don't move," Jim suggested.

"Luke! Luke, are you in there?" Uncle Evert called, knocking on the door again. "Is everything okay in there? Mr. Kleinschmidt? Hello?"

Luke darted to the door and opened it. I was relieved it was only Uncle Evert and not the skull tattoo guy. Luke led him down the hall and into the living room. My uncle said Lars had dutifully told him where we were as soon as my uncle returned from the grocery, so he immediately drove straight to Mr. Kleinschmidt's house to see what all of the commotion was about. When Uncle Evert saw Mr. Kleinschmidt passed out in the chair, he raced over to him.

"What's going on? What happened to him? Is he dead?" my uncle asked, searching for the old man's pulse and checking his pupils. "Why are you kids here?"

"Dad, it's a long, long story," Luke began. "I can explain it all to you later."

"Yes, indeed you shall, young man. Has anyone called an ambulance?" Uncle Evert asked, still examining Mr. Kleinschmidt.

"Yes, I called and Riverview is sending an ambulance right away," Daniel replied.

It seemed to take the ambulance a long time to get there, and I became fidgety waiting. Mr. Kleinschmidt was coming in and out of consciousness and coughing. Even with a lot of medical care, I didn't see how he'd be able to survive for long. It was a good thing Luke had agreed to take the documents and drawings to his contact at the State Fair tomorrow, but I couldn't shake my feelings of dread. Everyone knew you didn't mess with the Soviets, whether in international diplomacy or when it came to hiding and passing anti-gravity secrets to friendly scientists at a Midwestern state fair. I worried for Luke's safety. And to be honest, for my own.

After Mr. Kleinschmidt was loaded into the ambulance and on his way to the hospital, we collected Fritz to take him back to the farmhouse with us. I was relieved to get out of the old man's property before the Soviet returned. I realized, of course, that nothing prevented the skull tattoo guy from coming to my aunt and uncle's house if he wanted to. He was probably somewhere outside watching us and had seen that we came to Mr. Kleinschmidt's house frequently. He might surmise that we knew the truth about the old man and who he really was. If so, he might eliminate us just to shut us up.

"Okay, everyone. Let's have a little chat," Uncle Evert said as we rode back to the farmhouse. "Luke, you go first. Explain to me how you four ended up being at Mr. Kleinschmidt's house this afternoon."

"Didn't Lars tell you?" Luke asked, stalling.

"No, he didn't," Uncle Evert replied, being surprisingly patient. "He told me to get over to Kleinschmidt's house as fast as I could. That you four were over there and needed my help. So you take it from there. What's going on?"

We hadn't had time to strategize what we'd reveal to Uncle Evert or to anyone else. I was relieved when Uncle Evert directed all of his questions to Luke. My cousin, generally speaking, had no problem shading, bending, and modifying the truth, as needed. This time, as usual, he shamelessly spun quite a sanitized version of what had happened at the old German's house.

"So, you're saying that a random burglar broke into Mr. Kleinschmidt's house while you were there at *his* invitation this morning—a man who's warned you previously to stay away—and that you chased the burglar into our barn, but he got away without a trace. Is that your story?" Uncle Evert summarized.

"Yep. That's absolutely correct, Dad. You have a very sharp memory for detail, if I may say so," Luke replied, piling on the flattery.

"And, the dog got out during this encounter and when you took it back, you found Mr. Kleinschmidt very ill and called for an ambulance. Is that the complete story?"

"Yep. Kind of a boring story, huh?" Luke answered. "I was just happy I could be there to give the old gentleman help when he needed it. That's the way you raised me."

Uncle Evert looked into his rear view mirror to check our reactions to the story as some sort of intuitive lie-detector test. I quickly shifted my gaze out the window to avoid giving anything away.

"What's that you're holding there? Is that a leather pouch or a folder or something?" Uncle Evert asked, peering down at the package of documents Luke was clutching in his lap as tightly as a football. "Where'd you get that? Did you take that from Mr. Kleinschmidt's house? I sure hope you didn't take anything without permission, Luke. I've taught you better than that."

"No, no, Dad. Mr. Kleinschmidt gave this to me," Luke replied. "I swear."

"What is it?" Uncle Evert asked, peering down at it again.

Luke looked down at the bundle and paused to come up with an answer. "It's just some old papers he thought I'd be interested in. You know, stories about the war and letters about the war. Stuff like that. I told him I was a big WWII buff, so he gave it to me," Luke fibbed. "I didn't really want the stuff and took it more or less as favor to him when he offered it to me so I wouldn't be rude by refusing, the way you taught me." He flashed another big smile at his father.

"Okay," Uncle Evert replied. "I must say I've never known you to be so friendly with the old man before. I thought the two of you hated each other. This is certainly a dramatic change of heart—for both of you."

"Well, I've grown a lot as a person lately. I've learned to forgive and to see the good in people," Luke replied with a straight face. I did the best

I could to keep my composure. I heard Jim let out a chortle, and I nudged him in the arm to be quiet. He replied with a playful nudge back.

When we arrived at the farmhouse, Lars was at the piano in the living room playing something complex and classical, while Emma was outside sitting at the table eating freshly baked chocolate-chip cookies and drumming her fingers in rhythm with "Pleasant Valley Sunday" by The Monkees on the radio. She appeared slightly annoyed when I walked over to greet her.

"Where've you been all day?" she complained. "I thought you were just going to watch Luke and Daniel repair the roof on the old Nazi's shed. How long does that take, anyway? I've been waiting for you so we could go down to Glendale Shopping Center to shop and hang out. Dad said he'd take us. He kept asking me where you were, and I was running out of excuses."

"Hey, don't call Mr. Kleinschmidt an old Nazi," Luke corrected her after taking a seat at the table and grabbing a cookie from a stack arranged on a platter. "Labels like that aren't nice. Hey, these cookies are good. For once you didn't screw things up in the kitchen, little sister."

"Luke, be nice to your sister," Jim said as he reached for a cookie.

"I didn't bake these cookies, you moron. Bunny Bibble did," Emma replied tartly to Luke. "She just came by to drop them off and say hi to you, although why she'd want to do that, I have no idea."

Luke ducked as though the mere mention of Bunny's name was synonymous with an anvil falling on his head. "What? Bernie the Bruiser was here? Where is she? Is she still around?" He gazed around anxiously.

"Relax, Casanova. You just missed her. She hung around for a while, but had to go. And stop calling her by that horrible name. Her name is Bunny, and I like her," Emma said.

"I like her, too. Anyone who can make fabulous chocolate-chip cookies like these is my kind of woman!" Daniel chimed in, speaking with his mouth full.

"And she's good at self-defense, too. In my book she has everything a guy could ever want in a woman," Jim added, smiling slyly as he licked melted chocolate off his fingers.

"Except good taste in men!" Emma added. Everyone burst into laughter except Luke.

"Knock it off, you guys," Luke scolded. "If it weren't for me and my irresistible magnetism, you'd be eating stale Chips Ahoy cookies out of a bag instead of these great cookies. So give me a little respect, will ya?"

"Your irresistible— *what*?" Jim asked, laughing again. "Did you say barbarism?"

Luke made a gesture toward Jim and then went to the garage where I assumed he stashed the leather folder in that disgusting cooler as he promised the old German he'd do. It made me nervous to think important information like that was being hidden in a place so easily accessible to anyone with the fortitude to endure the stench to look there. I hoped the Soviet didn't know Luke had the documents. Every now and then I glanced at the woods lining the edge of the backyard and along the creek, worried I'd see his disturbing face. So far, so good. There was no sign of him. At least Mr. Kleinschmidt was in the hospital where he'd be safe, and I didn't need to worry that he was home alone where Igor would surely return.

I wondered if one of us should tell Uncle Evert about what we knew so he could get the legal authorities to help us, even though Mr. Kleinschmidt told us not to. Kleinschmidt was old and ill, and his judgment may have been impaired about what we should do. But none of my cousins seemed to want to tell Uncle Evert, so I remained silent and tried to push it out of my thoughts.

Aunt Louise brought out a big bowl of water for Fritz and placed it on the grass near the table. The German shepherd was much friendlier now than I'd ever imagined he could be. We fed him bits of the cookies, which he wolfed down almost as gladly as Doritos. Luke went into the house and returned with a package of Eckrich brand hot dogs and fed them to the hungry dog one at a time. Each time Fritz consumed a hot dog, he'd place his right paw on Luke's knee, and Luke would dutifully reach into the package and produce another one for him.

"Slow down there, boy," Luke coached the canine. "I know you're hungry, but don't choke."

"You're getting soft on that dog," Daniel observed. "I never thought I'd see the day you'd be best buddies."

"He's okay, but I'm not getting dopey over him or anything like that. I know Mr. Kleinschmidt will want him back when he gets out of the hospital," Luke said, sounding wistful as he petted the German shepherd's head and gazed fondly at him. "He's not a bad dog, really. He's brave and takes charge. He's loyal, too. He's got a lot going for him."

"Yeah, when you think about it, you two are a lot alike," Daniel jabbed. "You're both brazen and egotistical!"

"What? Are you asking for me teach you a lesson of the five-minute treatment variety?" Luke threatened.

"Calm down, O brash one. I have to go home now, so you'll have to give me the five-minute treatment some other time. My mom probably wants to know where I am, and I'm hungry for her mac and cheese. If I know her, she's made a big batch, and it's just waiting for me!"

"Okay, but you're going to the fair with us tomorrow, aren't you?" Luke reminded him.

"Yeah, I guess so," Daniel confirmed. "Take it easy and stay safe tonight. Call me if you need anything."

"Stay safe? What do you mean?" Emma chirped up. "Is there something going on that you and Luke haven't told me about? Why are you guys so worried about staying safe tonight?" She looked stressed.

"Because it's always a good idea to stay safe, silly. It's just something people say when they say good night," Luke replied.

"Right. See you guys tomorrow," Daniel replied. He walked across the backyard and down the path.

I didn't see any reason not to include Emma in our plans. I knew it would make my life easier if we did. That way I wouldn't have to keep watching what I said all of the time, which wasn't my strong suit. In addition, I didn't like keeping a major secret from her. As my close friend in addition to being my cousin, I wanted to be able to share my concerns with her.

"Why don't you tell her?" I suggested to Luke in front of Emma. He looked stunned and angry I was spilling the beans. "Well, she needs to know, doesn't she? I'm worried the skull tattoo guy may come here tonight. How are we going to defend ourselves if he does?"

"What do you mean? Why would he come here? Have you seen him again?" Emma asked. Her voice was tinged with panic.

Luke looked over his shoulder to see who else was around. Satisfied that only he, Jim, Emma, and I were within earshot, he proceeded to tell Emma an abridged version of what had happened today with the Soviet. After he finished the story, Emma became even more agitated and worried.

"We've got to tell Dad. We *have* to," Emma insisted. "He'll know what to do to keep us safe. He'll call the sheriff and ask him to come back out here tonight. They'll protect us. We need them. I'll go get him."

She jumped up, but Luke grabbed her arm and pulled her back down into her seat. "See, Sis? That's exactly why I didn't want you to know anything about this. I knew you'd get hysterical and spoil everything."

"What are you talking about? We can't just sit here and wait for the Soviet to return. We're just kids. We need help," she argued, pulling her arm away from him. "Why don't you want Dad to know the whole story?"

"Because Kleinschmidt said anyone we tell about what he was really researching and about the data will be in danger. So we've got to leave Mom and Dad out of this. Lars and Margret, too. Understand? We'll be okay tonight. I know we will. I'll stand watch all night. Won't that make you feel safe? If the skull tattoo guy makes trouble, I'll return as much or more to him," Luke bragged. "So he'd better not come nosing around here if he knows what's good for him."

"Sorry, brother, but nothing you're saying makes me feel safe at all," Emma replied, looking cross. "How can you defend us? You're just a kid with an attitude. It takes more than that to keep me safe."

"I'll help you stand guard, Luke. We can take turns. You can't do it alone," Jim volunteered.

"Thanks, dude, but why not go home where it's safe? You don't want to be in this mess, do you?" Luke replied.

"I don't mind hanging around here tonight. Being at home listening to my parents go at each other about moving away would be far worse. I'll call my mom and tell her I'm spending the night here. She won't mind. I'll be right back." Jim got up and walked into the house to use the phone.

"Moving away? What does he mean by that?" Luke asked, looking at me.

"Don't know," I replied, which wasn't true. But Jim had asked me to let him handle breaking the news to Luke in his own way, so I panicked and didn't give Luke a straight answer. I was becoming like Luke when it came to telling the truth, and I felt uncomfortable. Fortunately, Luke just shrugged and dropped the subject.

"I still don't understand why we can't tell Mom and Dad, but I won't say anything for now. I feel as though I've been living in a nightmare lately, and it just keeps getting worse. I'll be glad when school starts again and things go back to normal," Emma lamented. "I don't see how I'll be able to sleep a wink tonight, not that you care." She looked at me for support, and I returned a perplexed look. I didn't know what to do.

After dinner, Luke took his position at the dining room table outside with the BB gun lying across his lap. Aunt Louise asked him why he was sitting there with the gun, and I heard him tell her a confusing story about waiting for a coyote that he'd seen prowling around that might try to prey on Karma. She appeared to accept his tale, although I'd never heard of a coyote being that far north. Jim sat in a chair next to him facing the yard and the barn. The two of them wiled away the time talking about whether the Boston Red Sox would make it to the World Series and other sports stuff.

Emma and I went inside and watched summer re-runs of *The Green Hornet*, *The Time Tunnel*, and *Hogan's Heroes*. After that, it was time for *Nightmare Theater with Sammy Terry* on Channel 4. The movie *Them!* was the first feature shown tonight. It was about a nest of gigantic irradiated ants living in the concrete spillways and sewers of Los Angeles. The actor Edmund Gwenn, who was also Santa in the holiday movie *Miracle on 34th Street*, portrayed a myrmecologist who knew how to get rid of the killer ants. After several tense moments with lots of dead people crushed by their giant antennae, the ants were finally cornered beneath Los Angeles and torched with flame throwers. As the movie credits rolled on the screen, I turned to speak to Emma, and saw she'd fallen asleep on the couch. So I went outside to sit with Luke and Jim. They were discussing school. Jim had finally told Luke about his impending move to Arizona.

"I was going to be on the varsity baseball team this year," Jim sighed. "Do kids in Arizona even play baseball?"

"I can't believe you're really moving, but if you have to go, this is probably the time to do it. With Fishers High School closing and everyone being sent to Hamilton Southeastern High School, you were going to start over in a new high school anyway," Luke observed.

"Why are they closing Fishers High School?" I asked. This is the first I'd heard about it.

"Haven't you heard? They're going to tear it down and expand the elementary school next door," Luke explained. "A real genius idea, huh? Our beautiful school with the arches and the tower will be smashed to smithereens."

That was sad news, indeed. My mother had attended Fishers High School, as had Aunt Louise and several other aunts and my Uncle Forrest, not to mention all of my cousins. It was an important part of the Fishers community. Jim and Luke reminisced about the time they converted practically the entire school into a giant haunted house as a fund raiser at Halloween, the last basketball game ever played in the gym built at the back of the main building only a few years ago, and lots of other stories. It made me sad for them. It seemed that change was in the air, and that it inevitably touched each one of us in one way or another.

Suddenly, there was an odd rustling sound in the bushes not far from the edge of the yard. It was too dark to see anything. Luke cocked his BB gun and stared into the distance. Fritz, who was lying at Luke's feet, sat up and growled.

"Come on, you Russkie devil. Come out and show yourself. I dare you!" Luke shouted, stabbing at the air with the barrel of the BB gun.

There was another slight rustling sound, and then the sound stopped.

CHAPTER TWENTY-ONE

I'm Off to Join the Circus

Whatever we'd heard in the bushes as Jim, Luke, and I sat outside didn't come out into the open, even though we waited and visually scrutinized the area for quite a while from our respective positions at the dining room table. None of us had the nerve to actually wander into the woods to investigate. Jim suggested it was probably just a possum or raccoon. Luke disagreed and was certain it'd been the skull tattoo guy, and that his own tough words and aggressive demeanor had scared him off. Unlikely as that was, Jim and I didn't challenge him. If indeed it'd been the skull tattoo guy, it was more likely that Fritz's presence lying at Luke's feet and the memory of his stinging bite was the reason he left us alone.

As we resumed talking, I tried to relax, which was difficult. Every so often Luke suddenly stopped in mid-sentence and tensed up when he thought he'd heard or seen something. Then he'd relax and resume where he'd left off. It was exhausting. But I wanted to stay outside with the boys as late as possible, so I hung on. Uncle Evert came to the screen door at one point and asked if we were planning to sit at the dining room table all night. Luke had already told Aunt Louise that crazy tale about looking for a coyote rumored to be roaming the area. Luke didn't mention the coyote or give any other particular reason to his father, though. Uncle Evert probably wondered what we were really up to, but he left us alone and didn't question us further.

The time ebbed away, and eventually I was almost too tired to get myself into the house to go to bed. It was difficult to argue that I could offer anything more in this situation than moral support, so I reluctantly gave up my post and went inside for the night. Emma had already gone to bed and was blissfully sound asleep. My mind drifted to thoughts of the two large bedroom windows facing the back yard. Their curtains had been removed and sent to the laundry. If the skull tattoo guy looked in, he'd be able to see us, but even worse, I'd be able to see his hideous face in return. In addition, the windows were open and large enough for anyone to crawl through if they wanted.

I was afraid we'd all end up murdered while sleeping in our beds, just like the Herbert Clutter family written about in Truman Capote's best-selling novel, *In Cold Blood*, that came out just last year. The brutal true story of two drifters who killed the entire Clutter family while looking for non-existent money scared the bejesus out of country people everywhere, who thereafter began locking their doors at night. This was a practice I urgently wished my aunt and uncle would adopt.

I convinced myself that I had to stay awake to listen for the telltale sounds of footsteps so the Soviet couldn't get the drop on us. As I lay there listening intently, I fell asleep. Yes, sweet sleep, once again, had rescued me from thinking and worrying too much.

When I opened my eyes the next morning, it was sunny and, judging from the sounds in the house, everything was normal. The record player in the living room played "With a Little Help from My Friends" and then "Lucy in the Sky with Diamonds" from the Beatles' new album, *Sgt. Pepper's Lonely Hearts Club Band*, with the volume turned low. That could only mean one thing—Margret was home. She loved to listen to her Beatles albums. Emma was still asleep with her head under her bed pillow.

I quickly grabbed my brown Capri slacks and yellow-and-brown striped top, and ran into the bathroom to get dressed. I brushed my hair and placed my tortoise-colored headband on, choosing to wear my hair loose today instead of up in a ponytail as I often did. After I swiped the Slickers cotton candy pink lip gloss across my lips, I was ready for anything the day might bring, which I knew included going to the Indiana State Fair.

I walked into the kitchen where Margret was cooking at the stove. "Hi, Vanessa. I'm making french toast. Would you like some?" she asked. She looked very nautical in trendy bell bottom jeans and a short sleeved blue knit top with a large pointy white collar.

"Sure!" I replied. "You sure look cute in that outfit," I added. There was no hiding that I envied her trendy fashions.

"Oh, these things?" she replied, gazing down at herself. "Wendy let me borrow them while my clothes are being cleaned. I don't know what I'd have done if she hadn't taken me in the way she has—letting me stay at her house and borrow her clothes. Everything I own is damaged, ruined, or at the dry cleaners." The expression on her face changed from cheerful to troubled as she continued. "I'm just about at the end of my rope, if you want to know the truth. Don't even ask me how I'm going to be able to pull everything together in time to return to college in a few days. My stomach is in knots over it!"

Margret was always so calm and self-sufficient, it hadn't occurred to me that she was suffering from having her life disrupted by the fire, just like everyone else.

"Oh, listen to me go on," she chastised herself. "Mom and Dad have enough to worry about without me getting all dramatic. Just forget all I just said. I'm fine. Here you go."

She handed me a plate with two slices hot out of the frying pan, and I smothered them with Mrs. Butterworth's maple syrup from the amber-colored glass bottle sitting on the kitchen table. I headed for the door, but paused just before going down the steps, and turned.

"I'm sorry I've taken your share of the bed," I said. "I didn't mean to make you have to stay someplace else."

Margret smiled, still holding the spatula. "It's no problem kiddo. You're always welcome here. Now go on outside and eat your french toast before it gets cold."

I nodded and went out the door. Lars and Jim were seated at the dining room table when I walked outside. Jim was finishing his french toast, while Lars was reading a book entitled *The Heart of Man: Its Genius for Good and Evil* by Erich Fromm, which I found oddly appropriate. "Goodbye Cruel World" sung by James Darren was playing on the radio outside.

I took my plate and sat down in the empty chair next to Jim. I was surprised how awake and fresh he appeared. Not at all rumpled and half-awake as I'd expected him to be after a sleepless night of endless waiting, watching, and listening.

"How'd it go last night?" I asked as I sliced my French toast. "Did anything else happen after I went to bed? I'm sorry I was such a light-weight and had to go in when I did."

"No, nothing happened. Luke and I ended up going inside to sleep on the floor in the living room about an hour and a half after you did," Jim confessed. "So, no need to apologize."

"Speaking of the devil, where is Luke?" I asked gazing around the area. "Is he still in bed? He'd better get going if he's going to make that appointment of his."

"I haven't seen him yet this morning," Jim answered. "If he doesn't show soon, I'm going to go inside and find him."

Emma stumbled out the door holding a plate of french toast, her chin-length blonde hair tousled as if she'd just been in a wind tunnel. Everyone noticed and chuckled.

"Sis, what happened to *you*?" Lars asked. "Were you out all night partying or something?"

"Oh, stuff it," Emma replied, sounding grumpy. She plopped down at the table and stared at her plate in a sleepy stupor. "I always sleep hard when I'm stressed, and I'm stressed."

"What's got you so stressed out?" Lars inquired.

Emma paused. "Life," she answered flatly.

Finally, Luke bolted out the screen door, looking disheveled and slightly off-kilter as though he'd just endured a long, hard night.

"Hi everyone. I guess I fell asleep there for a minute or two and forgot what time it was. That bed in my parents' room looked so darned comfy when I walked by and looked in. I couldn't resist," he explained. "I've been sleeping on the floor so much lately. That ol' floor gets mighty uncomfortable after a while."

Fritz ran to greet him and jumped up and down happily as though doing a dance. Luke sat down at the table and took several small pieces of french toast from his plate and put them down on the grass for Fritz. This went on for some time until Aunt Louise emerged from the house with a pitcher of orange juice, which she placed on the table.

"Luke, stop feeding that dog at the table," Aunt Louise commanded. "That's a very bad habit to get started." Luke continued feeding the dog as though he hadn't heard her.

Lars couldn't contain himself and chose to offer his own observations. "You're developing a passive-aggressive co-dependency with that dog, and you'll be sorry. You know Mom will never let you keep him, right Mom?" he commented. "You're headed for a good dose of separation anxiety."

"I'm developing a what? No one's ever called me passive before," Luke scoffed. "Are you picking up that mumbo-jumbo from that book you're reading? A *Thor* comic book would do you a whole lot more good than that Erich Fromm psycho-babble you're reading there."

"All I can say is that as soon as that Mr. Kleinschmidt is out of the hospital, that dog is going right back to that man's house where he belongs," Aunt Louise said as she went back into the house. "It can't happen soon enough to suit me," she remarked just as the screen door closed behind her.

"Well, I'm your fan, even if that mean lady who lives here isn't," Luke said, cupping the dog's face in his two hands as it sat looking up at him.

I looked at the driveway and was surprised not see the van parked there. What was the game plan for going to the fair today? It was already past nine-thirty according to my watch. Time was a-wasting.

"Hey, where's Dad," Luke asked as he continued to scratch Fritz's scruff. "I don't see his van in the driveway. Is he around?"

"Nope. He left for a job in Tipton about an hour ago," Lars replied casually.

"*What*?" Luke exclaimed loudly. "He and I had an understanding he was taking me to the State Fair this morning. Did he forget? How could he do this?"

"He said he had an emergency and would be back around eleven o'clock," Lars continued.

"Around *eleven*?" Luke repeated. "Oh, this is terrible. I'm doomed. It'll take us at least an hour to get down there and parked. Maybe longer. Oh, this is bad. This is very, *very* bad. Dad's betrayed me."

"Calm down, will you? What's gotten into you?" Lars remarked. "There's always tomorrow. The fair doesn't close until Monday. You can go tomorrow if he gets back too late today. What's the hurry?"

"No. No. No. I can't go tomorrow. I have to go today. It's very important," Luke continued. "I can't believe this!" He sat with his head in his hands, running his fingers anxiously through his curly blonde hair. "What will I do now?"

"Will you take us this morning, Lars?" Emma asked, trying to be helpful. "In Mom's Bel Air? We should all be able to fit in that."

"No, sorry Emma, I can't. Dad has me going to Mrs. Haygood for him in about an hour to make a repair in her bathroom. Margret can't take you, either, I'm afraid, if you were thinking of asking her. She told me in the kitchen that Mrs. Patterson asked her to work today," Lars replied. "But you'll see. Dad'll be back in an hour or so, and you can go then. But if I were you, I'd wait until tomorrow and go early to beat the crowds."

Lars got up and walked inside with his book, passing Aunt Louise as she walked out of the house carrying a plastic laundry basket filled with clothes. She walked to the Bel Air parked in the driveway, placed the basket in the trunk, and then returned to walk back inside.

"Uh, Mom. Will you please run me down to the State Fair this morning?" Luke asked with a phony sweetness that made me smile it was so obvious.

Turning, she replied, "No, your father will be home later on to take you. He mentioned it to me before he left for his appointment, and he's looking forward to it. He'll be back soon. Just find your inner calm and don't fret so much. It's not good for your health." She smiled and walked inside the house.

"This is terrible. This totally louses me up," Luke muttered, his eyes cast down at the plastic gingham tablecloth. "Dad and I had this worked out. Then he changed everything on me. I can't believe it!"

"Let's just wait and see what happens," Jim encouraged him. "Maybe your Dad will return sooner than he thought he would. You never know."

"What time is it, Nessie Monster?" Luke asked. "The time please?"

I gazed down at my watch. "Ten after ten," I replied solemnly.

"Oh, this is terrible, terrible," Luke repeated, slapping the table hard.

"I'd better get ready to go," Emma suggested, taking her plate and going inside.

Jim, Luke, and I sat quietly. I was almost as upset by this development as Luke, but I kept my mouth shut to avoid adding to the drama.

"By the way, what is that smell? It's horrible," Jim asked, making a sour face. "It smells like your cooler, but I don't see it anywhere. Did you put that thing under the table?" He lifted up the edge of the tablecloth and looked beneath the table.

"No, but take a look at this," Luke replied, smiling.

He pulled up his shirt slightly to reveal Mr. Kleinschmidt's leather pouch strapped to his midsection. He quickly lowered his shirt and beamed. "Pretty smart, eh?" he boasted.

"What's that?" Jim asked. "Did you tape that thing to yourself? I thought you looked a little paunchy today."

"I sure did. Another one of my genius moves, if I may brag. I used the super-adhesive tape Dad uses on his jobs and some string and other stuff. No one will know it's there but us. Truly inspired, don't you think?"

"Yeah, dude, but you smell a bit overly ripe," Jim said. "The leather must have taken on the cooler's stench. Is there something you can do about that?"

"Maybe," Luke suggested. He went into the garage and emerged with two Christmas tree-shaped paper car deodorizers and held them up. "I borrowed these from the Bel Air. Mom'll never notice. Excuse me while I tape them on." He left and went inside, leaving Jim and me alone.

"I hope they're industrial strength!" Jim shouted after him.

After Luke was gone, Jim turned his attention back to me. "You look extra pretty today," he said, looking at me with his smiling eyes. "Your hair looks really nice worn down like that." He was wearing a dark green T-shirt that showed off his lean athletic build and late-summer tan.

"Gee, thanks," I answered. His compliment was unexpected and made me smile. "I can't believe this might be the last day we have to spend together for a long, long time. It makes me sad."

"Yeah. My mom wanted me to come home and help her pack today, but I told her I had plans to go to the fair with you guys, so she said it could wait," he replied, sighing deeply and spinning a spoon on the table. "I can't take all the heavy stuff my family's going through right now. I've been thinking lately that I'll run away from it all and join the circus. Wouldn't that be something? I could get a job cleaning up after the elephants. They always need someone to clean up after the elephants, don't they?"

"I'll come with you and join the circus, too!" I replied. "I could take care of the trapeze lady's wardrobe. I'm good at sewing sequins and gluing feathers. They always need someone to take care of the trapeze lady's outfits, don't they?"

We looked at each other and laughed. It felt good to laugh, especially with him.

Suddenly, Daniel walked up from the back yard. He was wearing a Western-style plaid shirt with snap closures and jeans, and not his frontier fringed jacket or Civil War shirt. It was one of the few times I'd seen him in "civilian" clothing. "What's going on? Are we leaving for the fair soon?" he asked.

"No, we're waiting for Uncle Evert to return from a job," I replied.

"What?" Daniel exclaimed. "It's almost eleven! How will Luke make his appointment by one?"

Jim and I nodded. "Yeah, how will he?" I asked.

Daniel sat down, and eventually Luke and Emma came out and joined us. The five us drummed our fingers and fidgeted as we waited for Uncle Evert to return. Every ten minutes or so Luke asked me what time it was, to which I'd try to give him a straight answer, instead of replying, "ten minutes since you last asked."

Eleven o'clock rolled around and still there was no sign of Uncle Evert. Then it was ten after and then fifteen after. Time was passing too quickly.

"What rides do you want to go on at the fair?" Jim asked. I sensed he was trying to distract us and help pass the time.

"I really love the Ferris Wheel," I answered eagerly. "But I like lots of other rides, too. It'd sure be fun if we all rode the bumper cars together at the same time, wouldn't it? We could drive around crashing into each other, as long as we don't hit each other too hard, that is."

"Well, I'm not signing any treaties. If you're riding on the bumper cars when I am, you're taking your chances," Luke warned. "I hit hard."

"Why do you always have to sound like such a caveman?" Daniel remarked. Luke looked at him and smirked.

"I'm really looking forward to having an elephant ear. Mmm! They're so good!" Emma said, making a blissful face. She placed her hand on her stomach for emphasis.

"Have a few of those and you'll look like a real elephant, Sis," Luke taunted. She glowered back at him in response.

Finally, at eleven thirty, there was the sound of the crunching gravel and Uncle Evert's blue van pulled up. Luke's eyes became big, and he jumped up and ran to greet his father.

"Come on, Dad. Let's go. We have to get to the fair. Everybody get in! Come on everyone!" Luke sputtered, gesturing for everyone to get into the van.

"What's this? Don't you want to wait until tomorrow to get an earlier start?" Uncle Evert asked as he opened the door and stepped out.

"No. The Percherons show is today at the Coliseum, not tomorrow. Got to see those Percherons. I'm a big draft horse fan, you know," Luke babbled. "Time to go! Into the van, everyone. Chop chop!" He clapped his hands together.

"All right. If it means that much to you. I'll be right back," Uncle Evert replied. He walked down the sidewalk and went into the house.

Luke hastily took Fritz, who'd shadowed his every move, over to the barn and put him inside a small fenced area and left a plate of food and a water bowl for him. Fritz was definitely Luke's dog at this point. His big brown eyes almost looked sad as he watched Luke hurry back to the van.

Jim, Emma, and I went to the van and dutifully took our positions in the second seat. Daniel made his way back to the third seat which Uncle Evert sometimes installed for occasions like this. Luke jumped into the passenger seat up front, keeping all of the doors open to capture whatever breezes blew through. Impatient, he laid on the horn and tooted it over and over again.

"Cut that out!" someone shouted loudly from inside the house. Uncle Evert appeared moments later looking annoyed, followed by Aunt Louise wearing a summery white dress and pretty flat sandals. She carried a straw bag with three-dimensional straw fruit and vegetables on one side.

"Get in the back, mister, and make room for your mother, before I wring your neck for making all that racket!" Uncle Evert said. Luke made his way to the very back and sat next to Daniel.

"Mom went shopping for some new clothes. Aren't they pretty?" Emma whispered to me. I nodded in agreement.

Now we were finally ready to go. It was eleven forty-five. Uncle Evert turned south on Allisonville Road and we began the long drive down to the state fairgrounds in Indianapolis. We'd only been underway a few moments when Uncle Evert made a face.

"What in blazes is that terrible smell?" he exclaimed, twisting his face in disgust. "Luke! You don't have that cooler in this van, do you? You remember what I said about never putting that thing in this vehicle, don't you? Luke!"

"No, Dad. I remember what you said and wouldn't dare bring the cooler. I swear! Maybe there's a dead a squirrel in the transmission," Luke shouted from the back. "Those can be pretty smelly."

"Shoo! That's strong whatever it is. Everyone open the windows and let's get some fresh air in here," Uncle Evert instructed. "Funny I didn't smell that when I was out just now."

We opened every window as wide as possible. I turned and gave Luke a knowing look, and he winked back.

We finally reached Fall Creek Parkway in Indianapolis. Uncle Evert turned on it and proceeded for several blocks and then turned again onto 42nd Street to look for parking. Traffic was already badly backed up. Moving slowly bumper-to-bumper, we made our way west toward the grassy fields where general parking for the fair was provided. Workers were posted every so often waving red flags, directing vehicles where to go. Several residents living along 42nd Street allowed visitors to park in their small yards for fifty cents a vehicle, which was double the price to park in the fields. They sat in lawn chairs with their homemade signs waving energetically at the stream of cars passing by, some shouting like carnival barkers to "park now." Many of those yards were already completely filled.

"Let's park in one of these yards, Dad," Luke suggested from the back of the van. "Easy in and out for just an additional twenty-five cents. What a deal. Whaddaya say? We could save time that way."

"No, siree," Uncle Evert replied, his eyes riveted on the road. "I don't trust most of them. You could come looking for your car at the end of the day and find it's gone and no one has the slightest idea where it went."

He pulled up to an attendant and gave him a quarter, then drove on. We bounced along the bumpy and dusty road etched in the grass until we were finally directed by a man with a red flag to the next parking space in a sea of parked vehicles. I looked at my watch. It was now twelve thirty-five. Luke had to hurry if he was going to get to the Reynolds Farm Equipment display by one o'clock.

We walked together to the north gate of the fairgrounds directly on the other side of 42nd Street and stood in a long line to get in. Luke was anxious and couldn't stand still. When we'd finally made it to the front of the line, Luke produced the coupon clipped from the newspaper that allowed free entry for groups of any size. We were allowed in and walked through the gate. I could hear the loud roar of farm equipment firing up not far from us, and could smell the sweet aroma of caramel corn being popped in a nearby red-and-white food stand. The spectacle of the other fairgoers in various sizes, shapes, and ages, some wearing skimpy clothing, others pushing strollers and chasing their screaming children, fascinated me.

Uncle Evert herded us to the edge of the sidewalk and then reached for his wallet and gave each one of us a dollar to spend as we pleased. He generously included Jim, Daniel, and me in the distribution.

"Be sure to meet back here at this exact spot at four o'clock. Four o'clock, everyone. Got that?" He looked each of us in the eye to make certain he'd been heard above the noise that seemed to come from every direction.

"Ah, Dad. That's awfully early. How about five?" Luke suggested. He fidgeted with his hands in his pockets, anxious to get started.

"Well, all right. Five it is, but not a minute later or you'll have to catch a ride home in a cattle truck," he said, smiling.

"Evert, let's go over to the Woman's Building. I read in the paper this morning there's a gladiola show there. I'd like to see them," Aunt Louise suggested.

Uncle Evert seemed to agree with her suggestion and they strolled away together. After they had merged into the crowd, Luke turned and spoke to us excitedly.

"Okay, people. Let's go find the Reynolds Farm Equipment display, shall we?" He patted the bulge under his shirt and smiled slyly. "It's getting pretty close to one o'clock. It's *showtime*!"

I looked at my watch. It was now twelve forty-six.

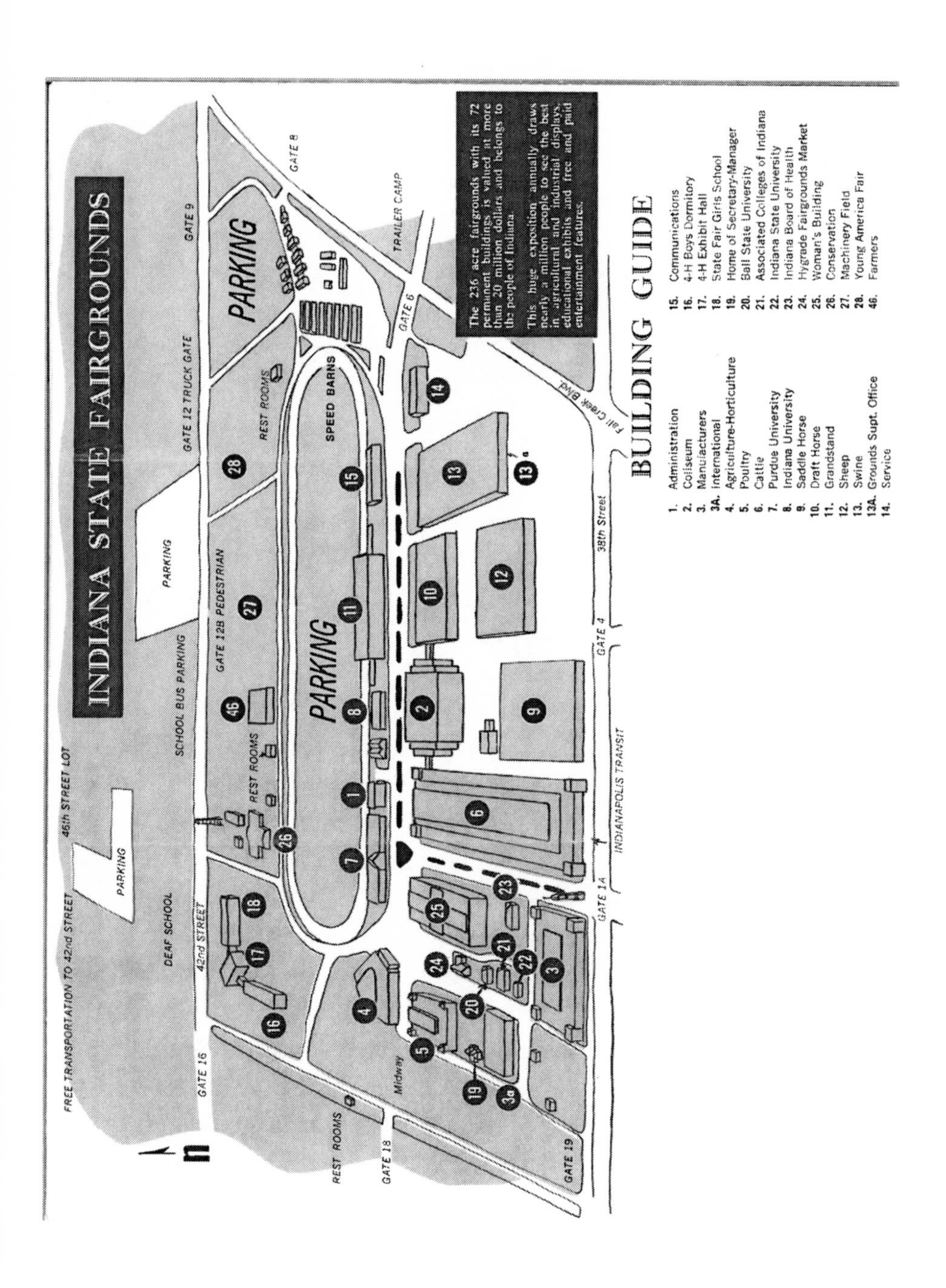

1967 Map of the Indiana State Fairgrounds.

CHAPTER TWENTY-TWO

The Boy From F.I.S.H.E.R.S.

The Indiana State Fairgrounds extends from 42nd Street on the north, south to 38th Street, and from Winthrop Avenue on the west to Fall Creek Parkway on the east. In the middle of this expanse is a one-mile oval dirt track on which harness racing, concerts, rodeos, and other outdoor events take place. The Grandstand on the south side of the track accommodates approximately 14,000 spectators. During the fair, the road ringing the outside of the track, also known as the ring road, is lined with vendors selling lemon shake-ups, elephant ears, caramel corn, taffy, funnel cakes, corn dogs, and other assorted foods and trinkets designed to entice fairgoers. These particular vendors are in addition to scores of other vendors scattered throughout the fair.

As we proceeded beyond the gate where we entered, shuttles dubbed people movers, that is, wagons lined with benches on both sides pulled by farm tractors, came one after the other along the ring road, all going in a clockwise direction. Each one bore a distinctive orange Hygrade Food Products Corporation logo on its tractor. We hurried out to the first one we saw and walked the length of its numerous wagons looking for seats. We couldn't find enough for all five of us, so we gave up and waited for the next one. Jim argued Luke didn't have time to wait and should get on the next one alone if he had to so he wouldn't be late.

"I think I can walk to the farm equipment area faster than trying to get on one of these darned shuttles," Luke observed in frustration.

Fortunately, the next shuttle arrived less than two minutes later. We quickly fanned out, walking both sides of the wagons, and at last were able to find enough scattered seats in the very last wagon for all of us. The tractor fired up just as we sat down. We finally moved forward. My heart was racing as the minutes ticked by and the meeting time approached. I turned and located Luke sitting on the other side, trying to adjust the bundle around his midsection without being noticed. I could imagine that by now the special tape was starting to pull at his skin and itch uncomfortably. Emma and I sat together. Jim and Daniel weren't too far from us, and they waved back cheerfully when I looked over at them.

The shuttle proceeded slowly and seemed to stop every few hundred yards to let people on and off. The endless stopping and starting made me unbearably anxious. It was now ten 'til one. Luke had only ten minutes left to find *Herr* Richter.

People of all ages and sizes walked alongside the shuttle as we rolled along at almost the same plodding speed as they. Some pedestrians were oblivious to the shuttle's presence. So much so that occasionally the driver had to toot his horn to get a particularly unaware person to move out of the way. We came upon one such man wearing a knit cap, a garment that seemed strangely out of place on such a hot day. He appeared to be alone and was walking almost directly in the path of the shuttle. After the driver tooted his horn, the man stepped aside and scowled back at the driver as we proceeded through. I was stunned to notice that he looked a lot like the man with the skull tattoo. I couldn't be certain because he had the knit cap on. Still, I became concerned and jabbed Emma in the side.

"Is that the Soviet? He sure looks a lot like him," I whispered after we'd rolled past him. "Over there." I pointed toward him with my hand low in my lap so as not to be noticed.

She turned to look, but the man didn't turn around, and we'd traveled too far away to be able to see him well.

"I've never seen him, but that's probably not him," she replied, turning back around. "Why would the Soviet come to a fair with a bunch of Indiana farm stuff?"

She had a point, but I turned to warn Luke anyway. His seat was too far away on the other side to be able to hear me. It bothered me to think the skull tattoo guy might be at the fair. He couldn't be there for pleasure.

That meant he was either following us, or somehow knew there was to be a rendezvous with *Herr* Richter today. Maybe it was he we heard last night when there was rustling in the woods as we sat at the dining room table. Could he have overheard Luke and Jim discussing the details of today's meeting? I had a bad feeling about this. Of course, it was always possible the man in the knit hat wasn't the Soviet. I hoped with all my heart I was mistaken.

As we approached the expansive grassy area where large farm equipment was displayed, Luke stood on the wagon's narrow running board and gestured for everyone to get off at the next stop. The shuttle finally stopped and we hopped off. We were in front of what looked like a giant parking lot filled with new tractors, cultivators, balers, plows, threshers, and other farm equipment.

"Where's the Reynolds Farm Equipment display?" Daniel asked, looking around. "I don't see any signs."

"It's got to be around here pretty close by," Luke replied, doing a three-sixty. "Wait! I think I see the word 'Reynolds' over there." He pointed to a spot behind a giant combine harvester. "What time is it now, Nessie?"

I looked at my watch. "One o'clock on the nose," I reported. "But Luke, I need to tell you something."

"Not now, Nessie. It's time to meet *Herr* Richter," Luke said as he took a deep breath and took off in the direction of the sign.

We followed him as he made his way quickly through the yard filled with shiny red International Harvester tractors of all sizes, and with green John Deere combine harvesters, rotary tillers, and drill planters. At the back behind all of the massive equipment was a sign that read "Reynolds Farm Equipment – a John Deere distributor."

"There it is!" Emma shouted, pointing gleefully. "At last! I hope we're not late."

We rushed over to the sign like thirsty cattle to a stream. I looked around for a man with an extra-bushy moustache and a loden green hat, but no one remotely fitting that description was in the area. Only a handful of people were there—people who looked like farmers and other regular fair-goers, and not like a German-born scientist with a bushy moustache waiting to receive anti-gravity secrets. Luke walked around looking for the gentleman, and then paced up and down, too anxious to stand still. The minutes ticked by.

"Maybe we've missed him," Emma suggested. "Or maybe he cancelled the appointment and there was no way for us to know."

"No. He'll be here. I know he will. He just *has* to show," Luke insisted, looking stressed. He wandered around behind some tractors and then came back, looking perplexed and pursing his lips. Where could the infamous *Herr* Richter be? More time passed.

"You kids need something?" a man wearing a short-sleeved white shirt with a narrow black tie and black slacks asked as he walked by. He had on a name tag that said "Len Chambers - Salesman."

"No, thanks," Luke replied. Then, thinking further, he asked, "Excuse me, sir. Do you possibly know a man by the name of Otto Richter? He works for the Modern Propulsion Company. We're supposed to meet him here."

"No, can't say that I do," the man said, shaking his head. "Never heard of that company, either. But you're welcome to hang out around here until he shows up." He looked at us as though we were lost children.

"Oh, okay. Thanks," Luke said. He looked disappointed, and absent-mindedly kicked a clod of dirt in a depression in the grass left by heavy machinery passing through.

The salesman walked away and struck up a conversation with a man and woman several feet away standing near a combine. While Luke continued pacing, it seemed like a good time to tell him about the man with the knit cap.

"Luke, I might have seen Igor—you know, the Soviet—when we were on the shuttle. The man I saw had on a knit cap so I couldn't be sure," I advised him. "Maybe I was seeing things and it wasn't him. I don't know."

"What? No, it couldn't have been him. Why would that ugly bastard be at the State Fair?" Luke blustered. "Nah. If you ask me, the Soviet's probably breaking into Mr. Kleinschmidt's lab right now looking for these documents I have right here. The misguided sucker! There's no way he knows I have them." He smugly tapped the pouch under his shirt.

"Okay. Whatever you say," I replied, but fearing he was being too quick to dismiss the possibility.

"What time is it now, Nessie? I want to get this over with," he asked, getting back to business.

I checked my watch. "One forty-five," I replied. *Herr* Richter was now exactly forty-five minutes late. I was starting to doubt he was coming.

"I'll give Richter at least one hour before I start worrying about him standing me up," Luke said, doing his best to sound positive. "He could be stuck in traffic or have some other reason to be late. You never know. Heck, we were almost late getting here ourselves."

I wanted to agree with him, but something didn't feel quite right. We stood at the Reynolds Farm Equipment display for several more minutes. Now my watch indicated it was two fifteen. No one except families and old farmers walked through the display. Even Len Chambers, the salesman, looked over a couple of times and offered a sympathetic smile. I could tell by Luke's manner that his optimism *Herr* Richter would turn up was starting to erode. Then, Jim had an idea.

"Didn't Kleinschmidt give you a code word to use? *Frieden* or something like that? Maybe if you walk around and say that word Mr. Richter will come forward," Jim suggested. "Maybe Richter shaved his moustache, and left his hat at home. He may look completely different. You've got to realize there's no way he knows Kleinschmidt sent us in his place."

"What are you suggesting? That I should walk around here like a fool saying that word in strangers' faces? No way. I'll sound like I just busted out of Central State," Luke replied, waving his hand dismissively.

"Well, what then?" Daniel asked impatiently. He climbed up on a John Deere tractor on display and sat in the seat.

"I'll come up with something. What time is it now, Nessie?" Luke asked again.

"Two thirty-five," I replied.

"You're being stood up," Daniel insisted, looking down from his high vantage point on the tractor. "Richter isn't coming. Face it. He's over an hour-and-a-half late. I don't see anyone from up here that could be him."

"Don't say that. He'll turn up. Come on, you guys. Everyone fan out and look for him. He's got to be around," Luke urged. "I'll stay here by the Reynolds sign in case he comes over here. Go find him before it gets any later."

"I'm bored with this, Luke. That man isn't here, and I don't think he's coming. Mr. Kleinschmidt must have been mistaken about when the meeting was supposed to be," Emma complained. "Let's go have some fun in the Midway. We can't hang around here all day. Dad only gave us until five o'clock. I want to get an elephant ear."

"Emma has a point. Let's go for now. Richter might show up while we're enjoying the rest of the fair. I'll come back with you later to look for him. He may still show up. Maybe something came up or he got the meeting time mixed up," Jim suggested to the crestfallen Luke.

"I can't believe he didn't come," Luke lamented, still peering intently at every person who walked nearby. "Something must have gone wrong. I'll tell that salesman that I have something to give Richter when he shows up, and that he should tell him to stick around and wait for me."

"Do you think you should? Can you trust that guy? We don't know who he is," Daniel warned, jumping down from the tractor.

"Sure. He must be okay if he works for Reynolds. I'll be right back," Luke said.

He walked over and spoke to Len Chambers, who nodded and appeared to understand. Then he ran back to where we were standing.

"Okay, I'm ready. Let's go," Luke said with a sigh. "But I'll be back, and Richter will be here when I do. I know he will."

We walked through the farm equipment area to the ring road and looked for a shuttle to take us all the way around to the Midway. As we did, I overheard Luke whisper "*Frieden*" quietly under his breath to an older gentleman as he passed by. The man looked back at Luke and frowned, confused, then continued on.

"Freakin' *Frieden*," Luke groused. "Some lousy freakin' secret code word if there ever was one."

CHAPTER TWENTY-THREE

Cat and Mouse

Luke, Emma, Jim, Daniel, and I ambled along the ring road toward the Midway, our destination. We decided to walk instead of ride the shuttle. This allowed us to check out the various vendors selling elephant ears, cotton candy, sunglasses, lemonade, pineapple whip, personalized license plates, plastic jewelry, and other treats and goods as we slowly made our way along with the crowd. The track was just on the other side of the chain-link fence running along the edge of the ring road. I could hear the muffled voice of an announcer on the loud speakers at the Grandstand as Jack Kochman's Hell Drivers prepared to present a stunt car show on the other side of the dirt track.

Emma stopped to purchase an elephant ear, and then we continued on. We walked past the Farmers Building, the Conservation Building, the 4-H Exhibit Hall and 4-H Boys Dormitory, and the State Fair Girls School, until we rounded the bend and passed over the bridge under which cars passed to access the parking lot inside the track.

We finally came to the colorful archway bearing the word *Midway*. At last we were at the official gateway to thrilling rides, hokey funhouses, and games of skill, all flanked by the giant Ferris Wheel at the western edge. A twelve-foot clock with a long, rectangular face and a Coca-Cola sign underneath was temporarily erected in the middle just for the run of the fair. Luke ran up to the first ticket stand he saw and purchased a strip of tickets. The rest of us got in line behind him and did the same. Now armed with official State Fair currency, we began walking through the noisy, colorful chaos looking for appealing rides to spend them on.

"Hey there, young man. You're strong," the operator of a game solicited Luke as he passed near him. "I'll bet you can knock down all of those bottles on the table over there on your first try. Sure you can. Here you go, three balls for just one ticket."

Luke slowed down and seemed to consider the proposition. The barker, a bald man with a large gut and a cigarette dangling from his mouth, held three white balls the size of tennis balls in one hand, his fingers curled around them in such a way that the balls fanned out. It was both impressive and mildly creepy.

"Just one ticket. Win one of these fine prizes for your lovely young lady there. Which prize would you like, young lady?" the barker asked. I was standing next to Luke and he recoiled when he realized the barker thought I was his girlfriend.

"Her? Oh no. *She's* not my young lady!" Luke said with a look of disdain.

He walked over to the long table where contestants stood to throw the balls, and checked out the set up. A table stood at the opposite side of the booth with three white milk bottles stacked on it like a small pyramid.

"There you go, young man. See how easy it is? Go ahead. Take these balls and knock 'em down," the man said, handing the three balls to Luke.

Luke ripped a ticket off the end of his strip of tickets and handed it to the man. After a brief pause, he threw a ball with the force of a hurricane toward the three stacked bottles. It slammed against the canvas sheet hanging at the back of the booth, missing the bottles by several inches. He quickly threw a second ball, which sped by the stacked bottles by several inches on the opposite side of where his first ball had flown.

"What an arm you have!" the barker exclaimed. "One more."

Luke picked up the last ball and stuck out his tongue as he concentrated in preparation to throw it. This was his last chance to win something, as well as to prove his athletic ability to the rest of us watching.

"I think this game is rigged," Daniel whispered to Jim. "Those bottles have weights in them or something to keep them upright." Jim nodded in agreement.

Suddenly, there was a familiar voice from behind us. I turned and saw it was Hawes, the boy who'd picked on Luke at the drive-in, and his two dubious friends.

"Well, look who it is, guys," Hawes said in his high-pitched twang. "Can't hit the side of a barn, can you, Larsson? Let's watch, guys. This should be worth a good laugh."

"Get out of here, Hawes. You, too, Clyde and Roscoe. Move along," Luke chided.

"Hey, it's a free country. Who's going to make us?" Hawes mocked. "I don't see your bodyguard Bunny around here anywhere." He laughed in a high-pitched, nasal tone.

"Why you!" Luke exclaimed. He turned and appeared about to swing at Hawes, but Jim prevented it by quickly moving between them.

"Come on you guys. Move along, will you?" Jim said. "Don't make trouble."

"Who's making trouble?" Hawes said with a sneer. He was tall and very thin, and stood with his shoulders hunched forward. "We're just making chitchat." Hawes chortled and exchanged mocking glances with his two friends.

The barker grew impatient for Luke to get on with it. "Come on kid. Throw the ball. I'm trying to make a living here. Move it," he said, flicking his cigarette ashes on the ground.

Luke turned back to the table, and without pausing, hurled the third ball toward the bottles. It hit the top bottle and knocked it off with a loud "pop!"

"Yeah!" I exclaimed, clapping my hands together. "You did it!"

Seeing that Luke had success, Hawes and his two friends slowly strolled away without further comment.

"I hate that guy," Luke muttered, watching them as they left.

"Just ignore him," Jim replied. "Bullies like Hawes eventually get their comeuppance."

"Yeah, but it's taking too long for him to get his," Luke lamented angrily. "I'd sure like to be the one to give it to him."

Luke turned toward the barker with a look of pride. "Here you go kid," the barker said, handing Luke a pair of pink, clown-sized plastic sunglasses. "Nice job."

Luke looked crestfallen. "What's this? What about the stuffed animals?" he said, rejecting the sunglasses. "I want that one." He pointed to a bright yellow Tweety Bird hanging on a wall covered with colorful stuffed animals.

"You got to knock down all three milk bottles to get one of those," the barker said, flicking his cigarette. "Want to try again? I'll bet you can do it this time. That'll be another ticket." He put his hand out to take the ticket as Luke reached into his back pocket to retrieve one.

"Luke, we've really got to move along now," Daniel whispered in Luke's ear. "Take the sunglasses and let's go."

"Oh, all right," Luke grumbled, picking up the sunglasses. "But what am I supposed to do with these?"

"Wear them," Emma said, grabbing the sunglasses out of Luke's hand and sliding them on her face. They were so large she had to tilt her head back to keep them on. It was a funny sight, and we burst out laughing.

Once we collected ourselves, we continued walking through the Midway. We passed the Tilt-A-Whirl as it spun people in clamshell-shaped cars while moving continuously up and down in a circle, and the Scrambler, a large pendulum that rocked screaming riders ten stories high and then dropped them almost to the pavement only to swing them up ten stories again.

Even though it was a very warm day, there was a pleasant breeze, and the sky was clear blue with white fluffy clouds. I felt happy and nudged Jim's arm playfully. He took my hand and we walked along hand-in-hand. I took a deep breath and felt content.

"I'll always remember this day," Emma purred. "All of us being at the State Fair like this having fun." Emma wasn't usually a sentimental person, at least not as far as I could tell.

"Me, too," I replied with a happy sigh. I looked up at Jim and he smiled back.

Unfortunately, our happy state was about to be interrupted. We had just stopped at the Spider to consider riding it, when the man with the skull tattoo suddenly came into view. He was standing on the other side of the Midway by the bumper cars. We all seemed to spot him at the same time. He was staring into the crowd, oblivious to the river of people with packages, children, and strollers swirling around him. Now that I had a good look at him, there was no doubting that it was him, even though he was wearing the navy knit hat that completely concealed his skull tattoo.

"Oh, my god! There's the skull tattoo guy!" Luke exclaimed. "I hope he hasn't seen us."

Almost as if he had radar, the Soviet's gaze slowly redirected itself toward us. I knew he'd seen us when a look of recognition suddenly animated his face. His countenance was sinister and haunting. He immediately started walking toward us. His jaw and mouth were set with the look of raw determination. It was clear he meant business.

"Oh, my god! What should we do?" I shouted. "Why is he here?"

"We've got to split up. He can't chase us all at the same time. I'm probably the one he wants. Emma and Vanessa, go find Mom and Dad and tell them we need help. They're probably still in the Woman's Building. Find them and stay with them where it's safe," Luke directed. "Daniel, Jim, and I will fan out through the fair and try to lose him."

"Luke, why don't you ditch that package before it's too late?" Jim suggested earnestly. "Throw it into that thresher they're demonstrating back there and shred it. That way at least the skull tattoo guy and the Soviets will never get their hands on it and use it to harm the world. If you don't have it on you, he'll surely leave you alone."

"No, I could never do that!" Luke insisted. "These documents contain the results of years of research by a genius physicist. They're the key to unlocking the mystery of anti-gravity! How could I destroy that? This stuff is too important. No, if I can't find Richter to give them to him, then I've got to get them safely back to Mr. Kleinschmidt. It's my solemn duty. I gave him my word."

"Enough talking already," Emma shouted. "Let's get out of here!"

She grabbed my hand and pulled me along with her, while the boys ran in the opposite direction. She and I wove our way through the rides and vendors selling food and finally emerged at the ring road. I looked back and saw the Soviet getting closer. He appeared to be coming after Emma and me, not the boys. A shuttle stopped right in front of us, and we ran around to the opposite side where we had the best chance not to be seen. We got on the shuttle without thinking or caring where it was going. I just wanted out of there. Once we were under way, I realized the shuttle was going to the back side of the fair where we'd just been, instead of toward the front side where the Woman's Building was and where my aunt and uncle would most likely be.

We jumped off when it stopped in front of the Conservation Building and ran in through the side door of the limestone-clad building. We emerged in a large room with a high ceiling in which crowds were clustered along the outer walls looking at fish in large tanks built into the walls. We weren't there long when the Soviet came through the front door and scanned the room looking for us. It was bright out and it took a moment for his eyes to adjust to the dark interior. We quickly joined in with a group of people looking at a tank filled with flathead catfish and black bullhead fish and turned our backs.

"Just act natural and maybe he won't recognize us," I whispered to Emma, barely able to choke out the words in my panic. We turned our faces away and pushed even more closely into the crowd.

The Soviet walked slowly around the room, examining people's faces in a fairly direct and bold way as he went, prompting odd looks in return. As he proceeded with his investigation along the opposite side of the room, Emma and I made our way through a room in the back filled with antique farm implements. We found a back door and exited the building. Not long after, our pursuer came out through the same door. I couldn't tell if he'd seen us leave or if it was a coincidence he left through the same door, but he seemed to be closing in just the same. We had to do something more creative if we were going to elude him.

"We've got to split up," I shouted to Emma as she ran ahead of me through a tent where colorful scarves and woven bed coverlets were sold. "He's right behind us."

She ran out of the tent and veered off behind a small stage where young girls were in the middle of a tap-dance competition, and crouched behind a speaker and other sound equipment.

"Split up?" Emma asked, looking puzzled. "But why?"

"You can get around faster than I can, and he thinks he's looking for two girls, not one. Let's give it a try. I'll catch up with you later, I promise."

"Well, if that's what you want, I guess it's okay. Just be careful and don't let anything happen to you. Okay?" she said, shooting me an encouraging smile.

"You, too, Emmie. Take care of yourself," I replied, feeling unexpectedly emotional.

She paused to consider her next move, then moved out and walked along the edge of the stage, cut behind a shuttle, and joined a group of teenagers walking up the driveway that ran along the edge of the large grassy yard in front of the 4-H Building and 4-H Boys Dormitory. They were walking toward its main entrance, and she easily blended in with them.

As for me, I remained crouched along to the edge of the stage while I contemplated what I should do. A wagon drawn by two massive oxen carrying a large load of hay appeared nearby. When it passed directly beside me, I hustled out and walked along on the opposite side of it for several yards as it rolled out to the ring road and then toward the infield bridge. Its tall load of hay provided an excellent shield. Just before the wagon reached the bridge, I broke away and scurried down the embankment to the underpass where cars were steadily entering and leaving the infield parking lot. To my surprise, Jim and Luke were also down there, standing together on the concrete sidewalk in the shadow of the bridge overhead.

"Nessie! What are you doing here? Did Igor see you come down here?" Luke scolded. "I sure hope you didn't lead him straight to us. I bet you did."

"Ignore him, Vanessa. It's good to see you. Where's Emma?" Jim asked, looking behind me for her.

"The Soviet followed Emma and me into the Conservation Building, so we ran out the back and separated. I hid beside an ox wagon to get here. I don't think he saw me. He won't look for us down here, will he? It's kinda out of the way." I was having a difficult time pulling my eyes away from the top of the embankment where the skull tattoo guy might appear at any moment.

"He might. Maybe we should keep moving, especially now that there're three of us," Luke proposed.

"Why don't we give it a second? If he crosses the bridge, we'll have a tactical advantage being behind him where we can keep an eye on him," Jim suggested.

"Okay. That's a good idea," Luke agreed, settling back.

The three of us lined up side-by-side against the wall. Cars drove beside us as they came and went, unaware of the grave predicament we were in. In one of the cars leaving the parking lot, a gaudy sunflower garden stake purchased at the fair was visible through an open window.

"Wish I had one of those lovely sunflower things. I bet it'd make a good weapon," Luke quipped. I nervously laughed in response, but the reality of what he said made me pause to wonder. Could things possibly come to that?

Suddenly, a deep voice spoke. I looked up, and saw the skull tattoo guy looking down at us from the edge of the bridge.

"There you are, my little mice!" he snarled. He began loping down the embankment toward us.

"Run!" Luke shouted as he took off sprinting toward the in-field parking lot.

Jim and I followed Luke as he took a zigzag course through the parked cars, going down one aisle, cutting through the parked cars to the next aisle, and then down that aisle to the next. We ran flat out as fast as we could, and finally made it to a pedestrian tunnel running under the track. We ran down the steps, through the long concrete corridor, and back up the steps to the ground level, emerging behind the Indiana University Building opposite the Coliseum. This area of the fair was the most popular. The sidewalks were crowded with slow-moving fair-goers and vendors selling food from their white trailers and tents, making it easier to disappear, but also more difficult to move through quickly.

"Luke! The Coliseum!" Jim yelled as we made our way through the crowd.

Luke dutifully complied and darted across the ring road in front of a stopped shuttle and bolted to the other side. He cut through a line of people waiting to purchase pork tenderloin sandwiches, ran to the front doors of the Coliseum, pulled open the heavy brass doors, and went inside. Jim and I followed close behind.

One of the gates, or portals, into the Coliseum's giant arena was straight ahead, and we ran up the ramp and climbed several steps until we emerged into the cavernous space where basketball games, animal shows, and rock concerts were held from time to time. It was illuminated by light from several large windows filled with glass block, and had cloth banners advertising various farm products hanging on the outer walls high above the seats. Luke turned and continued up a flight of concrete steps until we came to a walkway separating the lower and upper seats all around the arena.

A Percheron draft horse show was in progress down on the floor. The enormous horses were fitted out in silver harnesses and yoked in teams of six to fancy farm wagons with chrome embellishments, each with a male driver in dressy attire and a female passenger in an evening gown. One at a time, the farm wagons pulled by their teams sped around the arena. The sound of the thunderous clopping of the hooves of the massive animals on the dirt floor filled the air, as did the earthy odors of horses and hay.

"Should we sit?" Luke whispered.

"Might as well. Let's find a group we can blend in with," Jim suggested.

We proceeded along the walkway to the opposite side, and then Luke walked down an aisle to a row near the front where most of the spectators were seated. He selected seats next to two extremely heavy men in overalls wearing farm caps with the iconic red and black International Harvester logo on them, and sat down. At last I could relax for a moment and collect myself.

As if on cue, the Soviet entered the arena on the opposite side. He paused to look around, and then slowly walked along the walkway dividing the upper and lower sections of seats, peering up and down the aisles. His tall, muscular physique was silhouetted against the light-colored wall behind him. I could spot him easily, especially with the knit cap he wore. I was glad Luke had chosen seats on our side of the stands, but we needed to get out of there now that he'd arrived.

"Oh, my god. I'm so scared," I fretted. "What will we do when he finds us over here? It's only a matter of minutes until he does."

"Take it easy. It'll take him some time to work his way over here. We need to get out of here, but let's not get up and leave right away. We'll have to choose just the right moment so we don't draw attention to ourselves," Luke strategized.

My eyes were riveted on the sinister form as he slowly and methodically made his way around the gigantic space, studying almost every person he passed. It wasn't too long before I noticed another man who seemed to be acting rather suspiciously also. This other man wore sunglasses and a baseball cap, and stood off by himself near an emergency exit. I recalled that this man had entered the arena not long after the skull tattoo guy. The thing that caught my attention was that the man in the baseball cap didn't take a seat, and didn't appear at all interested in the competition unfolding on the Coliseum floor. He just stood off to the side, calmly smoking and watching the skull tattoo guy. As the Soviet moved along, the mystery man would move along also, each time finding a new out-of-the-way spot from which to continue his observations.

"Do you see that man over there with the baseball cap and sunglasses?" I asked the guys.

"Who? That guy?" Luke asked, pointing toward the mystery man. "Not until now. Why? Kinda weird that he's wearing sunglasses indoors. Who does he think he is—a rock star?"

"I don't know. This may sound crazy, but I think he might be shadowing the Soviet," I suggested. Luke looked unconvinced. "No, really," I added. "He came in right after him, and hasn't paid any attention to the horse show."

"Maybe he came in here to get out of the heat, and couldn't care less about the Percherons or the Russkie. It's pretty hot out there today, you know. It's not too bad in here," Luke said.

"Maybe he's a security guard or a cop hired to keep an eye on things at the fair," Jim suggested.

"Does a security guard or a cop wear a baseball cap?" I asked.

"I see what you mean, Nessie," Luke said after observing the two men a while longer. "Something's up with that guy in the baseball cap, that's for sure. I hope he's not going to make trouble for us. It's bad enough to have to run from a Soviet thug without adding another bad guy into the mix."

Just then, the two large men in overalls sitting next to us got up and scooted by us to leave.

"Up you guys! Moe and Curly are leaving. Let's go!" Luke said softly as he bounced up and followed the two men up the aisle.

The three of us followed the men to the exit, walking extra-close to them as we went to try to minimize our presence. The men didn't appear to notice us or care, and probably thought we were just being silly teenagers. Before I walked out, I took one last peek back into the arena. A chill came over me when I saw the skull tattoo guy staring back at me across the vast stadium, and the mystery man, in turn, watching the skull tattoo guy.

CHAPTER TWENTY-FOUR

The Unexpected Hero

Luke, Jim, and I ran down the steps to the gate leading out to the lobby, scurried around the lobby to the front door, and ran outside as quickly as we could. I didn't know how close the Soviet was and didn't want to know. All I knew was that I had to get out of there as fast as I could without knocking anyone down. Dodging people and strollers, we ran past the red brick Cattle Barn and across State Fair Boulevard to a wide paved area in front of the Purdue University Building and the Dairy Bar where there was a large Sutter's taffy stand the size of a small store. Large crowds milled around several packed shuttles making their circuit around the ring road. Luke ran behind a giant pretzel stand and stopped to discuss our next move.

"Luke, we need to find your parents and get their help," Jim said, breathing hard. "That guy's just too dangerous for us to handle alone. Didn't your parents say they were going to the Woman's Building? Maybe we should go there and try to find them." The Woman's Building wasn't too far from where we were.

"I'm not convinced yet that I should give up and let them in on Mr. Kleinschmidt's secret," Luke resisted. "He warned me not to tell them anything, remember? He said they'd be in danger if I did."

"But I'm scared of that man," I chimed in. "I'd feel better if we found Uncle Evert and Aunt Louise and got their help. Or, maybe we should go to the police. I know you don't want to, but...."

"I'm definitely not going to bring the police into this. Besides, I haven't seen a cop since we passed those guys directing traffic when we first got here. No, let's just keep going through the fair and see what happens. Who knows? We might get lucky and shake that goon off our tails."

"Fat chance," I replied sarcastically.

"City Slicker—you're getting on my nerves!" Luke replied with pursed lips. "Get with the program—or else!"

I made an apologetic face. Luke returned a stern look. A moment later we were back out in the flow of the throng as it moved slowly forward at the pace of a Sunday stroll. We passed the red brick Poultry Building and the yellow Agriculture/Horticulture Building with its red tile roof. We finally found ourselves at the arch to the Midway again and walked through. Luke looked back to check on the Soviet's whereabouts and spotted the top of his knit hat bobbing above the heads of the crowd coming toward us.

"Quick! Back here you guys!" Luke shouted, ducking behind the two-story Mardi Gras fun house. "That sucker's not giving up. He must have seen us and knows we're over in this part of the fair."

"Where do we go now?" Jim pondered.

"We need to find a ride where you don't see the people on it, and real quick," Luke suggested.

"I don't think there are any like that," Jim said, gazing around the area.

"What about this one?" I suggested, looking up at the fun house structure adjacent to us. "He wouldn't see us in there, would he?"

"I hate fun houses, but let's give it a try," Luke said. "We don't have a lot of choices."

We ran up the Mardi Gras ramp and each quickly plucked two tickets off our string of tickets. We handed them to the attendant and ran inside. We entered into a passageway that rolled like a barrel. We careened against the walls, but staggered successfully through, and then moved into a dark room where cheesy, glow-in-the-dark jesters with distorted features lunged at people as they passed by. After that there was a room with a floor that moved, and then a hall of mirrors where Luke and Jim goofed around pretending to be confused about which way was out. It was dimly lit and had mirrors covering every wall, with some even in the middle of the room. I wasn't too far behind the boys when a blonde girl about five years old stopped me and asked for help to get out. She tearfully told me she'd become separated from her older sister.

"Let's see," I said to the panicked girl who was practically clinging to me. "Only one of these panels is the real door. Which one could it be?"

I was about to push on one of the mirrored panels, when I saw the hideous face of the skull tattoo guy reflected in the mirror in front of me. I screamed and pushed the panel. Thankfully, it pivoted, allowing me and the little girl to escape the room. Her sister was standing on the other side, and the little girl rushed into her arms. A set of stairs that wobbled back and forth appeared next, and I scaled them as fast as I could, hoping not to feel the icy hand of the skull tattoo guy grab me from behind.

"Help! Luke! Jim! The skull tattoo guy is in here!" I screamed as I navigated the undulating steps, holding the handrail for balance.

"What?!" Luke yelled back. "Quick! This way!"

I reached the top of the stairs and looked around and saw Jim and Luke running across a balcony spanning the front of the building. They ran to the end of it and seamlessly jumped over the railing and began climbing down the white wrought iron decorative trim that extended to the ground.

"Down here, Nessie!" Luke shouted from down on the pavement, looking up at me as I paused at the edge of the balcony. "Hurry!"

It seemed rather rickety, but I had no choice. I put my leg over the railing and carefully made my way down one step at a time. The wrought iron swayed slightly with each movement I made. I was relieved when my feet finally touched the pavement. The Soviet rushed to the railing and peered over as I stood with Jim and Luke.

"I've got you now," he boomed in his thick accent. "You can't escape."

He climbed over the railing and began making his way down. I was alarmed he was so close and so persistent. How would we be able to make him stop?

"Come on. Let's go!" Luke bellowed.

We turned and ran. Just as we did, I heard someone speak, and paused and looked back to see what was happening.

"Hey, you. You can't climb down like that!" an older man yelled at the Soviet. The man speaking appeared to be in charge at the Mardi Gras. "Get back up to that balcony immediately. That's not the way out. What you're doing is unsafe and illegal."

It was fortunate we'd been able to climb down unnoticed, unlike the Soviet. Surprisingly, he did as he was told, and climbed back up to the balcony and went back inside the fun house to exit. I suppose the extreme girth and intimidating demeanor of the man yelling at him had something to do with it. Whatever the reason, this was a lucky break and gave us precious seconds to get away.

We continued walking as quickly as we could and passed the bumper cars, the Crazy Mouse roller coaster, the Cuckoo Haus fun house, the Yoyo, and numerous other rides and games. We eventually arrived at the Ferris Wheel towering over the other rides on the western edge of the fairgrounds. A line consisting mostly of teenagers was waiting to board. Hawes and his friends were at the end of it and didn't notice us right away, for which I was grateful.

"Shall we take a spin?" Luke asked, gazing up at the giant wheel with a big smile. "Get it? Wheel—spin. That's a little joke. But seriously, shall we?"

"What about the skull tattoo guy?" Jim replied. "He can't be too far behind us, and might see us on it."

"I'm tired of running from that Soviet thug," Luke grumbled. "He's ruining my State Fair fun." Luke fussed at the pouch under his shirt. It must have been getting very uncomfortable.

The line to get on the Ferris Wheel started moving as groups of two and three people were placed and secured in a car, and then the next car was brought forward for boarding. Hawes and his friends were finally seated in a car, after which they spent the time waiting for the ride to begin by harassing two girls in the car in front of them with what I supposed was a clumsy attempt at flirtation. When Hawes finally spotted Luke in the crowd, he redirected his attention to him.

"Hey Larsson. Where's Bunny?" Hawes yelled down at Luke. "She getting your tickets for you?" He snickered and his friends laughed.

"Why do I keep running into that guy?" Luke lamented under his breath. "He's such a jerk!"

Luke looked back at the crowd, and as I feared, spotted the skull tattoo guy coming toward us about two hundred yards away and closing in fast.

"The Russkie's coming," Luke blared. "Get on the ride! *Now*!"

Miraculously, the line was completely gone and there was an empty car sitting in the boarding area practically waiting for us. We ran up the ramp and through the gate, jammed our tickets into the attendant's hand,

and clambered aboard. The dark-haired boy running the ride snapped the security bar in place across our laps and hit the red button on the control panel to start the ride. He closed and latched the gate just as the skull tattoo guy ran up. Frustrated, the Soviet slammed his hand against the gate and glowered angrily. In a split second, the big wheel moved with a jerk, and we began to ascend. I was relieved when we'd climbed high enough to be out of his reach should he somehow have been able to get over the gate.

Up, up we went, almost silently, to the crest of the fifteen-story wheel. Then, back around and down to the boarding area where we were swept through and then lifted upward again to the top to complete a rotation. Each time we came to the crest of the big wheel, the Indianapolis skyline emerged in the distance, and then fell from view as we descended.

The skull tattoo guy stood at the gate and glared at us each time we passed by. Luke, not one to be intimidated, shot him a defiant grin with each pass.

"That Soviet dude is one unhappy man," Luke remarked. "What a pout! Hard to believe a mother ever loved that ugly mug of his."

"Hey, you guys. What are we going to do when this ride ends?" I asked. "We're toast unless we come up with a plan."

"Ah, Nessie. Stop thinking and just enjoy the ride, why don't you?" Luke replied, sitting back and resting his folded hands on the bulge under his shirt. I was perplexed about his attitude. He was remarkably relaxed under the circumstances.

I gazed down at the crowd and searched frantically for Uncle Evert and Aunt Louise among the scores of people milling around. I would have been delighted to have seen them or Emma or Daniel. I was concerned about what would happen to us, and especially to Luke, when the ride ended. That moment was coming quickly, and our pursuer would be right there when it did. He looked mean enough to do just about anything to just about anybody, so I didn't know what to expect. Would he let us go if Luke handed the documents over to him? Would Luke ever part with the documents, even if his life depended on it? It was fruitless to wonder, because I knew Luke would never voluntarily give up the precious documents to anyone but *Herr* Richter. He was too stubborn.

As we came around to complete yet another revolution, I saw the mystery man in the baseball cap that I'd seen in the Coliseum. He cut in the line that had already formed for the next ride, and ran up the ramp behind the Soviet. They spoke briefly, and then, to my surprise, they began scuffling and fighting right there at the gate. The attendant and people standing in line gasped and drew back. Then, without warning, the skull tattoo guy leaped over the gate and grabbed onto a car just as it swooshed through the boarding area and began its climb. He hung on for dear life as it went ever higher. I was astonished when I saw that the car to which he was clinging was the car containing Hawes and his buddies.

"Hey! Hey you! What do you think you're doing!" the young attendant yelled as the skull tattoo guy was carried upward with his legs dangling from the car. "That's not allowed!"

The Soviet struggled to get into Hawes' car and finally managed to get a foothold on the side of it. He pulled himself up and stood with the help of a nearby metal brace as the ride took him upward to the top, over, and then down. Hawes didn't react to the intrusion at first, but then threw a punch in the air that missed the skull tattoo guy by several inches. This appeared to provoke the Soviet, and he pulled a pistol from his waistband and aimed it at Hawes' head.

"Help! *Mommy!*" Hawes screamed at the top of his lungs so loudly that not only could everyone on the ride hear him, but so, too, could everyone on the ground.

"Shut up, kid," the skull tattoo guy barked to Hawes, who promptly shrank away and became silent. I couldn't be certain, but it looked as though Hawes was crying.

The attendant hit the stop button and the ride came to an abrupt halt that almost caused the skull tattoo guy to fall from his precarious perch. After he regained his balance, he stuffed his gun back into his waistband and began to slowly scoot along a cross brace like a high wire artist. He came to a place where he could pull himself up to the next section of the wheel and then moved across a long spoke of the wheel to the next car with the concentration and daring of a circus performer. I couldn't believe anyone would crawl around the structure the way he did so many feet above the ground. He methodically executed this maneuver with such skill and precision that, to my amazement, he was eventually only two cars away from us and closing in fast.

"You there! You're in violation of Indiana State Fair laws and regulations," a burly State Fair public safety officer in a beige uniform yelled to the Soviet from below. "You are hereby ordered to come down immediately or to return to the car on the ride you previously occupied," the officer commanded.

The Soviet ignored the directive and continued his steady and persistent climb across the wheel's skeleton, getting closer to us by the second. I looked down and felt a queasy feeling in the pit of my stomach and held on even more tightly.

"You there, sir! I'm talking to you. I order you to immediately cease and desist in your unlawful actions," the law officer yelled again. He reached back and took out a revolver from his holster.

The Soviet looked down and spat at the officer in an exaggerated and gleeful manner, and then laughed in a raspy and menacing voice. He quickly resumed his maneuver across the structure, defying the officer's order. People from across the fair noticed the commotion and walked over to see what was going on, causing the crowd below to grow larger by the minute. Meanwhile, the Soviet was close enough to make eye contact with Luke. He pointed at Luke and grinned in a creepy and disquieting way as he moved along the spoke toward our car.

"I think he's coming to get those documents from you right here," Jim said.

"Looks that way," Luke agreed. "But I won't give them to him, no matter what."

"Luke, you've got to! Mr. Kleinschmidt wouldn't want you to get killed over this," I urged.

"No way, Jose. And, I'll tell you one more thing. I'm not going to just sit here and let him get me. I'll meet him on his own terms," Luke declared with a strange look in his eyes.

"What do you mean?" Jim asked.

The Soviet was only a few feet away sliding along the very spoke on which our car was suspended. In a flash, Luke jerked on the safety latch, pulled the safety bar up, and freed himself. Without saying a word he stood up and stepped out onto a nearby brace and began to make his way across an adjacent spoke, just barely avoiding the Soviet's clutches.

"Luke! What are you doing? That's too dangerous," Jim shouted. "Come back. It isn't worth it. Stay in the car."

"A man's got to do what a man's got to do," Luke shouted over his shoulder.

"I'll get those documents from you," the Soviet uttered in his thick accent. "It's foolish to try to escape. You will only fall and die." The Soviet appeared almost delighted that Luke was meeting him out on the structure in some sort of duel of wills.

"Screw you!" Luke cracked.

Luke continued slowly and carefully sliding out on the spoke, holding onto an adjacent spoke for balance. I said a silent prayer for him. It was a long way down, and the spokes and braces were thin and didn't provide much room for feet. Luke continued on until the two spokes narrowed as they came to a point at the hub of the wheel. Not to be deterred, he changed directions and began climbing up and around the hub where the complex pattern of spokes and braces provided numerous surfaces on which to climb. The Soviet relentlessly followed on his heels.

After several gut-wrenching minutes, Luke finally came to the main girder that angled down to the ground stabilizing the giant wheel. He appeared to be contemplating which way to go when the Soviet reached out and grabbed his shirt tail from behind. Luke didn't see it coming and was taken off guard. He teetered and almost lost his footing, but managed to recover and stood strong. He turned around and faced the Soviet.

"I'm not going to give you these documents, Igor, or whatever your Russkie name is," Luke stated flatly. "So get lost."

"I'll take them off your mangled body after you fall, then," the Soviet snarled.

"That's big talk, Igor. I'd like to see you try," Luke bantered.

"Are those the documents under your shirt?" the Soviet asked, pointing.

"Maybe," Luke answered. "What's it to you? You're not going to get them. So turn around and scoot yourself back to Russia."

Luke was shorter and smaller than the Soviet, and in a match on the ground might have been easily overtaken by the older, stronger man. Up in the air where balance and reflexes were key, it was more of an even match. The skull tattoo guy moved forward to confront Luke like two gladiators meeting in the arena, but his foot slipped and he fell completely off the spoke. Everyone gasped. Fortunately for him, though, he was able to grab hold of the spoke with one hand at the last second. He hung on with one hand, dangling forty or so feet above the pavement.

"Help me! *Please*!" the Soviet pleaded to Luke as he flailed in the air, struggling to grab hold of the spoke with his other hand.

Luke didn't react at first. I wondered if he was going to allow the Soviet to fall. In some ways I wouldn't have blamed him if he had. Instead, Luke readjusted his own grip on the spoke with one hand so as not to fall, and then carefully crouched down as far as he could and extended his other hand to the Soviet.

"Grab my hand," Luke urged. "Hurry! I'm pretty strong. I can hold you."

The Soviet struggled and tried to grab Luke's hand, but failed, recoiling and dangling even more precariously by one hand.

"Come on. You can do it!" Luke encouraged. "Try again." Luke knelt even lower with his hand outstretched, straining to reach the man.

The Soviet, hanging high above the spellbound crowd captivated by the drama unfolding above them, made eye contact with Luke. Then, in what appeared to an effort to go for broke, he swung around and reached up with a quick thrust. But instead of grasping Luke's hand, he appeared to aim for Luke's midsection and grabbed the package still latched to Luke's stomach, almost pulling Luke off the spoke in the process.

"I've got them! I've got the zero gravity documents, at last!" the skull tattoo guy shouted triumphantly as he held onto the bulge under Luke's shirt with one hand.

"Let go! We'll both fall," Luke shouted, leaning so far over as the Soviet tugged on the package that I was sure he'd fall. "Let go! I'm losing my grip! I can't hold on. We'll both fall!"

After a momentary struggle, the string and tape securing the package to Luke's midsection began to give way. The skull tattoo guy, sensing he was in trouble, struggled to take Luke's hand or to grab the spoke or to grab *anything*, but it was too late. The tape and string securing the package finally gave way. Almost as if in slow motion, the Soviet fell backward, his arms and legs clutching at the air, his eyes wide with terror and his lips too stunned to make a sound. I turned away, unable to witness the horrifying spectacle. People screamed and shrieked in disbelief. Moments later I hesitantly peeked over the edge of the car and saw his broken form lying below, still tightly holding the pouch of documents in one hand.

There was a swirl of activity around the Soviet as people ran to his lifeless body. The mystery man suddenly emerged from the pandemonium and knelt down next to the dead man. He jerked the pouch of documents out of the Soviet's hand and then disappeared into the crowd. No one seemed to notice what he'd done. I wanted to shout for someone to go after him, but it was too noisy and chaotic for anyone to hear me.

As for Luke, he stood frozen on the spoke, his eyes fixed on the Soviet lying on the pavement in a hideous death pose below.

"Why didn't he take my hand? I told him to take my hand," he mumbled over and over as he stared down at the dead man. "*Why didn't he take my hand? Why? Why?*"

CHAPTER TWENTY-FIVE

Fitting Together the Puzzle Pieces

Luke remained out on the spoke talking to himself until he finally heard Jim and me shouting to come back to the car. We called to him for what seemed like ages. Even Uncle Evert tried to call up to him from the ground, but it was too difficult to hear anything in the commotion that followed the Soviet's fall. In addition, I think Luke must have been in a state of shock. It seemed as though he was re-living that fateful moment over and over in his thoughts and tuning everything else out. As for me, I feared I'd never be able to look at the Ferris Wheel again with the same happy associations I used to have for it. It would take a long time to erase that hideous scene from my mind. I'd never seen anyone die before, and it was something I wish I'd never experienced.

Once Luke was safely back in our car, the Ferris Wheel attendant, with the supervision of several law enforcement officers who seemed to have arrived from every corner of the fair, re-started the ride, and all of the riders were taken off one car at a time. Then they closed the ride for the day. They'd already covered the Soviet's body with somebody's coat. An ambulance came and took the Soviet away, and slowly the crowd began to disperse.

Uncle Evert, Aunt Louise, Emma, and Daniel were lined up waiting for us when we finally walked down the ramp to exit the ride. We eagerly ran to them. They said they'd seen most of what happened. Seeing their familiar faces was very comforting. Luke went straight to his father, who heartily embraced him without speaking. In a rare moment of sentimentality, Luke didn't resist, and even pushed his face a little into his father's chest. After a brief moment, though, he stepped away in his usual aloof and self-sufficient fashion, and was his old self again.

"Vanessa! Thank God you're okay," Emma gushed when I walked over to her. She embraced me quickly. "I told you we should stick together," she added, lovingly taking my hand.

"I told you I'd catch up with you later, and I did, didn't I?" I replied, smiling weakly.

Suddenly, now that I was safe—now that *everyone* was safe—I felt like crying. It came over me like an irrepressible wave. I bit my lip and worked hard not to give in to it. What would everyone think of me if I bawled like a child right there at the Indiana State Fair? A tear escaped down my cheek, and I quickly wiped it away before anyone could see it.

"Ah, Nessie. You aren't shedding a tear for your dear ol' cousin who was almost smashed like a pumpkin on the pavement today, are you?" Luke asked upon noticing my emotional state.

"Yes. To think—I was almost rid of you!" I replied, forcing a grin.

"That's the spirit! I do believe you're becoming one of us!" Luke said, returning the grin. He punched me lightly in the arm.

"Ouch!" I said, rubbing my arm playfully.

"*Seriously*, Nessie Monster? I guess some things and people never change!" he replied, rolling his eyes. We had a brief laugh together, which felt good and helped relieve the tension.

"I don't get it," Jim said, looking over at Daniel standing patiently nearby. "What're they laughing at? After all we've just been through, I don't see how they can be so giddy."

"It's family thing. Be glad you're not related to them," Daniel replied.

I turned toward Jim and gave him a warm smile. He pulled me toward him and we embraced. He kissed me on my cheek and then hugged me again. It felt good to be in his arms, to be safe, to be alive, and to be cared about. After just witnessing a life end, I knew that more than ever. Life was too short to hide my feelings any longer.

"Ooh!" Luke belittled us playfully as he watched. Jim and I laughed, and then exchanged a sweet kiss. "Gross," Luke remarked. "Don't forget where you are!"

Just then Hawes and his friends walked by on their way out. I could see by his demeanor that Luke's tormentor had a different attitude now. He was much less cocky, and almost appeared humble. When he saw Luke, he stopped to speak.

"Uh, Larsson. Uh, way to go up there, man. I mean—real brave stuff and all that," Hawes said meekly. "Sorry about all the trouble I've given you lately. Just joking around, you know? Uh, listen, maybe you could leave out some of the details when you tell the guys at school about what happened today. I mean—I'd really appreciate it—consider it a favor even, if you'd keep what I said up there just between us. Whaddaya say? Friends?" He stuck out his hand to shake on it.

Luke allowed Hawes to keep his hand extended while he considered the request. Then, he pursed his lips together, gazed downward at Hawes, and smiled broadly as if he'd just had a revelation.

"Hawes, not only will I most definitely tell my friends every detail of what happened up there today, I'm going to tell them about that!" Luke answered, pointing down at Hawes' pants.

Hawes looked down, turned beet red, and took off running through the crowd. His two friends looked confused and went trailing after him. Luke laughed uproariously.

The law enforcement officers standing nearby consisting of the State Fair public safety officer in the beige uniform, an Indiana State policeman, an Indianapolis policeman, and a man in a suit who appeared to be a police honcho of some sort, asked all of us to come along with them to the Communications Building on the east side of the fairgrounds to give a brief statement. Uncle Evert asked if we could have this meeting tomorrow after everyone'd had a chance to settle down and recover, but the police honcho said no. It was his opinion we'd remember more if we gave our statements right away.

So, we piled into the patrol cars lined up near the Agriculture/ Horticulture Building with their red lights flashing. Jim, Luke, and I squeezed into the back seat of one patrol car, while Daniel and Emma rode along with Uncle Evert and Aunt Louise in a second patrol car.

"Why didn't the Soviet take my hand?" Luke asked softly as we rode the brief distance through the dense crowd along the ring road. "I'll never forget watching him fall like that." Luke's eyes had a far-away look to them, as if he were still working through what had just happened.

"He wanted those documents at all costs, and didn't care if he died getting them or made you fall, too. Don't feel sorry for him," Jim said. "He wouldn't have felt sorry for you if things had been reversed."

"Yeah, I suppose so," Luke replied, nodding. "It's something I wish I'd never experienced, though. I can tell you that. Speaking of the documents, what happened to them?"

"I saw that mystery man we saw in the Coliseum take them out of the Soviet's hand and disappear," I reported. "Right after the fall. No one seemed to notice or tried to stop him."

"Crap!" Luke said wistfully. "After all I went through, and I end up losing them anyway. Mr. Kleinschmidt won't like this. Not one bit. I failed." He appeared to be taking it very hard.

"Well, at least the Soviet dude didn't get them," Jim pointed out. "Our national security would be a risk if he had. You deserve a lot of credit for that. You should feel good knowing you didn't climb out on that Ferris Wheel for nothing."

"Yes, but who took them? How do you know the Soviets didn't get them? Who exactly is this mystery dude and who does he work for? Maybe he works for the Soviets, too, for all we know," Luke said. "I don't like how he just shows up today out of the blue and now he's got the documents."

"Should we talk about the documents in front of these guys?" I asked softly, gesturing to the two police officers sitting in the front seat.

"Might as well. It doesn't matter now that I've lost them," Luke replied despondently.

We finally arrived at the Communications Building. We were led to a small conference room with orange plastic chairs and directed to sit. There was no air conditioning, and even though the window panes were pushed open, it was stuffy. An electric fan oscillated back and forth on a desk at the end of the room. The law enforcement officers assembled themselves on each the side of the desk, and then one directed another to tell someone in an adjoining room we were ready. A side door opened and a man walked in. I was shocked when I saw that the man they summoned was the mystery man in the baseball cap! He walked to the desk, propped himself on the edge, and took off his sunglasses. He was holding a cigarette and smudged it out in an ashtray on the desk.

"Ladies and gentlemen, allow me to introduce myself. I'm Special Agent Panerella of the Federal Bureau of Investigation. We're been tracking a Soviet citizen who illegally entered the United States several months ago by the name of Dmitry Azarov. He's the gentleman who fell from the Ferris Wheel today. We have reason to believe he was a member of a Soviet crime syndicate just beginning to operate throughout the Midwest. I'll have just a few questions for you about your relationship with this man, and then you'll be free to go."

"We don't have a relationship with him," Luke blurted. "He's been bothering an elderly friend of ours, and we were trying to help that friend. That's all."

"Okay, young man. Let's start at the beginning," Special Agent Panerella replied. "Go ahead and tell me what you know."

Luke told the whole story starting with the UFO he saw hovering over Kleinschmidt's farm, about Kleinschmidt being an ex-Nazi physicist doing research at Modern Propulsion for the U.S. government, changing his name from Karl Weidmann to Klaus Kleinschmidt so he could hide out in Fishers, and continue doing his research after he was forced to stop at Modern Propulsion, and about how Kleinschmidt lost his wife and son. He also shared how Kleinschmidt had given Luke all of his most important anti-gravity research documents to pass to Otto Richter at the Reynolds Farm Equipment display, but that Richter had never shown up. He related details about how this Azarov person had held Kleinschmidt hostage in his own home demanding the anti-gravity research data and chased Luke all over the State Fair today to get it.

"Azarov might have been a crook, but he was also a spy for the Soviets," Luke declared with a confident nod at the end of his recitation.

"We've gone through the documents I took off of Azarov's body—this special data you say this Kleinschmidt character gave you—and there's nothing in them but gibberish," Special Agent Panerella replied. "Sorry to disappoint you, but there's absolutely nothing worthwhile in them, much less anything as fanciful as anti-gravity research data. Perhaps, this Mr. Kleinschmidt was confused. You say he's elderly, so that's a possibility. Or, perhaps he was playing some kind of spy game with you kids, and you thought it was real. But I can assure you the F.B.I. has a dossier on Azarov, and he's a petty criminal and a whole list of heinous things, but he's not a spy."

I was stunned to hear Special Agent Panerella say those documents were worthless, and that Azarov wasn't a spy. What was going on?

"If those documents were just gibberish, then why did Azarov want them? He risked a lot to get them," Jim pointed out.

"Hard to say," Special Agent Panerella answered. "There's been a persistent rumor in recent years that several German ex-patriots who came to this country after the war were in possession of precious stones, gold, artwork, and other loot taken from people in occupied countries. Azarov and his colleagues must have believed your neighbor Kleinschmidt was one of those ex-patriots and had some of these things, and that you were carrying them for him."

"But when he grabbed the pouch, just before he fell, I could swear Azarov said something about finally having possession of the zero-gravity research," Luke insisted.

"Given the life-or-death situation you were in, I tend to doubt you could accurately understand what he said given the thick Russian accent he had, much less remember it," Special Agent Panerella argued. "Don't you agree?"

"Okay. Okay. Well, maybe so," Luke replied. He looked down and ran his hands anxiously through his tangled curly hair. You could see he was trying hard to make sense of all of these contradictory facts in light of what Kleinschmidt had told us. So was I.

Special Agent Panerella left the room for what seemed like a long time. It was getting very warm and uncomfortable, and I was anxious to leave. It'd been a stressful afternoon, and I wanted to get back to the farm where I could relax and clear my thoughts. Mental images of Azarov falling to his death kept playing over and over in my mind. I'd never seen a person get killed before, and I wanted to get far away from there and from reminders of what had just happened. I started to feel a bit queasy and walked to an open window for some air and looked out. A shuttle filled with happy fair-goers was just turning the corner heading to the Grandstand and the Coliseum. Those lucky people—they could enjoy a carefree day at the fair.

The State Fair public safety officer came in with a tray of paper Dixie cups filled with water and offered them to us. After we each drank one, Luke, Daniel, and Jim used the crumpled cups to pass the time shooting them into a wire wastebasket.

Finally, Special Agent Panerella re-entered the room. He was holding several sheets of paper with handwritten information on them. "Okay.

Here's the story. We've done some preliminary background checks on this Otto Richter, and he does in fact work at Modern Propulsion. We were able to locate him here at the fair, but he doesn't know anyone by the name of Kleinschmidt and doesn't know anything about a special meeting to get documents from Kleinschmidt," Panerella reported.

"*What*?!" Luke exclaimed. "No wonder he stood us up. I had a feeling he was never going to meet me. I knew it!"

"Calm down, Luke," Uncle Evert said. "Don't interrupt."

"Now, as for this Karl Weidmann, our research shows he was an engineer at Modern Propulsion several years ago, that his son Wilhelm died a tragic death, that his wife Hilde predeceased him, and that he himself died in a plane crash near Salt Lake City in 1962," Special Agent Panerella related. "As for Klaus Kleinschmidt, we're searching for information about him and haven't located anything so far. It's possible he's a run-of-the-mill retired farmer or engineer of some type, so we won't find much about him in any of our records. We're going to check immigration to see what we can find there. That will take some time."

Luke appeared crestfallen. "You mean—-was Kleinschmidt possibly trying to get even with me? Was this just a game to him? I can't believe it! I almost became an oil stain in the Midway just to protect those documents—those worthless, worthless, stinkin' documents!" His confusion appeared to be turning to anger.

"Special Agent Panerella, haven't you detained us long enough?" Uncle Evert demanded, suddenly standing. "These kids have been through enough for one day. Let us go now. You're free to get in touch with us later if you need anything further."

"Okay. But let me know if you remember anything else that might be material," Special Agent Panerella instructed us. He handed Uncle Evert and Aunt Louise his business card and opened the door. The State Fair public safety officer led us down a long corridor to the door and we walked out into the fresh air.

Uncle Evert suggested we eat something before we started the journey home, so he treated us to foot-long chili dogs and lemon shake-ups from a vendor located near the Communications Building. We sat at a picnic table to eat. My queasiness had passed. I hadn't realized how hungry I was, and it tasted especially good.

"Dad, I know you're probably sore about what I did today," Luke said between bites. "But I wanted to help the old guy. That's all. You've always said we should assist the elderly where we can. Right? And, I helped catch a bad guy in the process. I can't get in trouble for that, can I?"

Uncle Evert took off his glasses and looked directly at Luke. "I'm proud of your motives, but you need to stop and consider the consequences of your actions before you get involved in anything remotely like this in the future. Sometimes you're just too impetuous for your own good. We have some talking to do when we get home," he said.

"That's just what Mr. Kleinschmidt said!" Daniel mused. "The brash one—isn't that what he always calls you?"

Luke gave Daniel a dirty look which Daniel pretended to ignore. "Don't mention that old Nazi's name to me ever again," Luke grumbled. "He set me up with worthless papers, and I'll never forgive him."

We finished eating, then jumped on a shuttle that took us back to the gate on 42nd Street. I turned back toward the sights, sounds, and smells as we were about to exit the fair and said a silent good bye for another year. This would certainly be one I'd never forget.

When we got back to the farmhouse, Lars was sitting at the dining room table in the yard reading *Games People Play* by Eric Berne, M.D. Luke threw himself into a chair next to him, and Jim, Daniel, Emma, and I joined him while my aunt and uncle went into the house.

"You missed a really good time at the State Fair today, Lars. A *really* good time. By the way, where's Fritz?" Luke asked, gazing around the yard. "Fritz! *Komm hier*!"

"Uh, you can save your breath. Fritz isn't going to *komm hier*. Mr. Kleinschmidt just came by and picked him up," Lars replied. "So you can stop it with the Nazi dog commands."

"What? Mr. Kleinschmidt is out of the hospital already?" I remarked.

"Yes. They apparently told him he was okay to go home," Lars replied.

"Really? As sick as he was, I'm surprised to hear that," I continued.

"We didn't speak too long because he was in a big hurry. But he seemed the same as he always is," Lars replied, turning the page of his book.

"Darn it! I was looking forward to having Fritz around tonight," Luke complained. "I miss him."

"I told you not to get attached to that dog," Aunt Louise said as she walked out the door. "All we need is a dog around here to take care of in addition to everything else." She walked into the workroom and came back holding a large pot and took it into the house.

"Hey, I just thought of something. Now that old Nazi Kleinschmidt is home, I think I'll take a little walk over to his house and ask him why he lied to me and set me up to be killed the way he did," Luke said, drumming his fingers on the table. "Like Ricky always says to Lucy on *I Love Lucy*, the old guy has some '*splaining* to do."

"Set you up to be *killed*? What are you talking about? That must have been some State Fair. What happened?" Lars asked, putting his book down.

"The old guy just got home from the hospital. Maybe you should wait until tomorrow morning," Jim suggested, temporarily ignoring Lars. "Give him a break. You're pretty cranked up right now. Maybe you should take a day to cool off before you speak with him."

"Besides, what makes you think Special Agent Panerella was telling you the truth? Maybe Kleinschmidt didn't set you up. Did you every think of that?" Daniel suggested.

"What're you talking about?" Luke asked.

"Yeah. What on earth are you all talking about?" Lars asked, still confused.

"For all we know, Otto Richter was afraid to admit to the F.B.I. that he was going to meet Kleinschmidt, so he said he didn't know anything about the meeting and didn't know who Kleinschmidt was. If the F.B.I. asked me questions like that, I might say the same thing. He must have caught wind that the F.B.I. was in the picture, and that's probably why he didn't show up to meet us at the rendez-vous," Daniel explained.

"Come to think of it, I kinda thought one of those men with Agent Panerella looked a lot like that salesman at Reynolds Farm Equipment. You know—the man you told to tell Richter to wait for you? Maybe he was an F.B.I. agent and was just pretending to be a salesman so he could get Richter when he showed up," I suggested.

"I told you not to talk to that guy, remember?" Daniel said to Luke. "I knew he couldn't be trusted."

"But what about the documents? Panerella said the documents in that pouch were gibberish and worthless," Luke replied.

"That's what Panerella said, but how do we know he didn't say that just to throw us off?" Daniel continued. "You said the Soviet mentioned zero-gravity when he was pulling on the pouch up there, didn't you?"

"Yeah, that's what I think he said. I'm pretty sure that's what he said," Luke said. "Panerella's got me all confused."

"So, if that's what the Soviet—Azarov or whatever his name is—said just before he fell, that meant he was looking for anti-gravity documents, not the gold and jewels Panerella said he was probably after," Daniel concluded. "Would he look for anti-gravity secrets where they don't exist? Would he risk his life like that?"

"You've got a point there," Luke agreed. "Azarov must have heard Jim and me talking about the meeting with Richter when we were sitting outside last night. That sound I heard in the bushes could have been him sneaking around. That could explain why he came to the fair today."

"And, we've seen the UFO. How do you explain that? We know Kleinschmidt has the anti-gravity technology to make a craft fly like that," I reminded Luke. "Even Ryker says he saw it."

"But this would mean Panerella was lying to us about the documents being worthless. I can't believe a Special Agent for the F.B.I. would lie to us. Do you?" Luke asked.

The rest of, including Lars, who was riveted with interest listening to our conversation, smiled and exchanged knowing looks.

"Think of the Roswell, New Mexico, UFO crash in 1947 that the U.S. government said was a weather balloon. Think of the assassination of President Kennedy that the U.S. government says was accomplished by Lee Harvey Oswald all by himself," Lars replied. "Do you really need an answer to that question?"

"It's starting to add up," Jim said, getting excited. "The F.B.I. confirmed that Karl Weidmann worked at Modern Propulsion years ago and had a son named Wilhelm who died young and a wife named Hilde who's also deceased. That's consistent with what Kleinschmidt said about himself. I think he told us the truth when he said he used to be Karl Weidmann and that he changed his name to Klaus Kleinschmidt and moved here."

"But Panerella said Karl Weidmann died in a plane crash near Salt Lake City in 1962. How do you explain that away?" Luke challenged.

"Sometimes those plane crashes don't leave much in the way of people's remains to identify, and in this case they ended up identifying someone else's as Weidmann," Daniel suggested. "That'd give him a perfect cover so that no one would ever come looking for him. All he had to do was change his name and disappear here in Indiana where he could continue his research."

"So, that means those documents in the pouch I was carrying might have been the real deal? They were real anti-gravity research documents? Wow. I'm starting to feel a little better. I should have known that Mr. Kleinschmidt wouldn't try to make a fool of me," Luke said, smiling for the first time since we'd returned to the farm. "The old dude didn't lie to me after all. What do you know?"

"Don't tell me you didn't sneak a look at those documents, 'cause knowing you, I know you did. Did they look like anti-gravity documents? Well, did they?" I asked.

"Okay, to tell the truth, yes, I looked at them last night, but they didn't make any sense to me. They were formulas and diagrams and things like that," Luke admitted.

"That sounds like the real deal to me, and now they're in the hands of the F.B.I. Kleinschmidt won't like that," Jim said. "Didn't he say he didn't want those documents falling into the hands of *either* the Soviets or the U.S. government?"

"Oh, boy. You're right. I'm going to have to explain this to Mr. Kleinschmidt, and he won't like it. I guess I'm the one who owes *him* the apology, not the other way around," Luke said, now sitting straighter and looking more like his old self again.

"Well, do it in the morning. It's getting late. I have to go now. My mother probably thinks I've been kidnapped," Jim replied, standing. "Can I borrow one of your bikes if I bring it back tomorrow?"

"Sure. I'll go with you to the barn to help pick one out. Some of the tires aren't in the best shape," Luke said.

Jim and Luke started across the yard toward the barn. Jim turned and waved good-bye to me and tripped over a pot of flowers and almost fell. After he regained his balance, he made a goofy face, and I giggled. As he walked on to the barn, I felt melancholy realizing I might never see him again after tomorrow. We'd had our ups and downs, but I still cared about him as much as ever. Life and love were more complicated than I thought, and love, in particular, was more painful than I ever anticipated.

"I've got to go, too. See you guys later. It's been barrels of fun," Daniel said. He walked across the backyard and disappeared down the path to the road.

"At least the skull tattoo guy—Azarov—won't be a problem for Kleinschmidt ever again. Now the old man can live out the rest of his life in peace," I said to Lars and Emma.

"Perhaps," Lars replied, looking pensive. "I've been listening to you guys, and while I seriously doubt Mr. Kleinschmidt has conquered the anti-gravity challenge that Hitler and dozens of gifted scientists have wrestled with for decades, if the Soviets believe he has, they'll send more people to steal his research from him. That Azarov won't be the last. Not to mention the F.B.I."

"But those documents Luke was carrying to give to Otto Richter—those were the only documents containing the research data," I said. "That's what the old German said."

"He might have made copies and just not told you guys," Lars suggested.

I knew people kept copies of just about everything, but it never occurred to me the way Kleinschmidt spoke that he'd made copies of his research. He spoke of what he gave to Luke so solemnly, that I assumed those were the only documents containing the coveted anti-gravity solution. Was there to be an endless string of Soviets lurking around Mr. Kleinschmidt's property trying to steal his anti-gravity secrets? I couldn't fathom how he would ever find peace.

Despite that, for tonight at least, I felt a sense of relief knowing that the episode with Azarov was over. There'd no longer be a need to watch for him every second or to worry that he was lurking in the woods or along the creek. My last night at the farm would be peaceful and calm, and I'd finally be able to enjoy a blissful, carefree sleep before I had to pack up tomorrow and return to the routine of my suburban, junior high life.

Almost everyone went to bed a little on the early side that night. The day's excitement had taken its toll. I'd been asleep for only about only an hour when I was awakened by the disquieting sounds of fire truck sirens in the distance and the staccato of electricity arcing out of power lines the way they do when a building is on fire.

I sat up with a start. Emma was already awake. We darted through the gold curtains into the living room and found Uncle Evert and Aunt Louise standing outside the screen door in their robes facing the fields beyond the barn. The sky was lit up with the sickening gold and rose hues of a major fire, and the clouds were illuminated as if a giant spotlight were directed at them.

"What's going on?" Emma asked as she and I opened the screen door and stepped out. "What's on fire?"

Uncle Evert turned toward us with a concerned look on his face. "Kleinschmidt's farm," he answered solemnly. "The whole thing is going up in flames."

CHAPTER TWENTY-SIX

Homeward Bound

Uncle Evert drove over to Kleinschmidt's farm before sunup while the firemen were still dousing the last hot spots. He said he wanted to see if he could help out. I was glad he did. I was worried about Mr. Kleinschmidt and Fritz, and would be grateful to know if they were okay. He returned to the farmhouse just as Lars, Luke, Emma, and I were finishing breakfast at the dining room table outside. He appeared troubled when he walked over to us.

"The fire chief says the whole place is a total loss. The flames were especially hot because of all the chemicals Kleinschmidt had stored in his outbuildings. You wouldn't believe the complete devastation. Everything, including the house, was reduced to nothing more than a giant pile of ashes," he reported, shaking his head. "It looks like an atomic bomb went off."

"What do they think started it?" Luke asked.

"They don't know. It spread fast and jumped from building to building, so they'll probably never know for sure. Those chemicals could have started it. They were highly flammable. Who can say?"

"How is....how is Mr. Kleinschmidt?" Luke continued. "Did you talk to him? Did he get out okay? What about Fritz? Is Fritz okay? Did you see him?"

Uncle Evert paused, so I knew what he was said next wouldn't be good. "I don't think he got out, son. There was no trace of him or his dog anywhere. His truck was parked out by the road, so chances are he was home. The fire was so hot that—-well, let's just say, there's very little possibility the authorities will find any remains. It even melted metal. Some large machine he had in one outbuilding was completely melted and twisted. There's nothing left—-of anything."

Emma gasped. I did, too. It was horrible to think Mr. Kleinschmidt had met such a tragic end. I'd never known anyone who died in a fire before, and thoughts of the desperation he must have experienced popped into my head.

Luke slammed his hand on the table and got up and walked into the house. I didn't know if his reaction was about Mr. Kleinschmidt or about Fritz. Perhaps it was about both.

"Hey, Vanessa! Your Mom's on the phone," Margret shouted from the kitchen.

I went in to the living room and picked up the black receiver lying on the desk and said hello. Mom told me she was coming out in two hours to pick me up, and that I should be ready to go by the time she arrived. I knew there was no chance of negotiating an extension. Two hours was too short a time to adjust to leaving, but that's all I had.

After I hung up with Mom, I went straight to Emma's bedroom and jammed all of my things into my flowered suitcase, including the crocheted vest Margret gave me and my new transistor radio, but didn't pack my bright yellow A-line dress. For all I knew this might be the last day I'd ever see Jim, so I wanted to look as pretty as possible for him. I ran with the dress into the bathroom, cleaned my face, put on eyeliner and lip gloss, and brushed my hair. He said he liked my hair down loose, so I wore it that way with my tortoise headband. I slipped on my special blue flats with the silver buckles and then took inventory of myself. "Not too bad," I thought. "For *me*, that is!" I fastened a necklace with a little butterfly charm around my neck, and then took a deep breath and walked outside to join the others.

Jim, Daniel, and Luke were sitting at the dining room table talking about the fire. Jim's face brightened when he saw me, and he gestured that I should sit next to him, which I gladly did.

"That's a pretty dress you have on," Jim whispered. "You look very pretty."

It was just like him to notice. I smiled self-consciously.

"Look at the bright side. Now you won't have to apologize to him for letting the F.B.I. get his research," Daniel pointed out.

"Yeah. I guess so, but I wish I'd had a chance to get to know him better and to ask him more questions. You know, about his research and his life in Germany and the war," Luke said wistfully. "Now I'll never know about all that. His UFO is destroyed, and Fritz is gone, too. He was a cool dog—a really cool dog. I loved that mutt. The whole thing bites." His voice trailed off as he spoke, choked with rare emotion for him.

"I wonder what started it," I remarked. "At least we can rule out Azarov."

"We could walk back there if you want, you know, and look around," Daniel suggested. He seemed eager to go.

"Nah, not right now," Luke replied, being surprisingly reticent and a bit listless. "Dad said we should stay away for a day or so to allow the firemen to do their thing and let the place cool off. He said the fire chief thought those chemicals released in the fire might have made it unsafe to be there."

"Okay. Nothing's stopping us from going up in the haymow to see what we can see from there, is there?" Daniel asked. "I bet we can see *something* from up there."

Everyone agreed, so, Emma, Luke, Daniel, Jim, and I went to the barn and climbed up into the haymow. I had to be careful with my dress as far as how I moved and sat down. It wasn't exactly the best thing to wear to sit on the haymow floor, but I managed. We sat along the back edge where the wall had once been and dangled our legs over the side. Jim sat next to me. I looked off across the fields and could just barely see some blackened trees and parts of one or two charred exterior walls. I could tell even from a distance that it'd been a catastrophic event.

"You know, Lars said the Soviets probably would have sent more spies to steal Kleinschmidt's anti-gravity secrets. Azarov wouldn't have been the only one," I pointed out.

"Makes sense," Luke said, nodding absent-mindedly.

"I just got an idea," Jim exclaimed. "What if Kleinschmidt set the fire—you know—to fake his death? Think about it. Your dad said they'll probably never find any of his remains because of how freakishly hot the fire was. Maybe he didn't die in the fire, but the authorities will assume he did. That would mean he can return to Germany like he wanted, and no one will ever connect the dots and look for Klaus Kleinschmidt. Think about it. That'd sure be one way to get the Soviets and the U.S. government off his back, wouldn't it?"

"I don't know. That seems a little far-fetched," Luke reasoned. "He was awfully sick to be able to travel that far. And what about Fritz? Where'd he go? He couldn't take a dog with him all the way back to Augsburg, Germany, can he? No, he probably died last night, and took all of his secrets with him, except those in the documents the F.B.I. took, assuming there was anything more than gibberish in them."

"As far as his ability to travel, didn't Lars say Kleinschmidt didn't appear to be that sick when he picked up Fritz yesterday?" I reminded them. "Maybe he was exaggerating how sick he was when we were over at his house. You know, to throw us off."

"Kleinschmidt faked his death once before—that plane crash near Salt Lake City in 1962 that Special Agent Panerella told us about. So, he could do it again, couldn't he?" Daniel argued. "And, people travel with dogs all the time. That's no big deal."

"You're assuming that Karl Weidmann and Klaus Kleinschmidt are the same person," Luke said.

"I thought that was a given," Daniel replied.

"The other benefit of the fire is that now he can be certain no one will ever get their hands on his lab, his research, or that UFO he built," Jim continued. "It's a beautiful plan, really, when you think about it."

I looked off across the field and thought about what Jim and Daniel were proposing. Had Kleinschmidt set the fire to make it appear he'd died just so he could escape back to Germany? I'd like to think so, because that meant he was still alive and finally going home. But there'd never be a way to know for sure. It was probably too far-fetched to be true.

"I'll miss Fritz, no matter what really happened," Luke lamented. "He was a neat dog—-smart and didn't take crap from anybody, but had a good and loyal heart underneath."

"Hmm.... Who do we know who's like that?" Daniel asked playfully. "Except the smart part, that is!"

"Look dude—do you want me to throw you off of here?" Luke threatened playfully.

Luke pretended to push at Daniel to get him to fall off the edge, but Daniel held on and jumped to his feet to get away from him.

"Cut it out, Luke!" Emma scolded, pounding her brother on the arm. "You're going to make us all fall off, you dumb ox!"

"Okay, okay. Stop hitting me!" Luke made a peace gesture, and then continued speaking. "I could train that dog so easily. He was getting the hang of shaking hands and balancing Dorito chips on his nose. If only Kleinschmidt hadn't picked him up last night, he'd still be alive today," Luke grieved.

Suddenly, in the distance, the dark form of an animal running across the field toward us caught my eye. It was too far away to see what it was, but it resembled a coyote or a fox.

"What's that out there?" Daniel asked, pointing.

"Is it a coyote?" I asked. "Are there coyotes this far north?"

"It's probably a chupacabra," Daniel joked, reminding me of the hazing I experienced the first night I ever stayed at the farm by referring to the mythical beast my cousins had convinced me was lurking in the fields.

"Very funny," I replied.

"No, it's probably the Everharts' dog. He gets out all the time and runs over here," Emma suggested. "Mom won't like that."

"Yeah, it's definitely a dog," Jim said.

"I don't know. It kinda looks like...." Luke stopped and peered intently. Then he stood to get a better look. "It's.... could it be.... no, wait ...can it be? Yes it is! It's Fritz! Fritzie! You're back!"

Luke flew down the ladder so quickly he barely touched the rungs, and ran to embrace the panting dog who eagerly jumped into his arms. Fritz's smiling face and wagging tail were a welcome sight, but where did he come from? How had he escaped the fire? Fritz smothered Luke's face in dog kisses as Luke playfully roughed up the canine's fur.

"Where've you been big fella?" Luke asked. He looked him over and checked his front paws. "Were you hiding during the fire? Thank goodness you were so smart you knew how to survive without getting hurt. Your paws aren't burned at all."

"Interesting coincidence, Fritz turning up like that without a scratch," Jim said, standing at the edge of the haymow looking down at the reunion below. "What do you think of my theory now? You can bet Kleinschmidt had that dog stashed someplace safe during the fire as part of his plan."

"So, why is Fritz here now? Did he run away from Kleinschmidt or something?" Luke asked, still rubbing the dog's fur.

"No, silly. It's a plain as day. Kleinschmidt sent Fritz to you as a gift," I said. "To pay you back for being his friend, and for trying to get those documents to Richter."

"You think so? Why that crazy Nazi! What a guy," Luke said, kneeling down to hug the dog again. "I sure hope my mom lets me keep my gift."

I became concerned my mother might have arrived, so we all climbed down from the haymow and walked back to the house with Fritz happily running and jumping alongside Luke the whole way. I was correct, and my mother, Aunt Louise, and Uncle Evert were sitting at the dining room table when the five of us approached the house. I ran over to my mother and hugged her. Even though I didn't want to go home, I was glad to see her, especially after all I'd been through. The front page of the *Indianapolis Star* was unfolded in the middle of the table. The headline read "Fishers Teen Nabs Soviet Criminal at State Fair."

"Luke, did you know you're written about on the front page of the newspaper today?" my mother asked as he walked by. He glanced down at the newspaper and grimaced.

"Yeah, he's a real Secret Agent Man!" Daniel joked.

"What're you doing with that dog?" Aunt Louise asked sternly. "You know what I told you. We're not going to have a dog around here."

"Oh, Mom. He survived the fire. That must mean he belongs to us! The cosmos wants us to have him," Luke begged. "I'll take care of him. I promise."

Aunt Louise looked down at the dog with a steely gaze. Almost as if on cue, Fritz lifted his paw to do a handshake with her. Everyone burst out laughing. Aunt Louise's reserve melted, and she smiled and shook his paw good-naturedly.

"*Please* let me keep him, Mom. I'll do all the work, I swear. You can see what a smart animal he is," Luke pleaded. "He'll make a great pet. Really he will. Please?"

Aunt Louise paused and studied the face of the canine. "Well, all right. He seems to have more positive energy than I first thought. We'll take it a day at a time. But I'm not making any promises young man," she said. "Just remember your promise. He's your pet to take care of, not mine."

"Thanks, Mom!" Luke exclaimed, kissing her on the cheek. "You're the best mom ever!"

I introduced Jim to my mother, and then she told me to get my things and we'd leave. Jim walked with me to the front of the house, while Emma, Daniel, and Luke ran around to the back yard to play with Fritz.

"Well, gorgeous, looks like this is it for now," Jim said, taking my hand and looking into my eyes. "I hope you have a really good year at school."

"I can't believe you're moving away and that this might be the last time we'll see each other for a really long time—maybe forever," I lamented. "This can't be happening." I leaned forward and hugged him. It was good to be close to him. I closed my eyes and tried to drink in the moment and to memorize the feeling of his arms around me and of mine around him. A tear trickled down my cheek, which I quickly flicked away. I was embarrassed to be so emotional.

"Oh, you never know. Maybe my parents will change their minds and we'll end up staying around here," he said, wiping away what remained of my tear. "They're acting kinda crazy right now. Anything is possible."

"Oh, if only they would. My dream would come true," I said, smiling weakly and looking into his handsome eyes.

He gently swept my hair off my shoulder. "That's your dream? I'm flattered." He kissed me sweetly. Oh, how I wished we had more time to be alone together!

"Cut the mush, you guys!" Luke shouted though the dining room window. "Fritz is too young to witness such wanton behavior!" Fritz barked, probably because Luke was holding a Dorito chip high over his head.

"Get away from the window you perv!" Jim shouted back. "Let us have a moment to ourselves, will you?"

Luke said something I couldn't make out and walked away from the window.

"Please send me a postcard with your address on it when you get to Phoenix so I know where to write to you," I said. "I know you don't like to write letters, but I like writing them and it'll be okay if you don't write back if you don't want to. I mean it. At least if I write to you, I'll feel we're still connected."

"I'll write back, I promise. I can write letters when I have the right motivation," he said with a knowing look.

We kissed and hugged one more time, and then he walked over to the garage where his bike was propped against the wall. "Tell Luke I'll be back later today," he said. He got on the bike and started down the driveway. "Well, this is really it this time. Stay your fierce self no matter what. And don't be so hard on yourself. You're a very special lady." Then, he added, "And sexy!"

I let out a burst of laughter.

"Yes, you are! *Very* sexy!" he shouted over his shoulder, raising his eyebrows playfully.

"Shh! Luke will hear you!" I shouted back, shaking my head and giggling. No one had ever called me sexy before, and it was nice.

When he was almost out of sight, he turned and waved good-bye again one last time and blew me a kiss. I waved back and returned the air kiss. Moments later he was gone, perhaps, forever. It felt strange and I wanted to cry. I'd met him only a few months ago, yet he'd become very important to me. He was the first person I'd ever felt so deeply about. Could we be finished so soon? I felt stunned and undone, with a raw emptiness deep inside that actually hurt.

After a few minutes I collected myself and walked into the house to Emma's bedroom to get my suitcase. She was combing her hair in front of the large mirror over the dresser. "Bye, Cuz," she said, hugging me. "We've had a great summer together, haven't we? We've survived some pretty great adventures."

"Yeah, really great. Luke hasn't called me City Slicker in a really long time. I think I've earned my stripes and he won't call me that horrible name anymore," I said. "As far as I'm concerned, that's my big accomplishment of the summer."

We laughed and then walked into the living room arm-in-arm. Luke was busy teaching Fritz to sit up and beg. The dog was rewarded with a Bugle snack chip every time he performed the trick. "I ran out of Doritos," Luke explained as he gave the dog another cone-shaped snack.

"Bye, Luke. It's been fun. Glad you didn't fall and die," I said. I started to walk over to hug him good-bye, but he stepped back and waved his hand dismissively.

"City Slicker, get a hold of yourself! I'm not into that mushy stuff," he said. My ears stung when I heard him use the name I thought I'd proven I didn't deserve.

"Take that back you roughneck hayseed! She's not a City Slicker anymore!" Daniel proclaimed, entering the room.

"What? How dare you speak to me like that!" Luke reprimanded him. "You're begging for the five-minute treatment, mister."

"Well, she's not," Emma joined in. "And you know it, so stop calling her that!"

"Is this a conspiracy?" Luke asked, looking at Daniel and then Emma. "I was just kidding. You know how I feel about the Nessie Monster."

"Then say it, you lug head!" Daniel pressed.

"Okay, okay. Don't get your jammies in a twist. Geez. Everyone's so edgy around here lately," he said. He took a deep breath and continued. "I hereby declare that Nessie Monster is no longer City Slicker. From now on I'll refer to her as Nessie, Nessie Monster, or Big Red. There! Are you morons happy now?"

"Thanks Lukie," I exclaimed. "That means a lot!"

"*Lukie*?" Luke repeated, raising his eyebrow with disapproval. "I'm not so sure I like that."

"Oh, sure you do, Lukie," Daniel said, slapping him on the back.

Daniel and I hugged, and then I walked over to Luke again. He looked at me with suspicion. "What is it?" he asked. "Isn't it time for you to go home yet?"

"Not until I tell you how much you mean to me," I said.

"Oh crap. Here comes the mush. I knew it." He looked away with a pained expression on his face.

"That's it. That's all I wanted to say," I said, and then started toward the kitchen with my suitcase to leave.

"Hey, Nessie Monster," Luke said from behind me. I turned and he hugged me quickly and then stepped away. "Don't make this a habit," he said. I smiled and nodded.

I said farewell to Lars and Margret, and then to Aunt Louise and Uncle Evert. Then Mom and I got into the beige 1966 Chevrolet Impala and I waved to everyone through my open window as we rolled slowly down the driveway. I continued waving until we came to the end of the driveway and turned south on Allisonville Road to make the journey home.

"So, sounds as though you had an exciting time again visiting your cousins," Mom said as we rode along. "Are you looking forward to returning to school on Tuesday?"

"Yeah. I guess so," I replied. I leaned over the seat and unzipped my suitcase and pulled out my transistor radio. I turned it on, and out came the strains of "Homeward Bound" by Simon and Garfunkel. Yep. The DJs at that radio station always knew just the right song to play.

EPILOGUE

Three weeks later two letters arrived for me on the same day. My mother handed them to me while I was watching the late-afternoon movie on TV after school. I was delighted and surprised that one of them was from Jim. The other one was from Emma. I dashed into my bedroom, closed the door, and plopped down on my bed. I decided to read the one from Jim first.

His letter was handwritten on one side of a piece of stationery imprinted at the top with the words "Desert Inn Motel" and a drawing of a small cactus.

"*Dear Vanessa:*

Well, here I am in Phoenix! On the way out, Dad's car broke down just outside of Albuquerque, and we had to stay there a couple of days while it was being repaired. That's where I picked up this stationery. We finally made it here, though. We're staying at my uncle's house in a neighborhood called Paradise Gardens. I'm not sure how it got its name. There aren't any gardens, at least not the kind you see back home. The house isn't large, but we're getting along okay. I've written the address on the envelope so you have it and can write back, if you want to.

Dad's been spending a lot time looking for a job, and says he thinks he'll land one soon. I hope so. He's not so easy to get along with when he's out of work. It's so hot here that I swear you could fry an egg on the sidewalk. I'm getting used to it, though. My new school is okay, I guess. They play baseball out here, just like back home, so I'm happy enough. There's a boy named Juan on my team who's teaching me a few Spanish phrases. Señora bonita. Muchas gracias. Stuff like that. I miss home and the people back there. We're coming to Indiana for a visit around Thanksgiving. Maybe if you're not too busy then we could get together? I'd really like that. I'll call you.

Well, that's about it for now. I told you I can write a letter when I have the right motivation. I guess I have the right motivation where you're concerned. Take care of yourself, and let me know how you're getting along.

Fondly, your Jim."

I clutched the letter to my chest and beamed. He'd closed with the word "fondly," and used "your" with his name. Both of those had to mean something good! I quickly tabulated how many weeks there were until Thanksgiving. I counted seven. I didn't know how I'd find enough patience to live through all those weeks until I saw him again.

I carefully placed Jim's letter back in its envelope, then eagerly tore open Emma's envelope with embossed pink flowers on it, and read her letter.

"*Dear Vanessa:*

Greetings, cousin. How are you? I'm fine. Things at our house are almost back to the way they were before the fire, and boy am I glad. The painters finished painting all the rooms and fixing up Luke and Lars's bedroom this week. My bedroom curtains came back from the cleaners, and Mom hung them yesterday. There are lots of new things in the house, like rugs and bedspreads. Lars says we should have a fire more often so we're forced to make everything look nice like it does now. Mom didn't think that was so funny.

Dad said the fire chief finally declared that the fire at our house was caused by bad wiring. I really thought he was going to say that the Soviet set it. Speaking of the Soviet, Lars and Buzz have begun rebuilding and cleaning up the little house, and it's almost as good as new. It could be my imagination, but Luke has been nicer lately. I think it's because of what happened at the State Fair. I heard he sat with Bunny Bibble at lunch last week and once the week before that. Can you believe it? I also heard that Luke lent Todd Yamaguchi his history class notes when Todd was out with the flu for a few days. I don't know if I was more shocked by Luke being nice to Todd, or learning that Luke takes notes in class! I asked Luke about Hawes, and he said Hawes and his friends steer clear of him now, which makes him happy, of course.

Ryker still says goofy things to me all the time, like calling me Enchanted Emma. I can't seem to make him stop. I guess he's funny, but he's also so weird! He asked if I wanted to get a Coke with him sometime, and I told him I don't think so. I think he's going to keep asking me, though, because he asked a second time. I told him no then, too.

Did I tell you I made it into the swing choir? It's been lots of fun so far. That girl I wrote about in my diary who made my life miserable last year didn't make the swing choir, so I don't see her much, which is great. I heard Jim and his father left Indiana and are already in Phoenix. I'm so sorry he moved away. I hope you're not too broken up about it. I liked having him around, myself. He was always pretty nice to me, and helped keep Luke from going too crazy.

You won't believe how close Mom and Fritz have become! Luke isn't happy about it, either. Fritz follows Mom around, and usually sits at her feet when she watches TV or reads. Luke is feeling left out. (But Fritz is still devoted to Luke and always will be!) As for Mr. Kleinschmidt, they never found his remains, and officially declared he died in the fire.

I've saved the biggest news for the end of this letter. Two weeks to the day after the fire at Mr. Kleinschmidt's farm, Luke received a postcard with a postmark from Augsburg, Germany. It had no signature, no return address, and no name on it. I saw it myself. There was just one word handwritten on it—Frieden. Can you believe that? Frieden! I guess Jim was right.

Well, got to go now, dear cousin. I'll write again soon.

Love,

Emma."

I fell back on my bed and smiled.

CPSIA information can be obtained
at www.ICGtesting.com
Printed in the USA
FFOW05n1533260916

9 781457 550249